ICONOCLASTS OF AURALIN

IVAN METLIKOVEC

I suppose I should put something here,

So here's to the first one.

Thanks for being a part of that,

and hopefully many more to come.

PART ONE

Traveller

Chapter One
Days of Fog

The morning was quiet and while low lying fields were beginning to harden from their bogs in the coming of warmer weather, the darker hours brought a chill along with cold fog to settle over the paths and tombstones of the graveyard above. Any who would walk among them would be obscured from a view of the city of Churl, the great stone castle itself barely to be seen rising up on the slope beside it.

In the earliest moments of daylight did the swaddled figure of an old, slumped crone, walking with a stave in hand make her lone way through the fog and past the dew hanging off grass to walk into the graveyard, a small hill flattened above the fields, picketed with metal stakes and paths paved with stone.

The crone's face was as gnarled and weathered as the trees around her and to herself she talked in a hushed voice with tones of worry.

"The Minister, the Minister, why does he make a mockery of sermons sung when these trees were newly planted saplings, whipful and young? To bring falsity to the faith that has served him and the land in days past so righteously, his forked tongue honeyed to make his words seem bold and full of truth?"

The words spoken by the Minister had been heard by many people and such words should have been adhered to by all those in the kingdom of Alegan none the less. The people had reached out and taken his words as they always had, even when what was said changed to not at all be the same as what had been. Where were the words of the blind that should have been?

The old woman didn't understand these recent words she was hearing from the church and those that frequented its halls, but a bad feeling was settling into those old bones of hers. Not that old, familiar feeling which had caused her to hide away and keep herself secluded while walking out her troubles at hours such as these. Instead it was one that made her worry at the size that would be needed for such a graveyard which would come to be necessary from such a future she had heard being whispered in the streets.

Frequenters to the graveyard in which she walked would have stopped to wonder at a giant suit of black armour standing several heads taller than any ordinary man, beside some headstones so weathered that it no longer could be read who they belonged to. Under its palms rested a gargantuan sword, as curved, black and metal as the armour itself, planted at its feet.

The crone noticed the armour and a shaking breath came from her withered frame as she held on to her stave for support. She shook her head, righting herself.

"Really, it seems you have nothing better to do these days then walk around in the shadows, haunting people like a ghost. When all is becoming wicked and dangerous the world could use one like you to stand against the coming chaos of the Minister."

In reply from within the armour came a deep, echoing voice rising up out of the visor which broke the sound of the morning all around.

"That is altogether another matter entirely as to why I am here, and the choice to be here is mine. Is there anything in particular you wish to say to me? Neither of us have anything to gain from pointless discussion, do not take me as one who would reminisce about years long gone, Lara. Or was this nothing more than a chance encounter during a walk to you?"

There was much they could have talked about, as the land of Alegan had become stale, the population at its fringes looking for a spectacle if rumour could be believed. The peace those deeper within the kingdom enjoyed was brought on by a long and hard road few of them had bothered to tread or even remember correctly.

After all, this land was special and here was the center of the Land of the Light, a place which long ago let the blind see. It had been that difference which everyday folk believed would have saved them during the war, but there had been those few who had tread a road and sacrificed all that they could so those far away would not have seen how wrong they were. Now that road was being trampled by believers led astray, told that it had been through their faith that they had been spared. Those that listened would lay down bricks along the road to make it a more permanent path, but each of those laid bricks increasingly came from a terrifying furnace fuelled from the deaths of so many, all due to fear and sulphurous words. The stench had only grown in recent years and increasingly the old woman called Lara found herself unhappy with the long forgotten loss of her comrades and friends, even if one such as the Black Knight might remember.

"The city stinks, so I do this to clear my head and I think my surprise should have been enough to tell you that I did not expect you here. There's little to say, we are too late to save our countryside even if elsewhere will go on. Churl was chosen as the new capital by the king himself but why with what halfway hovel we had here the choice was made I can not say."

The Black Knight remained immobile but from within the voice rumbled.

"It is entirely convenient for a king falling out of favour with his people. He consolidates the church and kingdom in one place so as to not create a separate place of power that surely would have happened if he had stayed in Autumn. Here he would seek to make himself most absolutely a person of worship, to appear when the time is right."

"To save the world the way only he can? I didn't want to consider it as that's a danger others might not ignore, making it far less problematic than it sounds, people believing in divine selfhood. Be that as it may, the Minister and the king hold a divide in power few will be willing to admit. Held so apart I am unsure what the king might be able to do, so we wait and see, if that would be at all possible. The Minister has found his power growing ever since the king's arrival, being the mouthpiece of the king's words now more directly than ever before when surely the reverse should have occurred."

"For what little that power is now it is fortunate, so that I do not have to keep my sight in two places at once nor employ the eyes of others to assist me. We can not risk the same fate happening here as did before."

Both had travelled on that road a long time ago, yet they and all the others could have only done so much, as none of them were nobles or kings who had the ears of all people. They waited for the ones who had the attention of others, who were now making loud decrees that were not just a call to the massacre of those with an affinity for the magical use of fire as they had years ago, in Alegan and beyond. For over the years she had seen fewer and fewer people coming from northern or southern lands and the ones who did come were still as full of fervour as some had ever been.

It seemed then that the world grew as a result, expanding out from the borders to become wild and unknown. Or maybe those in the lands beyond were giving Alegan a wide birth, after the war and the exile of those who were still able to leave there would be only bitter memories remaining that burned in fire.

Lara knew what it was like to stay, while having such memories close to home and heart in a way she had never fully realised and would never show again. So perhaps for everyone the world was shrinking instead and when their sight pushed up against the vastness of a world unknown did people look around for what they knew as a comfort.

She didn't want to see the sights around her or feel the darkness, so her gaze was set out far into the distance, to the plains beyond while hoping that around her the darkness would not spread. What a barren and quiet world this had become from that of her youth. Lara shook her head and looked sadly at the world around her.

"Is this all that is left for us after the destruction of Malleau? All that is left for old Auralin to become? Where the space between each of us grows ever larger, the world ever colder and ever distant, for the silence in that sorrowful place has found itself a home here in Alegan and in the lands far away. It has made the powerful mad to fill that howling empty space with fear and hate and action must be taken to prevent drawing in that awful looming darkness, by finding brighter sources of light that do not rely on the words of a firebrand preacher or that other source most foully directed. Even then, mine is just one option, one chance, me raising my hand and casting my own lot in hope for our fates, merely one along with all the rest. Here it is said that Churl is the hallowed place of light but I will never forget first setting eyes on Malleau, and how it shone in the sun. She is so much the same that she reminds me of it daily with the light in her eyes."

The knight's head turned to face her.

"Ahh, the girl. What do you intend to do with her?"

A smile wrung on Lara's face and dry laugh escaped her.

"That kitten will have to learn on her own. She won't grow into her keen senses if she's kept coddled in comfort. Yet sadly I fear that sufferance shall be the surest stone on which to sharpen those claws of steel."

"Yet you still hold her back and see her as some idyllic pet, I do not envy your sentimentality in such things. Nor being in your precarious situation, planning a trap for the prince so early while you yourself have so little time left. Do not think I can not see through you."

Lara rewrapped her ancient gown around herself.

"It is rude for you to say as such. But you once said that you would kill the prince if it came to it, and I would certainly rather that you did not."

"Indeed I did, but surely you know that you will not be around to see if he takes the bait many years from now that would save him from me."

"Then can I entrust her safety to you?"

The voice came from within the armour heavy and piercing.

"I refuse. The future you envision could fall apart so easily were the Minister to lash out in his fall into madness and I will not entrust the safety of the future to a wide eyed girl taken to falling into hysterics. I suggest you finish up your matters in this world and find a quiet hole to die in, for you have caused far too much heresy by your own hands in this world already. Your body would only add to the raging fire just beneath the surface that you wasted your life away here to avoid."

"We can't be that far behind already?"

The Black Knight was amused by this.

"Oh, haven't you heard? All the preaching from the pulpit is reaching the ears of the masses. Even now it is being written and rewritten as men go about their way from this place to spread the new words that vomit right from the Minister's mouth."

Lara gasped and bowed her head, gripping her stave so as to not tremble. This was it, then. There was no more time to plan or prepare as she really had run out of time. Falsity taking note of and writing over falsity, while the truth drifted ever further away.

Scornful eyes glared at the knight as they once had, although without the grit toothed snarl she could no longer make. Instead she turned up her chin to leave with a scrap of dignity.

She left as she had come in the morning light, leaving the Black Knight to resume his position of standing alone in the graveyard, immobile and impassive. The knight's thoughts were in the past, but in regards of the coming future and all he might have to do, he knew Lara had been right. He would wait and see, allowing her plan the chance it needed in case it did succeed.

Along with the sword in his grip he had travelled and seen much and still was seeing that people made the choices he could expect them to make. He had made his own choices and would let others make theirs, for their lives were much briefer than his.

There had been a man once, and though the man was no more, not a shred of any person inside, he could still remember the way that man would have thought about this in his slow, mortal thoughts. That man would have cried once, for all that had been lost. Instead he remained standing and only raised his head to stare at the sky above, where hiding within the clouds twisted a dark and oily shape that left the knight thinking furthermore.

Chapter Two
Zelda

The day was clear and the sounds of construction were heard throughout the city where in the most rural of outskirts were gantry being assembled and pits being dug. Stone was being carted from far away to become new walls and towers. Those walls and towers had been slowly built up around the city in a great outward ring, and once completed there would be two unbroken rings surrounding Churl.

They were thick enough to walk atop of and with their cold stone faces sent a warning to any who might give this burgeoning city the wrong sort of attention. The king had assured them all that this would never happen as long as they kept evil beyond their lands. Evil ones were not those who were blind to tragedy, merely those who worshipped darker things or the light and heat of flame to be hosted in dark and foolish lands far away. Among those fools would also be people who worshipped nothing at all.

As such, these fortifications were a curiosity to the folk on the outer edges who knew that they were safe heeding the words of the king's messenger, quoted from the faith of the blind. Being brought into the realm of the city proper did only to reduce the view they had enjoyed of the hills and plains of the countryside, now obscured by the walls being built up. Of course they could just walk outside those walls by walking underneath those imposing arched gates but to those who now found their dwellings hidden in the shade it was not the same feeling of home that they had known.

Once, there had been a water mill that during the summer, children would play around, watching the great wheel turn and play in the river while adults watched on. The miller would sometimes come out and shoo away the children for being so careless but occasionally he would just watch. With this most recent ring, the water wheel of the mill had been built around, a tower added over it, not sparing a single place that could be used to stare outside and beyond the walls.

Down below, a metal grate separated the town from the outside, so while there was a gap, none could get through to the outside or play in the river. Yet still there was building and industry going on in the mill, there was work to be done and everyone's lives continued mostly unabated. Those who now lived in the shade found themselves moving further afield to stay in the sunlight, opening their shutters to keep their homes free of dirt. They could not stay in their homes as day came later and night approached quicker and it was always nicer to walk in the sun.

In one of these buildings there had lived until some recent years an old woman, the passing of whom had left the young woman in her care in possession of the residence, as well as a solemn sadness for a time. The change of deed to one so young might have been worrying but the townsfolk, now city folk, agreed that the girl was modest and kind.

Unless she made herself an irritation there were only mild words of worry and jealousy for the good fortune one so young should have on owning a scrap of land with a house. The church held it for her and allowed her to reside there with good graces that extended to the understanding of her needing to be taken in by another and given time to grieve, so that the house was often empty.

Even after recovering from those years, it was not often that she was found there. Atop the water mill was her favourite place to be, where she would stroll over the walls and could see the countryside around her.

Zelda was revelling in the weather while listening to the sound of the water go around. She wore simple clothing, a brown top that matched her hair, which she had tied back in a short pony tail. Her eyes were the same as her skirt, of a slightly darker brown, but all in all such clothing was of a sort most people could afford and even those within the inner ring had it little better as Churl had not known wealth for long. There were other places more suited to take advantage of the style of river trade.

As the walls had been built, people were now being employed to stand guard on the wall, although what for, no one could see the reason why. Their lands were safe, as theirs they all knew was the largest and most prosperous kingdom and the king had brought that prosperity with him, no matter however slowly it had begun to show in those who lived there. So it must have been idyllic, really, to be an archer overlooking the wide beyond, higher than any tree, watching for an enemy that would never come.

One such man looked thoroughly uncomfortable and fidgeted with his bow. He raised the visor of his helmet, under which he must have been sweating for it must have been such a restrictive thing to wear in such heat and addressed the young woman, who up until then had been minding her own business.

"I'm sorry miss, but do you have to spend so much time up here?"

Zelda did not seem taken aback, on the contrary was rather amused at the question. Warmth radiated from her smile as brilliant as the mid day glow.

"Why of course. I need to be making the most of this day while it lasts."

The man stood up straight, all proper and serious as if practising standing to attention.

"It is only, that we have been told to report instances of lingering or strange behaviour."

She right nearly huffed because he was being far too serious. Instead, Zelda put her hands on her hips.

"But you know who I am. And I've spent all morning helping the blacksmith move his wares to his new home. Quite exciting to hear all the new work he's getting, although I do hope we won't be seeing any of it in uses most terrible here."

The sun was shining, yet they knew there was an air of discontent about the world of Auralin in far off places, so much so that king Raylen forbid his people needlessly travel due to the danger. To trust the king they had to do as he said, all leaving for far away lands had to have a reason to leave. But that wasn't a cause for concern, for why should she leave? Especially since there had been much in the way of work. Even since the king had arrived Churl had become a buzzing thrum of all sorts of activity as one of the most important aspects of making it a suitable capital was by making it safer.

If the king had meant to use this as a means of escape from being pestered from those in the north he had succeeded, as scarcely had she seen any from there, or even an increase from the south for that matter but that just meant good news, if everyone was just too busy dealing with themselves.

Then there was the matter of the prince. People were expecting to see more of him and after the last five years, that pudgy boy would nearly be a man by now. As young women often did, Zelda wondered what it would be like to marry a prince and be taken high up into the castle. However, the whole family had been hidden on arriving to Churl, just as they had been hidden before.

Looking out at the great beyond, Zelda knew she wouldn't be able to take the madness of being shut away up in that castle and she was sure that there was already some royal girl somewhere who was destined for that lonely life where their every whim was satisfied. Would you even need the outside world if your every need was taken care of, or would it just mean placating your mind until you forgot that you were useless?

She suppressed a shudder. Even though the king had rejuvenated the city somewhat, there was regret about the need of these walls at all as they just shut people away from each other and stopped them easily looking out at the wide open world.

"A wall is only a wall if you can't climb over it." The archer said, words shaking her out of her dazed thoughts.

"You read my mind." Zelda said, causing the man to stutter.

"N-not with magic, of course. Besides, getting to know people's thoughts is not too difficult, especially since most people tend to think about the same things up here with everything else moving so quickly. It's a nice bit of peace and quiet, I'll admit. You could walk through a gate to look out there again of course, but one thing you can say is that we never used to get this view down here."

"Maybe a wizard could have lifted people up above their houses for a better look. There's nothing wrong with a little bit of magic from those who know how to use it properly."

The man fumbled with his helmet straps.

"I don't want people getting the wrong idea. And be careful with what you're saying, thinking carelessly like that could lead to problems for you."

There were no worries in that regard. Lara had told her many stories of powerful magics and the reasons people sought them out. Almost always for no good reason. Of course the war had not been for that reason but there could have been a spark in someone's eyes that burned out of control, no one knew just why it had come about. There was nothing wrong with magic, just fire magic and who needed that anyway?

She said goodbye to the bored soldier who she rather hadn't meant to tease and went down to the streets below. The stones that made up the roads and paths of these ramshackle parts of Churl that she wound through only covered the middle of them so that the sides were dusty and dirty which she avoided walking in. She really should not have minded and only a few years ago she would not have at all as few of the paths down here had been afforded the stones that were now set in it to give it just a little more the appearance of a coherent city.

Her boots scuffed over the stones and today's sun was bright and shining and Zelda looked for days such as today when she thought of Lara, and her spirits dipped. These days felt so much quieter than those she had when she was younger. Perhaps as she grew older and needed to ask less questions her voice was rarely at the tip of her tongue any more. She was busy, feeling her life rushing ahead and on some days Zelda did not want to leave the past behind, yet still these recent days were just as bright, when sunlight was not obscured by clouds that was and it meant she could carry those past days with her just as clearly as the sky. Those past sunlit days had to be behind her in one way or another as she was cautious of years disappearing while thinking of them.

She was thankful, having been given the place where she had spent so much of her life, even if since the walls had gone up right next to it there was no longer any view out into the farmlands or mountains far away. The house once had a back porch that went right up to the river, but that had been removed to make way for the wall. To reach the river now she had to walk some distance to the nearest gate and then back around where it was shallow enough for her to stand in.

People were checking their nets and heaving up buckets of water for cleaning or scrubbing, chatting as they went. How far removed she now felt from all that conversation, not because she was being excluded, but because once again she had the feeling of the world passing along as people got on with their lives. During Lara's time, the warring and fighting had kept people plenty busy. Zelda wondered what she would have been made to do during those times then shook out her head from those thoughts.

That wasn't fair, it was over, this was a time for peace and she certainly wasn't going to look for the lack of a war as an excuse that she had nothing to do with her life. It was just that all the tales she had been told were so exciting and full of danger that the thought of her sitting down and joining the communal washing line for the rest of her days made her sigh at its dullness. Perhaps if she pestered the guards enough she could train to be an archer and spend all the time she liked looking out to the world beyond. She liked the thought of that.

So distracted in her thoughts was she that Zelda had to halt, finding herself suddenly surrounded as she had not notice the approach of a group of young children that now swarmed around the street. Some were so small they barely made it past her legs in height, while others who were older and taller were not moving as fast as the younger ones. They all wore an odd assortment of clothing of different sizes and faded colours that had been stitched up to fit them in a mismatched fashion. More fortunate children might have worn something more uniform, but orphans got what they could, as she knew well.

"Look who it is. Look who it is." Said one little girl.

"Can you tell us a story? We know the old woman told you lots of stories and we used to hear them from her when we were little." Said a little boy.

Zelda was unable to keep a smile off her face, as their eyes and faces were bright, looking up at her expectantly.

"Well I'm sure I didn't hear all her stories and of the ones I did, some of them are not suited for your young ears just yet. I'm sure stories about the war wouldn't be appropriate for you either."

The children voiced their disappointment, another crossing their arm in front of her.

"But she told us lots of things about her adventures and the places she went to and the monsters she fought." They said as a fourth child tugged at her sleeve.

"Yeah, why are you keeping the stories all to yourself? Do you want to tell your own stories instead?"

"I didn't say I wasn't going to tell you one, just let me think for a moment."

They really do need to give me a moment.

Just when she thought she was going to be overwhelmed, a woman's voice called out to the youngsters. The voice was a little strained, words rolling at the end with the remnants of an accent from the north.

"That's enough you lot, stop harassing the poor girl for a tale and get moving. I'm sure she'll tell you one another time."

A pale woman a little over ten years older made her way up the street, flanked by still more kids, these ones some years older than the rest. She wore a white top and a thick black skirt. Despite the tone in her voice, there was a smile between the dark, straggly hair that graced her shoulders. Her face was a little thin and there were shadows under those light blue eyes that shone brightly, although that could have been because there were two little children hoisted at her hips, with another being carried by an older boy. She sighed, shaking her head as she walked over.

"Scamps, the lot of you. I'm sure one day you'll stop being a mischief to everyone but until then we all have to put up with you. Hopefully you'll grow out of that before you do your next set of clothes."

Zelda greeted her as the children detached themselves from her own limbs.

"Good morning Kieke. How are you today?"

Kieke chuckled.

"Busy as ever but I'll manage. These here ones, they're not getting any smaller and ever since the grown ones have left it's been back to me, really. I can't rely on these older kids now to do too much."

One older boy puffed out his chest.

"I can help, I'm responsible."

"Well you can show me just how much of that you really are by keeping the younger ones in line over there by the corner quietly now because we're off to keep everyone preoccupied. I don't know what work they'll have for us today but I can't have y'all causing a fuss or speaking when someone's asking for some silence. And on top of that, did someone just volunteer to do all the yard cleaning for us when we get back?"

"Um...actually."

The boy pulled a face to which both women giggled. Kieke ruffled his hair.

"Too bad, it's yours. You need to get used to just doing the things that need doing. Girls like that you know, so it's best to get the habit started. Without complaining."

Defeated, the boy walked to the front of the line and Kieke ushered the younger ones further up the road behind him. Zelda watched them all slowly march off.

"Maybe if they see what the price is for being helpful they will stay scamps for longer."

"A good tale should put them in line every now and then. Some of these ones haven't heard anything from Lara herself after all, so like it or not they'll be hearing it from you first."

"That sounds familiar."

"Yes, we used to be able to just sit and talk about things, me talking you out of your moods, trying to be who I could in place of someone who wasn't around for you any more. Zelda, getting you to help me with the young ones did you good. We can't sit and talk while admiring the view with the walls here but maybe another time we'll catch up outside them and there'll be view enough. I feel I'm being squeezed some days when I bring them all in here and that I might never see the horizon again. At least from higher up we can peak over the walls a bit."

Kieke stuck a hand in a pocket, producing a small brown stone, glancing down the road to toss the object to Zelda.

"Here, have this. It's a gift. Better I give it to you than I just drop it somewhere, this one will just use it to harass the birds and then I just know I'll get in trouble for it."

One of the older boys became red faced, embarrassed to having been singled out, so Zelda switched her focus to the stone, which was round, slightly flattened and very smooth, fitting nicely into her palm. There was nothing else particularly notable about it that she could find. It was after all, just a stone.

As the two parted ways, Zelda went on her own out to the front gate, where the memory of when there had not been a gate came into her mind. It was a heavy, crude metal thing that was lifted up by some chained contraption, the inner working of which eluded her. She imagined a place where something of the sort might be necessary. A far off land no doubt in peril, being fought over by ruthless nobles and greedy kings. That was not this place, with the king keeping the peace. People were going about their business with the only concern being dodging needy pilgrims and directing carts that carried what they needed for the church.

"Really now." She said.

Out the front wall was an entire caravan of pilgrims setting up tents along the wall and the fields, while others were looking for places to tie their horses. This never happened in the years beforehand, but when the king had moved in, much of the space around where people could have lodged was taken away by arrivals moving from Autumn. So those who had come merely to see the place where they placed their faith resorted to making their own spaces to rest.

Some of them looked out at her from their tents and she did her best not to meet their eyes, she did not want to stare rudely as one of those lucky ones who lived within those walls.

Zelda followed the thin old road that snaked out along some fields where hedges had been planted to create a tall barrier between the fields on either side of the road. Zelda pushed through the part she knew she could to get to the other side, where there were people farming the produce that would be important for the city.

Two older people, a man and a woman, were arguing but stopped when she approached. The woman made her way back inside while the farmer forced a friendly expression even if he did not smile.

"Ah, Zelda, you're here. That's good. I don't have much for you to work on today, there's less here than I thought and it's only getting worse each passing year, the land just isn't being helpful I'm afraid. Do you mind cutting up the beets for me?"

In front of him were boxes of farmed produce, red rounded beets. The fields around the home had been turned to mounds of dirt that had been dug up. The woman returned with jars that had been cleaned and emptied. Inside, a large pot bubbled away. At Zelda's confused expression, the farmer explained.

"We will need to pickle all this to make it last so that it doesn't go to waste. If we don't do this ourselves you know what will happen. It'll all just rot in wagons so that's my idea for the year. Taking matters into my own hands, or yours rather."

"On the matter of hands, aren't you worried about the pilgrims sneaking into your fields at night?"

"Something else getting worse every year." He said quietly, rubbing his jaw, eyes narrowing at the space past the fields as if he could see right through them.

"To get a munch of my crop on holy ground I'm sure some of them would do it, the journey here can't have been easy, though suppose these ones came from the south so have less to complain about. That being said I'd be more worried for the farm master over the other side. They're right up against his fields and he tells me they're taking water straight out of his irrigation but once word gets around to this new batch of sycophants that the fields are strictly church land I'm sure they'll all cut it out. Some of these people worry me though, they come from so far away it's hard to know if we can trust them."

"Well we just have to let them be and hope they let us be."

The farmer looked down at his boxes of produce.

"Really, it's all so different now, we don't know who our friends are out there these days in those other accursed lands, so it's best to be careful. Now go get started on the crops for me, they won't cut up themselves."

Chapter Three
When Darkness Comes

Zelda was on her way home from the inner city ring as the sun was setting, drawing gold light down that was cut off by the tops of both wooden and stone buildings in places where long squares of dark shadow spread across streets and off of walls. Among these shadows were people and Zelda had found herself being followed by them. They were keeping their distance and were trying to hide out of sight but she was able to tell, due to that feeling of being watched. It would already be quite dark back at the streets and the thought of that hurried her along, more than it usually did so she wasn't stumbling around blindly in the dark, or knocking on doors pleading with someone to lend her a torch for the night to make the remaining journey. The sparkling of the water as it peeked in between houses in the lowering light often had guided her home, but not since the walls had gone up had she been guided such.

There was a danger with the walls which there was no way for her to fix. They were all in a way trapped, as further to the edge the houses went the further from any outside gate or road they were, wedged between the old wall and the new. The longer she walked the more she knew that her chances to shake off the ones following her were gradually declining. If it came to trying a door to see if someone would let her in, she only hoped that no one would hassle those she had gone to for some aid.

The path that led home turned left and right, and even though Zelda kept her attention on that as much as she could, noticed people still lingering about, which was not something they usually did. Even though they kept their distance from her, she didn't need to see their faces to know they were not people she knew. This road that she walked was a frequently trod path by her and she knew who everyone here was by the way they stood and what they wore. Everyone had worn clothes these days and these ones wore clothes scuffed and worn from travel, but most of all it was the silence between them which set these people apart from those that she knew.

They're not talking, they're only waiting, watching, quite unlike most here and certainly not usual for people to be out this late in the afternoon.

Unfamiliar faces were not at all uncommon, with pilgrims such as them coming and going, from this place. However there was something about the way she spied one, then two following her, to have the first leave only to then be watching her later along the road that made her take notice.

I could round on them. She thought.

But I don't know what good that would do these people. As far as I know I haven't done anything, and they haven't done anything either apart from being a bit too interested in me.

Of course she did her best to ignore their presence, if someone was pulling a bad joke then they would not get the satisfaction from her, though Zelda doubted that anyone would go to this amount of effort to unnerve her. There were no parts of town through which she would not walk but she began to wonder if this was what people meant when they said that there were places best avoided, those places she imagined being lawless and grim, filled with people all with their own ends to fill and letting no other person being allowed to get in the way of the filling.

Here in this city, everyone who lived in the surrounds understood that they had to put other people first and that was what they all believed. There would be no survival for anyone otherwise if they did not all stick together so the saying went, as such, she among the others who lived in the city would tolerate those who came to show their faith.

There were a new lot of pilgrims lately, however. And she thought to herself that these new ones were simply sitting about the place with their glaring, rather unsettling eyes as if she were the one intruding on their space, of which there was plenty to go around that wasn't directly in the ways of other people.

There was an opening in the path where it split into a small group of houses, none of which were hers, as her path would be walking behind on the right leading slightly further down to other rows of homes, where the outer wall loomed overhead in the distance. In front of this circle of houses was a man with a grubby brown coat and white fisherman's hat. He was talking in a low voice to more of these people who had congregated in the space near the buildings to the left.

Zelda was thankful that at least one person from the church was around to order these disordered groups.

I wonder when they will be encouraged to move along or decide on a place to stay, it would be nice for someone to do their part and get these people to where they very much should be.

There were no more people following behind her after that and ducking behind a house to follow the old path home she walked in silence and dim light that made her squint, until she came to the circle of houses with the old one backed up against the wall, made of black wood, with two stories and a heavy, latched door.

In the middle of this circle was a tree with a stone post, off which hung a lamp to allow those who lived around here to see at night. The other paths to her left and a little way further down were slightly illuminated by the post but shadows swallowed up the light only some steps away. High up above her the castle was still bathed in the last of the sunlight, shining in orange gold. There were no walls obscuring those views up on high. Zelda knew that light gave the king the wisdom to make his judgements and so it was right that he had such access to the light whose shining glory had once revealed itself to help the blind in a long gone hour of darkness and uncertainty. A time long past indeed.

She unlatched the door and made her way inside. If Zelda had simply closed the door it would have left her mostly in darkness, so she took a candle outside to the lamp and lit it with its flame, being careful not to disturb the lamplight or let it go out. With that she took one last look around at the empty streets, silent and still with not a soul in sight, and walked back inside, shutting the door behind her.

Zelda did as the faith suggested and took a moment to be thankful that she had made it to her home as all should be thankful for. The entire bottom floor was just one large room with two thick supports barely counting as walls in the middle. The back walls held a door and windows which now were permanently shut as the views beyond them no longer existed. The fireplace along the wall on the right that had once been generous was now bricked up to half the size that it used to be, the loose bricks sitting inside it would not be needed for some time. On a thick wooden table nearby the fireplace was where she prepared food and around it was where she kept her supplies but Zelda preferred to spend more time on the top story where many precious things were kept.

Such things included written scribblings of Lara, some of which she could barely read, scrolled away carefully up the back wall. Sometimes she would take one out just to read it, then put it away in the slot she had found it. There were still entire chests of writings that were not rolled up, merely stacked on top of each other that she did her best to sort through in her spare time, but she would eventually come across pieces she could not read in some other language amongst the rest, and that always dulled her enthusiasm somewhat for a time.

After starting a fire in the fireplace and setting a small pot on it, she headed upstairs where there was one of those writings on the desk which she had been looking over, wondering where to store it. It spoke of a faded old land in the far north just under the Northlands that had fallen into ruin, having been abandoned by its people. Some of the writing scrawled from one time to the next, going back between winter and summer as if the days themselves were interchangeable.

Zelda had been having trouble working out if this was intended or if Lara had simply been using old paper to write two memories of the same place together. But then that did not explain the large gaps on the paper between what would have been the first tale and the second, and the fact that both of them wound and twisted together a little too much for her to fully convince herself that they were separate. Winter and summer were different times of the year, not daily occurrences as this writing almost made it seem to be. Such a strange place, unless there had been magic involved, but there was no discussion of that on the page, just a memory then, perhaps of two times.

She opened the blinds above the desk to look out into the night's sky where she could see the castle off in the distance, now lit up by torches as the sun had passed from it.

Certainly up there in the castle there would be many wonderful things going on behind closed doors, yet with the king being so secretive it was hard to tell how they lived. Looking at the high, unmoving place made her wonder if they were all kept shut away from the world by some overzealous guardian, or if the king himself was overly paranoid. But, enough people had reportedly come from other places who had met him and after all there was the Minister himself who's words were taken from the king as if the king had said them himself.

That man could not have said a thing unless approved by the king after all, and ever since they had come together in the same place, it seemed that much more could be said, and that was to help his people weather these strange, thin times. With word of trouble all around in other lands it was best to be safe in the one which had taken charge of its own people.

Zelda closed the blinds and went about her business for the evening, pouring over the words of regret and loss that were painful to read, because as was often the case they were not at all to her the words of the woman she had known. These would have been days real lifetimes ago, if what was written was the truth. It made herself regret what little she had done in almost eighteen of her own years. As the candle flickered, Zelda felt tiredness overtaking her and while hoping that she would not dream of far off places being followed by people she had never known, eventually fell asleep at the table.

There came a sudden popping noise which roused her from sleep. Judging from the downstairs glow, the fire was nearly out, the light inside down to a few remaining sticks that smouldered. That wasn't where the sound had come from, she thought. In her grogginess she strained to hear a shuffling sound that followed along the walls with an odd creaking. This was rather strange, as here it was not likely to have wild critters walking over people's houses at the middle of the night.

Zelda stuck an ear to the wall and heard further creaking, certainly too loud and heavy to be some field mouse who should be well on the other side of the fields by now. She took a new candle and went to the door, pausing a moment before opening it as quietly as she could to peer out. When she could see no one at the door she opened it wider, silently as she could without making a sound. The lamp in the street was running out of oil, so was dim and faint and the dark of night hung off of everything and the air was still. The noise had stopped.

Regardless, she stepped outside.

"Hello?" She called out to the night.

There was nothing in reply.

She took a breath in and silently moved to the right edge of the house so she would be able to peek around the side. Somewhere at the back of the house a thump was heard and she whirled around. There was a person standing on the other edge of the house, they must have been tall for where they were she was still looking up to see them. Standing in the dark as they were she could not see their face.

"Now what might you be after?" She asked them.

They did not speak, only slowly begin to walk forward. Zelda realised he would soon be between her and the door.

She lurched forwards so that she could reach it, but she knew there would be no making herself to the door in time if he were to do the same, maybe just being able to squeeze in and try her hardest to force the door shut. Just as she was about to reach it the door opened wider and another man just as large walked out from inside the house, right in her path with arms outstretched. There was little she could do to stop in her tracks than throw herself to the ground to avoid running into them and being caught.

As she did she dropped the candle which broke in half and she scooped it up in her bare hands to keep the light from going out. Even though she had to grab hold of it and the hot wax burned, she did not let go.

She stood with the candle in front of her, hoping to see their faces but behind her she sensed a presence and stooped, barely in time to avoid a club to the head. The swing went wide past her and struck the stone pole against which it splintered loudly.

Zelda looked for a way out, and while backing up away from the three found another appear from around the house, and again another emerging from the shadows to block her escape up the north path. The road she had travelled on earlier was bare of people so she did the only thing she could and run up the road, as the light in her hand flickered dangerously low and the sounds of boots followed after her.

Hoping that her path would not be blocked, knowing that she was still being followed, she saw movement to her side and realised that they had split up to further trap her. Zelda made it out of the web of streets and found herself at a main road that cut cleanly from higher up the hill to the distances down below. Now would she go up or down? She gave herself a moment to think.

I can't stay in these streets I don't want to be caught out and I just know that's going to happen if I don't make a choice soon. I'm going to be spotted here, I don't have the time.

Well if she went down the road that would take her out of the lower gate into the fields. Somehow there was no one on duty at the gates that she could see, and those torches were out.

Why is there no one there?

The sound of crunching boots made her choose and she ran up the road further into town. Here the buildings were a little bigger and taller, made of thicker brown wood than the old farm houses. At least here there were lights still burning along every few of these buildings and she was able to finally throw away the candle down in front of a path on the other side of the street, hoping most desperately that it would lead her pursuers astray.

Wax stuck to her fingers and she tried to carefully remove it. Where she did there were burning red lines of skin so raw that in places little points of blood began oozing through.

She did not have long to look at these as movement came from below, where one of the men who had chased her now made his way onto the street, a sharp knife in his hand and he wasted little time running up the road towards her.

Further up the road was a sign for a tavern but her pursuer was gaining on her and she would not make the entranceway in time. There was a gap between the tavern and the building beside it where she hoped she could find a space to crawl, putting her out of reach but found only an open path to the back of the building. As the man with the knife appeared in the alleyway, she knew there was no choice for her but to run down it. Then Zelda tripped and fell, crying out as she saw the arm with the knife ready to plunge down.

But another dark shape stood over her before it could, and the blade of a sword that could barely be seen in the light thrust forward, plunging into the chest of her assailant. The man with the sword in his chest shuddered for a moment in a spasm then fell motionless. The figure before her was already sliding the body off the blade carefully, using the dead man's clothes to stop blood getting on his hands.

He turned to her but she could see little of his appearance in the dark. When he spoke, his voice was gruff and clear, but most alarming of all to Zelda, it sounded rather lifeless.

"Best get up from the ground, it is about time to get off the street, just for a moment."

He did not even help her to her feet, only walk back the short distance he had come, appearing to want to get back into the tavern, but Zelda didn't think on it as she found herself in such an urgent rush to follow that it took everything else from her mind, as long as she was not left alone.

Chapter Four
A Fortunate Meeting

Zelda followed the man, his sword already back in its sheath, as he led her without further words to the inside of the tavern, where it was bright and most of all warm. Despite the earliness of the morning it was filled with burning orange firelight from lamps and a fireplace. Here she was able to get her first view of him, or at least a view from the back, his head covered in thin dark brown hair shaved close to appear almost balding. The rest of his body he had covered, wrapped in dark leather clothing which was thin, torn and dirty down to the boots, all of which clashed with the clean and light brown interior of the tavern walls.

Without checking to see if she were following, he left her alone just inside the landing, heading to one of the round tables in the far back corner to join three other men.

A beefy man with a handlebar moustache was leaning on the server's bench, head turned behind to the man who had walked past him with a sword. Seemingly satisfied with his own safety, he turned his attention to her, with an expectant gesturing of his head in the man's direction.

"An early morning for someone such as yourself. With them, are we?"

"I...don't know." Zelda replied.

The man hadn't suggested anything of the sort that she join them and the way he had dispatched her attacker and the clothes he wore made her pause and think carefully about whether she shouldn't find herself a corner and hide out the remaining hours to wait for a guard to stumble in. That dead man wasn't going to go anywhere either.

This man will soon find that a body has been left behind his tavern and will be in trouble. I can't just tell him, I'll look suspicious. Or the man who just brought me in will be made suspect. While he did do the deed I'm not quite sure yet if he deserves to be caught, knowing nothing about him.

She diverted her gaze over to the corner and chanced a glance at the round table where the four people now sat in conversation. A different man to the one who she had encountered, one with more hair on his head and a thin moustache that stretched out to the furthest corners of his face, noticed her stare with a quick smile and beckoned to her over with a wave of his hand. Without a word she nodded to the tavern keeper and made her way over to the table.

The smiling man was wearing fairly plain traveller's clothes that might have once been white under a leather jacket, but were now all dirty. He gestured to the empty space on the bench next to him, but for a moment Zelda remained standing, if shakily so at that. She stayed where she was even when the man, closing on forty or so years, spoke in a calm and pleasant voice to introduce himself.

"Come and sit over here with us. My name is Findal, what's yours?"

"Zelda." Said Zelda.

"Well Zelda, I'm just a trader by trade, or once was, a little while ago before now making my way with these fine people. You looked as lost over there by yourself as I once did before happening upon them, that's all, so thought to myself it a shame."

Zelda kept her voice down.

"They may be quite fine people for you I am sure, although for me if being rescued meant anything other than witnessing a murder I would have much preferred that, thank you very much."

Her legs felt a little weak as the happening was still burning fresh in her mind, and so she found herself sitting down on the bench as a realisation began to occupy more of her mind.

Someone is dead. If nothing had happened I would be dead. But someone is dead and I have seen it.

The man seated with his back against the furthest wall raised his eyebrows, even if to Zelda he didn't appear at all surprised by this news. A little older than the man who had offered her a seat, his mouth was hidden within a great brown beard that wove in with his with messy hair. He wore tough light brown leathers and had hair on the middles of his fingers. He spoke up at this in a calm and clear manner.

"So that means you're the one Survel helped. Well whatever it is you may feel towards him, at the very least you are still alive, and importantly for us by his account are someone who knows their way around, unlike those who tried to catch you."

Now she could see Survel's face, which put him around the same age as the previous man. His was covered in a short beard and held tired eyes that were not, she suspected, due to the earliness of the morning. She could not help but glare at that face which maintained an air of disinterest so strong she could almost smell it, sickening her in a sensation that trickled down her neck just by looking at him.

"Had he been able to tell you that because he was following me? Not that I would have been able to guess that one more was following as there have been more than a few eyes on me recently."

Survel scratched his jaw unenthusiastically at the attention, and replied to her with the same flat tone as he had before, not at all the appearance of a man who had so recently taken a life with his sword.

"I happened to realise you were being followed and decided to watch. As far as that matter goes it would have been senseless to watch you die, though it's possible he didn't have to die, but it was dark, I didn't want to merely graze him to then have him then turn to me. This place has its fair share of problems."

"Such as the body now lying next to us, which will no doubt be found by morning?"

The larger, bearded man hummed to himself for a moment, and seemed to put aside that question for the time being, leaning forward on his elbows.

"Listen lass, my name is Gunter, and I'm wondering if I could ask you where something is. Someone, rather on the off chance you have seen them. I have been looking for a place where an old acquaintance of mine lives and haven't been able to find it in such a big city. Previously we've always met a little further outside, and I must say I am surprised to see these new constructs having gone up since I was last here which has confused me most admittedly. The person we're after, is a friend of mine, an old woman who was a particular teller of stories by the name of Lara."

Zelda could not stop her face showing sadness, and Gunter frowned.

"You know of her?"

Her head slumped to stare into the burned hands on her lap, and her eyes began burning just as much with tears.

"Well I knew of one. How can it be that in such a place as this you would seek out perhaps the person it just so happens I might have known? I'm terribly sorry to say this but if it is her you're after you have arrived too late, as she has been dead for some three years. If you had a message or something to tell her I'm sorry it turned out this way. I can take you to her house, as that is where I still live and have kept her things if you would wish to see them to be proof enough. Of course too can I take you to her grave."

Gunter rested his face on his clasped hands while his eyes narrowed, becoming clouded as the frown deepened into shadowy lines that appeared on his face.

"Well, that is certainly not what I expected to hear. Despite her age I always thought her as being so strong. But I realise now that even those memories take place many years ago. Perhaps it was foolish of me to not have expected this. Worse more is that we made quite the detour to come here, and we're short on time."

All present were silent for a time, until Zelda found she could no longer hold in her words. Her hands stung, her eyes stung and her heart stung too.

"How can it be that these things are happening to me? What have I done that I have found myself here in the early hours of the morning?"

Gunter caught her looking at her hands and gently examined the burns.

"These injuries are very light."

He picked at his teeth and picked out a seed, crushing it between his fingers, covering them in a small ground up paste. He then took her hands and gently held them in front of him. A numb sensation passed through Zelda's hand, as if the insides were warming and expanding, more fuzzy at the tips, and although there was no wind, it felt to her that a breeze had wrapped itself around her hands, cooling them. The red burnt skin had healed over as if it had never been. She examined her hands with wide eyes.

Smiling sadly, Gunter leaned back in his seat.

"A pleasing reaction to the power of the world. I should have said earlier. The four of us are druids, Zelda. We have come here for our own reasons but know that the pain you feel is shared. Where possible we do our utmost to prevent such heart pain from causing further anguish and harm."

"I've never seen a druid before."

"That would be most likely, as people deafen their ears to our words, of the ways of the world. We avoid places such as this where we are most certainly unwelcome, where people are strongly devout to their faith and would not turn from it and would probably turn on us, which is why we come during the night, with our heads low. Still, as I have said, there were reasons for coming here but I am tragically too late. There is still the matter of yourself, however and one other thing."

His eyes then turned to the last person who had not been introduced, a younger man than the rest with darker hair and brown mud covered leathers. It almost appeared that it had been painted or smeared in mud, such was the roughness of the leather. While he had a young face and the scowl that set around his eyes at being given attention was something more a scolded boy might pull, he appeared several years older than her, although he was probably no more than five such years if she had to guess.

"Peter?"

Peter rose to his feet and stepped out of the circle. His voice was as much as she had guessed from the expression on his face, drawling more like an irritated boy than a man displeased at his task.

"Yes I'll get rid of it. Try not to go anywhere else without me. I don't want to discover that I've been waiting around only to find you're all in the next town over spending Findal's gold in a tavern."

The man left at a haste, and how exactly he would dispose of the body she thought it best not to wonder on.

"There are others out there." Zelda said, concerned.

Gunter's eyes showed that he did not share in her fears, however.

"That won't be a problem."

Findal's eyes went from the door back to Zelda. He began twirling the end of his moustache.

"Who went after you again?"

Zelda half shrugged, half shook her head.

"They were not familiar to me I am sure, they could be pilgrims but why they would be coming after me I don't know."

"Is there anywhere else you could go where they might not find you?"

"If they were watching me so intently during the day I know they would know my face. I can't hide here forever and I don't know if I would want to."

Gunter was frowning again.

"It is unlikely that this is the case, but I don't like the possibility that they went after you because of Lara. We might have been discovered and you are nothing more than a lure to trap us."

"Who would trap druids?"

"There are many who would seek to give rise to a world filled with darkness. Allow us a moment, if you would."

Without waiting for her to get up, the remaining three put their heads together, although Zelda found there was little reason for this, as due to her closeness she could still hear every word they said. She wondered if she should be minding her own business by stepping out but she still listened intently, while at least doing her best to appear distracted.

Gunter spoke first.

"Should we take her with us or leave her here?"

Findal spoke.

"I wouldn't mind another companion for the road. She is seemingly being targeted and her home here is no longer safe. I suggest that being her Lara's friend is enough for me, as she was enough of a friend of yours."

Survel responded.

"We could make it safe. And after all, she's just ordinary. This is not a task for ordinary people we are on here and she would slow us down, surely."

Gunter sounded thoughtful in reply.

"Yet who is to say that she is? We could find ourself with an ally or at least a helpful person. I think it is clear to say that for her own protection we could take her out of the city at least a little while and find a place for her along the way. Also, despite our lack of rest we should endeavour to leave as soon as we can if this is indeed a trap for us. If not for her sake Survel, make it for our own."

Survel nodded.

"I do not wish for any wasteful conflicts here."

Gunter rose to his feet.

"Zelda we have come to a decision. You may not understand why it is that you have found yourself here this early morning, where many would make the choice to look the other way to your plight, such has it been in places I have walked and being able to resume our journey and make up for lost time is of utmost importance, but nevertheless you are being hunted and it would be amiss for us to look ahead so blindly. So I would ask you as Lara's friend if you would travel with us for a time. We are more than able to keep you safe and will be leaving this place shortly and have decided that for the moment you should come with us. We know of places you could hide for a time, perhaps returning here when it is safe to do so if that is your wish."

"You're not staying here for the morning?" She asked.

"No, we have a quest to undertake, an important one. And we must leave, soon, travelling on to the solstice in the coming year. It is most important that we be there, for a great gathering of our kind has been ordered and we shall go. No longer can we idly stand by while the people of the world do not listen to us."

There were no disagreements to this between any of them, the other two were eager to get moving just as much.

"Well isn't that just rude of everybody?" Zelda said.

"I'll listen, and I'll go with you and I'll pay attention. Please, I must go with you and away from this place while I still can."

Gunter nodded.

"That is the right course of action. Do not be discouraged if you do not understand everything you hear, especially if you put the effort in to listen. The world has been waiting for more people like you who would listen with what I can feel is a glad heart, while the rest are ignoring the pleas of the world and look inwards. Because nobody listens, the world you know falters, and is set to fall deeper into a vile stagnation of a world long past the days of glory. We druids know of this truth and have often sent ourselves out into your world of kings to right what wrongs we can. So make no mistake, we will proceed beyond the place where we will leave you, but this is not a favour we will require you to repay, for our quest is one of a worth beyond any other."

The others stood, and Zelda herself had quite already made up her mind. She was concious of walking just a bit too quickly to the door, where she was forced to linger as the others caught up. Before they did, Peter reappeared, fading in silently from the dark. He took her presence without comment as they all made their way into the cold morning, breath turning to mist. She turned to look at the ones who would take her away.

"I don't quite understand, but you have somewhere else to be rather quickly it seems. I'm just in the way while you have to deal with other problems far larger than mine."

"Indeed." Gunter said.

"But as you have chosen to walk aside us do not be concerned. We have other things to do and we can not force you to travel with us. For now I will seek out the graveyard and see with my own eyes the stone of the dead that covers my friend and shield her from rising into foul unlife. Even though surely such a curse is not here, it is just safe that we do such, as we know how to keep her soul at rest. However, you must instead gather some things for the journey we would ask of you to retrieve so you will not be such a burden on us. If you could find a few tools needed for mending clothing, objects such as rope, twine and some lasting food if possible. You will meet us outside the road beyond the lower gate a little later. "

Zelda's eyes widened and it was not only the chill air she could feel in her chest.

"I was going to back home to find some things, some of the things you ask for would be there, as well as some of Lara's stories I wanted to take with me but you're leaving me alone? What about the others out there who were after me?"

Peter shook his head.

"It shouldn't be a problem."

Gunter nodded in his direction.

"If he says it is so then it is so. People who would do us harm are one of the many things we must attempt to look out for and we shall check the roads carefully for any who might, so now go do your part. I'll take a look around the house myself and see what I can find that might be of use but do not return to it now, they could be waiting for you there."

"Thank you Gunter, I suppose I shall do what I can to assist." Zelda said.

After giving them directions, which they insisted they now would not need due to the understanding of where it was that she lived, the four fanned out down the road, disappearing into the darkness that made them all seem to have merely been from her imagination. Regardless, the words echoed in her mind, reminding her that she had spoken them to somebody.

I shall do what I can.

Of course, the matter still remained of who precisely she had spoken to, as Zelda had found herself inexplicably alone once again. The encounter she had just been part of had been real, even if there was no body behind the tavern when she had checked, which might have been another thing to tell her that nothing at all had happened if it wasn't for the fact that one of those people, one of those druids, had apparently gone to dispose of it.

Now Zelda was cautiously seeking for what they had asked of her. She didn't want to stay, and these people were willing to help and were already on the move, which was what her feet wanted. All she had to do was gather some things for them that she knew she would be able to return, but staying around here with the dark corners holding unknown threats wanted her to make for the front gates and never look back.

Instead she was sorting around the gutters and side alleys for what the druid had asked for, finding a sack that went under her arm and inside it was a spool of rope and some fishing thread that she had found, along with some carpenter's tools left around that she had been lucky to find. Not lucky for the person who would find that their tools would be gone in the morning.

There was a noise some feet behind her and Zelda whipped around to see Kieke staring at her, an expression most grave on her face and in those eyes was a look of bleak worry.

"What are you doing?" She asked.

Zelda looked down at the things in her hands. The sack over her shoulder began to feel heavy.

"Oh, Kieke, I'm not stealing, I'm definitely not stealing."

What is she doing out and about?

The woman flinched.

"You're leaving. Why are you leaving?"

"I'm sorry Kieke, I don't have time right now I have to get out of this place."

"Who is making you doing this?"

"Please, there's no time for me to explain. They'll come after you too if they suspect anything, you'll get hurt, they'll kill you as they've tried with me."

"What do you mean they'll hurt me? Has someone hurt you? Nothing else is going to happen, here's what you need to do. You need to stay, come with me, we'll wait this whole thing out, whatever it is and you can tell me about it in the meantime."

Zelda shook her head and moved past her. The woman left where she stood but her voice called out from the distance.

"It's going to be ok, it all is. Just you wait." And then she dashed off without another word.

Yes, better that she go keep herself safe. The kids needed her desperately and it was better that she made sure they were safe right now.

Zelda looked down at the things in her hands, finding herself momentarily struck dumb. What was she to be doing with these? Wasn't this stealing, what she was doing? She wasn't sure how badly the others needed these things but surely not enough to ask her to just take the property right off people's doorsteps.

Maybe I shall find a place and hand these things in. But as nothing is open this early and I have yet to see a single guard I have nowhere to hand these into.

Then she thought of where she had been.

Of course, there is a place, just returning to the tavern should be fine, I'm sure the tavern master will have it all sorted out during the day, nothing to worry about.

There was, however, something to worry about that put her on edge, a feeling of caution rising in her gut as she approached the doorway. The place had gone dim, the light coming from the open door not as bright. If the place were closed for the remaining hours then surely all lights would be out but that was not so.

Deciding to be sure, Zelda took a tentative step inside, finding that there was also no sound of any sort, the place was silent, and cold. The fire having been put out, only a few glowing lamps were left to cast shadows along every wall, yet she could see the tables and benches upturned, bottles smashed.

Then it was that she laid her eyes on the tavern master, or what was left of him alongside his assistant. Their bodies were in many pieces and the larger of those were little more than pulped, slashed meat.

It was is if the air had suddenly left her and she choked, stumbling back outside hoping that out here she could at least breathe again, as she could not remove the sight from her eyes and went running as fast as she could down the road.

She could not keep it up, stopping to a halt so fast she nearly toppled forward, as before her there were two people standing with their backs to her a little way further down the main road. From where she stood she was having trouble identifying them, but they didn't appear to be any of the druids.

Both men were talking quietly amongst themselves and she could not hear what they were saying, only tell that they appeared distracted enough for her to divert herself away from them. At the same moment she sought to avoid their attention, to turn left into a side street, both turned back and saw her. One pointed and both started running at her, so she dove left, remembering to watch her footing, as she was sure that she would not get lucky a second time were she to fall.

She came out to the road which would lead her to the lower gate were she to take it all the way down. The road turned into a right bending curve on the way up, disappearing quickly under an archway, while the way down was a more or less straight line that dipped sharply but would have left her more or less visible.

Risking a look behind she saw that neither one who were chasing her had yet to enter the laneway so threw herself underneath a wagon of large grain sacks and hid under the wheels, where yet more bags that would have otherwise overburdened the wagon were placed. There she remained silent, mouth covered as the sounds of two pairs of boots approached, along with another pair from down the road running up to meet them. It was the man with the grubby jacket and white hat.

"Did you lose her? She didn't come down the road." He said, voice coarse.

None of them took more than a moment to decide that she had run further up the hill. When they disappeared around the bend, Zelda emerged from her hiding place and ran down the road instead.

As she made her way to the front gates, she did feel a burning guilt for the things she had taken. Then the thought that if she was not going very far, she should be able to return the things she took, entered back into her head and moved her on. Each sound put her on edge and the opened gate was just another step to freedom. Even at this hour there should have been guards at this gate and yet there were none of those. Someone else was waiting for her at the gate instead.

"Kieke!"

Kieke looked so sad and her voice wavered as she spoke.

"You were serious when you said you were leaving. Why are you doing this Zelda? It doesn't have to be this way, I'll take care of everything. Just you wait a little longer, I'll fix this."

"I can't wait, I'm not going to be shut away somewhere and hide, I'm going to get as far away from here as I need to so I don't have to be looking over my shoulder and you don't have to either, I have people helping me."

She only meant to push her gently but Kieke leapt back as if she had been struck. There were tears in her eyes.

"I see. You don't know what you're doing. Please understand."

Zelda fought back her own tears.

"I have to do this, I'm not safe here and the people I've been around aren't safe. There's a tavern back up the road, don't go in there. You should be making sure the kids are safe."

Kieke turned to look up the road and Zelda used the time to run, hoping she wouldn't follow. Even when she glanced back, Zelda saw Kieke remained where she was, staring. Then the woman again went back to looking quizzically up the road.

Chapter Five
Leaving Home

Zelda was out the gate and running past the farms and straight down the dirt path, where the open fields were replaced with orchards and trees that lined every side, so that the path was dark where the morning light would have otherwise been. Shadows moved out from underneath them so she skidded to a halt, but after all that it was only the druids. They all moved onto the road and looked behind her.

She did not like being frightened so, but still found herself thankful to be around company.

"One of you could have come and stayed with me. I nearly had a run in with more of those strange men. And all the people at the tavern we were at are dead. Is this because of me? What do they want from me?"

The druids all shared worried faces as they looked to the city, especially Gunter.

"We went to search the graveyard. It is a place I simply did not wish to be left alone. I still do not know the answer to your questions but that is disturbing to hear. I would be tempted to turn back if that weren't going to put you in more danger. Danger that had we stayed with you, probably would have found us in larger numbers. At least you made it this far by yourself, we can deal with the rest if it comes to that from here. Did you manage to get everything we needed?"

She nodded. She had managed to get her hands on all of the tools, the food, some round stones and string. She held the bag out but none of them seemed terribly interested in checking the contents.

"Good. I feel I must tell you something."

They all set off along the road and as they walked on past farm houses and storage huts, he continued talking in a casual way.

"Far from here and out of this kingdom there is a town where we will leave you be. It should be far enough out of the way that none should find you if any were to come looking. As I said earlier you can only come with us so far, as the journey is much too dangerous. The place we travel to is not one that looks kindly on strangers."

"Well in that case, what were you able to find in Lara's house?"

"As for that, I was unable to find anything that we might be able to take with us."

"None of her work or stories?"

"There will be no stories left to tell of any sort if we are to fail at the task set before us. You must understand, the world is in peril, Zelda. The cycle of nature that holds this world together is slowing, and after its time there shall be only death. Here in this place of places I had come seeking advice that is now dead on the wind, so you tell me the worth of those words. A harsher buried truth can not be found here. For that, we must depart this place while I go holding my heaviness with me, knowing it is nothing against the weight of the coming stillness that threatens all that live in this world."

Zelda looked around.

"Is everyone in danger? Are we in trouble?"

He sighed sadly before looking back at her.

"More than you could possibly know. Perhaps you can not feel it yet and perhaps you never will, I think, but there is a coldness creeping over this world and we must act in our place as watchers of the land. Caretakers of the trees and forests, stewards of the streams and guardians of the mountains and plains and the creatures that dwell within them all are what we are. Unlike us, this kingdom and its people have their way of looking at the world which is selfish, inward. They do not see, or do not care, I am not sure which. But to that end fades the world and the hope of all who live fade along with it. So we must be careful and move onwards swiftly. None of us wish to stay in such a place for no reason. For that, we must be on our way, and you will come with us and perhaps see what it is I mean, for a time."

They followed the twisting road until they came to a split where it connected to the next. Under the signpost, with its arrows pointing up, down and along, was someone else there waiting.

Oh how did she get here so quickly?

"Kieke! You can't be doing this, this isn't funny, I'm mean it."

The woman looked up at the group, tired lines of resignation on her face as her eyes darted from one person to the next.

"A-ah, I thought there was going to be less of you. Zelda, you can still listen to me, can't you?"

"I can't go back home."

"Well of course you can't, there are people crawling all over it. But is it so hard to just trust in me again?"

She took a step forward and all the druids pulled out weapons, simple swords that were crude, short and straight.

Zelda put her arms up to lower the weapons.

"No, don't kill her, she's a friend, she's a friend and she's got kids to look after. And I'm not one of them any more, Kieke. I was never really a child when you helped me. This is my choice, to go."

The woman herself was edging away from the others along the road.

"Then there's really nothing else I can do for you."

And so it was that they left her there, the others taking to the north west path without a backwards glance and Zelda watched her while she walked, half expecting her to follow them, but instead Kieke stayed where she was, so Zelda turned away. Only, an instant later she found she could not help herself, taking a moment to look back and by then Kieke was gone.

They were all making haste along the road when Zelda stopped walking.

Gunter turned to her.

"What is wrong?"

"So much has happened and I've never seen her act like that before. Never in my life have I seen someone become so twisted and odd."

"I would hesitate to call that twisted, yet it would appear that the darkness that spreads across the world has found a home in her heart. It was right for you to come with us if you surely thought yourself amongst her presence most safe. It has also occurred to me that our hasty departure and the unfortunate fates of those you have come across could be seen as reason enough for us to be framed, unless that too was an outcome those dark workings hoped for."

"It is if everyone suddenly went mad and on my account and if only I could understand why. I don't want anyone else to get hurt or injured, or lose their life all because of me. My life was fine, but it's all fallen apart so quickly and now if it is as you say, I'm on the run, accused of murder alongside all of you. This is all too much."

Findal looked over the road, checking back along the way they had come.

"Does she need a minute? We might be able to stop."

Zelda took some shuddering breaths and realised that it was not just tears blurring her vision.

"I think I'm going to be sick."

Survel looked around.

"We have a long way to go, but maybe the next town will be far enough, the fate of the world depends on us all."

Then suddenly, the four did something strange, their heads looking up to peer at the sky. Zelda could see nothing out of the ordinary in that dark grey sky, although the stern, uncaring coldness of it baring down on her did make her want to cry even more.

They had walked on, but she remained bleary eyed for much of the remaining early hours and even a little into the ones where the sun had risen fully in the sky, the cloudy morning passing into a blue far above the green fields. The long country road where the trees had some time ago separated out gave them a view of the land around which they now travelled and they had passed people as small as dots off in the distance who went about their business tending to their herds and farms.

There had never been a reason for her to leave her home before and by her own guess had walked longer already in an almost straight line than she had in her entire life. It was much as she had imagined it from looking out over long green fields with the mountains being these fuzzy green blue mounds off in the distance.

The road steadily took them further west and turned away from the north, where a wide plain beckoned off in the horizon, as far away as she could see.

I almost didn't see this morning. She realised.

The sounds of briskly walking feet were in her ears, and she found herself trying not to bump into anyone to keep up the pace, while staying in the middle of the group. Peter and Findal were in front while Zelda found herself next to Gunter and for all his words, Survel was last in the line, only a little further back than the others. He noticed her looking out at the farmers.

"There's no telling what is in the minds of these folk. You see them rounding up those animals? While they are certainly for food, the control over nature they are exercising shows their dark hearts at work. Nature is not a tool to be exploited and used to make the lives of thankless minds easier."

Zelda unhooked the sack to look inside it properly herself.

"This reminds me. I just wanted to make sure everything I've got here was enough, all these tools."

He chuckled.

"Oh we don't actually have any use of those things, those are part of a way of life we have all long left behind."

Her eyes went wide.

"So you're telling me you didn't need half of this stuff to begin with? Why did you get me to steal it all then?"

Peter turned to her. His face had not changed from gloomy annoyance since she had first seen him.

"To see if you would do something that most would consider against their morals. For you see, outside of the world in which you have lived there are many things you might find to be considered immoral. You need to be prepared for choices that may not suit you. And we'll find use for some of this stuff."

"Morals?"

"Yes, you see it as wrong, because those objects don't belong to you, but the way we see it, all things will return to the ground. The ground is the only true owner of anything, even all of us belong to it and are tied to it. The objects that pass through all these hands are meaningless to such a greater power, their value tied to a worth nature itself does not consider worthy. The hand and the object are the same to it, you must seek importance elsewhere when it concerns objects and things or possessions, you might say."

Findal looked into the bag as he spoke.

"Even gold passes from one hand to the next. The value placed upon it is arbitrary and false, only because it shines beautifully and is hard to come by is it sought and clutched and held in locked coffers. While gold has its worth in bribes and much of Auralin has lived off it, I look forward to a world where it can all be left behind."

The others were in agreement, and Gunter spoke back to him.

"Words a older version of yourself would have been horrified to hear. But behold in the sky the great disk. There in the sky is the greatest source of gold and warmth that metal can not provide, and all may benefit from it and none may take it away or bring it low. Those who try are the ones we seek to stop, those who would dim the world and turn it to darkness. In such an hour all things will be without value or meaning and the world will come to a meaningless end. Already this darkness spreads in the hearts of these cities where people find that the worth of their own lives, believing that they are so tied to their valueless creeds, is failing."

Zelda retied the sack.

"Well then, at the very least I can use what I have here for a time."

But she could not help but think to herself.

Have I wandered into a gang of thieves? Their words and ways are quite peculiar.

She did her best to stop those thoughts from making her legs heavy, any heavier than they already were after having been up since the early hours of the morning. As it turned out, she did not get terribly long to think of the possible consequences of having done just that and wandered into a gang of thieves, before an opportunity came and presented itself to test her worry.

Ahead of them was an upturned wagon by the side of the road, the left wheel had come loose causing the wagon to have toppled, spilling the contents of the wagon onto the road. The spindles inside the lost wheel were splintered and broken, which looked to be beyond all hope of repair. As they came closer noises of a grumpy man could be heard, becoming louder and louder as they approached.

"Why is it that my luck is so poor?" Came the voice.

"All this way I have come with my load now I must think that I should abandon it to the wild creatures as I can not make this journey on one wheel."

The sound of metal tools being thrown against wood and clattering to the ground followed the man as he walked from around the back of the wagon, to freeze upon seeing others on the road. The man was not happy at being caught unawares, staring at each of them with a grim, down turned mouth while his arms hung loosely by his sides, as if waiting for the inevitable.

"Just get your thieving and banditry over and done with, I'll have trouble enough as it is moving even several of my bags of stock on my mule, that is if you don't take him too.

Gunter held up his hands.

"We are not thieves, nor are we interested in anything in this land that might be yours, as nothing you own is needed. All we need is that which comes from the land itself."

"Well I beg your pardon but all I need is to get all this stock to the cities ahead. Having come from Gandagar I'm supposed to be stopping off at Churl first but it might be as far as I go."

The man went back to attempting to mend the wagon, moaning and muttering all the while he did so.

Once he was out of sight, Findal stroked his moustache.

"I think we could take this moment to rest our feet and at the same time benefit from this misfortune. Let us try to help this man on his way. Perhaps in doing so we could convince him to say that he did not see us on his travels, as there is only one way along here and if we are being followed I would rather not have someone following us on this road knowing that we travel on it. We should assist him and find out if he would do that for us."

Gunter looked at Zelda.

"Well what do you want to do Zelda?"

Zelda had been looking back at the road, a creeping sensation increasing down her spine that made her legs want to move very fast.

More quietly than she intended but loud enough to be heard she spoke.

"I say we stop." She said.

This isn't what I want at all but if I did say to keep going I would be obviously overruled by all the others, absolutely four to one. There's really nothing I could have said to keep them moving. Oh and after all that man does need help.

While Zelda paced around the road, Peter was busy observing the sturdy grey mule, which was obliviously munching on grass at the side of the road.

"You say that we might be able to convince him Findal, but how can we be sure of his word if he is to agree? Trusting people who look to line their pockets with the wealth of the world are hard to trust. I didn't say impossible though." He added as Findal peered at him from the corner of his eyes. Findal continued in the silence.

"Yes, people change. I'm sure we can bring this man around. If we show our good intentions all should be well."

They went around to the back of the wagon and Gunter cleared his throat and spoke to the man.

"Sir we would like to fix your wagon, if that would be fine for you?"

The man glared at them rather irritably.

"Yes, yes, help if you can, although I can't see anything on you which would help my wagon in this state, and there are not any trees around here large enough to make a proper wheel out of. And you are sure of what you tell me, that none of you need wealth for doing so?"

"None at all." He assured the man.

"While an odd thing to say, from my perspective at least, I thank you for whatever effort you can put in. I'm not one for such things, the world is more than what you are. Where are people going to get the things they need to live if we're all to be like you, with our heads stuck in the trees, you who would think to know what it is like out in the wide world?"

"It is possible that the world conspired to break the wagon, so that you might never find your way to the end of the journey you find yourself on, but we are kind, so will do what we can. Leaving a man abandoned on the road is not an option. Feel free to rest your legs while we get this done."

Zelda sat down to watch the others work, wondering how it was they might get this job done.

Gunter stuck his head out of the wagon to look at Zelda.

"Was I speaking to you when I said you could sit down?" He smiled through his chuckles before she could reply.

"Of course you can. Just don't fall asleep."

Looking back along the road filled her with a light headed dizziness. There was no one she could see, so she focussed on watching the others work to keep her eyes away from staring at the way they had come or falling asleep, which felt rather tempting indeed, but the curiosity of how they were going to fix the wheel intrigued her enough. Zelda saw that while there were trees around, there were no tools that they had brought to bring down a tree.

This turned out not to be a problem, for as she watched, Zelda saw them pick several small trees which they could bend the branches together into the shape of a wheel. They then grew the trees until they became large and the branches grew together, twisting thick. Using their swords they cut the new wheel they had just grown off the trees and left it to Survel to remove the outer bark and wood so that it could be steady and flat on the road.

"If farmers could do that I think we would all be better off." She exclaimed.

Peter shook his head. She was sure he was trying to be serious but with his age and countenance in such contrasts how could she possibly take him that way?

"I don't know why you think anyone can learn what we do. Because what could be better than using what we know for the benefit of those who would not care? The world does not look kindly on those who use it without reverence. They would only cause a glut, an over abundance that would be dismissed as they scrape the soil raw. And who would be the cause of such a benefit? Not us, not the world. Back in Churl and these lands you would all keep being liars claiming it to be from above."

Survel finished checking the woodwork.

"So our lessons aren't lost on you, Peter, good to know as always."

The new wheel fit perfectly and once it was in position could be attached where the other had broken. The wagon was removed of the rest of its load and the men hauled it upright and began to replace the wares. Wanting to do something, Zelda jumped to her feet and took a sack to place in the wagon. It wasn't hefty enough to be troublesome and by the feel of the contents was full of grain, as was most of his other bags.

After retrieving and saddling the mule, who looked most unenthusiastic at having to resume its duties, the man looked to make his way quickly, but stopped to look over those who had helped him.

"I take it you have no love for our church. Not being native to this land makes druids a rare sight around these parts, if you ever had a reason to come here at all."

Gunter nodded, and he pointed down the road.

"Will you go forth without revealing that you saw us? We are druids, indeed, and go about our days wandering around as you see here. We have concerns that there are those who would seek to stop us, merely for being who we are."

"The girl looks a little lost in the clouds for one to be tagging along compared to the rest of you. I can't help feel something is amiss."

"She'll find her walking feet soon enough and all we are doing is taking her to a place where she could rest after becoming restless in her own home."

"That all, is it? People should indeed move about if they feel that way. But don't think I won't warn you to keep a proper eye out on her and don't you go ditching her by the side of some road, sir. I've encountered no brigands or bandits thankfully on my journey but to the roads where there are, well I know a person out of their place when I see one and it would be a cruelty to leave her be without good cause."

"There is no such cause. I am taking her along a path to a place I must travel to regardless. Leaving her would only leave me holding a heavy heart for the rest of the journey, which would be most unwise. You too should not allow this misfortune to bring you down, or the darkness of the world will grip your own heart gladly." He explained.

The man laughed.

"Oh don't get yourselves down in the dumps now by talking that dark talk, business is good when it is good. You're all a bunch of the weirdest folk that I ever heard. Although, as you said, I saw you none and not at all. You saved my profits you did. The light be upon you."

The party started off again, and Zelda was left thinking about how much time they had taken and whether it was worth the good deed, for they had helped a man along his way and had no reason to do so.

"Surely we didn't have to stop?" Survel said.

"It is unfortunate we could not have just done away with him as we pleased. Do you agree, Zelda? One key thing you must learn is that all things must be beholden to nature and that is the true way of the world. Sometimes it is best to not interfere or meddle in the misfortunes of others because you deny them the struggle needed to pull themselves out of their own woes along with the triumph and understanding that comes with successfully mastering an issue at hand. If they fail then they fail, so it is in the wild, and while some animals leave those in distress, there are those beasts that prey on the ones who are weak and fallen."

Her feet hurt but she did not agree.

"While we do need to keep moving, I'm most against violence, no matter how fast it resolves a problem. That being said I don't want anyone to catch up with me, or find out that we can be caught up upon because I'm afraid if that happens we won't make it out alive."

Gunter grumbled at this.

"We're not even behind half a day of travel because of this. If we had been caught on the road then surely we would have had to leave that man to a death he may not have come across had he not been in our presence. Yet that would have been the least of our problems. Certainly we would have to fight to make it out alive because we would have to make sure we were protecting you."

"I just want to leave it all behind."

That did make her think, however, that if they had not stopped for her they would have been well on their way by now rather than only a little way along. But then it was entirely possible they might have not stopped for that man either, missed him on the road having gone past him before he had his mishap. So in a way she was happy to have been some assistance to a stranger.

When he got to the town at the roads hopefully he would help them if anyone did ask if he had seen any others on the road. She had to admit that there was no way to know if he would do so, even if that would put her mind at ease. And while that left a darkness hanging in her mind from the way they had come, there were other things that had begun to darken the road ahead for her.

"Are there really bandits out here?" Zelda asked Gunter.

"Oh not this close to Churl, but it is a possibility we might come across some a little further on our way through Alegan. There's nothing to worry about. You are the only piece of a certain part of my past I have left, a faint one at that but I will see to your safety as will the others, of course."

After a day of walking, the place she had known was gone, to be replaced by the ground sloping upwards on her right, while they all continued to walk along the road which had become narrower and narrower as the ground rose up higher so that she couldn't see what lay at the top.

She imagined shadowy figures leaping out from behind trees and rocks to come and drag her back home. But there were none of the sort, and as they descended for a time she felt that they were walking into the ground itself and the further they went the more the shade covered them.

Zelda felt herself shaking not out of fear or the fact the sun was off her back, but a promise that as she walked further into the dark along a road she did not know, that each step she took they were all descending into the belly of the world itself and would never be seen again.

As she tried looking ahead she wondered if the world was welcoming her. Then again she was walking into the unknown, and wouldn't anyone feel the way that she did, wanting to be a part of where they went? After all, if the place they left her was amongst mountains she would have to force herself to get used to them. She took a breath and tried not to imagine being smothered by the dark as she let herself sink into the shade.

Chapter Six
On the Road to Gandagar

The days that followed were not so cold as to be troubling but a wind blew in from the north and Zelda found it to be cold. She shivered, but that wasn't what made her shiver most. From the words of the others she had heard them speak amongst themselves to discuss the presence of shadows on the road and she took that to mean that they were being followed in a way she could not see.

That must have been it. Not wishing to alarm her they walked alongside the road, and sometimes off the road entirely, so that they might avoid those who would choose to follow them. Her boots had never been in such a sorry state for so long and her feet ached from the distance walked in them.

Many days had passed in this manner, steadily as they travelled west then north, then west again and as they did she began to see changes in the countryside around her. More trees with green leaves and thicker bark on browner trunks were along the road as the ground became steeper and more wild. While they still travelled down the same road that descended through gullies and turned to climb upwards, the mountains now behind them were replaced with hills that steadied as they travelled until the road pushed upwards, setting them on a long, flat stretch of road that was carved out of the top of the hills.

Down the left of the road there was ground that dropped off sharply after a few paces into a forest of dark green hills that crossed into each other as far as she could see. Where the hills connected low, further down, there were dark ravines that set them apart that reminded Zelda of a spider's web. On the right, poking through the trees, their view was of the hills alongside them elevated slightly higher and it was these hills that the road was gradually turning to meet. It felt that they would quite likely not be nearing their destination soon for there were no obvious signs of life along the road. Unless the life was in those dark shadows being talked about that were creeping where she couldn't see.

To distract herself from those horrid thoughts, Zelda spent her time watching the others go about their business as they tested trees and ground. To the druids this appeared to be of some utmost importance, as they happened to make these stops with some frequency with which she had first observed with fascination but now, well it was more to make sure they were actually doing anything at all. Sometimes they would stop suddenly and Gunter would say that they had to check on a cluster of trees or the insects that lived in a hollow trunk amongst them.

"Why do you do such things?" She asked on one of these occasions.

"To ensure that all is as it should be." Came the reply. And then he would knit his brows and elaborate further.

"That is only to the extent that it can be, of course. We are on our quest to right a wrong greater than a slight straying of the cycle. Where a single colony of insects might overwhelm the equilibrium of a small place such as this cluster of trees, none of this matters in the face of such dark adversity that you yourself have felt."

She had not felt anything of the sort of which he was saying.

"I've had to run away and now for days we have been walking and a part of me wants to be sure, absolutely, that I would not have a confrontation of the likes again. So of course I have to keep going. Perhaps if there could be some certainty in safety I could find myself returning but in the meantime do wonder if I should indeed be camping out in trees to be hidden from sight."

"You'll do so as long as it takes us to get to the place I have in mind, a place quite a way away from here still, but one where you should be able to hide without worrying yourself of where it is you sleep. We are not thoroughly out in the open as we would have been were we to take the north road out of Churl and travel that way. We would have also been surrounded by people who's minds would have been unknown to us but nonetheless darkened and troubled by life on such roads and towns that told them to live for themselves and disregard nature. Do you worry that we will be caught unawares one night by such people?"

She shook her head.

"Not that. I have a bad feeling about this, as if just beyond me some horror that I have yet to see is catching up with us. It comes and goes, however I may just be jumpy and looking for excuses in the things I see and hear, but we definitely need to keep moving. Every time we stop I have to turn my head back to the road and wonder if now will be the time we are caught upon. Not when we're sleeping because everyone has to sleep."

Gunter and Survel looked to each other and both men shrugged, and without saying a further word left her alone while they went about their business.

Zelda wandered to the road and looked along it in both directions. The way they had come was very far away and through twists and turns there was only so far she could see into the distance and all she could see ahead were hills that she could not decide were mighty or small. Not knowing which made her feel small. Smaller than she was already. Occasionally, staring out over the vastness of the plains had made her stop in awe of them, especially when the sun shone off them, and had reminded her importantly of those around her, made her think of home, where everything she had known had been. These hills that rolled on were not familiar, the land looked as if it were moving, not flat on stable ground. A stable place was her home no longer though, and perhaps it wasn't terribly fair to call these hills an unstable place, they were just different.

I need to withdraw from the world, some place away from the eyes of others. If I had stayed instead of walking on this road I would have died without the help of anyone around me, or they would have tried to help and perished too. All for me being a person used to reaching out my hand and asking for help.

Zelda had once managed to pull herself out of her younger sorrows after being left alone, there remained that hand held out waiting but not expecting, for someone to grab it or put something in it. Now though, as she was surrounded by strange men who talked to trees, she wasn't sure if she should ever hold out her hand to reach again.

She felt she could not do so, and instead would use her hands to support herself, to hold onto the short sword she had been given, a weapon she had no intention of using. She supposed that there were those that lived their lives with these as their friends, all the support they needed and all the world they saw would balance on its edge. Zelda wondered what Gunter would think of that but decided against asking him, not wanting him to think that she was interested in a sword in the way Survel was.

A dead man had swung out a sword to that hand and by doing so all she had known in her pleasant life had gone in an instant. That had been the moment, she realised, even if there were many moments along this road where she could have decided that her old life was behind her, that someone would take their sword to her was when it had happened. She had no interest in the violence that she had suddenly found in the world and while she could not use the sword as an excuse, Zelda knew that there might come times where it would be useful.

Had she been a warrior with a sword then no man would have caught her unawares or helpless, that was not who she was, however. That at least was what she believed, as anyone could swing a sword and Zelda found inside herself no fascination for it. What did that mean for those who did? If she searched inside them she could guess at what she would find, either the same coldness in that of the alleyway death or some twisted fascination for the object as some might, having nothing else to turn their affection too.

If I had a sword and knew how to use it I would have not had to see such coldness in others, such as one I'm now journeying with, and relying on for my own protection. However, I am thankful for that at least, and the reassurance from knowing those cold eyes and metal edges won't be turned on me.

Zelda had only seen the world as being so cold once before when Lara had died, despite not being family hers had been the face of the only one she had known. There the world might have stayed looking at her, surrounding her as to be cold seemingly forever and there she would have stayed were it not for the kindness of another who had taken her in and had not seen her as an orphan returning to the fold. Quiet the opposite, and there Zelda had found happiness again with a shoulder to lean on, and where she had learned to be that same shoulder for others.

Home had been a sleepy little place before the king had arrived and it seemed that so much had happened so quickly that she hadn't realised she had been growing up. For the little that had all meant in the end, as growing up while the walls had been raised had happened not just to her home, but to herself too, and she had trusted them to keep her looking at a place she had found to be safe, as neither had lasted in the face of true danger, or perhaps the druids would simply call that a thankful clearing of her mind.

"The king must be right to hide himself away." She said.

Findal raised his eyebrows.

"Whatever do you say that for?"

"Outside the walls of his castle the world is a terror, at least to those who don't know better. But he must know better, mustn't he?"

"As far as you should see it, anyone back there is all the same. They're cold, dark people, all willing to do to you again what they nearly did to you before. That king just allows it to happen, watching from up on high like the foolish magicians of old. Mind you he is no such man, just a man who thinks himself holy, whatever that means to you these days."

Whatever it meant to Zelda was not something she had honestly thought much about. Clearly the king had power, that she had always known, but it had never been dark or cold power, at least in her mind. In all truth the world had seemed so much brighter on their arrival. Trying to get a glimpse of the prince, or wondering what life was like now beyond those closed off walls, that had added a sense of wonder in questioning the lives of those they could not see and no one was fearful of them or for them. There had been no terrible change that had made her question the warmth that came from all people before. As long as that warmth was not from fire after all and there had not been any of those people to question why they might be around either. They had all been protected while the king had brought his foresight to their city and with it, a warm increase and buzz of life.

With the increase in people she had gone about her days holding her arms out for others and had found happiness in it. Even at the memory of it, her worry subsided to be replaced with that glad happiness that was given to her on a good day's work. A happiness that choked and died in her throat.

Those people were getting further and further away, a distance she could no longer see in her mind as she had quite lost track of the pace that had been set. A part of her didn't even want to know, as the distance might halt her just by thinking about it. Having never travelled out of the city was one thing but to have a destination so far as to almost leave the land in which she was born behind, that was unthinkable. It almost didn't feel right, as if the very steps she took would be severing her from a place that had sustained her and to which she would not be able to return.

Zelda looked down at the sword. There was nothing special about this weapon, yet here in her hands was proof that she was leaving her old self behind whether she wanted to or not. Perhaps returning would mean relying on such a thing. She was not a person who wanted at all to rely on such a thing, so what was she supposed to do with it? Brandish it at other people or threaten them? Certainly she found herself questioning for how long she would be in a place where she needed one but Gunter seemed to believe that she needed it, even if they themselves surely should have been enough to guard her from anything.

I'm cautious at having a man such as Survel as my teacher. Would those cold eyes rub off on me too? And the fact of the matter is I'm going to be left in a town while they proceed onwards with their quest. If they leave without me completing my training would that not leave me in danger of making mistakes while training on my own? Also, I wouldn't want to be spotted and thrust into a militia if there was any sort of war. If I remain as I am they would have no reason to enlist me and march me off.

Zelda suddenly had a vivid image of herself marched off into some northern conflict where she would die alone amongst all others who would be sent off to die in such a place. Lara had often told stories of many such soldiers. Unknown faces that she had not known were left in the aftermath of such battles, staring blankly with nothing left at all to say. For some she had thought up and wrote about what she had imagined their lives must have been like. They were nobodies on doomed battlefields who would never come home, so in her mind had given them places to be in her own world, even if that past was most likely not the case and those places had never been, nor would ever be.

Zelda had listened to these tales hoping that nothing would ever come of them that she could compare with her own life, yet here she was mulling them over, wondering if she might ever find herself in one, which was an ever growing possibility in her mind.

The only problem here is I can't see any of them picking up a pen and scribbling away with ink to tell of all of this. And if I was to die why would they record such a failure? It would be nice to be remembered but after all I'm just a traveller trying to look after my own head.

Had she died, Zelda was sure that she would have been remembered. There were only few who had turned up to help her bury Lara, however, and for herself she would have to expect nothing more than that. If she never came home, who would know that she had died and who would care? As some girl who ran away in the early morning with no words or outward understanding of who she was, only that she was in danger, to which she might still be looked over if she perished alone on some road without having learnt a single lesson. Even the druids had more than that. People they met might not know their names, but what they stood for, which was so strange and different was well known and journeyed ahead of them as they travelled. Or so it seemed to her at least. Then again, she certainly did not look the part of some druid and found herself aloft in their conversations from time to time, unable to find a point on which she might speak.

All the druids knew what it was they were doing and saying when they went about those things such as talking to trees. Certainly they were not brutes and the more she watched their slow, deliberate study of the trees and the animals knew that they took their time where it was needed most.

But the slowness of their journey perturbed her. Grim and grizzle were the moods of the days when it suited them which turned end on end and many nights passed overhead where at the least of it she was thankful for such guardians. Safety was not a thing that one got from walls alone. There still had to be people willing to stand and defend those behind them and none had come to her aid when she had needed it. The world beyond those walls was no different, full of people who would do nothing while caught up in their own lives showing how little any of them truly mattered.

In the face of such things as the mountains and rivers and other natural wonders, it was easy for Zelda to see why it was that the druids spent time surrounded by them and tried to make others understand their ways of thinking when coming into civilised lands. The fact that they would take anyone else along at all, Zelda felt was special and showed to her that despite their ways they were not as cold as they appeared. They still had to concentrate on their tasks, yet she was here, showing to everyone that might look that they were concerned in matters beyond their own.

Where was that concern now in everyone else? Who stopped to watch the sun set, or the wind blowing through the trees gently swaying their branches in its wake? They stopped and made their own time to remind themselves what it was they were on their way to defend. And here she was just watching them do so, while occasionally sneaking in some moments of happiness amongst the sights and the sunsets that she felt guilty about later because she herself was one of those others to them, she knew she shared the complacency that came with not knowing their ways and was waiting for others to carry out their journeys.

If what they said was true, then there was nothing she could accomplish among them that they could not do themselves. Merely a girl who ran away from home, perhaps now with a sword in her hands with which she could at least defend herself, but not understand what was at stake the way they did.

Even so, one could not hide behind a sword, and Zelda found herself unwilling to hide behind one that she herself would hold. That wasn't her, couldn't be her. Perhaps she would write instead of this part of her life where she met these strange people who went off and defeated a darkness that even they shuddered to speak of. Often she had found herself looking out at the world on a bright day, but it occurred to her that she had never been worried by not seeing others do the same. If dark days were approaching it would be best for everyone if they were around to do something about it. Who else had she seen, or heard that had this duty? There had been nothing, not a drop in the rumour mill or in the water from anywhere. If none of this had happened to her she felt that she would have been left quite unawares and that wasn't something she wanted to be caught as any longer.

So here she was with a sword in her hands, being given what might as well be all the time in the world to glance behind to make sure none were following who had come to finish what they had started with her. And yet the druids were still going about their way, humming amongst themselves and she held in herself a shaking breath that escaped more than a sigh, almost as a plea to any that might hear. None of the others could hear it as the sound was masked through the wind, which was cold, so she had to think that there might be something else out there that would listen.

I guess that was the old me. The one who could stand by and watch the world go by. Now all I wish for is the speed and haste to go forward without such distractions making me stop, but that isn't for me to decide. The druids, they should be deserving of me putting my trust in them for saving me and having kept their word so far. I also have no reason to doubt them still. But if that is so, then I should not feel better holding this sword.

There was nothing so peculiar about wanting the world to pass them by even if that wasn't where she found herself now and the road ahead held places unknown which prevented the urge from walking on by herself from being any stronger than a mild form of interest, quickly dashed. Instead of walking on, some feeling inside her forced her to look around and think things through, even if her eyes darted to spaces hidden in shadow that appeared so much more dangerous when standing alone on that road with only a sword for company. The sheath dug into her hands which brought to her a sense of comfort and Zelda found she was hating herself for it.

Chapter Seven
The Warlock

In the middle of the night, a person ran out through the fields outside of Churl until they could run no more. This would have been a sight to see, were anyone outside at this time to see it. Even so, she had always been careful to avoid being spotted, most absolutely, especially on nights such as this one, where both the moons were up and shining, where she hoped no one would bother to be awake and notice her. Not one to rely on such influence, sometimes her master would stroke her mind to let her know that someone had become just a little too interested in her and she would be thankful and invite the stranger into her home so that their curiosity could forever be sated.

But now, Kieke was being punished, as she keeled over in the moonlight and vomited. The girl had been a key which had slipped through her fingers. On an unassuming encounter a few years ago her master had told her, warned her, that the girl was important. Now she was gone. Far out of reach, hidden behind the blades of free minded, tree addled cowards. Surely they would turn her over at the nearest convenience to themselves.

There was always the possibility that they had suspected something, that they had noticed that feeling that made her special. Her master had not been one to elaborate further than he had and she herself had done her part and gone along with his words, being so careful to be someone Zelda had needed. Not careful enough.

As her body wracked and twisted with pain, she collapsed in a heap, a few yards short of the old farm house. It had to be tonight this happened, not just because it was the night immediately after her failure, but because this was how they would punish her in a way that could be most severe. With both moons full her master's power was strongest and most clear on these nights, even though she had not always found him to be receptive during those times, since when were he ever at her calling?

No, Kieke would sometimes find herself alone for weeks, months at a time only to be checked up on during the oddest of moments and at other times her master had hung around enough in her head to be a second voice in the back of her mind, correcting her notions of right and wrong, for which she had always been thankful. Most of all she greatly enjoyed using the magic given to her but wasn't having fun now. She couldn't even feel her legs.

That to her was a sign that she had greatly aggrieved her master. Well now she had to bear the lesson that was being meted out on her, but here of all places? Farmers on their morning routes would easily spot her if she were to lose conciousness. Hopefully she would be able to crawl the rest of the way so that she would not be spotted in such a position. Surely her master didn't want that, because then everything would be over. Word would get out and that would be the end of her, sneaking around the place in the middle of the night, deeply suspicious as it was, wouldn't stop one such as her from being dragged in front of the people, to be decided what it was she could be guilty of. They would not need to wonder if they took a look inside the house, however.

Oh let me not succumb this night to be spotted out here in the morning!

Kieke gritted her teeth with effort and braced herself to stand, hoping her body would obey. In response, she heaved and threw up again. Sweat trickled down the side of her face and inside each little bead heard her master's voice, muttering faintly, each one with different words she could not completely hear and each one was an extra eye that could see her and had turned to look at her in the eyes to know her fear. Her ears were filled with a swarm of her master's words while her head was swimming with both light and darkness swirling in her vision. When it cleared, Kieke was left staring down at the puddle she had just made.

What a waste of good vomit.

The rippling voice of her master spoke, as a great powerful voice that rose in a great tremor, from deep depths of water disturbed far across a great ocean. The voice wasn't just in front of her, it was in her head and she could feel it under her skin, through her body.

'And yet I can feel you through it. You speak of waste? Look at what you had, what you could have had if you had not failed.'

It was never all mine. She thought to the voice.

The magic wasn't hers, it belonging to her master, the deep one. Kieke merely made use of it to further the goals of her master.

'But you could have have had it. Was it not enough? Were my powers not enough for you? Were you wanting more? Hoping that by this failure I would give you more?'

No.

'All for you to hide from you own inadequacy. By daring to suggest what I would give you was inadequate.'

No!

Her master was holding all that power in front of her, just out of her reach. A power that had never been hers fully, but Kieke was painfully aware that what she had was slowly draining away. There up in the sky shining so full and bright were the twin moons and she imagined they were his eyes and she dared not look at them. Regardless, she could feel the power buzzing in her belly that made pins and needles set into her legs. As for the rest of her body, there was no strength in her limbs, which weighed heavy, so she found herself unable to get up.

Now wouldn't that be a sight if I were to collapse right now, instead of crawling my way to the house. I really don't want to have to crawl.

She didn't have to, not if she didn't want to. After a moment of steadily tucking her legs under herself to push herself up, she found herself staggering to her feet, making the rest of the way to the farm house light headed on uneasy legs. Once inside she collapsed with her back against the door. Anyone else would have fallen lame at the dripping stench held within these walls but Kieke took a moment to breathe it all in.

There would be some investigation into the people in the tavern who went missing, absolutely, but she decided she might as well cut herself a break from ambushing senseless pilgrims and farmers.

She had to drag them through the swampy mud all the way back to the house at the edge of the fields, but she had hoped that they would be worth something to her master. They were not. She had trusted too much in herself. Her master had done so too, so now she suffered in the dark alongside the bodies of the recently and not so recently dead as the voice of her master rippled through all the pools on the floor.

'What are these you have brought before me? You know better than to try and placate me after your failures. Your continued existence shall be my decision alone.'

Kieke opened her mouth to speak.

"I tried to do as you asked master. Three times I tried. I know she needed to stay, she's the key to get me into the castle. I didn't tie her up I know but I didn't want to accidentally kill her, and there have been so many of those accidents I did not want to risk mishandling her."

'Complacency, overconfidence.'

Such words rolled in her head as her master made her writhe. Her body was cramping up all over the place and among the stress and the sweat found she could not move.

'These things from you? Do better.'

"It has been years since my last-"

'Your years mean nothing.'

The voice cut into her like a knife while she groaned.

'It is too late now for the key, you must find another way in.'

"To get closer to the king. I have the kids. If I fail then surely then over the years one of them could succeed."

'It must be you. Your tide is receding yet I will set it right. The darkness approaches and you no longer have the years. You must succeed or the world will perish to darkness.'

Feeling weak and angry about her lameness, she asked her master a question.

"Then what am I going to do about myself now?"

'What you always do. As you are told.'

Kieke was left alone hearing only the slow lapping of small red tides steadily receding, much as her own had been. She knew of the endless ocean but she was not a part of that ocean far from home, there would be no home as long as the king lived. Years, years she had been getting closer, only to now have the most certain means of success slip through her fingers. Now she had to make do with what she had all over again from the start. For that, however, she would start in the morning.

***

The archer had been stationed at the top of the wall for some time, he had seen people come and go. In his boredom he had taken to recognising people as they made their ways to and from the city. Farmers who would angrily shake their fists at the wall that added a fair distance to the walk back to their homes, people going to and from market with their particular orders, the woman who ran the orphanage.

He was still a fair way back from the actual city, when he turned around he could see the second wall behind him far beyond the buildings and trees that had now been enclosed. It was hard for him to believe that they had actually enclosed the whole town here, as keeping everyone safe was one thing, walling land off from the outside was another.

Well that wasn't his decision and those castle walls were so far away it made him question who he really was protecting. There had never been a need for people in armour roaming the streets.

The people behind me shouldn't need my help and yet they say something had happened in the early hours of the last morning, or so the rumour has spread.

It seemed that bandits had made their way into the city, ransacked a tavern before leaving, at least not west according to the word of one, yet not without having taken a few things here and there from some people before doing so. A sad tale but back behind the second wall, how would any of those think to care about such an act happening beyond their walls? They would not. The outside was still the outside to them, so the town beyond Churl, with its grass, clusters of houses and trees, would likely never be accepted into the city proper, at least that was how he saw it.

How accepting they could be of people had not changed. The king had come, so had people from all around come with him, filling the place out, making it grow with a sound that had been scarcely heard for years, of people and all kinds rumbling within. None of the king's men would be expected to live out here, and he knew of none who did. He didn't expect them to keep a low profile either, being who they were.

Looking down, he saw the small swarm of children that followed that woman around. Impossible for such a person to keep their own profile low surrounded like that. He didn't know how she did it and couldn't have stood the constant attention himself.

"Off to church are we?" He called down.

She looked up and called up to him.

"Ha, funny you to ask. There's business to be done there today for sure, but whisking these ones off to keep them out of harm's way if they were to stray around the farm comes first."

"I don't see the humour, if it's all the same to you. You would think the grim hearts out there in the fields would be warmed a bit by such a bunch as yours. Farmers giving you much trouble out there?"

It was that he more often saw their faces to be unhappy, he himself did not understand why, as there was enough food he thought, at least to go around, even for everyone there was enough, not that he himself was going to be taking up that sort of work.

Kieke responded to him with a shrug and a look of admittance coming and passing over her face.

"I was myself one of them so I know where they're coming from this time of year. Did some toiling out there for a while until I took this up because no one else would. In honesty lately I did offer to swap my residence with those of the farmers who dwell within one of them nice little town houses cause the orphanage is right next to the fields they work in all day but apparently that costs more effort than it is worth. They own those pieces of land in here, not what I live on though, so aren't eager to give them up."

"Their loss."

"Aye yeah. I'd even hold the doors of the church open to them if I had to, to make sure everyone got inside to have a chat."

"And yet the doors shut at night. You'd be forced out eventually."

"Yes I would be." She said.

Kieke shuffled off with the kids in tow. There was time to spare and she let them loose in what had once been the center of town, until the services moved further up behind the second wall. At least here they could play in reasonable quiet without disturbing anybody.

She had a place she wanted to be so slipped away and made her way along paths on the right to the wall close to the river, below the lower gate.

Just before she reached the old house she was heading for, she peeked around the corner to make sure that there was no one there who would be guarding it. After all for most of yesterday the house had been covered in people snooping all over it. Whether there was anything left inside wasn't entirely her concern, the place itself was more of what she was after. Yet if there was anything left there she might be able to find signs or clues as to where Zelda had gone. Not a hope that she could do much about all that right now but it would steady her to know a little more than the smallest scraps she was spending far too much time wrapping herself up in a headache for while trying to piece together what she knew.

Her master would know, for he knew where all the water went and might pick a trace of the girl up at a river or stream. Yet to tell her, that would not happen. Her master had already put the key behind them, so anything she could find herself was most appreciable.

With the coast clear, Kieke made her way up to the door and found it unbolted. Most of these buildings had been converted into storehouses that were out of the way, but anyone could just walk down the street and take a look around, with the doors being locked shut of course. Not this one though and she pushed her way inside to find the place had been turned over. More or less to be expected with all the activity going on recently and a part of Kieke found herself not wanting to disturb it further.

Still, she sorted through a few strewn books and scrolls of paper briefly without finding anything that would have compelled her to continue and she put everything back down as she had found it carefully. She had been searching for somewhere else to stay and knew she would have to convince the Church to allow her to move the orphans, if not into a farmer's town house then somewhere such as this.

Dust floating in the air, catching the sunlight made her cough and she knew she had to leave. It wouldn't do to have anyone catch her stalking the place out.

The farm house was getting a bit too big for the few or so left under her care and there were plenty of houses that the king had brought from people that were not being used for anything other than the storage of grain. Back outside she felt the walls rise up behind her, just as they did stare at her up ahead.

This was what she saw everyday. That place so close yet so far. Did she have dreams of it too? None certainly the way I do. Well if she did it is likely that they will never come to pass. Dreams are only dreams after all, and it is likely those ones are over.

No one answered her silent questioning, in fact Kieke could not hear a soul, this place was quiet and she was alone. She ripped her eyes away from the castle to peer over her shoulder. There would have been a time when a wall had not obscured the river and fields and she could have seen and heard all sorts of things. People fishing along the river, people walking along the roads and she had watched years back with steady, horrified interest as the two walls gradually went up. The only wall stopping her was the one that stopped her and everyone else from getting into the castle and prying into the grounds. No matter how frustrating, she knew there were others out there with similar needs, not necessarily similar intentions yet still all the same looking and longing.

It's a pity I can't leverage that at all to get into the castle. As one voice amongst all the others, what is mine compared to dignitaries and far off royalty? I'm certainly not going to be able to slip in with one of those.

That hadn't stopped her from trying before, although it had turned out that trying to sell herself into slavery by begging at the heels of the rich and wealthy only made her appear far too desperate for their attention so that doing so again was no longer an option. Moving in closer one step at a time would have to be the way to go, meaning she would have to go through the church to get this place and regardless how much in her mind she looked for an answer to her troubles today she had to treat this day as any other.

Further out from the first wall the enclosed town was bustling and bright in the sun and people were living their lives none the wiser, or perhaps just a little concerned at the roughness of the fates of those who had gone missing. And now she was looking for a place that would put her and the others out of the way, trying not to appear too opportunistic. Kieke could hear her voice now.

"I did happen to notice that a residence has opened up in a rather convenient location and appears unoccupied..."

So the days passed and Kieke was happy that everything had gone well. She had managed to grab hold of that house, a new place she now had available for the kids, more often than not they would be found in that old black wood house on the rim of the outer wall and much of their time was spent there. That old farm house was falling to pieces while this old house was in much a better, sturdy shape. Also, being inside the walls gave Kieke peace of mind and was another talking point for her and all the others who spent their time chatting, because she had known the one who the house had belonged to and seemed to have been passed from person to person as if by fate.

"I wish I could believe in such a thing as fate." She told one of the other women, who were both minding their kids.

Often it was important to get the younger ones together so they could play in the fields and socialise, let them just go out and be kids for a brief time. Kieke could not relate to it herself, letting them loose to make their own fun together as a requirement for city living, even if others told her they might get lost wandering the city in their boredom if nothing else.

"So, you don't believe in being sent messages and being told what your life has in store? What a strange way to live. You aught to keep your head down more."

"I know you're not being serious but for me it is only right to believe in what I see and hear, not because the clouds make the light shine down a certain way. Sometimes future events are determined for us, other times it is clear what direction we will go only because we have tasks to complete that have preferred outcomes so we're compelled to do them."

Kieke smiled out at all the playing kids.

"I just want them to be happy, not to be knowing that feeling again of abandonment and aloneness that some of them have felt. It's good to be part of something, even if it's make believe."

"It's rare that we would get such cold comments from you."

"I'm serious about all of it. A person can see themselves as part of something and not really be a part of it at all. Maybe that's because they are not acknowledged by the group who truly are part of it, or it could be that they're doing something wrong themselves and are not worthy of the support. Some people will look out and only see a group of abandoned children, so it's up to me to turn their attention away from such thoughts and focus instead on being a part of this family. I don't want them to see themselves the way that the world sees them."

At first she had been welcomed as anyone else was looking for a home and eager to work. She hadn't been aware of the underside at the time while tilling the fields but had to admit her alarm when she took up the church's offer of looking after the orphans. Why people would come to another country and simply abandon their children and move on was reasoning beyond her and many others where efforts to rehome them even amongst their own people had been impossible. There was nothing wrong with any of these kids, they just weren't wanted for one reason or another and she and her master were happy to have them.

"You only need one person to start the doubt, the feeling that you don't belong follows close behind. It is all fine to talk about my fate, because I couldn't care less what anyone else thinks of me, however I don't believe that their fates were written as such sad stories. That being so, I allow them to have their choices because ultimately the choices of others led them to my care for reasons I'll never know. And if I were to choose, then they wouldn't have these fates at all. They would be out there, glad and well, without worries."

And it seemed as if they had no worries out in the fields, the children of Churl would mix with the pilgrim children and they would all get along just fine. She noticed some of the children looking and playing with an object poking it with sticks. It took both women a moment to see clothes being held up and played with for both of them to go running over.

In the part of the field where there was a ditch stank the body of some unfortunate soul, likely uncovered by some creature during the night thanks to the shallow burial. No, it wasn't her work, she'd not toss such a specimen and she had to ignore the little spark in the back of her mind. This was supposed to be an unfortunate sight after all. Then she realised that it was, because she couldn't haul this one off and make use of it.

Both women ushered the kids away from the scene and after debating what to do Kieke pointed back to the city.

"I have to go to the church and see if I can get more assistance, some of the things in the farm house are not mine and I can not take them from there to the city so I'm short of supplies. I should go now, early, they will want to know about this. Can you see to the young ones for the time being? Don't worry, they'll do what they're told."

The other woman agreed and Kieke left her with the kids as she made her way to the church. She didn't have to tell them what to do, they just knew to behave, like her. Exactly like her.

Chapter Eight
Tidings at the Church of Churl

Kieke tipped off a guard as she went through the gates but as was frequently the case these days they just shrugged and went about their lazy way. She had a sneaking suspicion she knew where all these pilgrims were suddenly getting work. Their pilgrimage over, they would not return home and who better to guard such a holy city than those who had proven their devotion beyond all doubt?

These people are guarding a city, not its people.

The thought turned over in her head. You could take out all the people and a city would still be just that, a city, one that would be rather empty and devoid of anything that made the standing structures worthwhile. Would people still roam such a place? Would they still come to such a place? Of course they would, for this place was the special, holy place of the pilgrimage for which they would be thankful for the light which they could not see.

People do not need a city to exist and yet that's exactly what recent history shows us.

There were conveniences that came with staying around other people who could do what you could not because life worked better that way. Why separate yourself from those you had known if you could continue to live alongside them?

As she passed people in the streets, some in little clusters praying, Kieke knew that taking these people out of their place would ruin them. The desire to belong was strong and that made it too easy for a person to lose themselves in the significance of their own homes. It was as if they never stopped to think that a pilgrimage was just that for a reason, you had to eventually return home.

One only needed a strong enough anchor to where they came from to be rid of this notion. Kieke's own home was far, far away, and while there was nothing wrong with joining in and being happy and honest as one could be she missed the sea and had never thought to remain here forever. To live in a way so simply and earnestly among those others who were not even looking at you twice, well there was little sympathy she could find in the matter for those who did and found their own selves lacking, or disappearing entirely into the dark. When she was done and the king was dead, the people would make their own choices whether to stay or go and whether to take the left over pieces of their faith with them.

Enough of them did when they departed with their pilgrimage completed, into the north, into the east, and into the lands below. How they would cope and how far they would go she did not know. Then again, it was possible that they would all curl up and moan, the way some did now that she passed, not for any sadness, but to remind themselves that they were weak.

Almost time for me to play the part again.

She would not play that part of weakness that others did, one where she would be tempering her courage and self conviction to be reminded that she should cower before the king. Her part was one not even rehearsed, as this was her life, not some woeful play. Long ago had Kieke let the grit settle in and over time had made herself get used to the feel of it that had left her chafed red and raw in the flesh on many occasions but a little pain to her was just that, pain. The church talked about pain too as the truth of life, a ray of light in their lives to know if it was lived well. Something to set them apart from all those soft peoples in lands they would never see. If only they knew the story as it was from the ancient beginning.

In all honesty, Kieke didn't know the whole story either, as it pre dated her master's awareness of this world, but all together felt very much aware it was not what Churl was preaching. It had been so long that the old truth had been cut up and buried with none thinking otherwise, if they ever thought at all. Did a bunch of blind men really find their sight restored? Certain magic could do that, magic that had not been seen in these lands for a long, ancient time. If that were so then it became clear how to justify looking the other way and keeping magic out of these lands as all the miraculous doings had to come from within. And after all there was that reminder of who stepped forward to guide the people after that terrible time and flame.

As she often did, she wondered where those words were out in the wider world of Auralin and if they had reached her home. If so they certainly would not have been written down, unlike the case here. People out in the lands beyond knew what life meant, whereas life was whatever the the king told you it was in Churl. Normalised suffering made her sick, more than any dead body ever would and one thing would lead to another if she did not fulfil her mission, as this foul darkness would spread. First, she had to be another person, one who might just be sick at the sight of a dead body and one who relied heavily on the church that told her just how much she should suffer.

And here she was, standing in front of the place she had needed to be, reached with feet that had walked more than what most in this wretched land ever would. The followers of the church were something else entirely. Years ago she had first encountered it and it never ceased to make her scratch her head how people followed in the words of a pack of overly forgiving once blind men some many hundreds on hundreds of years dead.

The building was enormous, built off the side of the castle and interred through the inner wall so people in the castle could come and go whenever they wanted within daylight hours. How keen she was to find that door, to then slip away into the shadows and use it to gain entrance into the castle and finally reach the king himself.

As much as she would have liked to have been, Kieke would not be left alone for a moment to go snooping whenever she came here. There were always guards and preachers bustling about that would spot her and few would keep her waiting if she needed to meet with them, leaving not enough time to search all the places she wanted to. As it was with bolting in unannounced and early, it meant that she would be forced to wait.

From her entrance on the left, she could see the main chamber was empty of people, the stone walls with their side walkways separated by pillars and the levels above. She could hear and almost feel the scurrying of people beyond these walls like mice and here and there a robed person might appear for a moment while going about their business at a frenetic pace for whatever reason they might be.

While she waited for one to stick their head out into the main building, she roamed the main chamber, which was large enough to seat over one thousand at a time. There were rows of low wood tables at which people could kneel at, facing the front of the room where a stone slab low to the ground was placed for all to see. Choosing a row on the left, she knelt down close to the isle and Kieke pretended to pray.

No words came to her mind as she knelt there waiting for someone to come. She could always say she was thinking of the one who was now dead out in the fields if someone were to ask her for what she prayed, but to say that would not have been the truth. Far too many people died for her to care and far more would from a source beyond these walls and halls. The words might echo out from the chambers into the cold hearts of those who heard them, but not hers. It was important to leave space in her head for herself with her thoughts, where she could spend some time alone in her own head. For that at least, this place was most helpful.

Thinking about herself wasn't something Kieke did often. She was more often than not at the behest of her master's words and choices, or dealing with the children. Time truly alone was precious, but such things were often put on shelves high out of reach, only to be looked at and admired, maybe to be taken down once in a while to be examined before being put away again. Such things were not for her, surrounded by children and the voices near and far, voices that might all turn silent later if she were to fail. Did any of those other preachers within these walls worry about the darkness that came their way? No, of course not, they were blind, thankless, and they ate and drank the words of the king as if it alone could sustain them. Kieke had seen too many sad, thin little faces to believe that was possible.

When will it be my body that someone discovers in a ditch, when all this is done?

Unless there was no one left by the time she had her chance for anyone to even look upon it, and all that would be left would be her and all those that she had gathered, silently watching the blood of the king drain into the ground. If only that would be enough by then. Oh let it be enough.

Yet there was only so much she could do on this side of the wall, a wall she could not climb or otherwise use her magic to remove this obstacle in her path. Some time coming she would have to make her own way in whether anyone wanted her to or not.

Showing herself for what she was, that was not a pleasant thought. She had resisted doing so for so long it would have been foolish for her to change that now, as each person she took away brought her closer to her mission.

You can't take it back, the things you do. It's not in your nature to hide in the dark, that is the realm of foolish kings and those who are foul and dead.

It was mandatory, the acts needing to be done. Her master demanded it and she felt no sadness when doing so, for after all it did slowly aid in her mission. And after so many years she had this silent longing to see its end and be done with it finally. What Kieke would do after she wasn't sure of, but there would be no need for this place which she now found herself in. All the grand frivolity amounting to nothing but the wealth only royalty could afford.

Pity they couldn't use their gold on other things, that might honestly open their eyes. She was thankful that in this time there was no army they could buy with such coin to go spread their lies further, strengthening the darkness. This entire place reeked of the king's vomit, even if it came out of the mouth of another.

Once she was done she would turn the whole place over into a storehouse or another useful space, just as the king had done with the houses at the city's edges. If anything she felt somewhat inspired. That's all the good it was now anyway, a glorified slab of stone where she could perhaps sneak past the watchers and the guards and make her way inside then watch everything fall to pieces the way she wanted it to from the roof.

She rose off sore knees when someone finally came to her, a man in a white hat with a few days of careless growth around his face. Enough grey hairs sprouting amongst the black to make him appear older than he perhaps was, with watery eyes that he levelled to squint at her even though it wasn't so terribly bright in the room that he should have needed to.

His mouth twisted down into a grimace as some did when they saw her. The way she saw it, it was nothing particular, as she was tired and worn out as the rest, despite never having seen him before she could understand his reasons why, as that woman willingly doing the job which everyone else despised, clearly there had to be something wrong with her.

You're new. She thought.

Kieke decided to speak before he had a chance to, as she had the sudden feeling that she would not get one otherwise.

"Finally someone has come. I'm here to request some more help. First however, a body has been found out in the fields. Children saw it and I shudder to think what incident caused this foul happening along with others so recently."

The man continued to peer at her. His voice was cracked and hoarse as if he had been shouting. This didn't seem to be from the cause of some upset and he sounded far more irritated speaking to her then she thought he should have.

"Yes we know. Everyone should stop sticking their heads where they don't belong. I do thank you for your concern but you're rather late."

"But I was here early."

"And yet you're late giving me that information, which I no longer need as the problem has been dealt with. I only recently arrived from Gandagar but I know enough about you to not need to worry for whatever it is you might ask, it's not my business after all. I do not want to be dealing with your particular goings on amongst us."

And there we go. She thought.

"If you were in the area and had prior knowledge then I did not know and apologise as most here are too busy to talk, however."

She was led her familiar way through to the right of the room and down a corridor to a room that connected them to all the other places of prayer that the more common folk were not allowed to reach on their own, where the Minister was waiting for her. A tall, broad shouldered man with a gruff beard and dark hair beginning to bald, around him were other people, attending to him after after making a sermon, removing his holy garments that made him resemble a swaddled beggar. Only a beggar would never wear such richly knitted clothes, such was the recreation of the first landing of the Light, quite a generous farce, at least as Kieke knew it to be.

The story went that blind beggars had been gifted old clothing by someone along their harsh road, and when finding that they had been given such clothes, with their sight restored, they forgave all those who had been cruel to them along the road and sought to make all see as they did.

So over the centuries a land had formed with a king at their head, an ancestor of one of those who had been blind and such it had been until they could no longer properly handle their power. Merely a few years ago the citizens of this land had been blindly forgetting their king, with the Minister being seen as the head of the church until the king had made his move and in doing so reminded everyone where it was he was seated while forgiving them all the same.

In turn they forgave him for being so invisible, even as the king shut himself and his family away all over again. Well he was right to be afraid if he was. It didn't matter who he surrounded himself with to slow her down, Kieke would make her way past or through them one way or another.

Despite losing this near absolute position of power, the Minister always appeared in good spirits, with one slight crease in his indomitable appearance. Kieke was used to dealing with children with sunken eyes that lacked spark but it continued to surprise her on seeing a man in such a position of supposed divine clarity and reach appear so constantly exhausted. When compared to herself he appeared to have the easy life, yet even so, the tiredness never showed in his voice or passed beyond his eyes and never had as long as she had know him.

Even so, there was only so much of his time she wanted at all as she found that insane preacher to be someone entirely irksome. The Minister of the Church of Churl had clarified Churl as being the religious capital and the ruling family had scrambled to relocate to keep their absolute power in one place. With such a man yapping at the heels of the king she could understand better why one might hide away. Despite this, he was just a guard dog who didn't know what it was he was guarding.

Regardless of the circumstances, his eyes always looked ahead and his voice was always loud and clear as one might as expect from one who's voice was a carefully crafted tool and he turned to her to speak.

"What is wrong, child? We've already heard of the matter you came here all concerned with but I sense there is more than just that you have come here for today."

Kieke took a breath and began talking, looking into those staring eyes.

"What's wrong is that people have chased a dear friend of mine away from this city and her senses. Now she's gone off with others and I know they are suspected, but I still don't know whether we're safe from whatever else might come."

"Hmmm, we all should be safe in this city, but nevertheless I shall send men to make sure that we are all safe as we should be. Such lapses in safety should not be tolerated. As for your friend I am not sure what it is we can do but pray. You should really try that."

"Even so, she is gone now, I doubt there is anything that can be done for her. I am very upset and sad, wondering who these people are that frightened her so."

I never did get an answer from her, did I? She thought sadly.

Whoever they were, they wanted her and anyone else she might have come across that night dead. I wonder if they did not like her telling stories? There were plenty who had not liked Lara when she was alive, quite possibly even been fearful of her but it's been so long since her death, it doesn't make sense as to why now they came upon her place and the one last girl still living in her house with murder on their minds. If only I had been there to begin with this could have all been so different.

"Are you still with us?" The Minister asked politely.

Kieke blinked.

"Of course, I was just wondering how to ask also for more aid in a generous manner. We have been given a house within the walls now but still there are things not quite as they should be."

The man smiled, satisfied.

"Do you think that you can eat off our words? Be honest, you can not. Yet in far off places people eat because of them, those words carried home by those who come to our fair city to pay their respects, however much I must admit that some come here these days to communicate with the king on other matters. Your matter of aid shall be looked into if you say what is required, but you must live for things, if possible, not merely receive them."

"Where is he?" Kieke asked.

"Tell me where the king is when people meet so that I might speak with him if others are able to do so, it would be appreciable."

The Minister stroked his beard.

"Hmmm, that is an obvious question. He came here as the castle is much more easily defended and has since taken up residency inside it. There he relies on his good citizens such as you to do what he cannot from inside the walls. So keep at it. After all, times are hardly worse than before and you need to be an example to others on how to hold yourself together. Unless you think someone else can do what you do?"

There really is this liveliness to the man which disturbs me.

It gave her trouble working out if he was being blunt or if he simply lived his own life without caring for others. Certainly he had a role and performed it well, but he too was just a puppet like any of the others and if he was happy enough then that was up to him to be ignorant. She would not be ignorant in thinking that if she removed him there would not be another ready and waiting to take his place.

On striking him down she could see herself becoming the king's ideal vessel for woe cloaked in well meaning intentions, not from the church, as some other darkness to grow that this world would fill. The wave of death and despair coming from herself, growing out of the filth uncontrollable by her if she were even still alive and all this would be for nothing. She couldn't stand to see herself used as such a figurehead of death so deep and far reaching that it would lead to the end of the world.

Back outside, Kieke saw how everyone went about their day in the brightness of the morning while up above in the castle the king's heart continued to beat and only after being silenced, leading the world away from that awful end that was coming for them would Kieke let someone else figure out what to do with the leftovers.

That was if she had the time and while it seemed that she was going about her days as any other, she was reminded how that was not so. Up above, the sky behind the clouds pulsed and seethed with a blackness only she among them could see.

Chapter Nine
The Bell City of Gandagar

It had been some weeks while mountains rose up on the south ever closer to their left to meet the party yet they had veered ever further north to walk next to them. This saved them all a difficult walk over the mountains and after a twisting and turning journey, the path began to climb slightly where the stone ruins of six towers came into view. Each of them were sitting on the top of their own hill over a north eastern rise that together completely hid the land beyond them.

The land itself dipped steeply downwards from the top of those hills and it could be seen that far down below at the bottom of the dip created by those hills was a flat basin, within which rested a city of orange stone basking in the sunlight, sheltered and protected by the mountains and the slopes on either side.

There was no great castle or fortress to defend it, but most of the buildings inside rested between two dusty orange walls along the south east and the north west, blocking the road directly in their path.

A river ran alongside the mountains to act as a natural barrier along the south west side, while forking around the back to the other side a trench had been dug from the river around that fed into irrigated fields. There were houses of a different colour that sat in the spaces left of the river and right of the fields, spilling out up the sides of the mountains a little way, little squares of white among the green.

While Peter and Findal went on ahead to go to the river, as they needed to fill up everybody's water bottles and bags, the other three rested at the top of the hill where they could still admire the view down below.

Zelda in particular was taking a good, hard look over the place. If the walls were anything to go by, as well as one large building near the back of the city that had collapsed in the middle which itself was surrounded by other buildings with their own roofing caved in, the place appeared to be falling apart.

Squinting to look further ahead past the city, she could just barely see a road continuing behind the far wall to twist out of sight, between the hills and past the river.

"Are we here? Where you'll leave me already?" She asked, to which Gunter shook his head.

"No, this is the Bell City of Gandagar. In days long past if a king needed to come down to Churl they would find themselves here, using it as a place to rest and remain while whatever they needed to do was carried out elsewhere. We have further to go than here before I would consider you safe. I do hope we can move through this place with some speed as this city has within it words of that foul church that I do not like the feel of. Something inside me tells me that they are here as I suppose they should be in some way. Let me tell you more while we wait."

She learned that along the left was the river Gan which split far north before the sea into the same river that ran through Churl. For the reason the city was named, there had once been guardians standing watch and those towers, the Dargars, had been constructed here to guard the river on its way south. The river certainly was an important piece of land, but up on those hills when the towers would have been standing, they could have been used to see in all directions, particularly from the north.

"Once there would have been watch towers up on all those mountains, created by elf hands long ago to be solid, standing sentinels but over time the people here have found they had no need of such protection and let them fall into ruin. The war certainly would have made them nervous without those eyes looking north on the hills but it came nowhere near this place. There was even a great bell tower you can see in the city that has since collapsed. That is why you people call it the Bell City, even if beyond these lands it is still called the Sentinel City and there is no bell to be rung."

"So nothing that has fallen into ruins here has been rebuilt?"

"Sadness fills me that we must wait until we can use our words properly against the people here in a manner that will convince them to abandon such living spaces."

Zelda held a concerned frown on her face.

"These people have done nothing wrong. Why should it be that they lose their homes?"

Survel gestured, pointing to the furthest ends beyond the houses.

"It is not the homes but the nature of the walls and the memories of those towers. If they wish to see as birds then they should learn to live as they do. There are plenty of trees around here within which they could make their homes but instead they live in this ditch."

They all sat under the trees as the day passed on and only after some time when neither Peter or Findal had returned did Gunter decide it best for them to make their own way into the city.

"It would not be entirely unlike either of them to get distracted." He said. "We should find each other eventually, there is no worry but a drink of water would have been nice."

They all descended down the hill to the gates and from where they were there was nobody to be seen and it was not only the sight of people that was missing.

Where are the sounds of people going about their days? Zelda wondered.

Now that she was closer, Zelda could see that these walls were not built as thick as the ones back in Churl and indeed had cracks, gaps and even missing pieces.

Walking close to the gate, from the wall stuck up several armoured heads, simple domed helmets but alongside those helmets were dark brown bows and the tips of arrows pointed at the three of them below, ready to be drawn if needed.

One of those helmets called.

"Halt, you who would approach our city. Goings on stir in the dark and there are rumours of wicked folk coming our way. While we ensure that all is well and nothing is amiss you must make a choice to either turn back the way you have come or proceed within with all haste. There shall be no skirting around the edges of our city so if you mean to pass through then I hope you make peace with the delay in your travels unless your journey was to end here. If that is so, welcome to Gandagar. Now enter through the gate if you may, the lot of you. You've got somewhere to be for your own safety."

Walking underneath the dagger sharp gate gave Zelda an ill feeling that grew until they made it through to the other side, stepping out into a completely empty square that was dirty, dusty and silent, the eyes of those standing on the wall looking down on them and those men were silent too.

From this side it could be seen that each of them wore a single piece of plate over their shirts, with those underneath appearing black in the upper left and lower right quarters while the other patches were yellow. Their pants were all brown which left to them a strange uniform, one that could have identified them on a battlefield but that seemed unnecessary for such duties as theirs.

The arrows were still notched in their bows and the three of them were looking to get out of reach of those as soon as possible.

Before they could get to that distance the sound of chains clanging and a crashing sound brought their attention behind them as the gate slammed shut. This did not seem to worry the others as much as Zelda thought it should. Their emotionless faces helped keep her calm believing she should behave the same. Gunter's mouth twisted open slightly when he looked at her, however.

"You see, the open skies mean that we could fly away quite simply in the form of birds but this is not so simple to achieve for yourself."

Survel merely shook his head.

Into the square marched more soldiers, this time armed with spears and as such the three of them were taken further into the city, more to its right, away from the river. She then very much hoped that such a thing would not become a problem.

Well this certainly isn't at all ominous. They seem well trained if nothing else but I wonder what has all these people taking such precautions?

They were shoved into a storehouse, finding themselves in the company of many other people who had been rounded up into open feeding pens where animals and other beasts might have had their hay stored in different times. The faces of the people were fearful and worried, keeping away from those with the spears. Some held injuries that had been tied up with cloth as best they could.

Gunter spoke to the man about the observation.

"Some of the people here look unwell."

That included the man he spoke to, his face was gaunt, not helped by the ill fitting helmet that was a size too large on his head.

"Never mind them, mind yourselves, it is the right thing to do. You would be right to be careful as us, for we look to make sure that we do not hide or harbour that which would bring down wrath on us all and keep us from our better days."

And with that the man shut the stable doors in his face.

While a few eyes turned to the newcomers, most kept to themselves. Some were close to the open door up the other end leading to a courtyard, with the sky outside in the distance looking grey and bleak, as if to walk through there was to enter a new land other than that which they had just come. It appeared as one without hope where only those who hid sheltered in these pens had explored only to come crawling back to the comforting smell of rotting wood and musty hay.

A moment later Gunter chose to break his silence, speaking loud enough to be heard but in a most casual and calm manner. He did not sound like a man who had been locked away unjustly.

"I hope that these people will not be left in such sorry states."

A dishevelled man rounded on him.

"What are you, vagabond looking preacher? I've had enough of people of your likes and your sad, earnest words. Some of us just want to get out there and live."

"I'm no preacher of that sort, but I am a druid." He replied politely.

The man scoffed.

"Just what we need, more people who take some moral high ground. Where is that now? Nowhere that will get you out of here. The church has decreed that none shall leave while they go from house to house. Only those with the proper allowances may leave and walk about, but not even then freely."

"You must all need to eat though. How do you get fed?"

"Farmers may come and go to see that we don't starve, but they too are watched."

"Most unfortunate."

The three moved as far as they could to find some space for themselves away from the throng of people, up a ramp to one side of the pens that was overlooking the outside if they pulled themselves up to look out though spaces too small to crawl through. Zelda was able to see out beyond to the fields where down below there were groups of armoured men gathering together, sharing information, then parting ways to continue their lookouts.

"If only they would tell us what it is they are looking for." She sighed.

Gunter did not sound as if he agreed.

"We can't help everyone with a problem. I hope the problem isn't us,"

They then heard Peter's voice from below them.

"If it was we would be in trouble by now."

His head appeared from the level below and he lifted himself up to the next floor. Findal's head appeared next, having had to lift up Peter, and with slightly more effort made himself join the rest of the party.

"I did not get very far in negotiating, unfortunately, but we did manage to refill the water bottles."

Zelda found herself hardly amused at both of them.

"Couldn't have you two just used the ramp instead of tiring yourselves out?"

"Well when I saw Peter was going to do something so silly, I just knew I couldn't have him doing that while leaving me to just walk around. It had to be done, if he could do it I should have be able to as well."

"If you want to talk about useful effort, I saw people out in the fields and the clouds above are becoming dark. Are they really going to force the farmers to work out in the rain?" she said.

Gunter nodded.

"Those who farm must be there to do their work. Perhaps we could get some information from them. Yes, I do think so. We will return shortly."

After making sure that no one else was around, Gunter and Survel turned themselves into small brown birds. Doing so cause Zelda to drop from her hand hold in shock and fall to the floor. The two little birds easily fitted through the bars with a little jump and took flight, leaving her mind blank as she continued to stare at the window and the sky above.

"Could I be taught to do that?" Zelda asked.

Peter spoke up, his voice oozing so much with the stroppy tone of a child that she cringed because really, that was too much.

"Taught? It's not a matter of being taught. It's more of how far you're willing to go in your understanding. That would be if you could even do that and then would require you to want to learn. If you don't want to learn then it can't be done."

"But I do want to learn."

"Then you'll have to ask the only druid here who is able to teach you anything."

Findal smiled apologetically.

"I won't be much help here, as it took me many years of dabbling and research before I was able to find someone to actually show me the right ways of doing such things. Who knows? I could have been missing out on years of experience just because of that. That is, I'm sure, what he is trying to say."

"Does that mean that without anyone to teach you, no one would know how to use the magic?" Zelda asked.

"Well it certainly wouldn't be easy. There are many ways one can get closer to nature and form a better understanding but in my journeying I discovered many wrong ways to go about it and what that did to people. Best that you learn from those who know a bit clearer than I and they might even know you better than you yourself. Deep inside, I mean, where our connection to the world all rests."

Peter had sat down and curled up and he became somewhat even more sullen at hearing this, his gaze was to the wall, distant, not looking away from it.

"That's not something everyone has and even if you did it would be up to people to want to train you in the first place. Do you think he's going to do that? We've got a mission to do, we can't afford to be wasting our time and yet here we are, doing just that, all for you."

He sighed, all the air out of his lungs. Maybe he was just trying to keep his composure.

"You talk about wanting to learn then fine. If there really is a lesson here for you I hold myself in absolute hope that you learn it. Because there's nothing else for any of us to get out of being here."

***

The two birds flew out to a nearby field free of guard patrols and resumed their human shapes. Neither had much of a plan as to who they would like to talk to, so with that waved down the first person they could see. He was a stern faced fellow, who if had he held a weapon would have given the pair a cause for a different action rather than standing and waiting for him to wander over.

The man was wondering where the pair had just come from but did not wish to ask, it might make him look inattentive or even stupid and he couldn't afford to be either of those things.

"You two after something? If so I've got nothing else left to give. They'll leave me out here so you lot don't starve come the chilling but I bet not a grain will reach our mouths in the harsher months ahead."

Gunter raised his hands.

"We are not whoever it is you think we are but we would ask a question as to what is going on in this place."

"If you're not with them, heed my advice and take no further steps onto the road or you'll be hustled up and lost inside." The farmer said.

"Perhaps it is nothing to fear, but when did this start?"

The farmer thumbed a finger east.

"Came that way and started surrounding us. First it was just a few men on horses wanting to refill and rest, then more came and joined the others as they were leaving, who then took up positions outside. They said something about the king and that was it really. For no other reason could men armed with such quality be provided and nobody wants to look like they've gone about disobeyed the king now."

"Too late you all realised, hmmm? Well to be the bearer of bad news their claim is quite legitimate as that is what you have forced upon yourselves, to kneel down to a mortal man. We came from the capital and I at least have no doubt that the actions here are the same as in that place. It all reeks the same."

The man shook heavily and leaned on his knees.

"Leave me alone. Leave us all alone. I don't want to get into trouble. Do not go to anyone else and mock us for you don't seem to care at all for us. Did I not say they came from the capital?"

"You did not exactly say so." Gunter replied.

By then however, the man was hurriedly making his way back across the field, just as the rain began to fall. And fall it did with a crackle of lightning and boom of thunder, pleasantly natural to the ears of the druids.

Both then spotted another man standing in the fields, wearing a dark brown cloak of some thick material that covered his whole body. Perhaps, they wondered, if he had been crouching down and had not been visible it would have been the reason for missing him before, even if they had not spotted him from the skies.

The man pointed back to underneath the buildings where between eves that overlapped they would be sheltered and hidden. The three of them wordlessly made for the space to get out of the rain and under cover, where the two could see the man's face.

He was older than the pair, with sagging lines down his face, which was thinned to a point that made the sides of his forehead rather pronounced. His brown hair was going grey and balding, having been shaved low in an attempt to disguise the fact. His brown eyes were steady however and he looked around with a searching gaze about him. Satisfied, he returned his attention to the pair.

"What are people like you doing here?"

The man's voice was not yet cracked with age but it probably wasn't going to be long before it was.

Gunter chewed at his words slowly.

"It seems this place is under some restrictions on who comes and who goes and we are caught up in it, whatever that may be."

The cloaked man nodded.

"Indeed, and I must say that the sound of our arrival has reached the ears of this place sooner than we had expected."

Survel frowned.

"There is no 'we'. You are not of our kind and are the only one here of yours."

Gunter put a hand on his shoulder and spoke level headedly to the man.

"So you say this has nothing to do with some illness, that is helpful to know as I was beginning to worry that we were running out of time."

"Yet if you go to the houses above you shall see that I could not tell you the exactness of what has befallen here for the houses are empty. While you might guess that they have all been rounded up to be interrogated as to catch us, I feel that is not the case. Needless to say no one here has spotted us as much of the houses you see behind you beyond the fields have been abandoned completely, for a long time at that. Nobody lives in them, after having been explored they have been found to be barren and empty and I have yet to see if that is still so the case across the river."

The rain soaking into their clothes suddenly felt very cold indeed. Gunter raised his eyebrows.

"Abandoned?"

"Quite, and you shall find much of the surrounds beyond here as such. The roads in the north are not safe and there are only two close by, relatively speaking, one to the north west beyond here and the other much further north but it would be faster to reach it from this side of the mountains rather than attempting the journey along the east road and then be taking the Great North Road. To travel through the centre of this land is not advised as all know why."

"How much does the surrounds cover, exactly, by your reckoning?"

"Everywhere we have been along the west side of these mountains from far in the north."

The reply made Survel growl.

"You're rather close to being rather unhelpful you know that? If you are giving us the run around, know that there has been plenty of that already on this journey for us. We too came from the north, by the way of the west some time ago."

Before either of them could step forward, another person pushed themselves rudely in between the way of both, who while short was not helped in this way by carrying a wooden staff suited for someone much taller than them. They wore common brown clothes taken to yellowing, blackened and frayed at the collar with the sleeves and trousers, both too long, tied up so they would not trip. Over these garments was a black, untied cloak with the hood thrown back so everyone could see her face.

Both druids took in the appearance of the sudden newcomer and froze, as her skin was a tanned brown that reached all the way up pointed ears that angled past her head. Two golden orbs shone in her eyes and her flaxen hair was tied by a white band in a low horsetail that hung half her length down her back. Everyone had to look down, even when she spoke in a clear, bell-chimed voice, because although fully grown, the elf was only five feet tall.

"Yet you two appeared almost as if out of thin air yourselves, even though you did not, as I saw you come here. This is yours, thank you for letting me borrow it." She returned the staff to the man, where it looked much more at home in his grasp.

Gunter barely found his voice.

"Elf, I want to know what it is you have done, for you certainly must have done something. And sir, be you a wizard of some kind matters not to me more than whether you know what have you done in giving that staff to such a creature. I wish to know what it is you two are planning for your presence looms over this place as a stench full of bad tidings, even while I can not sense any wickedness about it on its own."

The elf turned her eyes on him.

"That's because I haven't *done* anything. There's no need to worry, I only used the staff to help myself turn invisible briefly, as I'm not so good at that simply standing in an alleyway." She affected a thin smile to hide those pointy teeth then frowned as she paused to readjust her sleeves.

"As a personal preference, these do not help. Obviously they are not mine and perhaps for a moment I could fit in without needing to worry about it but they were all I could leave with."

"If those clothes are not yours, who do they belong to?"

"Someone you would be glad not to meet and you will not have to, because of me. You should be thankful. On another matter, the method of your leaving means you have a way in? As do I, but it is best not to be using yours when you don't know what's around the bend, or if some rotten archer is bored and looking for sport."

There were many people out in the world that the druids did not want to meet, most particularly people who might lock them up and take them away. Druids had been rather fortunate in the last few decades not to suffer the same fates as mages and elf kind, but there were still those who would lock them away in dark and foul places where no light would enter. And in the darkest of those putrid places there were creatures of vermin that would come to feast on their bones.

In those far off lands where such people and vermin roamed openly, anyone travelling there would have to be careful, where as in Alegan, well, the lack of people as told by the wizard could proof of the need for just that.

Gunter did not like those places, especially because one of the best ways to help with getting out of those places was to make a source of light and none was so readily available if one knew how to make it than fire. But most of all what he did not like was the fact that a creature with such a certain affinity for it was right before him and that there were many other problems that one so self persuaded could decide to solve with fire.

"We should clarify, we are not actually in the need to get in or out with help, we have that managed quite fine. Yet what you say and what I see is of concern, there is an arrogance that rots this land where people care little for others."

The wizard stopped short of saying how little one person's life mattered in the grand scheme of things, instead the wizard shrugged his thin shoulders.

"Well how much have you seen of the people that believe the church and their king? They're just waiting for a miracle now that will never come. Anything that does will not save this world and those who believe are foolish for doing so. It's all different up in the Northlands anyway. None of them care about some church of light as it is so far away and they think nothing of the doom that will come from this land to spread across all of Auralin."

"Then that which would cause it needs to be removed."

The wizard sighed, raising his free hand to the sky.

"Removed? Have you seen that which hides above us? You must be aware of it as men of magic, that darkness overhead. I'm of the opinion that there in that place of worship is the cause of all that makes this land go cold and dark. As you suspect there is a disease that affects this land and it is not one of the body but one of the mind. I travel east to break down all that would spread it, and am looking for people to do so with. You hold it in low regard. Would you come east and tear it down with me?"

Gunter shook his head.

"The world needs to change. We can't go on like this but the snares are too deep in the soil to believe that doing merely as you suggest would destroy people's faith, such is the way it spreads. That dark warning of which you speak merely tells us the final days are getting close. To that end people must come to their own understandings of how they live, it can not be forced entirely upon them but their minds are clouded and their ears are blocked. Yet take heed for that matter as they already have little faith in this world. You want to bring their churches down because you're worried that you'll all be lumped in with those damn pyromancers eventually. I can't blame you for that but what those in Alegan believe is weak, frail. We picked up a girl who lived at that false centre of the world her whole life and she spares no thought for it, although admittedly we need to make sure she knows enough to escape from it fully before leaving her behind."

"And what is it she needs exactly?" The elf asked.

"Something you can't help with. It is our own business what we do and as such we do not intend to go back to that place nor take a single step backwards as we believe utterly in the way set before us. Were the circumstances different I gather that we would go with you and could leave her behind here to whatever fate and have it be no cruelty."

"Not an elf I hope?" The elf asked with eyes narrowed.

"No, not an elf. Certainly not that we see many this far south anyway, but she's an oddity none the less. Do not be concerned, as fate would have it that I felt the particulars of our meeting to be more than coincidence, encountering her as I did. As such I'm taking it upon myself to leave her somewhere safe."

The wizard pressed his head firmly up against his staff.

"Your refusal is unfortunate, as is the fact engrained deeply in your being that you can not be persuaded otherwise."

The elf directed her gaze to the wizard.

"A change of plans then Bernard. I shall go from here south as far as I can to make it out of these lands. I do not wish to tread further or incite this land further into darkness. My very presence makes this so, as I feel the power in the world thin evermore. You must take the fight to the darkness without me."

A choking noise escaped the wizard and his face was drawn aghast.

"You too? What is it that I have done in my travels or otherwise that I might be cursed with such luck? I would have thought that breaking you out of gaol would have been enough to show my sincerity but you say it is not."

The elf was distracted by her own nails.

"My choice. You will find others who would follow you on your quest. I dare say you have been nothing but unfortunate which is fixable neither here nor there in a magical fashion. In other words, look elsewhere, but do please look hard, for the fate of this land rests on your success."

Survel groaned.

"I'm quite done talking with people who care nothing of what it is we set out to accomplish, a world free of vermin, shackles and chains. We waste out time talking with you, but it is not for me to care that you waste your own time among us."

Bernard could only hold onto his staff to keep himself standing as tall as he did.

"In regards to the foolish church I agree with what you wish for. You expect the end to come and would like to see all people free of the boundaries you have seen as if that would turn their heads into a world free of darkness. I have seen the boundaries you speak of but I have seen many more beyond that. What you seek to accomplish will not save this world. To you it is lost."

The druids had heard enough of the wizard's prattle. Each turned themselves into a bird and flew away from the pair. A moment after that, only one person remained, very much thinking of himself a fool.

Chapter Ten
Taking Flight

On the return of those two druids, the others gathered around to find out what they had learned. Findal was busy playing with some coins that he had traded off one of the other people who were here, but even with his eyes on the Items being turned over his restless fingers he frowned.

"So there is an elf here, at least one so you say and one is far troubling enough. Could it be they who are being searching for?"

Gunter nodded.

"They say it is so themselves, as the church needs to make sure there is no sanctuary for them here. Cutting off this place to them as somewhere they can stay safely ensures that they must move on to find help elsewhere and may fall into another trap, not that such a thing is our concern."

"What a mess they've put us in. With all the soldiers being cautious we can't just stage an escape. No way to get out for us, or at least one of us. I suppose I could try bribe the guards then maybe we could all escape."

"I'm not sure that would work with an elf on the loose."

"I suppose not."

Zelda spoke up.

"Can I not learn to become a bird as you can? That would make everything so much simpler for everybody."

Gunter held a distant look on his face.

"You are too far from the truth of nature. No matter the wish one might have, one can not merely think of the possibility and achieve such knowledge, there are understandings that you must first come to possess."

Peter nodded.

"I told her as such. There's nothing wrong with pleading if you think it suits you though."

"There will be no more pleading from anybody. We will stay until we think of a way to get her out of here. We will take Zelda with us. It would be a victory for the darkness which sought to take her life if she were to be left here. Such a thing should not happen as we should never leave one who could tip the balance of the world."

Zelda didn't think that pleading suited anyone at all. She hadn't done much pleading herself and didn't intend to start as that would prove Peter right. For the moment she would let such a topic of conversation rest. It wasn't about giving up, just waiting for the right time to bring it up again. Right now there was another thought stuck in her mind.

She had not saved herself out of any particular duty that she thought she had, there wasn't a task or quest she was undertaking that demanded her own survival, merely her survival itself, yet here she was being talked to as if she were part of something larger and for that thought she rather wanted an explanation.

"What do you mean by me tipping the balance?" Zelda asked.

Gunter stroked his beard.

"More understandings that can not be seen by you, so only concern yourself with the fact that the darkness we have so spoken of would grow and it would be most irresponsible of us to allow that to happen. It is not you yourself, merely the actions that would result from such things. The very notion of bad deeds is a poison that poisons the well of well wishes and that makes the world all the more unwell."

And that was all he or any of the others would say on the matter.

When the hours passed it increasingly became clearer that they were not going to get out so easily. With the druids sitting apart humming with lowered heads, each appearing to be meditating, Zelda found herself alone and for a while she decided to keep a watch on them as the humming was beginning to attract the attention of the other city people, who had moved to give the band of dirty, out of tune men a wide birth. After some time she found herself picking at the sheath of her sword absent mindedly and quickly made to find something else for herself to do and decided to head outside to get some fresh air.

As the rain was coming and going, Zelda took a moment to look at the ground and became rather concious of the mud under her feet. The ground was mostly bare aside from some patches of grass that had not been trampled and there was no view, only the other barn doors that along with the one she walked out of made up a half circle up against a wall that blocked her from seeing the fields outside. None of the other doors were open and when she put an ear to each of them she could not hear anyone inside, nor could she see inside through any cracks in the doors or underneath them.

Then from inside her head came a clear, bell sounding voice.

"There's no use looking in. All those rooms are as empty as I believe some people think your mind is. But don't worry about what they say, it's not so hard."

"Who's there?" She called out. Looking around she was completely alone save for some birds minding their own business over on the grass.

"You can't see me but I am outside somewhere. We are connected through the ground that is also part of all things."

"Are you a druid, like the others?"

"A druid?" Amused laughter floated inside her head.

"Truly what a funny way humans have of seeing the world. Dividing the things they can't understand together in their heads so that they may conquer it. You're just holding a piece of a greater understanding."

"But I'm not a druid myself, I haven't learnt anything to do with them. I'm not a part of anything at all, really."

"It is not necessary to feel that you must belong. In order to be who you are all you have to do is get out there and show them."

The voice fell silent and after a little while Zelda stood up slowly. Over the other side of the yard there were birds on the ground, pecking at the patches of grass. Zelda was not entirely sure why but she made her way over to them. She leaned over and smiled at the little creatures going about their carefree lives, free of all the troubles she had been covered in lately.

"Hello little birds. Are you going to teach me all about yourselves?"

The birds looked up at her, and she felt a strange unease above her.

"What's wrong?"

One of the birds held a seed in its beak and flew up onto her right arm, staring at her. Zelda kept herself still as the bird hopped down it as if her arm were a branch, and she opened her palm, to which the bird jumped into it, as if it was offering her the seed. The very next moment it promptly pecked her in the hand.

"Ouch!" Zelda said, waving her arm so that the bird flew off a few paces to join its friends, where it just stood, watching her.

"Now what was that for?" She asked, upset.

But the bird just stood there and said nothing. Because it was a bird.

Looking at her palm, she could see the seed had been embedded deeply within and a small pool of blood was welling up around the injury. Zelda tried to poke out the seed and found she could not, being left staring at the hole in her hand. As rain began to fall again and the birds flew away, there was an odd restless sensation within her palm and as the blood was washed away she saw the seed split and grow. It grew upwards into a seedling sprouting about an inch tall and she covered it with her free hand against the rain.

As she did so a shadow stood over her and she turned her head around to see that Gunter had followed her out into the rain. He noticed that she was holding something in her hand.

"What are you doing?" Said the druid.

She ignored the sudden surge of reluctance that rose in her chest and showed him. His face was creased with a dark concern that nearly made her fear come true.

"How did you do that? You should stop."

"You said that I would need to learn, so here I am, learning, or trying."

"Indeed but this is not how you should go about doing it. You'll turn yourself into a tree."

"I don't feel like a tree." Zelda said.

However the seedling was beginning to grow and she did wonder what she would have to do if it did not stop growing. Carefully, she dislodged the seedling from her palm, careful to keep its thin roots from breaking that had grown under the skin. Pulling it free stung and little lights swam about in her vision as her palm welled up with blood again. However, as the rain continued to wash it away she found it entirely healed.

"But you can't have known how to do that." Gunter said and it sounded that he complained in a way rather strained.

She doesn't know what she's doing, or I hope she does not and that she is not doing anything purposefully. To find something hidden in her mind after all these years for us suddenly to bring that forth? No, that's thinking too much of those who would cause the death of the world. Not for them to use us like so.

Zelda was far too transfixed on her hand to care about the incredulity in his voice.

"Yes, you are right to suggest that I have no idea what I am doing, because I truly have no idea just what it is I am doing. Now I must do something with my plant, that would be the right thing to do."

Zelda looked around and dug a muddy little hole with her fingers slightly away from the wall and planted the little seedling into it. She looked up at Gunter, who's face seemed to have frozen completely.

"There. So if you were going to teach me whatever the right way to do something is can we get started? Out of the rain would be nice."

However when she shared the news with the others, they appeared to be tired and subdued, each with great thoughts on their minds. Only Peter appeared alert and he looked at her strangely, blinking slowly as if to make sure that she was there in front of him at all and Zelda rather wished he did not.

The excited rush of what she had done faded away, because she couldn't help but feel that she had done something wrong, even if she didn't know why and not one of them seemed interested in telling her what it was.

Perhaps they themselves do not know exactly what I've done wrong. Findal did tell me that there was a wrong way of doing things so maybe I will be finding out what that is.

That voice she had heard made her wonder at exactly what it was she needed to understand in the first place about making a tree and planting a tree as she had done. She had seen Gunter fix her burned hands earlier and hadn't meant to copy him here, it had all seemed to happen together, unless there was something special about the rain.

Still, looking down at her hands was enough to illicit a feeling of wonder even if she couldn't quite feel anything different about herself.

***

The next morning, Zelda was surprised to see that the tree had grown rather large through the night. Certainly it would have otherwise been impossible to grow a tree to the size it should have taken several years to do, but something she had thought quite impossible had only happened yesterday so she felt she could be excused for being surprised again.

I think I should be allowed to be pleased for what I have been able to do.

Many people were surrounding the tree and talking about it, asking questions, such as why was it there and how it could be. So of course the five were sent to stand in front of the tree, as it was likely that they had something to do with this, most could say.

An old man of the church was there standing before them in his robes with his hands on his hips and an angry look on his face. His voice was much too loud for how close he was standing to them.

"Why is there a tree here that was not previously? When a tithesman from the church comes here and demands to know where the tree came from so they may judge its worth properly, who should I say this tree came from? I have enough to worry about while having to consider the value of that which suddenly appears before me."

Zelda wondered again at the quietness of the others and suddenly did not find it surprising that the others might not speak. When nobody spoke, Zelda thought that she should. It was after all her doing and if no one would speak up for her she would do that herself as one who marvelled at her own handiwork.

"It was I. I made this tree."

The whole crowd turned to face her as if it was one creature with many heads. Some wore the same faces while others differed throughout the beast. Zelda realised she had to be careful not to provoke it. Best not to suggest that she herself had made part of the tree either. She had not thought of druid magic to be so dirty and she was certainly being leered at with the same intensity as the others.

The old man scratched the back of his head.

"Tell us how it is, girl, that you did this."

"You see all these men I travel with? They can do wondrous things but not I. Until last night they were unsure of what they could teach me, so I brought forth this tree to show that I too am able to learn. But as I am only new to learning, how I did this I do not know." She admitted.

Her words did not have the desired effect that she thought it would have as this brought groans and jeers from the crowd and she held her arms apart in an effort to silence them.

Other than the way a tree might grow, from the ground and the sky of course, so then I don't think anything is wrong with saying a druid did it.

The people here lived around trees and forests so one more tree should not have been a problem as much as they were saying. The old man certainly looked to her as if it were.

"Yet you were not given permission for such an act. How dare you think to provide for those who should suffer. You deny them the right to rise above their suffering. There will be those who will not be thanked for providing relief to those who were in need of shade."

Then can't they thank me instead for what I have done? She wondered.

"As such, you will be held here while we think up an appropriate punishment. For the church demands it."

I've never seen this side before. Didn't even think that it was like this at all. Scarcely enough did anyone ever do the wrong thing. Is this what it looks like to have it brought down on my head? How comfortable my life was for me not to realise or even care about how things would go. We just did as we were told and why would we not?

All of them were herded into the barn on the opposite of where they had come in, which was opened to allow them to be thrown in and the door hastily shut behind them. It was dark, apart from where some windows shined light beams down, small enough and so high that only birds or other crawling creatures could escape through. The barn was nearly completely empty apart from some large logs, so Gunter and Survel heaved up those logs and piled them against the door to block the way in.

It was also one of two ways out, Zelda thought, but figured it was best to let them keep doing what they believed needed to be done.

Findal went to the door up the other end and tested it, attempting to force it open. They could hear the old man's voice outside.

"Do you see this tree? Do you see what has been planted here? No one asked for this yet here it must remain for the time being. I hear your cries, you all yearn to be proven trustworthy and there are many ways to do this and among them most certainly is this. Any who would wish to be set free will be allowed to go if they take up a weapon and strike down all those who took part in this lightless creation for none of them can be blameless here."

Survel looked at the others.

"We're leaving now."

In that instant the door was opened and there were cries and complaints as others were urged to help clear the wood at their feet instead of piling on top of each other.

"Now, there is no later for any of us."

With that Survel turned into a small black bird and began to ascend as the noise of people rose, with Peter following suit without a single backwards glance or word a moment later.

Despite the pile not being completely removed, people were trying to get into the room, clambering over each other to get inside. It then seemed that thinking of them all as a beast with many heads was quite apt, as there was something inhuman and crazed about the way people got stuck on each other trying to get in.

On seeing this, Findal stepped away from the door he could not open with a look on his face of utmost apology, as he too turned into a bird and took flight.

Zelda had watched as one, two, three birds had reached a window and flown into the sky. She didn't know what to do, her knees were weak and her stomach turned.

Only Gunter was left behind with her and he looked down at her not appearing worried, merely sad. She reached out to him but he shook his head and she recoiled at the coldness in his eyes, for surely she was not imagining such a thing.

"You can't leave me here." She said.

"Nature gives and it also takes away." He said.

"You made a tree most magically without knowing what this would do to the balance of the world. Now after all you have done you mustn't ask for my help. You showed me something before that I wasn't quite sure of. Now show me something else. The world will live on with or without you, but only if we live."

"Who's we?" She cried, but he did not answer her as he had taken the shape of a black bird and had left with the others.

"Who?"

Her words were drowned out by the sound of the doors being ripped open from the other side and with swords, pitchforks and other farming tools were people rushing in with murderous intent.

Far above, it was much calmer up in the sky. Despite being covered in grey clouds, the sky held off from any further rain or other stormy weather. Creatures of the air such as birds were making their way to wherever it was they needed to be. Four such black birds were flying together with a very important purpose in mind.

And a little way behind them, a fifth.

Chapter Eleven
Those Who Understand Peril

The light was fading from the sky when he found her. Zelda was laying spread out on the grass beside a hill covered in trees, where rocky ground was beginning to leave patches of land around it where trees could not grow. Looking up at the sky as a dark figure stood over her, from where she lay Zelda could tell it was Gunter who stood over her, obscuring the view.

She sighed out a great breath, which she could do now without the pain she had felt after finding herself back on the ground. Even so, her arms and legs still ached, while the vestiges of a monumental headache were still steadily leaving her be.

Zelda could not quite feel her mouth when she opened it to talk. She wanted to tell him to stop blocking the sky. There wasn't much to see, but the grey sky above was calming, a constant slate she could just watch as the world passed her by while her mind felt heavy and her thoughts came out sluggish. However, she knew the desire to do nothing was momentary and selfish compared to the other larger problem that ate up space in her chest and made it hurt on the inside.

"I might as well say it, you all seemed rather uninterested by what I have done. Do tell, was this just a joke between the lot of you all along?"

Gunter's voice in reply sounded tired, keeping the same flat tone as he spoke.

"So that is what you say when you are like us now? Your answer to that should be 'no', by the way. There was a strange sense I did have when we first met but I could not have been sure what that was for. If this is where it has led you then after all this was a most fortunate encounter for all of us. Yet it almost was not so due to all the problems that were brought along with you. Such a thing made you weak, carrying with you the remains of a life you said you wanted to leave behind. Were you to settle down you would have made of whatever the place to be one for those weaknesses to grow. Regardless of your wish to depart such a place of weakness to begin with I am sure of that now."

You are berating me? Zelda thought.

She had not understood how it was she had done what she did. She had not told the bird to do as it did, if that had not happened then she would not have been here, at least as far as her head told her and she still could not piece together how to make any of what she had done after happen again. Becoming a bird had been based on a fear she could barely hold onto. One she did not wish to hold onto at all.

Most of all Zelda knew that because of fear she had not wanted to stay. Perhaps the others had all believed that she had picked up what she had from watching them go about their ways, but to say the she might as well be wallowing in the very type of place she wanted to run from, to seek shelter amongst those who on a word would call for her murder? Well, that sounded like someone who did not understand her at all.

Gunter took her lack of a response to as a means to continue talking.

"Fortune led me to you, so I took it upon myself to take you from there. Surrounded by the cold city walls as you had been your whole life, there would have been no reason to look upon the wider world favourably, which in a way is why we shun such places. They stifle the natural way of things and strangle it of worldly reason with false words from a false king or queen, among other reasons found in other lands. Auralin must be free and open to all and in your thoughts and words you must be an example to that, listening carefully to the words of the ones who do not understand, while telling them the way that it should be for the better of all. I did not see that in you before, you cowered before that false illusion of life you once knew."

Zelda was looking out to that sky above and her voice was just as grey.

"I could have died."

"There are many more certain ways in which people faced the realisation that the following moments were to be their last. That was not one of them. If you continue to push yourself you may amaze even me. In those last moments before you turned, I was not seeing one of us, I was seeing a desperate person with a clouded mind looking for help. Nature does not give help, unless by some sick twist of fortune luck smiles upon you."

"Then next time I shall take my sword and run head first into battle, there at least I might die quickly and save everyone the trouble if I really am nothing more than one who would help to ruin this world so they would say. But I do not want this, I have something and I want to use it. It would be a shame for me to throw it away."

The druid dragged his fingers through his hair.

"Then why did you not hold onto the seedling? You could have planted it somewhere important and not gotten us all into trouble by doing so."

"A part of me did not like the barren look of the place. It was a feeling. Is all this grumpiness really because I planted a tree and disrupted the balance of the world?"

That put the pleasant, knowing smile back on his face as well as a slight lift in his voice.

"You can see just how the people thanked you for it. That is why we journey as we do, Zelda, to find our strong voice by which people may first understand. Otherwise we're all just wasting our breath."

"How do I make my voice strong so people listen to me? What can be done for those places?"

"Keep journeying with us beyond where we were going to part ways and you will learn in time how such places that you flee from should be dealt with by us. We have talked before in manners of pulling down such places by force, yet the best course of action is not always so straightforward. It is good that you wish to learn, so that we can get started on this journey with you all over again, this time with new eyes for all of us."

He began to walk away, leaving her to look at the grey sky again, but turned to look back after a moment.

"There are still some more days ahead of us before we get to that last town. Our little flight cut off a few days, however I shall err on the side of caution and insist we all stay on our feet despite its expediency in travel. So don't worry about having to fly again so soon, but also make sure you don't find yourself in the position again where desperate flight was called for and I saw you appearing so helpless."

Then Zelda was left alone as the dark crept in. She still felt weak and disembodied after finding herself on the grass, her mind still a whirl as she began to settle into the acceptance of no longer being burdensome while not feeling excited about the whole prospect. When she dug her fingers into the grass came a heaviness that she felt throughout her body.

Ah yes, that was how I got here in the first place. After dropping to the ground I just became so tired. I guess there are plans for me to be useful after all.

Gradually, the blanket of clouds above was torn open and from those tears could stars be seen shining through. She thought how that was so very much like herself, with something deep and mysterious being hidden behind a grey cloud that one day might bring rain.

"I don't know, how will I be useful when I have so much to learn about everything? I feel that this magic has just been put into my hands and am not even moving them myself, with someone guiding them by holding my hand all the way. Should I not expect some sense of deeper worldliness? Something is missing but I don't know what."

So it was she spoke to the sky above, high and uncaring. Surely it would not judge her.

Then over by a tree a familiar voice chimed down to her.

"I told you before. You're just one piece of the whole thing, you're incomplete."

Zelda sat up fast with grass in her hair as an elf wearing human clothes, with tanned skin and flaxen hair jumped out of a tree to crouch on the ground before her in her baggy clothes.

Fear pushed against Zelda's chest and mind and had to stop herself from starting to shake, or crawl back along the grass, to instead stare at the elf. Shock made her mouth move before she told it to.

"You're an elf! Ah I feel tricked, after all this voice in my head was from a creature of fire."

The elf grinned happily in a most charming manner despite those wolfish teeth and sat herself down, lazily crossing her legs to get herself comfortable.

"Yes, yes I am. Although if I were to call myself a creature then it would only be fair for me to call you one too. Perhaps as a human you would be a creature of dirt, but I really can not tell. After all, where it was any of you came from has been long forgotten so I doubt anyone would know and even then, I wonder if it would be worth in the knowing, for look where fire gets us. I would hate for another to be labelled as such by one thing to be, such as all that it is we are known for and just understand so well."

Zelda eyed the elf not without suspicion, unwilling to make a move to get up and flee.

"You made me do something stupid and I'll have you know that I didn't have a single idea about what I was supposed to do in the dirt back there. I know about sticking a farming tool in the ground at least but that's as far as my knowledge goes in any sort of plant, to say the least of one made out of me."

"It was your choice, one based on something you wanted so much. Who knows what would have happened if that thing you searched your whole life for was never found. Do think of that, it is so important not to regret those moments."

Her own feet had carried her on the road out of her own need to live, yet Zelda thought it difficult to separate all that had happened as everything had been one big blur. She wasn't even sure when people had made the decisions that had changed her life, merely that she had walked into them and felt them herself and she had not known that something was wrong until it was almost too late.

How am I supposed to make room in my head after all that has happened? I can not pick away at the knot of tangled memories and unravel what I see into little moments.

Less chance of regretting then, if she could not pinpoint exactly when things were going to go wrong. Zelda knew when she had encountered the problems herself, on that night when everything had changed, but those people had all been acting on something and she did not believe that putting a face to that person would be worth imagining.

"I wanted to be useful and nearly missed the opportunity to be so. That's not to say I ever thought living in Churl and going about my life as I did meant I hadn't been useful. I suppose after the war there were plenty of people looking to pick up menial tasks to support themselves. But now in a small way I want to do something else."

The elf's smile disappeared as she tilted her head in thought.

"For those who had to flee, who hate being exiled from their homes, they would agree with wanting more from life. They also hate that just because they were useful at a certain something, they had no choice but to flee and hold their hate within them as they went, but I myself don't have the expansive restlessness to care. To be quite at peace is the best way possible for those of us who wish to put this terrible part of our legacy behind us."

"And who are you? My name is Zelda, what is your name?"

The smile reappeared and widened on the elf's face.

"If I tell you my name then you might speak of it and those who know of who's name you speak will never leave you alone ever again, being who I am. More importantly those who hear it might retrace your own steps to know where I have been and I want to keep all that a secret."

"Well someone seemed to know you were coming, as back in Gandagar the whole city was rounded up just for you. Or at least the one who leads us on our journey says so."

"I wonder if that was really so for all the people who were not there in their homes? I met that one while you were there. Be warned. You think you will know all that he will teach you and yet I must say that you shall find yourself quite under performing, so please temper your expectations of usefulness to this world. If I am being honest the concept of druids, of which I am sure you will call yourself among them soon, is rather a bit of a giggle for me and mine as you may have guessed. Going around playing the caretaker of nature and all for what?"

The elf reached her arms out wide in the air in a great stretch, encompassing all the sky above. A great grin was on her face that passed into her eyes as she looked above, eyes which were wide, twin golden orbs where Zelda could see the night's stars reflected in the blackness within.

"All of this, and none of it answers to you, because none of it is yours, never was, and never will be. Do remember that when going about your days, for there are reasons out there which will hold you to your magic most accountable."

"What sort of reasons?"

The elf lowered her arms and gaze into her lap, her ears drooping along with an expression of sadness on her face that to Zelda, for the briefest of moments appeared to be guilt.

"Foolish reasons. Ones I can't say are entirely human, but as a druid you will cling to them none the less."

Quite suddenly up in the sky there came a noise that to Zelda sounded like a splash of water, only as deep and rumbling as thunder and lasting just as long. She saw within the grey clouds a black, slinking something that looked watery. It twisted through the clouds as it came and went and the sound came and went along with the blackness like a pulse, one foul and black. Her head hurt to look at the thing, even after it vanished as quick as it had come, leaving the sky looking as if it had never been there at all.

Zelda's eyes were left seeking the sky, and when she was sure she could find no other trace of it ripped her gaze from above to look at the elf for answers.

"What was *that*?"

The elf stared thoughtfully above.

"Ahh, you have noticed the darkness. It is but one sign that the world of magic has finally found you but that is not the purpose of it, so I must run beyond its grasp. Yet I admit I have lingered here longer than I should have, being unable to resist getting a good look at you meant I had to follow you for a time."

Zelda clutched her head.

"The darkness hurts."

"Do not stare directly at such wickedness. That it give you pain means you can feel the evil and malice coming from it. If the pain persists, ask your companions to help you manage it, as I am sure they will know many things in regards to it. But I must say this, be careful of what they tell you, what any of them tell you, whoever it is you might meet who would use the word druid, because it's only part of a greater understanding that they will never reach."

"I do not know what is it about me that compels you to tell me all of this. You say they will not reach whatever this greater understanding is, but what about me?"

"What about you, sweet human child? All I'm saying is what I need to for you to save yourself."

And with that, the elf stood gracefully with a backwards step and disappeared silently into the night. There was something in the way that she had disappeared so completely that Zelda was sure that she would never see them again.

She then became aware of how dark it was. Her eyes could not pierce the darkness around her, as if this night was the darkest night that had ever been and Zelda could see all she had known in her mind's eye being swallowed up by the dark that without her knowing had hung so far and so low over her home and everyone she had known.

Was this the darkness they could see which I had been living my whole life under all along? I wonder if this is why the whole world is in danger, from something sneaking in the sky they can't even see. This could be what Gunter meant about me having a clouded mind looking for help. I've been staggering around in the dark and yet from what the elf is telling me I can't know if any of that will truly change.

Of course, there was no one to answer her thoughts. The sky rumbled far away but this she could feel was the coming of rain. As Zelda thought more about the darkness, she made sure to keep her own rain inside, as that would be most unbecoming of her new self. However she did shiver, and that made her stand and walk away from the trees and where she could see a burning point of light across the rocky plain on the other side of the hill, which after tripping and falling over a few times made her way to a small camp fire amongst a cluster of trees the druids had made.

This time she didn't question their emotionless faces, as all were tired, propped up against trees while Survel was the only one among them slumped over in sleep. Her own face mirrored the others and kept it that way to stop the thoughts bubbling inside her from showing. If she wanted to be like them then she would have to act like them too. Even after having slept for most of the afternoon, she soon found herself falling back into the embrace of sleep.

***

Once again, Bernard the wizard found himself left on his own.

Damn fools. Let them all go stick their heads in the trees if they think that will save them, even though it will not. Nobody could look away from such a sky and ignore the meaning of it.

Some people hid away willingly in shadows and from there were unable to see their own part in the end that would come for all. They were waiting for the sky to fall on their heads, as if to be punished for surviving the war. This punishment was not so divine as it was foul, raising the dread into a sense of uneasiness with each passing day.

He had begun forcing himself into sleep, even though he did not want to close his eyes, because there was darkness in sleep and he was very afraid of waking to find no light at all. Just as now where something that writhed far above their heads surrounded them all in a terrible darkness reaching down to get him to which he could not escape!

The wizard shuddered awake, his stave clattering to the ground. He was in one of the well lit corners at the inner wall in Gandagar, the overhanging walkway above creating cover from the weather for those underneath. It was late at night, with braziers burning along the walls and at the gates to show that they were still locked. Beyond that, darkness.

There were other people who had pulled up rugs and mats to sleep on along the wall, being kept out of their own homes. Thankfully, none had stirred due to his jolted waking. Many of them looked exhausted, even in sleep.

Bernard found himself suddenly restless so went for a walk, where the imperceptible blackness of the sky was above him, so high or so low he could not tell. Perhaps this was why people were worried with what they could see of the world, preferring in this land to play blind, but superstition of that kind was not like the people he knew. They wanted their belief to be attached to something and he was going to take it away from them. Make the king powerless, make the Minister powerless, to show the people of Alegan that the ones they revered were just like them. They too should fear the sky.

There are not many people left here. Bernard thought as he roamed the city.

He had spent the last few days exploring the houses along the river and had also tested the river itself with his stave, finding no ills within it. He did not want to go up into the mountains as he did not know what it would be he would find and did not want to get lost in them either. The task set before him was away from these mountains and each empty shell of a home that he had found had only reminded him of why he was here so far south. It was not quite the torn up destruction of some of those smaller villages he and the elf had come across on their way here, yet one day it might just be so, were Gandagar not to be emptied entirely and left to fall further into ruin.

And still the guards were given their orders and told to hold all who remained in the place. There had been some escapees recently which had only doubled the resolve of the guards to keep everyone else where they were, hardly an issue for a wizard such as he, yet he was sure that he would have to leave them to their fates at the hands of their loyal church watchers.

One such guard noticed him walking around and came to attention. Their voice was only hinting at the tiredness that clung to the man's eyes that stared at him wearily.

"What are you doing around here so late, old man?"

The wizard was polite while the guard tugged at his collar.

"The same as you, what I believe to be right. Walking around at this time is just what I need."

"Well you can do it somewhere else. No one leaves until the searches are complete. We have got to be vigilant to get through this madness, or else our futures will become dark and cloudy away from the light of all good things."

The guard was just one man with a rather simple outlook on things. In other lands such a way of looking out to the world would have been commendable but there was only one thing he would be putting his faith into.

I should hurry. The further fear and madness spreads the more treacherous it will be to move in these lands. This town is blockaded, yet others are ruined and how many more will suffer this fate I still do not know. But I wish for a person to rely on, so must first make some space between me and that place of worship. There are no others here I could convince to leave their posts, all too much like this man. Perhaps there is another place where people might be disillusioned, that I could find my ally not amongst the ruins of the dead, having arrived far too late.

Bernard bowed to the man.

"I understand, I shall try and get a little more rest, because we all are going to need it tomorrow."

"You won't have to do anything, you'll see. After every night there will be a morning for all but the wicked. So the church says and so it will be. Go back to sleep you worried old man."

The guard's own words seemed to have re-energised him, and he laughed as the wizard walked away.

Early in the morning light of the next day, a single black raven was seen flying away from the city. Of course, no one paid it any heed, although the bird did wonder if anyone would still be laughing if the sky fell about their heads.

Chapter Twelve
The Old Capital of Autumn

All the common folk in the lands were supposed to be dealing with their own problems, yet rarely did the wizard or any wizards see that to be the way it ever turned out. While far away in far off places there was no fear or worry, here these people held onto the hands of others, trusting in them to lead them through and away from such people who had such fears or worries. If that hand were to falter, if presented with another hand would they hide away in fear or take it cautiously even if it would send them further into ruin?

Some answers were unknowable until the time came where it would be too late to change anything at all. As such, Bernard counted amongst himself those in this land about him who should also bear the burden, should it come to pass, of holding the hand away and to play the part of the one who pulled the faith bound of Alegan away from their belief. In doing so, he would have to know if he made the right choice, as none should suffer for his mistakes.

He had made an awful lot of them in his time. It was best for him not to think about those too much for if he did he would be sent into a depression of falsities and over encouraged pain far more overblown than what had really happened in days long gone. His past mistakes were a thing that should remain unknowable to the most of people, because if they knew, then people might focus on what he had actually done, such as his use of magic.

Bernard's magical aptitude was only his after a fraught road long travelled of dangers and personal vices of a man he no longer was. In the end he hadn't so much as mastered magic as he had taken charge of it and that in itself had taken a very long time, to wrangle the secrets out from tomes and make them his own. If he had been given more time he would have liked to learn even more and be known for something specific, but here he was as a wizard of no particular craft, hiding in the shadows of Autumn, the old capital of the kingdom of Alegan.

There was an important distinction to be made, between wizards and other kinds of people who had access to the ways of the world some might consider spectacular while others might suggest cursed. The trappings of life were left aside while people devoted themselves to honing their crafts and whatever those might be was widely up to the interpretation of the individual or the teachers they would study under. That was the most different thing between them and a rogue mage, a guiding hand. At least that is what all wizards said, for that was what they knew.

To make matters clearer, it was easy to see the handiwork of one with no tutelage out and about in its raw and unrefined state. Easy too for people to make judgements and go about their days snarling at all sorts of magical talent, learned practitioner or not. Especially in Alegan where the church held the chains and rattled them menacingly and most like him kept their distance.

But to go around such land that they now controlled, if one needed to, would take a large amount of time so it was better to grit your teeth and go through them despite the danger of capture in places such as those it may have been foolish for even he to travel through. Coming here he had passed down through the north west kingdom of Kasynne, who held itself apart from Alegan and the trouble had not been worth the effort, he decided.

Bernard had made his way north east from Gandagar and then further north to come here and after a further moment of reluctance forced himself out of the shadows of a quiet, empty street into the warmthless daylight that stretched itself over the stone cobbling along the city's many paths and roads.

To his left was a short stone wall which behind it was the river dropping down quickly and across it was the second half of the city, yet those buildings were ones that did not have the strength of construction or forethought that those on the side closest to the old castle did. The uneven slope of the road arched up and down off to where he could see it no longer and where it ended up disappearing over one such bump. The shambled houses and buildings of Autumn, stacked atop each other precariously, while being packed tightly together, kept going long into the distance until they too were obscured by the slope. Stave in hand, he began to stroll along the cobbled road.

The city around him was bustling in the distance but right here it was quiet. This old city of the king, once so proud of the title was now the same as anywhere else. Throughout the first years they had endured the king's absence but now Bernard could feel the coldness that had caught up to this place. The people were now just people, even if they lived on a river that allowed them trade which was reasonably simple and easy to maintain. No king was needed to send a boat downriver.

And yet, how it was that this place was falling to pieces was clear to see and no one person such as himself could put it back together. The place was falling apart into blocks, divided up into both sides of the river, which should have been shared. Even on those sides were further divides, ones that did not make this place better, where there were divides between neighbours and houses.

They are swallowing their sickness here, even if it makes them increasingly ill. They carry on even as their bodies complain but now their minds are directed at each other. Me, being alone, should have little trouble passing through here unscathed and yet I worry for the foul habit that this place has picked up in its need to forge ahead with a new identity. I would like to come upon this place again once all is said and done, if even just for myself and yet I wonder if it is too late to hope for such stability.

As such he had so far avoided that side entirely and was thankful that his destinations were further off this well trod path on this side of the river. People were still coming and going from it, as they had to live, they had to trade, but tellingly no one fished in this river and on closer inspection the murk coming from its waters was evident.

Bernard regretted imagining himself eating fish caught from the river and found his appetite diminished to be replaced with a wavering nausea. That could have been helpful but he was not short on coin were he to demand food. With no one to complain to, he set about watching the morning flow of traffic to calm himself. Then again, the increase in people and their sounds did nothing to help in that regard.

Where the king and his family had once resided, some rich noble had taken over and was strutting around trying to keep order. They mostly likely knew what to do to keep themselves sane.

I'm sure that man knows his place in all of this. Not a king, not a diplomatic piece, not even the eyes of those here would turn to such a man and his family if he has them and ask them for advice. That all might be well yet what kind of person might dare to think himself fortunate for being given such a task?

The snubbing had well and truly set in, and in the minds of the people of Autumn they were now to their king as the sky was above him, covered in cloud with it raining every once in a while. Bernard paid the faces of discontent no heed, even when he could feel the violence in them and hear it as he passed homes and other dwellings where people were turning to the bottle then their family. He had no such vices. To be lost in a world addled and unpredictable was his own nightmare. That was why as a wizard he sought the fire and the shadows that cast from it. For more dangerous than the heat of the flames was the very darkness that it made and so he came to such a place as this where the fire would be rising, to prevent the darkness he knew would come.

He could not shake the feeling that all the coldness was all part of some grand design, that things were set in motion for this very reason where people would look elsewhere but oh for them to look again and look anywhere else but such dark and fiery death was of an utmost importance.

Bernard had no desire to reveal himself as the days of bombast and wonder were over, or so they were in his eyes, were too in the eyes of many who practised and taught magic properly. There was no need to state his intentions to all these people as the days were long past where such a man would be looked upon with wide, admiring eyes. Trust was very much on the outer, the rings on a pot yet to be moulded correctly and to have those rings smoothed out would require careful attention.

The wizards in the northern lands were still in control of the spinning of the pot, and were watching from their high tower intently the state of the world. That pot, the trust of all wizards, would have to go into the fire eventually, where carelessly it might be smashed after being set.

To avoid the fire outcome and keep the pot spinning, they would keep the clay in good supply so that all those over the many lands that had their hands on it would not be left with nothing. Still, the hand which would bake the pot would be a concern, even if that was supposed to be the real goal of any piece of workmanship that required hardening. But they were not there yet, any of them, even if the old days long past were the best days, there were still new days of hopes yet unborn ahead.

The world was still in motion and for that they were thankful, however people in this land he found himself were a certain beacon for the ceasing of such motions and the rest would surely follow along with it. So here he was, a lone wizard, doing his best to curb the collapse of all they held dear. The pot, in other words.

Indeed they all had a role to play, even the ones who were not taught, but the thing was that they could act out of turn, causing the world to fall into hatred and chaos. For them there was no pot, merely the mud to be flung at each other as the world faded away with them so distracted. No upstart mage had he found on his journey to come with him and that may have been for the best, as they would have drawn attention to themselves. Attention was not something he was accustomed to.

Ah, how those old wizards of ancient ages would be reeling at the notion and rolling in their crypts! What a time those ages were, where people would stop and stare at the sheer impossibility of all magical wonder being performed before them. Such an event might have proceeded a great procession of men marching through the streets inspiring greatness, enlisting the young folk to go out who would be lured underneath the flying banners of many colours that whipped in promising winds. Where they would wear armour, carrying lance and sword and shield. Then they would go off to defend their lands from great foes such as dragons or other such foes such as foul armies in clashes of bright magic and ringing steel.

These days there were no such clashes, no such battles, no such wars. Young men would rather run away or hide than enlist in a venture which would most likely end in a doomed patrol. Their superiors safe and sound to give the orders, would do so without nary a repercussion or thought for the ones they were sending to their deaths. It should be saying something that none would send their men south or west into Alegan, that was a far distance anyway, a long walk, and why fight over what would tear itself apart eventually?

Why indeed. But while they all turned away, some had to keep watch. No, this was not the age where he could spur men into a frenzy and send them here, with a mere monetary tithe to the lord of the land from who's able men he took. And so he, with the graces given to him to act by the tower and the wizards within went alone to muster something in this fading land that might resemble the wonder of the old days, knowing that they were long behind him. Others might try and certainly there were foul circles at work that had been waiting in the fringes ever since the war and the banishment of the elf people from Alegan and the surrounds, and of those circles he would not look for either inspiration or assistance.

How crude they were, how selfish to think that this world was beyond saving and should burn to the ground. They of fire and flame, the teachers of death as far as he was concerned. Those teaching that the inevitable was beyond hope of changing, were so very quiet now, hiding in the security of their Houses. Waiting, watching, smouldering. It was up to him as the learned one to deny these awful ones their chance at holding onto the world. Their grip was not quite there yet, a hovering hand waiting for the moment to grab and grasp, to doom all who lived in it. Even they would wait for that dark end to appear, to show themselves as rescuers and it was before that moment where he would stop them in their tracks if not before.

On spending time thinking of such thoughts, Bernard had successfully troubled himself, as among this city could be any manner of person and now here he was simply focussing on the worst outcome.

"I must be careful with staying unnoticed here. It would not do well to have people of a vicious and certain sort pluck my life away."

He whispered this to himself, knowing that speaking to himself lent to others the notion that he was little more than a crazy old man but it helped him to collect his own thoughts. He stopped in his tracks, narrowed his eyes and raised his voice to respond curtly to the silence.

"And you, on the other hand, need to work on your own personal stealth. Although I doubt you have a care for being discovered."

In the gap between two houses in front of which Bernard had stopped, a towering suit of black armour stood in the dark against a wall, arms crossed. The voice from it was as deep and as expansive as thunder.

"What are you doing here despite surely knowing what creeps in this place?"

"What does it look like, I'm snooping around. I can't lie to you." He responded dryly.

Does he seriously think that I don't know what he would do to me were he to think otherwise?

The Black Knight did not seem overall to be impressed.

"Know now that your eyes here will cause agitation, stoke the flames and have the potential to send the smoke far and wide, where it will rattle others. I warn you, do not do so."

"If I'm careful as I shall be, that will not happen. I thank you for your concern as I myself share in it, but you need to do something else with what power you have."

The knight was silent for a time.

"I watch and listen, acting when I wish. I have seen the world in chaos and would not have so happen again. As such I am mindful for any and all who would cause the world to fall into fire and shadow so enraptured that they can no longer see the mistakes in their own existence."

"Then our goals align." Bernard said.

The knight leaned back into the shadows, leaving the wizard alone. He wrapped up his robes and continued on his way.

"So I too shall go, mysterious one. But I shall go on here and hither be silent about it. I must know if this place is falling, as I fear the rest of the world shall follow in its example if the worst is to come to pass. I can only hope that there are others, Black Knight, that share in our goals for there are many off in their own wiles and ways who care nothing of a world but their own world, though it be a piece of the whole that will not survive by itself."

As he continued on his way alongside the buildings right next to the river, he wondered how carts or merchants would be able to get through these narrow walkways without being forced to turn around or jump into the river as there was very little room to walk. In this afternoon light people were sparse, it was getting darker sooner and most were likely already home to avoid the cold that would follow.

The buildings were sturdily made, boards locked close together with shutters held tight or sometimes open. Some buildings would have great wooden pillars on their edges or lower floors built up on stone to support the wood above. Despite all of that construction, there was something about the creeping state of disrepair he noticed in some of them that gave him pause for thought. Some buildings were worn from the weather and the closeness to the river, rotting wood crates and sacks of produce was left out to mould.

The people who live here should consider themselves lucky that they resided along such a river, that the trade would not dry up entirely with the ripped up prestige and yet for some I feel that is not enough.

He saw how they had squandered what they had and felt little pity for those eyes that he saw about him. Eyes could be everywhere and who knew what was beneath them, a person just waiting for the spark to set the world ablaze or fall apart in blindness? It was likely that such an act would burn out some of this rot. An act such as that would be good, yet the fire was not what good wizards worried about the most, it was the shadow beside it.

His nose twitched and he sniffed the air. There was something in it, a certain smell that came with fire that wasn't quite reliant on fuel to burn. In a strange way, this fire would ignite first then seek its meal. It only took a couple of times experiencing it to notice the difference.

Pyromancers.

His mind spat out the word, and now his mind keenly was on notice. Bernard rolled his knuckles, ready to thread together magic into anything he would need.

Then all of a sudden the sensation was gone, the smell replaced with the smell of sewer water. The wizard shivered, even though the weather wasn't that cold enough to chill, really.

He did not feel the sensation again while walking along the road, which was a bother for him as he wondered then if that meant he was going loopy or losing his touch. That wasn't something he had expected to happen for many more years, certainly. He decided that some veil had fallen or was testing itself on the minds all here. He would need to ask to see if anyone had just experienced what he had.

The sound of squeaking wheels reached his ears as he came to a crossroads. A bridge with low stone walls was on the left, on the right the road wound off further into the city. Directly ahead was a continuation of the riverside path he walked on and more houses. A man was crossing the bridge up into the darker part of the city with his barrow, so Bernard hurried to catch up, walking in front to stand ahead of him and waving for him to stop.

"I do say man, did you feel anything just before, any strange sensation?"

The barrow man leered at him under his hat.

"Nothing here out of the ordinary if I don't count your voice. Go back to your books you fool." He said.

Most unhappy at having his day interrupted, the man continued on to his route to mutter barely audibly to himself.

"And leave us in peace."

"What's going on here?" Bernard heard from a voice behind him, belonging to a stern man, thin faced, his expression irritable at being brought out of his warmth in this ruckas.

Ah, the watchman this man seems to be.

He remembered that on the corner of many of the streets were the houses or buildings of those expected to be as watchmen. No doubt that this man had come out to do his duty in case of the worst. If that were to be the case however, the wizard noted that he bared no weapon nor displayed any keen posture to defend himself, a slouching and downtrodden of face man to be judging him by the rings under his eyes, doing the least he could while observing the incident.

The man with the wagon shoved a finger towards Bernard.

"This damn bell-ringer is harassing me. Tell him to clear off and not ruin the evening of anyone else."

The newcomer had the appearance of wanting the very last thing for him to have to do being striking up a conversation with a stranger. He hooked his thumbs in his pants and strolled over without making direct eye contact, indeed seeming more interested in the surrounding buildings and the weather.

That was until the man's disinterested pivoting turned into a right hook squarely into the side of Bernard's head.

No more blows came falling to him, as he lay dizzy, thoughts unclear, but he could hear distant voices and wondered at them.

Are those the voices of the dead calling for me?

No, how wistful of a thought, the voices were of a gathering of few people, all now wondering what the mess was. It was him of course, aside the road, and while his vision was hazed over he could focus and still hear words. It hurt when he tried to think and while on the ground an old, uneasy voice floated down from somewhere above him.

"I keep telling you nothing good will come from being so ruthless with random strangers."

The voice of the second man came down on top of them.

"But they're here up to no good, that's what I've been saying. No one just comes here any more and does it look as if this man has coins to spare in your store? I think not."

The old voice sounded as if they admitted as much, a disquieting, shaking sigh escaping them.

"While you may be right and that those of us who cannot afford to pay the boat fee to make use of the river trade suffer, how many more must we turn away, waiting for the good days to return? They may not, in my lifetime. Or yours."

"Of course things will get better. The king will clear that whole mess up the church has put him in and return to reside here, bringing Autumn back to its rightful glory."

The wizard was regaining feeling and strength in his limbs. There once would have been a young and hot headed mage who would have seen that belligerent man fry like the most unfortunate of rats climbing up a lightning rod but he was not that young and quick to rage any more.

He pushed himself up and found a kind pair of hands easing him to his feet. Her voice was young and concerned and he very much hoped this was how he'd be treated by the youth when he was suitably elderly.

"I am sorry, for some of us do not take kindly how we have been treated and some of us take that anger and place it unfairly on others. Pay him no mind."

Bernard lightly touched the side of his head and fought back against the pain.

"I will do what I can, when I can. Letting opportunities for vengeance pass by is a show of restraint they need to learn but not through hands on teaching, I think. Yes. I however shall demonstrate it now, by doing nothing untoward him."

With a grabbing motion his stave shot from the ground into his grasp and the audible exclamation of all present was what one could expect, some with surprise, others with fear. He cared not which there were more of, for it did not matter. He did wave away the growing murmuring that followed, however.

"Restrain yourselves. I'm only using it to lean on, reason being courtesy of your friend over here who quite knocked me off my feet. See?"

He demonstrated his use of the wooden branch to keep him upright by holding on to it like a tree trunk, but even the warmth at his elbow left him, his vision clearing only to show him the backs of heads and hear the slamming of a door to his right.

The wizard was alone again, wondering if he should have pressed the matter, the sound of squeaking wheels in his ears, wondering about the wheels turning he hoped, away from the dark. An uneasy silence fell on this street.

Some sought fire, and it burned them. Others sought the comfort of oblivion and found something far worse waiting for them in the dark. And yet there were those still who sought something they could not understand, but knew that only peace would follow once they found it. That one was by far the worst, for the things people would do for it and the lengths they would go were as immeasurable as the burning gold stars in the night's sky.

Peace through eternal damnation and death for all must be avoided. Perhaps I should head to a place where I might be surrounded by those with keen minds.

He made his way to a great library that had been created at the insistence of a king some many years now past. Before leaving for Churl, the royal family had been quite restricted in their movements and had not ventured to it in years. Perhaps if the place had not been opened to the public it would have seen more use if they were so afraid of their own subjects. Where they had gone now surely was not as well equipped, where there would likely be only one book to read.

The structure was wide and white, standing three stories tall and carved out of polished rock. The wizard wondered how much longer it would remain standing, as a sign of importance and necessity it now was no longer, people had other things to worry about than hiding away within a book. He was not one of those people and as he walked within its walls he could smell the musty air inside of books that he had never entirely gotten used to.

The length of the building around every wall held books of all sorts and colours and the shelves ringed all the way up to the very top. Down on the first floor there were many long, tall rows that all crossed together to meet with benches where people could sit. There were still many more tables and chairs scattered around where people could read in peace and for the use of this place, only one would have been required.

An old librarian sat by a wall and had her head shoot up at his entrance, their eyes turned into a squint, but Bernard shook his head.

"No, you won't recognise me, for I come from far away to be here."

The wizard gestured his arms west. As the countenance of the librarian remained stony, he smiled warmly.

"It's quite alright, I just need a quiet place to be for a while to look for some books."

That was only half true, he was not looking for what was there, rather, what was missing. It was however more true than where he had implied he had come from.

Scouring the shelves for anything he could find that might have been out of place, he uncovered nothing while peering at other people pouring about books for a potential person he could take along. Some people weren't even reading, merely using the table as places to sleep or talk amongst themselves.

There was trouble when people neglected to read, but no history book would help him with his quest. A solemn stillness was coming over the world. That old war had been merely the beginning of the end, he felt, an ending that the world had never needed to record the like of before. Of course, if no one took heed and no one noticed, it would sneak up on them and it would all be over before they knew it. And there would be nothing to record as there would be nothing left.

He took some books off the shelves at random, hoping to use the time to watch others that might have been walking around. Hauling the stack over to the librarian, Bernard accepted a candlewick so he could find a dark corner to pour over them or at least pretend to do so and demonstratively took a match and lit the candle. This was all part of how the song and dance went, to prove that you were here reading certain books and not others.

His teacher could have lit a flame with her bare hands and had he attempted it he might have been able to, but he would not attempt magic in this land that was seen as cursed. As he sat down he saw other little glowing candles, knowing that the librarian had watched over the lighting of every single one.

Perhaps the world had been anticipating its own doom, and now some six decades later people had to have been wondering what had happened to that coming end. There were those who were looking for sparks to fan into flames to bring it about again and that to him was most grim.

He stroked his beard in thought.

Where else has the light gone out for this land? Not at all just a matter of the king leaving here, there are others that must share this fate, as it can not have trickled down from the north or blown in from the west on those foul dead winds of that dead land. Neither should have the words to turn the minds of people as people are quite on guard for influence from both of those directions.

That time after the war must have seemed so glorious to these people, no longer the forgotten child obscured by the golden light of that city, their own light could shine ever so brightly across all who were lost. And they had taken charge of this broken and fractured land, organised the round ups of those who used fire magic and the recovery of those who had nowhere to go, bringing them into the grasp of the power of their belief.

That should have been as far as it had gone for those who lived with the promise of a bright future yet in the end the whole world doused itself out of fear of the fire that had brought it so close to destruction. Now there was smoke that could be found everywhere amongst the shadows of an ever approaching night which Bernard admitted to himself left him with a sense of dread.

It could have been that the king had seen some of the danger and had tried to keep the whole land under his control. The kingdom capital had been moved to the religious capital, an old city that had collapsed into disuse, not unlike Gandagar but one that had seen pilgrims far and wide come, trickle in.

But it seemed the king could not control his church and the words coming forth from it bade his subjects to leave the rest of the world to rot. They in Alegan would be saved and all they had to do was wait, yet where people were choosing to wait he did not know, unless it was dead in the ground.

Or it could be in places such as this. He realised.

Bernard wondered what others who used this place as a refuge for their minds were reading and looking at. Perhaps they just read to pass the time, waiting for the end they thought they would deserve where they would be shown a world beyond that of the other lands. It must have been that the dead were not worthy and that those who had left had gone somewhere safe, he hoped. The church of Churl said that people were blind, but the light would make them see.

Well, that would only happen if he let it happen. It had occurred to him a few times that it might be far beyond himself to turn the opinion of an entire kingdom riddled with weak minded zealotry. He just hoped he wasn't alone and that someone else would be able to help. They didn't have to be scholars or learned people as he was, just those who were willing to stop the world from fading away, being choked out of existence.

It was that very existence and the wonder of that which was being taken for granted in the kingdom and they despised anyone outside it because it meant that if they could exist, then other terrors could too. Ones that looked human, or monstrous and they had to share the world with them, or admit that they were the same.

So even though they walked in the light there would be a darkness waiting alongside it, dark were their very actions and that would become them without them realising it. There would be no world after the dark took over, only an end that would be both cold and terrible in which the world that was would cease. To stop the cold, he knew some would turn to fire and from the darkness that sprang from such fire brought demons. A power once sought after that would have led the whole of Auralin into ruin. There were those who would prefer that.

The wizard sighed, thankful that the fate of this kingdom was not their decision to make, to which the candle's flame flickered merrily, itself perhaps thankful that there was some additional air directed at it and he frowned to himself. Perhaps there really was nothing else here other than people living in a place that was fading into obscurity, but even Churl had been that way for years until recently, all word of mouth considered.

He collected his stack of books, getting murmuring from some of the others seated as his chair scraped. He didn't care, there were other times to read and he had to get out of this place before he fell into a malaise of doubt and self loathing.

He certainly had not found anything here more than what would become kindling, books and people alike. After snuffing out the candle he went on his way and handed the candle back to her.

"Be careful to look after the books. In days such as these they could go up at any moment." He said.

The librarian still held a stony face.

"Take your books and hurry along with your doom saying elsewhere, we don't need it here. I think we've actually been spared the worst of it, don't you think? The war never reached us, the moving of our king has quite taken the heat off. Now we can be permitted some silence from all that rabble who comes and goes. So be gone along with them."

Chapter Thirteen
Searching for Allies

Bernard was out roaming the city and had come to the next place he had decided to visit. The church that sat in Autumn was a tall, stone building and rising up from its middle was a domed tower where a bell would be rung. It was nearing that hour as he made his way along the stone slabs of the great bridge to be met at a shuttered metal gate on his way in.

The holy man who he met was middle aged and wore a thick dark cloak around his shoulders, with a long hood that capped over their head and past their eyes. He was, however, friendly of expression, something Bernard admitted he had not yet seen since arriving. Some people, regardless of the trouble he would cause them, appeared as fair enough people to perhaps not fully deserve the fate that would find them.

"Oh, are you here to ring the bell?" The man said.

The wizard shook his head and leaned on his stave.

"The bells of the church of Churl will not be announced by any ringing on my behalf. May it be that I have the look of such a man, but that is not why I am here. I have just come from Gandagar and on the matter of bell ringing must say that the bell tower there is in such a state of disrepair that the sound can not be rung to those who might need to hear it. Now I am here having made it in all speed yet I see this place is falling apart at the very foundations of what makes a kingdom, its people."

"Then perhaps you are a wizard, might I ask? Come to solve our problems?"

The wizard cursed his words before continuing.

"Whatever problem the lord of Autumn is having surely can not be so large that he would imagine a wizard would be required for the fixing. And were that the case, surely a wizard would have better things to do, such are our own foundations of righteousness put forth for us and all to decide what it is a wizard should do best."

"Then state your intention and be plain about it. For rabble is not welcome here. We've had enough of the ill winded preachers and those who announce our doom, most lacking of trust that which would save them."

Then again, perhaps this man did deserve what would be coming for him, Bernard thought.

"This is not the first time today I have heard such similar words. Do tell, have there been people here causing a fuss in recent times?" He asked.

"A fuss to put it mildly, I do say. Some have been caged away as simply removing them from the city proved fruitless."

As leaving them outside might poison the other parts of the kingdom and make people think while truly opening their eyes. The wizard thought, keeping the comment rightfully to himself.

"Could I meet one of these people?" He instead asked, mildly, not wanting to come across as old and cantankerous to the first person who had not treated his person and that mood together as a forgone conclusion.

The man looked back inside behind him to see if they had been overheard.

"Hmm, well I suppose that's what you could have been here for, we shall say, otherwise you might not be allowed through. I don't see the harm in it other than to your own sanity. But be careful that your own words don't get you locked up, or me in trouble."

"Of course."

Yet half the kingdom would be in chains by that reckoning, with everyone chained together, isn't that how it is right now? We might as well all be prisoners regardless whether or not we're in a cage.

He was escorted to the prisons, a low underside where he could have told he was being led to by the decent down far below and the increasing stench of unwashed bodies, filthy cells and mildew.

What answers can I possibly find here? He wondered.

People hid things away, so it was here where he would search the minds of the mad for anything he could use. It was possible that anyone with anything to reveal had been dealt with prior, but he had to try and do whatever he could. Simply abandoning the world was not something he would do, even though it seemed everyone here were content to rot in their own filth, an act he was sure that those above would eventually join them in when the end came.

The last time he had done such a thing as break someone out of their confinement the lucky one had not hung around, however here he might have better luck, even if that took convincing another that all they had to do was follow along with him and all their problems would all be over.

He coughed, because that was so very familiar, after all it was the exact same situation he was trying to avoid. The coughing continued due to some irritation in his lungs. Perhaps there was something in the air.

Only after some time scouring the gaol had he relented to accepting that the mad had been no help. There had been those who had magic power, who had been tortured quite severely to madness, so that they would be of no help at all. While it hurt him deeply inside to leave those in such places and positions, he could not bear being the master holding the leading collar of anyone so far gone. None were pleading for release, they had been past the point of an open mind and all he had demanded answers from had been wallowing within the frail confines of their minds.

Once back outside and free of the musty cells, he took a moment for a breath of fresh air and to look around. The gaol opened into a flat patch of grass with a short stone fence around it lined with trees, thin and leafless, their white bark giving them the appearance of ghostly tendrils snaking up from the ground to the sky above, which remained cloudy and dull of colour. Past the wrought iron gate he had a fine view of the lines of houses and other buildings which sat on either side of the river. They stood tall, cold even, with the people so similar he knew must have been amongst them.

Despite the sensation he had felt of there being heat right around them he had to admit that there were those with the other kind of heat in them, that hate for others and lack of respect that were found in some people regardless of their circumstances.

How much longer do we have?

He could feel in the stillness of the air that clung onto the world that was failing, falling apart at the seams. The people were wrong to think that the world could not be lively and vibrant outside their own lives. Only the most scattered remnants of those who believed had ever bothered to make their way to the south, where the capital was, to Churl and its long gone light. Those glory days were in the past, the way it was supposed to be was not how it was any more and he did not have the heart to tell any of them the truth at all.

In another time, he could have turned such people to a worthy cause but now was not this time. People were too wary, too afraid of others and too suspicious. He could well see the reason behind their fears and the reasons for wanting to be away from all the worldly problems but their minds were self centred and their reasoning for helping others sparse.

He was not yet desperate for allies but so far had found none willing to stay and if none here were willing or able to assist then he would find help elsewhere. He did not think that leaving the elf had been the right thing for him to have done but to pull her arm along would not have been helpful. Leaving Alegan however would have been far worse. There were too many others off on their own wayward ways to be of help for him to join their number and it was rather likely that the elf had become one of those, but he had to make the most of what he had, which was very little other than his initial success of bringing himself here intact.

He searched his waist for his coin bag and assessed his situation. It was not terribly late but he rather did not want to be left without a place to sleep during the night. The wizard went to get some early supper at an inn well away from the river and found the hospitality lacking. The walls were thick wood that kept the inside warm and they certainly appeared sturdy but all present kept their guards up around him. The salted fish was bony and gritty. The potatoes were poor in size. The ale he found diluted. All these were further signs to him that not all was well, as no place that would have called itself the head of the kingdom would have served up food such as what he ate.

Perhaps if everyone looked at the food being brought to their plates they would realise what trouble everyone was in. To him this seemed unlikely to occur, after passing over his gold he found his room to be of similar quality to his food. It smelled just as bad, so he spent the remaining light against the window reading the books he had taken, and the night that followed was spent sleeping in the opposing corner most furthest from the door, where he could watch it.

The next morning he awoke to the sounds of a scuffle and looked down from his room window to peer below in the early morning light. Two people were arguing over that which he could not tell due to the width of the glass making the sounds unclear, so made his way to the street below. By the time he got down there, one of the people had left the dirty street behind.

"What was going on here just now? The shouting troubles my old bones." Bernard said.

He rather did not like pretending to be so old and clueless, yet he knew that there were uses for appearing as much as he could the wizened old man while being careful not to show the appearance of his interest so terribly.

The remaining person, a young man was dusting himself off.

"Faithless naysayers, old man, nothing you need concern yourself with."

A faithless naysayer might be just who I'm looking for. Bernard thought.

He moved past the lad to follow the back of a cloaked figure making their way down the street.

Unfortunately, the person was brisk and the wizard no longer quite so, which was rather infuriating and while he had attempted to maintain a respectable distance to not be caught he had to hurry in order not to lose them entirely. In doing so, he tripped over and fell face first onto the hard ground. A shadow stood over him and he looked up to see the person looking down at him, having walked back over to investigate. The man was thin and bald under the hood, a slight look of suspicion on his face.

"Why were you following me?"

"Because I believe that I can use your help." Bernard replied.

"Well you can get yourself off the ground. I have no reason to help you."

As the man turned away the wizard struggled to his feet.

"Wait, wait, hear me out this once if you may. The world is in peril and I look for allies in these times where all the world seeks to rot and fade away."

The man paused for a moment, considering the prospect.

"Come to my home. There we will discuss this peril you're so keen on."

Bernard was most relieved to hear this.

"Ah, you understand me completely. Very well then, I shall do so."

The man's house was little more than a square shack, boarded and locked up, that sat on a slight rise in a curve of the river. The river twisted off into the distance while the morning mist settled and the sun rays evaporated the moisture off the ground. The house would have had a view of it from the inside had it not been bordered up and showed the peeling, musty signs of it being so close to water, not unlike the buildings closer into the city. The man spent some time going through a heavy, rusted key chain to open all the locks that covered the door.

Once inside, the wizard could see that there were locks on the other side of the door too that the man promptly secured, to which the wizard did not mind, as he saw them as being no obstacle were he to wish to leave.

The man moved across the room to begin adjusting lamps to get them to burn, and with his back to the wizard he spoke.

"Do you hear the hustle and bustle of people going about their lives in carelessness and apathy? Awaiting the time for their faith to save them they await their end, for the dark is already here among them, growing in strength because of them and they don't even know it. Yes, yes, I understand. We can only ward it off as we have for so long. This nice house has been provided to me so that I may better watch in secret while I do what I can."

Bernard looked around, the room was almost empty save for a thick chair in one corner and a table.

"To have a place such as this is almost not needed. I went to the library and went over some books. I was surprised to find the place so abandoned."

"Well you wouldn't be finding much there these days. Everything that has been written down is only good for one purpose."

The wizard frowned.

"I suppose there are those cases where what has been written will only lead to hardship overall were it to spread and what might be divine salvation to only those who travel deep into this land on pilgrimage."

"Have you yourself seen the trouble along the northern borders?"

"And did nothing about it too. It is not only this land that suffers the slowing of the world but all others besides. The lines between rulers mean nothing to the coming darkness."

The man sighed.

"As I have told you, it is already here. Tell me, what do you feel about this place?" He gestured around the room.

The wizard was perplexed by the question. What he felt was that this was a person he might not be able to convince to leave his home, as he certainly liked his security. Unless he did something to force the man to leave, which would not be the right thing to do at all.

The man took a lamp with him as they moved into a second room where a sneer played on his face.

"You haven't answered my question. It doesn't matter what little we do, it's not enough, it is never enough. Don't you see, don't you feel what is going on up in the sky? That darkness is coming and the whole world is blind to it, doesn't matter where. None take our council and the prisons and gaols fill with the mad who can not speak of it to the masses, you know this."

"I have had first hand experience with all of these things, that is true. We have to be careful, as there's more than one place to keep our eyes on."

The wizard tilted his head. There was this creeping sensation that something was amiss.

And as for this house, I feel it is a nice old home, conveniently placed. I do feel something else, what is this I feel? Ah now I understand. He speaks in 'we' as in the manner of those in their Houses.

Bernard spoke carefully.

"I realise this myself, yet must still ask whether it is you realise what it is you would do here?"

"Of course. Where one succeeded others failed. The fire, it must have been so beautiful, but the direction those holding it took? No, they were foul minded. Why start a fire only to snuff it all out? We have been branded as evil but that is evil, power is power, not evil."

Bernard did not wish to entertain the idea.

"That magic is nothing but a weapon for someone who refuses to use their own hands. It is a danger to any who use it and a tool of the wicked. None who are whole of mind have any reason to use such magic."

"Who were we but the ones to try I'll never know." The man spat.

"That darkness is nothing like us. The world will burn if we have to prove it. Beyond this land the world does nothing, it doesn't even watch, they can't even fathom the end coming for them. Whereas here, the people of this kingdom sit blind expecting lies to save them but we will save them and start it all over from the ashes that remain."

He did not look mad. His voice did not shake but cracked at the end of his words as if something was effecting his lungs.

"Step into the light. That's what they say, that's where the dark comes from and the blind masses do so because they know no different. Throw them all to the fire and then they will be saved. Burnt, ruined, but do you think the evil dark will touch them then? No."

Bernard's fingers dug into his staff.

"Plans such as those shall be stopped before that happens. Those of us without addled heads on our shoulders shall open their eyes and there will be no need for a world of fire, a world of fear. You understand what it means to be beholden to such things. You solve nothing and merely exacerbate the problem."

The man snarled.

"A scared child's answer, one I hear so often from Illit and the like while we of House Maffer know the truth. All in all, people are being taught falsities and talk their lies all the while the truth is out there. You think the world can bear it? A cold and dark place? Look around you, the last gusts of air are being blown across this land to make their way out to the world beyond it and none here have the strength to get up and fight because none of them can breathe."

"You would burn it all to the ground and as such I am done talking to you. I fear there is nothing left to learn here. I would go to the place which might be the last to find hope, however misguided, and redirect them."

"You would attempt to leave?"

Bernard had no intention of letting the pyromancer leave, either.

The temperature in the room increased to searing degrees as the air itself lit up the room and sizzled as the man threw back a hand to grasp at the foul magic. Yet the wizard was ready and from his free hand came flying a single blue bolt that felled the man, his body crumpling to the ground. Even though his life was spent, blue ripples arced off him, making his body twitch.

Bernard looked briefly around the house as the temperature returned to normal but could not find anything else of use. So he fled to the front door and brought it down with a blast of air from his stave, the metal breaking and wood splintering. He did not see anyone else but knew that if he had not been heard before he certainly had been now.

If anyone had been watching this place, just as I have been watching, then it won't be long until I'm found out myself. So I must be gone from this place. Oh how I would rather have sent another in my stead to Churl.

He knew that the angry noise would have been heard in the distance, so chose to leave as fast as he was able. A quick glance around showed no one approaching yet he still made his way hastily to the stables. It would have been a simple matter to turn back into a bird, had he not been knocked around and forced to defend himself, so he was far too exhausted for any spells or incantations, and his night of rest had not allowed for him to properly gather himself for any other attempt.

Regret filled his chest but Bernard forced his legs to move.

I can not rely on others to do this for me. It saddens me that Autumn may be lost to those head first in the fire and would themselves rather sit in the dark awaiting the coming ashes than move forward with bright eyes and so must be left to its own devices, regrettably.

He approached a bored coach driver and his mooching beasts.

"You there, are you for hire? If so then take me from this place and I shall afford you my entire bag of gold."

On holding the bag in front of the man he snapped out of dull daydreams in an instant to have his eyes focused on the glinting gold, now dreaming of those things which he could spend it on.

"Aye sir I am, just tell me where we'd be off to and I won't say another word."

"Take me to the holy city, that place once nearly forgotten now esteemed and hallowed among the pilgrims and where king and church resides."

"A long journey but a one worth both our times I'm sure." Said the coachman, carefully putting the bag of coins inside a trunk which he then sat on.

As he pulled his beasts into reluctant compliance, the wizard hopped into the back and pulled shut the curtain and he was soon lost amongst the other travellers coming and going. Something festered in the place he went from but he knew that there was no more time to be dealing with it. At least the foolish pyromancer had been right about that.

Chapter Fourteen
In the Home of Kag

Often on their way the druids would come across the shells of towns and places long abandoned, ransacked for their wood and materials, leaving little left but the husks of hamlets whose residents were long since gone. What might have been vibrant places had all its people either scattered or dead. Or maybe those people had travelled west, beyond the furthest reaches into the forests and further still to a dark and horrific death, with no home left or place in the world gladly walking the way through.

If they did go, it was impossible to tell if they paved the way for others, as there were no warnings for others or even remnants of camps left by travellers willing to doom themselves. Such sad sights they saw made them all feel that perhaps it was best this road was forgotten, and gradually any indication of the path to travel disappeared, often completely for days at a time. This was the west road, or rather the east road, as it was the road to the place of pilgrimage for the pilgrims who had come from the city and land that no longer was, a place taken and destroyed by fire that brought foul demons out of the ground and into the world to ruin it utterly.

So this road was rarely used and the further and further they travelled, the more the stones worn into the ground had been overgrown by plants and had steadily been covered with dirt. It was always found again, sometimes spotted in the distance a little to one side, leading them on and pointing them on a cloudy day to the last lonely town on the trail all by itself before the trail disappeared entirely. So it was that a single town marked an end to the road, beyond which nature would take its due.

The more Zelda thought about it, she realised that travellers had always taken the north and south roads on which pilgrims and other dignified people had come to her home and through it to lower lands or the east, with only a few sorry traders making the journey west that she had ever spied along the road. It was that road she had now travelled beyond, her mind free of the need for gold or profit or any other sort of gain for that matter and she was not alone in that feeling growing deep in her chest that they were far away from many places people might willingly come in great numbers.

She craned her head around to look back at the mountains behind them.

"Tell me, why are we here? We're meant to be on our way north but this road has led us back south and at that downwards gradually too, that I have been feeling under my feet."

Gunter answered her.

"That is correct, however there is an old town here and an old friend here, one I would like to meet which is the reason why we come here. Do not be alarmed, for I have no fear in my lateness resulting in having missed such a friend in this instance. On what could be missed, this is our last chance to stop and resupply as nothing else lies further on our path for many leagues. If there is anything we can not scavenge that any of you feel you might need then here is your last chance. I believe you will find we are quite leaving the lands of human settlement behind after this. Come to think of it, not much else lies either west nor further south of here."

It certainly seemed that way, as she could see the path winding down slowly and Zelda looked ahead to see a bunch of old uneven stone buildings, around twenty judged by counting the roofing, sitting on top of a slope that cut away on the left to drop far down below into a valley and forest trees. In her mind it seemed rather wrong to call such place a town from this distance, a settlement perhaps indeed but with the way that everything was clumped together most haphazardly with a lack of good workmanship, it appeared far removed from anywhere else she had been.

Its aloneness might have been the only thing that would have given it any chance of being ignored against those in the pursuit of battle by those inclined, for the rocky slope looking out to a southern forest showed no sign of being a pathway to lands that were not wild and avoided.

I suppose it will be digging caves for me from here on out if I want something over my head that is not a tree when I sleep.

It was the time of the year when the wind and sky would turn cold and where people in turn would turn cold, as if they would turn to the cold for guidance, year after year. Sometimes, Zelda did not like it when this time of the year happened, people retreated into more than just their homes and by the time the land began to warm again she found herself around those very different than they had been before.

She knew they could not stay in this place throughout the winter and that was all well. The wind, the cold, the silence when the wind was not blowing, it etched into every last piece of her mind how she would not stay here either. Zelda didn't want to know anyone only to have them change over the winter. If they only kept moving, those around her could not surprise her with changes of heart, or words from a troubled, unbalanced mind. They could not outrun the cold, she knew that, yet it did make her wonder what would she have done if this place was to have been her new home.

Findal's voice brought her out of her thoughts of drudgery.

"It never used to be such a worry as there was once much that did lay beyond these lands a long time ago, such as a seaside city far in the south west along the water which was a key trading hub with the Northlands. It exists no longer, for it was where the linage of mine came from, fisherman with a wealth due to the trade of the sea, so I can be certain of that. I would not expect to have a claim to any of the ruins of the place now, as I am sure there are many equally as worthy by their own familial ties who have no knowledge of any of it but I would like to go there one day just to see it."

Peter shrugged.

"Even if it still stood that doesn't change the fact that it is very far away. Whether it still exists or not we would have to travel many more lengths south than we have already west to reach it and that is not where we are headed."

Zelda was still curious.

"Do you know what happened to the city?"

Findal hummed while scraping his jaw.

"Some say the sea dried up and an army marched across the water and sacked the city. Others blame foul sea witches for turning the waters vile and the minds of men to mush. The most likely explanation to me is that it relied too much on northern trade and gold and when those lands fell into their own conflicts there were none remaining who would trade with them. Without the gold that turned the port into a city to sustain it, the lives of those living day to day on the flow of gold became fraught. Not mine though, we tried to keep the trade up with the north which makes me the next in line, however I would prefer to warn everyone about the troubles of gold."

Gunter was nodding his head approvingly.

"And what would those rich merchants say, if they were to see that their ancestor has given up all wealth and riches for rags and a home amongst nature?"

Findal laughed.

"They'd be horrified, but I don't care. All I want is a place to call my own and be happy and if I get to take everyone along with me all will be the better for it, just as you have shown me. Zelda, you'll find once you have everything you truly need in life and are happy to stay that way the rest just comes naturally."

The land dropped down even further on the left side between mountains that rolled on into the distance, but closer to them dipped sharply into a gully far below that was dark and wild. Zelda hoped that they were not going down there as there was a feeling in the pit of her stomach that turned whenever she looked down it. Thankfully they didn't go near it and stayed on the steady downward slope into town, where a muddy path became one embedded with stones to become the streets which any good town should have had.

What Zelda had taken to be a mass of shambled buildings were in fact the houses of those that lived in the town. The town was rather smaller than she had thought, the buildings spaced closer together meaning each of them had to squeeze through in order to move forward. The wood such as that of the doors had once been painted white but were peeling and aged, with moss and other green plant life creeping and growing across the walls and the roofing, which itself was growing grass and drooping at the edges. Some even appeared to have been draped across several buildings at once to create some very dark passages indeed.

Up on this slope the wind whistled through no trees, only between the houses and under the eaves, ending in gusts that would attempt to blow under doors and chill people in their homes. The roofing was made from thick thatches of straw and the walls were piled stones with gaps in them that were stuffed with straw to prevent drafts as best they could.

This would have been my place. If what they say is true then this must be the distant place they were talking about. I'm not sure I like it, yet to hide away in this remoteness, it surely would have done its job for a girl looking to hide.

Zelda felt the silence was getting to her, and whispered to Gunter, not wishing for her words to be heard unless they might seem foolish, or even indeed if they were not.

"I hope nobody minds that we're just walking in here unannounced. It all feels rather private."

"Nobody minds. This village is like any other." He said.

"And someone does know that we're coming. In fact I'm sure they know we're here already, waiting for us."

They wound their way further between the crush of buildings, following the ever shrinking path and spaces on the sides of their shoulders as the buildings leaned into one another. There were gaps where the path widened here and there, where curved stone steps met together at the entrances for several houses yet from within them came no lights or sound. Zelda hoped that everyone was simply outside as they should be.

Eventually they came upon the middle of town, a wide open circle of ground completely covered in the stones that made up the paving. Blades of grass were sticking through the cracks and at the centre of this open space there stood a water pump leaving it otherwise not extraordinary.

All the houses and shops were crammed together and from first glance it was impossible for her to tell which was someone's home rather than a shop as all of them looked the same. Now being faced with many branching pathways, Zelda found herself at a loss for where they should proceed, as did the faces of the others but Gunter seemed to know where he was going.

He led them away from the circle down a side street that led out of the main block, where the slope curved off to the right and beyond a lone tree and a boulder a single row of older wooden houses followed it to the edge of a cliff.

Gunter stopped at the side of the street and looked back at his companions.

"The person I came here to see is not fond of a large amount of visitors. I should take only Zelda with me for the moment. After all, this was where I was planning to leave her to wait out the events that caused her departure, but of course our plans have further changed due to our unexpected good fortune."

She found that she could only nod at this.

"I might have to leave a few things in town then, I hadn't expected to be caught up in such a thing and had aimed to return them."

Findal shook his head.

"You can't always return the things you take from people. Best not to worry about a few lost tools here and there, one day you might find there were things less tangible you took that you hadn't realised and those things can't be replaced or given back. Those things can become a worry to you so don't concern yourself if you can't speak to those you wronged as others will not understand the weight behind your well meaning and even then you might not find the weight of such wrongness lifted from your back."

"Whatever do you mean?" She asked.

"Never mind, never mind, I said one day, but that's not today. I'm going to go busy myself around town, see what's making up the good of this place while the rest of you meet with this friend."

Peter sighed as both wandered off, him trailing a little bit behind, to explore the town as the rest continued on down the slope.

Survel shrugged with his bored, careless expression devoid of any warmth and sat on the large boulder under the shade of the tree, where he took out a stone from his bag to sit by himself, the still aired silence cut through by the slow *shink shink* sound of the stone against the edge of his sword as he sharpened it.

The two of them continued to the very last house and by virtue of it being on the very edge of town was the last at the edge of the drop off, which lent to it a distant feeling of abandonment. The feeling was increased when Zelda looked back up towards the rest of the village and the backs of houses were all so close together that it created the illusion of a wall that seemed to shut them out, with Survel the only other person in sight.

Gunter walked up to the door of the last house and knocked. After a moment the door opened and both walked inside to a rather well lit interior that appeared to be neat and tidy. There was no sign of who had let them in. There was, however, seated on a soft cushioned chair a rather large creature.

The beast was similar to a squat, grey mountain cat with giant grass green eyes, the colour of grass when put in a shallow pool with the full day's light upon it and those eyes appeared so deep to be two of such pools. What set it apart from a mountain cat was not only its size, which was at least double that of a conventional breed, but that protruding from the top of its head were stony horns, ringed and curving out and then in to point upwards. It observed the newcomers without fuss, remaining in its chair.

That must be someone's well behaved pet. Zelda thought.

A rather strange pet indeed.

She wondered then who it might be she would meet, who would keep such a pet. Then, most unexpectedly, with the voice of a curious old woman ever so slightly sounding similar to the voice of a cat, it began to speak.

"Well now, who is this you have brought before me I do wonder?"

Zelda could not help herself but speak.

"You're a cat?"

"Who is this *insolence* before me I do wonder?" The cat beast said, seemingly correcting itself.

Gunter took a step between the two.

"I hastily apologise for any wrong that she may have caused for it is not my intent to bring one to you who would cause you trouble."

He turned to Zelda, ushered her aside and whispered in her ear.

"There are those who would not be taken kindly at such words for they are much more than what they seem and are very old and tired. Do not take lightly their presence for although they are on our side, how long for they could care for this world remains to be seen."

The cat beast chuckled.

"No trouble is taken. I'd much rather it remain on your shoulders than mine."

The cat beast turned its entire head to look at Zelda with those large green eyes.

"I am not a cat and the entirety of what I am has passed so far through the years that even I can't say. I am Kag, and you may call me such. Some even call me older than the world itself, yet I must say they are suitably far off the mark as far as that is concerned. There are those who would laugh at the notion, myself among them sometimes. I admit I am rather catlike though." And she paused to lick her paw, to which Zelda could not help but giggle.

Kag returned her attention to Gunter.

"You have brought with you quite the companions. Odd to see you walk openly in these times, in Alegan of all places. The world is caught in its last pale light where people are suspicious and withdrawn, clutching at former glory while they turn on each other."

The druid nodded.

"Most regrettably we act as beggars and wanderers moreso than teachers now. None have reason to suspect or care what we do and indeed there are those who do not care that the world is thinning and is worn out, has forgotten the ways of the honest and is now only the grounds for which human greed and suffering sit. The core of what we are is in danger but hope remains if we are to succeed in bringing about a future green and full of life."

"I don't understand." Zelda said.

After a moment, Gunter spoke to her.

"We are after a world where the greater understandings of it are shared by all who live. We could still leave you here but you have shown to be able to grasp that understanding, so leaving you here is not going to happen. You're a valuable person beyond what anyone who tried to kill you could have thought, unless there was some other inkling or other inclination that you missed. As we all dim, you came out brightly, cloaked in the sun. But the cloud moves across us all and you are no exception."

"I think I am piecing this together. Do we have a plan to save the world that now includes me?"

"We do have a plan and have had one before your arrival. There is only so much even we can do for the moment, but I am determined not to keep it that way much longer, as such we seek the wise spirit that once resided in the forest of Atwixie, to return it to the place from which it fled. It is the source of our power and the longer it remains lost, the more our power to uphold the natural cycle of this world falters. We will ask it to give us the power to return the world to what it once was, moving it clear of the dark future that awaits it."

Zelda's eyes went wide.

"We're searching for one person in the whole world? Have there been others searching?"

"Many of us travelling far and wide have sought them, who could be in any shape they so choose, and some of those searchers have agreed to return and will share what they know, which is where we head to hopefully narrow down the search. A gathering of druids at the solstice."

Kag stretched out to lounge on the chair.

"There is not much I can provide for way of advice, only that you should avoid the valleys altogether and keep going along the north west as you should be. I have been keeping my eyes downcast south and must remain doing so. As for the forest when you get there you have been there before so you know what to do and who to be cautious of. I would offer this suggestion, however, to pick your place to approach the forest from carefully."

"The closer to the Great Tree the better."

"Of course."

Kag held up a paw, turning to peer into Zelda's eyes.

"The world is in trouble, girl. I do not know how much you still don't know, yet there is no doubt in my mind. I would implore you to travel with these men further into the forests of the west, on the edge of the north kingdom of Kasynne and see their task be done."

Zelda nodded.

"You speak of fearful things just as they do. Of darkness spreading across the land on the back of evil intentions and I think that no one should want this. So of course I'll go, being much more at peace knowing that I helped rather than reminding myself that I did nothing when I could have."

"Yes, that is why the hurry, to meet those who might avert the world from catastrophe before it is too late. Such people might already be among you, but who am I to say? Perhaps the spirit doubted itself hence why it fled and finding anything with such power that wants to hide is a monumental task. If it shall be that it will not turn this world away from its doom you must be ready to hold up that power with all your strength and yourself place it where it belongs."

Zelda held her head against a dull pain that had begun to grow within it.

"I need to think about what I've been told."

Gunter hummed.

"If you are concerned that you might not be there to save everyone, do not worry. If you try desperately to do so then you will live a life with tremors and shivers and you will sleep lightly until you die of exhaustion. Let some things be. Perhaps when we get to the spirit we can all get what we ask from it. Now go for a walk for a while and sort out your head. I might even meet you out there, so don't wait for me."

Zelda left the two to their peace. But she was left wondering what it was she might ask such a being as a spirit, conflicted over what might be the best thing for her to ask if it ever came to that. She wondered too why a spirit might even look down at them at all and decide that their wishes were worth listening to, after all the realm of nature did not seem to her to be the type of place to give favours.

***

When both were quite sure that she had left, Gunter and Kag resumed their conversation, the creature pawing at her ears.

"I envy her indecision. You don't get to make decisions like that if you have lived as long as I do. You can only influence so much, so have to make choices as to where you put your energy. Otherwise you might find yourself spread too thin and have all your ideas in a shallow sea. I come from an age far gone in the past, and in a way, there I remain. The world was a better place then and these days have been seeing it grow dark and things stir in it not seen before. For what you are trying to do I am thankful but this world has seen its best days come and go."

She stared at him with her endlessly deep green eyes.

"Where have you been these last few years Gunter? I hope you have not been spending it attempting to make people have favours of you as you would have been wasting your time."

It was with some reluctance that he admitted the truth.

"No, the only people to really have taken to me are here along on this journey, and some in the forest see eye to eye but is it the same for all of us."

The door opened and Survel walked in silently.

Gunter sighed, rubbing his temples before continuing.

"Besides, there has been quite the backlash, what with people being drawn up and taken away because of what they can do. Not even we are immune to scrutiny, as I myself know. We can't possibly stand in a crowded space and ask for aid. I don't want everyone to stop fighting if that means they're all fighting us instead."

Survel's voice joined the conversation.

"We will teach them the true way the world has to be once we regain the power to do so. Let everyone fight among themselves, there will be plenty of that afterwards anyway, where they will be forced to listen to us."
Kag looked around thoughtfully.

"When the eyes of the stalwart are fixed on each other it allows for such strangeness as the certain, sharp darkness that has come into this world to do so that none could fault for arriving. It is a curiosity that wraps a path through the sky uninvited and is ephemeral as the breeze. As I do not know what to make of it I am taking precautions, so this town is one such place secluded from it that I know and shall remain so for as long as I am here. What might you say to the possibility that the day may come where it would be ordinary to find one's peace in such things and let the world pass on by?"

"You always did see things differently." Gunter said.

"Oh I was nothing special once. We're not like you humans, the way the world spins up on high is different for us. You may have your own understanding, but for us it's more than the dirt and the trees and the sky above, more than the sun or the breeze that carries it, I'll have you remember. The world you want is the one that came before, but you don't know if it will allow you to turn it back. Those of us who lived through that old world can tell you that it is not all what you believe it to be. Furthermore, whenever there has been a wish for a new world it has been stopped by those who opposed the change. Do not mistake what you want for the will of the world. Some people like this place and will defend it appropriately, even if that means letting it die."

"The world is already dead to me. With the spirit returned to its rightful place in the heart of the Great Tree, it will be remade as I wish it to be."

"If others come for you I can not help. It is as I said and more, it is not the right path to will the world a certain way. I can remember a time where this was such and look where we are now. Heroes might save the world but at the end of their journey can't force the world to change along with them. No matter how you think of yourself your deeds will not have you be seen as a saviour."

"I don't care how people see me. If any are left they can call me a monster for all I care. If I'm the closest thing to a monster they'll have then my victory shall be absolute."

Kag's ears twitched. Once, someone had fled into the valley below, to be hidden while everyone else politely turned their heads from the subject of a missing person. A quiet curiosity for whatever was growing in the dark had in turn become a desperation of not wanting to be left behind, which was why Kag knew where it was they now lay, she had made sure of it. That person had not been ready to die, even though their death could have been many years away they had been scared of missing their chance to keep living. They had not cared what they would be called either.

Mistakes are being made and lessons are being forgotten. She thought.

"I gather the others don't know about the roles they will play in bringing about this new cycle of the world you wish for?"

"They need not know. For they don't understand, can't possibly understand the loss to begin with some of us have been through. This world will be remade and no one will have to live in a world ruled by others."

Survel nodded.

"A new world free of meddling is the only way to continue the cycle now. If those along with us survive then they will have fought for their own place in it. If they perish then the cycle is still being upheld as it should be. No one will interfere, I'll make sure of that."

***

Zelda had managed to find out that normal people did indeed live in this town. At the furthest end there was a slope that more safely slid down on the north side and wrapped around to the valley below on the west. Here it was she had found the people who went about their business as far as she could see at an unhurried pace. Some had horse drawn carts where they took wood from the trees at the edge of the valley below and carted it up where people waited to heave it into store houses.

From within those buildings were all the heady smells of freshly cut wood. She breathed in deeply and could feel the ripples in the wind, which was strange, because she had never felt that sensation before.

This place she decided, would be a start, a focus on what was to be saved. Zelda hoped that whatever would become of their goal, people would be able to continue living in places like this without any worry. Maybe they would even grow while keeping their charm. It certainly wasn't for her, but others seemed to like it, for here people were, working together.

People had worked together to get rid of me.

Zelda was most hopeful that everyone had done as they had only as a means to save each other. What Churl would have been without the church she did not know. If getting herself out of the city was all that was needed for everyone's life to be normal again then she would be happy until she knew when to return.

I was a threat to unity without knowing it, even when I thought I was a part of the place. Well it was a part of me, at least. I would very much like to return and let them all know what they are doing is making the world a worse place. Of course, some might attempt to kill me on sight again. Maybe it would be best if someone else goes, once we have the means to do so.

The others had thought it likely that someone had picked up her magic and affinity which was why she had been targeted. The spirit which would hand the world back to the druids would hopefully give her what she needed to be understood by such people.

It was some time later in the afternoon, when Zelda, Peter and Findal were eating what had been left of old, stale bread chunks and Findal was happily holding a hefty little bag that had the suspicious sound and shape of coins within it.

Zelda stared at him.

"Findal, what was all that you said earlier about the evils of gold?"

Peter yawned on the grass.

"Don't worry, I'm sure some of the shopkeepers thought they were given the best deals they had ever seen."

Findal scoffed.

"I am not swindling people! You just tell these country folk things and some are keen to buy what is being sold. It doesn't matter if the person across the street was selling it to begin with, if they won't talk to each other because of some petty disagreement I'll happily supply what they need with no worries for where it came from and all discounted of course. Learn this, there would have been no disagreement to begin with if there had been no gold. Even so, my words as a druid will not get through to everyone yet, so I should think a few coins here or there that might get us out of a tight spot should do us some good."

Eventually Gunter and Survel came to locate them and Zelda felt as if they had all been caught stuffing their faces.

"Did you find out what you wanted to find by coming here?" She asked.

The straggly haired man took a piece of bread, eyeing it distastefully.

"Yes, but it was a very personal reason to come here at all, hopefully the rest of you found yourselves to not be bored from the waiting."

"Not at all." Peter said.

"We stocked up on food and there are many strange places around here that people will tell you about if you ask. Another time we should explore the area in greater detail."

Gunter shook his head.

"I do not know what manner of things could be disturbed and I would not wish to intrude on my friend's peace."

"So this also means they can not help us?"

"Not directly, but I needed some advice and now with that I know the way that must be taken better than before. We head as far north as we can as soon as we can. We can't rest here the night."

With everything they needed, they all made their way out of the town, where on the edge of a vast slope that rolled steeply down, they headed north west, the wild expanse of untamed land standing before them.

Zelda looked back for a moment at the town, wondering how her life would have been were she just herself as she had known so recently. In such a little place she would have hid and perhaps lived for who knew how long and she would have stayed while being blind, deaf, senseless to the world, however one might put it. If she did not see the sky and feel the fear and evil coursing through it, what would she have done?

She instead put the thought aside as here she was, with a purpose, walking away from that life with a glad feeling in her heart into a world where there were no walls to be trapped behind or set paths to follow, a world she just knew was somewhere she could look forward to calling home.

I leave behind me a world where I could have told tales, old ones belonging to Lara as well as my own. However instead of telling tales, I have quite found myself a part in one and even if all I do is watch, in the end I hope I'll get to say that I was there.

PART TWO

Reflections

Chapter Fifteen
A Boy Named Brodie

It was approaching the time of the year where the warmer days made way for colder weather, where the wind more often then not began to bite at pieces of uncovered skin. Only on some days was it so, a day here or there steadily being more noticeable that was eventually enough to remind people that the world was moving towards another winter.

Kieke was making her way as she usually did during these days, walking to market where she could get food she might be able to store and keep for a little while before it was all gone. The chill wasn't a problem as she had been used to it since she was young, when she had lived amongst the sea which made up her earliest memories. Now that was real cold which people here wouldn't know of, at least for those who had lived in Alegan all their lives and never ventured beyond it.

She knew the measure of those who lived and stayed within the walls of Churl but the pilgrims were those of the sort she could never be sure of, the only thing she could tell about them was that from whatever distance they had come they were happy to arrive. And arrive they did, some shockingly impoverished even by her standards but the church usually sorted them out, gave them food, shelter, a quiet place to rest. This all to turn them into good, little slathering wordsmiths if they had not been already, so the king could be happy that people were listening of course and that others who heard such good people might do the same.

Every once in a while people would stay, those passing moments of lukewarm air making the longer gusts of wind feel much more chilly, because those that stayed never again strayed far from the walls or talked about their homes. Those were likely long forgotten and their families quite so too, if they came alone.

Kieke had been to places uninteresting and lacking in charm, but among those places had also been those which were homes for somebody and despite her own stay in this land with her mission to complete there were often thoughts of home she couldn't satisfy simply by walking down to the river to look into the water.

The sounds were too different, the smell, the taste of the water, which made her long for her home on the isle off of Shryke even more, off in the far north Ruthlands. It was an aching that she often replaced with the dull throb of scorn she held for a single man hiding away behind all these walls in his castle.

That man didn't have to care about what was going on down here. Kieke was sure he didn't even hear their voices. So for the pilgrims leaving to return to their homes she was mildly conflicted, as while she was thankful they had homes they could return to, the king still span his fanciful story and they took the words right back home with them.

Most of the time. Surely where those pilgrims had come from meant more to them than to have that place discarded completely and never talked about again. It wasn't as if they had anything to hide. Unless she got in under their skin then her master might glean something from the marrow in their bones, but she had never felt the urgent need to do such a thing. After all it might make her feel more ill in the knowing just how far gone some people were.

Kieke had something to hide of course and had always been careful to do exactly what it took not to be discovered. She wondered whether or not an outside observer would see her just the same as those pilgrims who stayed and knew she wasn't sure that she would like the comparison. If people did see her the same, then it would help her as she stayed amongst those other people who had lived their lives here. Among the rest she wouldn't stand out and have anyone question where it was she had come from until she opened her mouth.

All she ever told anyone about her home was that it had not been a nice place, which was only what someone would say if they didn't like the salty sea air and the rough, tough greenery or sand beneath their feet. No one in Churl could relate to living in a land such as that so she lied, because to her it was a very nice place. If she said that she had liked where she had come from then someone who had been little more than a pale northern girl at the time would have been sent packing.

It was true that the years had endeared her to those who knew she helped out the kids but she felt no need to give up the illusion that she was happy or at least content most of the time. Besides, it wouldn't do for the kids to have her moping around everyday she looked up and saw the castle out from her door.

Days such as this she would sigh.

This could be the last winter from which the world will not escape and still the castle remains closed to me. I have done what I can to get as close as I can, now all I ask for is some reason for those gates to open and allow me through. Or I would much rather that the king left, where along some road he could be taken unawares.

It was quite likely that the king himself was unaware of her and what it was she truly wanted, but she hoped that messengers were at least telling him of people such as her who were doing good in his city. She could not help but wonder at the silly guard dog of the church and whether he would be paying attention to anyone else at all. The Minister was far too wrapped up in his own misguided importance to allow her to speak directly to the king, yet the more she thought on it the more she had come to realise that was precisely the point of such a man being there. Another layer added to the all important means of communication, where saying nothing at all could also be a way to tell someone what you thought of them.

The people didn't seem to mind not hearing the king's words directly, but Kieke wanted to hear his voice, to hear the words of this person who's life had sent her on a mission so far away for so long. All for her to come here to put an end to that life. What words would those of a man be with no one else to speak them for him? What would he say to her?

She had always envisioned during the earlier years to quickly get in and get out after the deed was done. Over time this had changed and she now wanted to stay and have a few words, to then revel a little in the feeling of success afterwards.

Kieke wondered if she should bother staying behind to watch and see if anyone would pick up the words he left after his death. It was true that there would be nothing left to worry about afterwards, but regardless it still amused her to think of the sight, all those people scurrying around without a king to tell them what to do. And the rest of the world would thank those people for finally taking some matters into their own hands when they finally did.

Nobody would thank her, of course. Not for her the grandstanding and the notoriety of tearing a kingdom to pieces, nor did she want her sisters to suffer the wrath of people unknown just because she stuck her head out to dare proclaim who had done so. It was best that she remained to history one of those nobodies herself, one of those who stayed quiet. That didn't mean she had to shut herself away from the world to complete her mission, quite the opposite.

Ahh, but what if she didn't have the time? Well that would be unfortunate, but the mission was never about what it was she wanted, because while the king lived nobody would get what they wanted and the world would be led down a very dark path indeed. Somebody had to save the people of Alegan, along with the entire world. The prospect of leaving alone the ones to fend for themselves who had led the world on to its doom must have been tempting for those in other parts of the world who remained in their homes. Not wanting to get too close to have that burden thrust on them as such burdens so often were when no others came to answer the call.

It wasn't their fault, not yet. As it was they would ultimately have little to no say in the matter. This could be changed of course, depending who you were, as kids certainly could be useful. And nobody saw them hiding away in the corners because after all, they were just kids. None of the ones she kept around her had reported finding a way into the castle, though Kieke didn't mind doing what she did for them regardless.

While walking up the street, Kieke had been minding her own business when a loud noise of yelling and shouting came from further above, putting her on alert. This was not as out of sorts lately as it once would have been, even so, her mind twitched and she waited for a response as one by one the orphans counted off in her head, each little instances of curiosity from one through eight. From what she could feel it told her that none of them were nearby, as absolutely should have been the case with no exceptions. Not that it would have been the first time she caught one of them where they shouldn't have been, but for the moment all of them were safe from whatever the commotion was.

Don't come to the marketplace, was the message she told them, then let them be so they could go about their day as they should and so she could concentrate on carefully walking up ahead, where boots and voices were gathering in sound, coming directly towards her.

Kieke had intended to stand her ground until she walked a little further on and saw what was happening. There were men in silver armour grabbing anyone they could see, while others with swords brandished them and those people in their grasps were all being dragged against walls, bailed up left and right with their backs against the road, necks at the ready.

This including one man who she knew had seen her approach. In the mere instant she had to hide herself, Kieke jumped behind some boxes stacked next to the store on her right. Whoever owned the place might accuse her of hiding amongst those things in order to take items for themselves but there was no time to consider the consequences on this course of action.

Thankfully what followed were no sounds of horror that had in previous places accompanied the rounding up of people against walls. She hadn't considered this as one of those so lawless places and still it remained to be so. Were it not the case then a body separated from its head or three would have given her plenty to work with if the needs had needed to be.

I really hope that man doesn't say anything about me. There is an awful lot of yelling going on over there however and I really do need to consider the possibility that he'll let something out to get out of trouble.

It was at that moment she realised she wasn't alone behind the boxes. The person had remained so still and the clothes he wore were so crumpled and grubby that she had mistaken the young man for a pile of rags.

Not quite a man, yet he was not a mere boy at his age either with short, grubby black hair, even if she could not help but see him as such.

He eyed the marching group of men with suspicion, seemingly uncaring about the other person who had just jumped next to him, preferring to keep his eyes on the road and shoulder to the wall where he squatted.

Kieke peered through a gap between the boxes, which was as much as she dared to do, unless any more meant that she would be spotted and hauled off. It did not appear that she would be found but she much preferred to watch unfolding happenings from the outside rather than being in the middle of the violence.

And what if people actually sympathised with her in her helplessness were she to be caught? That would make her sick. Her stomach churned merely thinking about it.

She turned to the lad and whispered.

"I hope you don't mind that I hide here with you."

He didn't turn to her to speak, staying still and barely moving his mouth to reply.

"Only if you don't get me caught, I don't like the look of these ones."

There was a grim steel behind his words and along with that strange emphasis behind them was a guarded look behind his brown eyes.

Now what is it you have done? Kieke thought.

You're not like me. I suppose you could just be afraid, then what would you be afraid of? No reason to stay here at all if you are.

The young man continued in a low voice.

"I've seen them, they came down straight out of the castle and came around asking questions of people in the inner city, inspecting all sorts of places. The last time I came out of the inner wall into the townhouses they were out too, questioning people."

The castle! Anyone coming out of that gate from the castle itself, out from within that guarding wall, had to be sent by the king. What was he up to? Whenever anything new happened it rarely had no consequence, so Kieke did her best not to seem too interested too quickly.

"Asking questions? They certainly don't seem to be doing that here."

"They had been cordial enough at the time but this is different, even if they're chasing pyromancers out of the city. Dealing with this quickly, that's for the best I know but what of us just going about our lives? This isn't how people should live, not even nobodies like me."

The group of men were walking down the street and Kieke joined the lad against the wall, not wanting to be spotted through the cracks by chance. She kept her voice quiet even as those sounds passed down below, people being shook up for reasons unclear.

"Tell me then, what is it you do with your life? What's your name? I'm Kieke, I run the orphanage down past the lower gate. A lot of the kids think like you do, especially the abandoned ones, it's not good on the mind. "

The lad lurched, taken aback but answered politely enough.

"My name is Brodie if I suppose you want to know. I guess what you do makes you someone to somebody. I must be honest with you, having been living in the inner city, only coming down here when I want to stretch my legs, I haven't found much reason to leave beyond going outside of north or north east gate. So I'm sorry if I should know a little more about you if you're known around the west side."

To Kieke it didn't matter if he knew nothing at all, she was used to speaking to those whom she suspected of not knowing what it was she did at all. In one way she was thankful for their lack of care, eager to let her be the same as so many nobodies in the light of the king.

The footsteps had faded further into the distance and when she was quite sure they were gone stuck her head up. Back onto the street it had now resumed its quiet usualness, even so soon after the sounds of footsteps that only a few moments ago had carried men with weapons drawn through.

People were laying on the ground, appearing rather shaken, being helped up by those around them.

"What was all that about?" Kieke asked to one of the people on the ground who was testing her ankle.

"Nothing to do with me." She said.

Brodie nodded.

"A while ago there certainly was a strange instance of violence in the outer wall, chased someone out of town is what I heard. The people who left can't have been up to any good, that's for sure. I'm sure that's what all this is about in a similar way. They're searching for heretics, that's my guess. They made a big deal of this because they let one slip through their fingers before and we haven't heard of that happen for some time."

For a moment the words tugged as a tightness in Kieke's chest before receding.

Well we can't do anything about those people up to no good now. I have been wondering about that myself. Hopefully this'll be the end of it then. Don't think they were after me but it's always best to not be sorry for making the right decisions. A little more clarity on the matter would be most appreciated.

She turned to Brodie.

"Do you mind showing me where it was those people went last time you were here? That way you can go see a little more of the outer city as well."

He could not find a reason to disagree, wanting himself to take a further look around and spy out the places the men went.

If I get this woman to be my eyes down here I won't have to worry about the risk of being spotted by extending myself so much. Most of that lot won't know my face but I can't ignore the possibility that someone from inside will be taking a stroll and recognise me.

He nodded.

"Of course, we can go right now."

This was a fair walk but the pair made their way up to the northern inner wall and the gate that sat at that part of the ring. The giant gate was currently closed but it could be seen through, the metal bars had gaps where one could see into the inner city beyond.

On their side of the gate, wood buildings of a single story were pressed up against the walls and along the path to create a circle with three exits which were the closed gate, the way they had come, and the downward sloping path to the left where they could see much of the western part of the lands before them. Due to the north of the town being higher up the hill than the south, they could follow the wall along the decline all the way out to the west and southern plains in the distance.

There were some people out and about making the most out of their days, but the location at which the two found themselves was one that sounded quieter than Kieke was used to. A place such as this could have been full of people, instead of the slow paced morning that made up this part of town. Brodie showed her to the buildings and took a look around himself, soaking in the view.

"Anyway, here's where they were. I had just come out of the gate we can't now get through and there were a bunch of men going through these places, roughly searching. Didn't even look like they knew what for. Shouldn't they know what they're looking for?"

"No, that's what the church is here for. You saw what men with swords do, I suppose sometimes they talk but other times the hand that holds one gladly thinks of little else than using it. Even if all they did here is ask questions, a sword is one way to encourage answers. The king knows what he's doing, sending all sorts of people to do his bidding. They just have to make sure to clean up the mess they make afterwards. I'd much rather there wasn't anything of the sort for them to do. The church should focus on looking after its people, not minding those who should not need to be looked after because the king says to those who can not be trusted among us to go out and do his bidding. I would hate to think that the king would approve of such behaviour as we have seen."

"You have dealings with the church?"

"Absolutely. They're my lifeline to keeping the kids in shape and I can only hope that my deeds are being noticed."

Brodie just nodded.

There's a low chance of that happening. He thought.

He decided on keeping the thought to himself. Brodie knew a fair bit more than he was willing to tell this woman and he hoped that she had other motivations than having the king take notice of her. The king was shut far in his castle and Brodie had not seen him other than at a passing distance for quite some time.

He showed her to one of the shops that had been looked through earlier by the men. However, on asking around inside, there was little that they could get from the owner of the store, a straightforward talking man called Neemus.

"Sorry Kieke but I've got nothing to say about them. They come in here saying they're doing the right thing and that's just what I'll believe. A shock to us all certainly, but it's nothing we can't handle."

Brodie found himself surprised.

"Oh so you know her?"

Neemus shot a squint eyed frown at him.

"Well I don't know you, lad. So shove your questioning of me off that doesn't belong as part of the discussion."

He turned back to Kieke and snorted.

"Kids. I've lived here a long time, before any of these walls. People are more often coming than going and they don't always come up here but you know, I don't think we should mind the new folk. In a few more years we could find ourselves even more better off. The lands beyond Alegan need to recognise us and once they see what we have here, all will be better."

"Well for me it's becoming more and more of a one woman effort, granted we don't have the numbers of unfortunate ones that we used to any more but I thought that all was fine with policing each other when it came to knowing who our neighbours were. Guess I'm just wondering why the church's funds are going into armour and weapons, that's all. They keep telling me that there's only so much they can do to help me but I don't see the people staying to be struggling, even if most would rather camp out in tents then be on their way."

The shop owner scratched his jaw.

"All they did was go around asking questions and no matter however roughly, I had nothing to hide so they took a look around and were on their way. I understand the unease but there's other things to worry about, you know what I'm talking about."

"Having to teach the kids to hide in their own home is not something I thought I'd ever have to do here, is all. You can't trust some people when you give them authority."

"Talking from that past you don't want to tell us? Well if you've any understanding of what's going on here from another painful perspective that should help you put it all to rest for you."

Footsteps came from outside followed by a worried woman sticking her head through the door.

"I just thought you should know Neemus, there's a mob out again and they're coming up asking around for all sorts of things, maybe stay in for a bit."

"It's just the church, Maria and thank the Light that's all."

"But there's word going around they shook up some folks. That doesn't sound like the church at all and they're coming this way now."

Kieke's head lifted up.

"Oh? Well that's interesting. I think I'll look them in the face this time since I know I'm not going to lose my head. If you don't mind me, Neemus. Have a good day."

With that she stepped outside with a sheepish Brodie lingering at the door, to which she peered back at him.

"You comin' or what?" She asked.

Something was certainly up with this one, but she didn't have the time to bother getting to the bottom of it all just yet, even when he seemed to squirm around his reply.

"I suppose I could just stay around here without sticking my own neck out."

Kieke chuckled at that.

"I didn't say that as if I expected you to do anything. It's alright, have some faith, you."

She didn't have time to prod him further as advancing up from the road came the same ones whom both had avoided earlier. Their blades, while still drawn menacingly thankfully were not bloody and they certainly were not as rowdy as before, holding themselves with a little more restraint.

They had a man of the church now alongside them, perhaps curbing their ways to being a little nicer and more polite. Not that a single man robed in white could have done anything against a group of armed thugs, still it was nice to see how they were behaving more like she had expected guards to, even if Kieke would have rather had it be that none of them were around at all.

Now here it was she did stand her ground, waiting for the group to make its way up to her where they could notice her and hear her speak.

"The church just doing some searching aye? So if there had been nothing to worry about, what was the deal with the men among you who went about their ways in a manner not seen here yet? Disgraceful."

The man who had chased another down the street stuck out a finger to point at her.

"Now you listen here, you don't get to say we lessen the grace of the Light. Such words might be taken seriously."

Kieke shrugged.

"I only thought you'd be looking for someone in a manner all would be more accustomed to. Unless there is a change in the words of the church which then by all means proceed, as I nor anyone else shall stop you."

The robed man turned to the armoured men.

"The king is disappointed in you, hence why we are here, to disperse any ill will that might be floating around on behalf of the Minister. You and some with you have only recently come of Churl to prove your faith and I shall see our ways upheld."

Even the dog has a dog. Kieke thought bitterly, not wanting to have this man be another obstacle in her plans.

She must have been staring oddly for the man spoke in a slow, carefully worded manner.

"Is there something you were after to ask of me or the church?"

"An answer of all this would be nice." She gestured around.

"Tell me, robed one, you ain't looking for-"

Kieke stopped. She had been about to say 'a lad' yet found herself thinking better of it. What did it matter to her if they were looking for Brodie? If he was a problem he wasn't a dangerous problem, she could feel that there wasn't a magic bone in his body and if anyone else was going to rat on him then they would be sure to do so without her being able to do a thing about it.

The man tilted his head, waiting.

"Yes?"

She lowered her voice.

"You ain't really looking for fire magic are you? The rumour's gotten us all worried. Surely those who come here on the pilgrimage do so with holy intentions, but can it really be that there are those among us who would do us harm?"

"Careful Kieke, your Ruthlander ways are showing. This is the final stop on one's road to salvation, we shall do our part in guiding this world's people to a light that is true. I can not help who finds their path lead to Churl, for all paths should lead here but those of such terrible, burning evil we shall remove before they ruin the sight and minds of us all. The world beyond us does not fully share in our caution. Much of Auralin is a foul cesspit, the home of elves and wretches and as such our light shall guide the way for the worthy to see."

Kieke stowed her tongue against man's words.

Worthy? Only by having people stewing in this place while the king adds poison to the pot. Then the whole sorry mess is going to be tipped over the rest of the world or worse, force fed to the innocents who truly need the help such a place might bring were it not so foul as it supposed the rest of the world to be. Why can't they see that they're a stupid, ignorant vessel for hate? I suppose they believe I am supposed to feel glad that I have been made worthy from whatever barren place in the north I crawled in from.

So it was that she knew dipping her hands into the pot might be a disgusting task, that she might only be able to not speak her mind for so long before going insane but she had to do it. She had faith but it was not attached to such a place or man as was here and removing the man would leave some to be reaching for anything at all to believe, because they would be open to believe anything and that included the real truth.

I might steel this place yet, for it to become a place such like a shield against vile manipulation that it has seen. People should find their own strength, or at the least get a master that listens and speaks.

She was going to keep up the outward lie to the contrary, of course.

"Certainly I agree with you, Churl only shines light on the good places and people of the world, while piercing through the hearts and guises of the wicked."

The man beamed.

"And so it does! Now, you lot." He pointed to the followers behind him.

"You hear from her and others the same what you hear from me, it shows the good folk of Churl are many and more, that they believe. Go take the ones we have been told are not as they really are."

The men made their way into one of the shops where a commotion soon broke out inside. While they did so, Brodie inched outside and made his way over to Kieke's ear.

"So do you actually know your way around?"

"I live not too near these parts and I'm not sure what to make of what I'm seeing to be honest. It doesn't look good, nor does it bode well. This is new, this is different. Nobody should be staying on their own."

"So do you have a mysterious past?"

"Not really. Are you alone in this city?"

His eyes went wide.

"Oh no no no I'm not like that at all. Came from Hustag, in the east descending past the Haralands and stuck here now. No reason to return either, whatever it had was funnelled out years ago, years before I was born."

She understood that he was likely bored out of his mind and just wanted to explore. With what she had just suggested maybe he would prefer someone to walk around with.

Well that would be right, coming from out there I'm surprised he doesn't have another person already glued to his hip. That caution shouldn't have to be required here through. I suppose he's gotten used to wandering around on his own.

Intrigued as she was in this shabby looking somebody, he quite wasn't her type. She could consider doing some exploring herself in his mind later as this strapping young lad would be adequate as another set of eyes and ears. It would be for the best, so that she wouldn't have to worry about one more person and he wouldn't have to worry at all.

They watched the men pull everyone outside. There were three people, none she knew by name, who looked worse for wear with injuries about their arms and heads. The gate behind them opened and Brodie looked out with a frown.

"What makes a heretic these days I don't know. Maybe if more people freeze to death in the winter there will be less people to turn to such things, if indeed that is what they're doing."

Kieke did her best to shut out the cries of the people being taken away, their arms bound by ropes and chains as they were taken through the gate up into the inner city.

"You said before that these men are coming from the castle. I've always been fascinated with the place, though I've never been able to get in past the grounds since the king shut the gates. I wonder what's going on in there?"

"Oh believe me I've had the same thoughts myself. Haven't been able to find the answers though."

"If you've got nothing else to do in your spare time, how about we do a little information gathering? I'm not buying that everyone is fine with this either, but maybe that's just me speaking with all the kids looking for an excuse. Not too long ago people thought they were dirty you know? Don't want to go back to those days."

Brodie's appeared to be saddened on hearing such things.

"Really? That's awful. In that case I could help you out with them if you need it."

"That would be most kind of you. I have to warn you though, some are becoming right little devils."

"Considering the circumstances should you be saying that?"

They watched as the three people were dragged further into the city yelling and crying loudly in the distance, the gate slamming down behind them that prevented anyone from following.

"No." She said sadly.

"I should not."

Chapter Sixteen
The Prince of Alegan

It was a sunny day and the young man who was not in fact called Brodie, was following the light beam from the sun as it made its way across his room. The room was deep so that while he could have walked up to the window, much of the timber walling of the room around it was in a dull shadow that hurt his eyes. Every once in a while he would have to get up and move so he could be sitting in the sunlight so that he could read. It was best he made the most of the sun before it was gone for many long, cold months ahead.

When that happened, Rin would only have a few lamps for company. For the moment he had no one and the prince had been alone for quite some time. For the first few years after coming to Churl he had been allowed to roam the entirety of the castle interior but never take a peak outside, then he had started getting older and asking questions, to which he was locked out good and proper, which he could not entirely fault his minders for doing, looking back on it.

His old home within the city of Autumn had been well fortified and as such had not given him such a view of his surrounds or that of the river that flowed through it. The castle in Churl was far higher up than he had been back in Autumn and if he stacked up some books that lay about his room to form an impromptu staircase that took him several meters off the ground, he could look out from his window over to the rings of the city while admiring the lands beyond the castle walls in the morning light.

There was a nice view of the river that he could get from balancing at this height, a silver snake laying across the land off into the distance, where closer it cut into the outer ring of the city. Maybe the snake was only passing underneath, not caught, trapped in the claws of something awful.

As he attempted to further his line of sight beyond where the glass would allow, one of his feet kicked a book from the pile and so dislodged the lot and he fell awkwardly down on a cascade of books, some with rather pointy edges, which he then had to take the time to put away. From inside his room with his feet on the floor he could not see much of anything, because that way his father knew he was safe and all the tall walls looking out had people sitting on them, all keeping watch, which was all that mattered.

He smiled because he knew that they were likely as bored as he was, even if they had a view that didn't require them to balance constantly.

Despite being kept out from the deeper insides of the castle, he had been allowed to walk outside ever since arriving to stop himself from becoming pallid and restless, albeit in an enclosed yard. However it was up to chance whether or not the door to his room was unlocked at all on some days or he wouldn't be able to leave, as happened for days, on occasion weeks.

Today the door was unlocked, opening with a click, which allowed him to leave the room. The floors were all covered in red carpet with a long purple rug underneath. Down the right there was a corridor where he could waste time trying to open all the doors again, but the left was where he wanted to go, so after shutting the door behind him he made his way along the other side of the corridor, which opened out into a wide landing at the bottom of a slowly sweeping staircase. It was much brighter down here, with giant windows allowing light to flood the room.

There were no people where he was and paintings and statues left no empty spaces along the glass doors that could have been thrown open. From the inside this looked like a way out, instead this false exit only went down so far as a level or two before opening into a giant deck where all manner of the public had once been allowed to come and sit. Now nobody got to see that view as far as he knew.

He took another left which led to the small space allowed for him outside. There was much more space inside where he could walk around but after a while the carpet smell began to invade his senses so he much preferred the outside, where he could get an uninterrupted view of the sky. Even when standing outside so high up, the clouds in the sky were as far and unreachable as they ever were, while down below where he stood there was even grass growing, with trees which he could climb, some with strong enough branches for what he would use them for.

White paving stones cut through the grass and he made his way over to the small gate that could not be opened from the inside, only from the outside with a key, a key he had eventually obtained. He could not stick his hand through the gate and open it, so if he wanted to leave then he would have to climb a tree then jump to the wall if he wanted to. It had taken him quite a while for the first attempt, to build up the courage so that he wouldn't overshoot the wall and potentially plunge below, but his fears had been unfounded, as only a short drop below its base was another grassy square of ground, much like the one above it but without the walls. This gave the level down a much better view, not as high as the one he could get from his room, but one which was much more expansive, where he could see all around, apart from behind him where the castle rose up.

There was a metal bench against the wall he had just dropped down. Here, people would have been able to sit and take in the scenery and maybe be thankful that they lived in such a kingdom that allowed them to see such sights. Now the king had taken that from them, although Rin did wonder how many people cared. Such views were not what many living here wanted to see.

The king stopping by must have been such a novel event for them compared to living in the glory of a place that had once made the blind see. But the king had stayed and Rin often wondered if there were those down below who had not adjusted to his father taking over. Well it had all been his anyway and merely his presence reminded them who was really in charge of the kingdom.

If Rin looked out over the edge he knew that this was very close to the front courtyard if one disregarded the tremendous vertical distance one would have to travel and he never quite felt like wanting to risk that fall, much rather preferring to remain alive. He would eventually follow the ramps down and make his way there and sneak out, easy enough to convince the guards at a distance that he was a servant running an errand. None of those servants would be able to stop and take the time as he did to sit down and stretch out on this bench.

Someone has to cut the grass here. I suppose I have been rather fortunate to rarely run into anyone else.

There had been a few close calls but directly catching someone in the act of doing what they should not or being where they should not was all another thing entirely compared to being suspicious. If they caught him then suspicion would be what he would use against them. If you had a suspicion then you didn't know everything. And he was the prince. They should be more suspicious of the men bickering and scheming behind closed doors than himself. He might as well be among those who had no idea, for what little he saw of the bickering and the scheming those doing so certainly weren't supposed to see much of him.

His father had been adamant to keep the family all hidden away for as long as he could remember and had never received an answer as to why, but over the most recent years had found that the guard put on him had lapsed. His father either didn't care, or more likely expected him to be quiet and compliant by now so was ignoring him entirely. Unless it was the church who did not care. The Minister was often speaking in ways he did not think his father would, yet that had been the reason for coming here, one voice, one ruler for the whole of Alegan. Who's voice was he really hearing when words of the king were spoken?

It was hard for Rin to know exactly what passed for his father's words these days. Masked men roamed the streets looking for heretics when they should be out looking after the people or roaming the land, keeping it safe that way. But what had happened surely wasn't what his father had wanted in coming here, instead of a new life and security over his people, things had just made a turn for the worse.

People are talking in reverence about the church, not my father and throughout his realm are all being effected. What's he been so afraid of? All it is doing is holding him back.

He had scarcely seen his father, the king in all but the longest of times.

My father is forgetting his people. Well, that's nothing new for me to experience as myself, but why did I feel it so much, like an outsider before? I had dreams once, of what to make of myself here and of being someone special. If my father hoped for some of his own fears to run off to his subjects then he has succeeded. But you didn't need the church, just because you knew some would listen to them and not to you didn't give you the excuse to sell yourself out. When will this place be abandoned for your next dream, father? We're already leaving behind mother. What would she have told you to do?

She had been sick, unwell for some time. Her life had been drawing to a close even when they had arrived.

"The world had been done with her", the Minister had said once, trying to explain to a grief stricken young boy why his mother had to die.

He spent some time on the bench wondering when the world would be done with everyone else. Perhaps life would pass them all by and no one would have to worry about a thing. Certainly he had not made the most of his life to make the memories he wanted, those chances had come and gone, then there were instances such as this, where he just sat and watched the sky with no worry at all. This could become a memory, but there was nothing to say that it would, as many times had he sat here. Time was precious and that at least to him was where the hateful feelings came from when he was trapped indoors. The thought that he was wasting his life away.

Plenty of people he had come into contact with had been rich and noble, they had appeared to be people with a sadness or lack of grand purpose that their luck should have afforded them. Looking out at the sky he had to wonder how much it mattered that those people were not someone special either.

No matter who you were, the sky was there for everyone and many people came and went about their lives without experiencing anything spectacular. Yet they could still stop and look up and it didn't matter, unless you were blind of course. That was supposed to be what made this place special.

Everyone needed to be able to believe in the life they were living and the king was supposed to support that for everyone. Now Rin was getting an ill feeling that it wasn't about the people, only the ideal of what a kingdom had to be. Obviously there were those dangerous ones who had to be removed from the kingdom. Even if there were some of them here and there, people could be themselves while those who ruled could look down from overhead and make sure all was right and just.

Yet he could not convince himself of that and he decided that he could go further into town once again, because today was too nice to stay indoors. There might be days where he would suspect it not be the best time to stray away from the castle but this was his choice. It would all be his one day anyway, so he might as well wander around and get to know his people.

I can say one thing up here but down there experiencing it is another thing entirely. I could say that I am surprised, but I was foolish to think that there would be no divide between us and them. I'm sure there are those who long for the day of an active, facing king, so shall I be when I get there and whatever secret that has been hidden from me throughout my life will not stop me. I don't care if my life must be held in the trust of the people, with an axe at my neck, because if things are not right with the people then there is no kingdom to begin with.

***

He had found himself straying on the edge of the inner city. There would have once been nothing but the outside world before but now there was a ring to pass through and Rin did not wish to go much further beyond these first walls. In all honestly it didn't really matter where he went as in either the inner city or old outer town he got to play the part of another person. One where people didn't look at him twice and where those who did, did so to tell him off and even that was enjoyable because at least he was being noticed.

The citizens were often going about their days busy and that made him feel happy that they were able to do such things, as he had heard stories of far off lands where people were restricted in what it was they could do and where they could go.

There wasn't much point moving to other places now, as he very much knew.

Unless people had homes to return to there was no reason to set out to make a new home for yourself amongst some deserted place where there was no money or fortune to be had. You could not simply wish a place into being that would spring up with all the necessities of life around you as your life would end cold and hungry. You had to bring those things with you.

A king might demand that his subjects follow him to places unknown but a king he was not. He had no knights or servants that he might order to do as he wished, no power for him, no not yet. All he had were the people around him here as he walked through the inner city streets, who didn't even know who he was. He couldn't get them to do as he wished, however simply by being close to them he felt an attachment to those around him he would have otherwise lacked.

On seeing them being gathered up and taken away, it felt to him to be a threat, even though the notion was silly, because after all the men and the soldiers were all on his side. He wondered if he was jealous, because those people dragged back into the castle were probably seeing more of the insides than he was. The walk to the torture chambers and the dungeons went right through the middle after all. He hoped no one was actually being tortured and imprisoned and were given swift deaths instead.

Rin knew that he should be able to call upon his people and when the time came for such things would do so as much as he wished. He didn't think he would lead them on their way to some other lost place, away from Churl certainly but not to a place that was nowhere. Wherever he might end up deciding, it still had to be a place where people could recognise it as one suited for a king regardless of his whereabouts and would still be seen as the head of the kingdom were he absent off defending or ruling over his lands. Walls were nice for the purpose of defending a place that needed it, but he tried to remember the last time anyone had a proper castle constructed, which must have been such a long time ago that he could not think of it. Certainly long before he had come into the world.

The people working to bring all the stone to Churl had it turned into a wall with towers and not some other great or useful building with which they could be proud. His father wanted to bring the outer towns into the reach of all he controlled and to protect himself with an added layer of defence, but from who? Rin certainly could not see anyone marching down south to get here, certainly an army would be raised and sent to defend those places from anyone foolish enough to stand before them, so why the bother here he did not understand. If it was a precaution against those who might sneak in then those people were going to do that anyway, whether as a traveller or under the guise of a pilgrim and he had not seen anyone display such behaviour. Unless some of the people were more than what they seemed and such thoughts pained his head to have to think about, the possibility better suited for those who could then do something about it.

Rin knew there would be a day where he could, when he would be king and on that day all the secrecy and hidden agendas one might bring would be a thing of the past and that meant himself too. An open and noble king, that was what he aspired to be. There was no reason for him to lie to his people if there was a problem, he would help by telling them what to do so that they could move onwards. If he had to tell his people to build walls then that would be that, they would build walls and if he had to, then he would do so alongside them. If only to prove that the task was necessary, but not because he could. Others could lift buckets of water and place the pieces of stone. He couldn't possibly afford to look too much as if he existed among them. Who would take him seriously then?

He caught his reflection in a bucket of water alongside a street pump, peering in to see himself more clearly. Buckets were being put on a cart that would be sent around to provide water to those who needed it for uses such as cleaning or drinking.

I don't have any idea what that king will look like. I'm certainly not who I used to be and there's still a long way to go. I'd rather have my answers and not be thrust quickly into the role of king, whereby I might find myself manipulated by those hovering nuisances of my father's court who would be desperate for a scrap of power. They might be done away with entirely if none find themselves to my liking.

None of them had endeared themselves to a chubby little boy who had now grown up remembering the way they swarmed about his father, keeping him from getting close or most often speaking at all with the king. Over time that boy had turned from one who had never gone hungry his entire life, yet had known hunger quite strongly regardless of how much he ate, to the person he saw in front of him.

There had certainly been less to eat in Churl and that reason by itself could have been enough to make any child resent coming to a new place, full of days and nights of burning hunger where he dreamed that as king he would never have to feel that way again. Years later, with his skin stretching over his cheeks down the sides of his face he wondered whether or not he might have burst by now were he not to have stopped eating.

Now there was a different kind of hunger he found, one that his demands for books had only temporarily satisfied in his quest for knowledge to know more about the world. So he had taken to escaping out and roaming the streets. Now roaming the streets was not enough and he wanted to travel further and understand more about his land but how could he do that when concern tugged at his mind and brought it back home? So his mind turned to this problem where he would have to stay within the confines these walls as much as he dared.

If I were to vanish then what would become of the people here who would be mine? I would be returning to a place empty as all would have been upturned and destroyed in search for me. I can't have that happen, no matter how much I hate this place the people here must still be protected even if it is only one small, tiny part of a much wider kingdom that as a whole deserves far more recognition than it has on the back of one little speck of light, however bright. Were I to leave there might be none on my return, nor any who could be seen as being worthy subjects of a king. Yet those who should mind me do not come out in search of me, or I doubt I would have been able to leave my room.

He certainly could not have made the acrobatic feats required to have some freedom if he were overweight. With all the isolation, no one out here had to see him grow and change, so there had been little shame in seeing himself slowly change. Every once in a while it shocked him though, as a part of his mind was still that where he remembered having a rounder face and thicker arms. How people would be shocked to realise that the prince had been among them the whole time.

Rin had some time ago decided to take note of the ones who helped him or were otherwise kind. Those who were not, unless they were extremely vexing, he decided would be tolerated. Besides, he needed to prove he was a stable ruler, and it would not do for him to cull this place of the ones who had troubled him as his last act before leaving. The words of his deeds would follow in his wake and he didn't want to be known as one who ruled through fearsome means.

He picked up the bucket and carried it over to the water cart and a squat man came out with his hands on his hips.

"I had this sorted, thank you very much. I wouldn't want to be responsible for any spilled buckets. I could only fill them once and there's a price on every one. I doubt you have the coin to pay me back were any to spill, boy."

Brodie smiled.

"It is quite fine, I can help with that. That being said I could do other work. If you know of a tavern that needs supplies delivered or stables that need cleaning out I'll be more than willing to do what I can."

"You'll get a kick if you go down there unannounced and just start scraping up the place and I'm not talking about from the beasts. As for me I've got no use for you, I can't spare coin on you and I'd rather do my work myself and save the expense then waste time on you."

"Maybe I'll give it a miss then if it sounds like trouble. Speaking of which, what is your opinion on all this most recent trouble?"

"You're one for words without thinking, aren't you? Well you're going to have to be quite more specific, as there have been enough people running around for me to lose track. I must say it is most suspicious that there are people so suddenly not of a stable or honest mind. They could be enchanted by witches or other foul things to do worse deeds."

Rin scratched at the hair growing on his face, shedding dust.

"I've seen no sign of such evils in this hallowed place. Perhaps all have been caught and got what they deserved but I still don't like the fact that they're here and could be anyone. Doesn't that bother you?"

The man rolled his eyes.

"The church will sort out those who should be here and those who should not."

"And what of those of us in their sights?"

"What's to say any of us are? Have some faith, they'll need it."

The man gestured behind him and Rin quietly shrunk down next to the cart as the footsteps of armed men came closer. There was several of these men, including a man of the church who was desperate to remain among them as following him were a group of angry people. That man chose to direct his guards over to the water pump and Rin kept his head down as the group walked over and he found himself stuck between the pump and the cart, hoping he would be spared their attention.

If any of them got a closer look at his face it was possible one or two might recognise him if they were castle guards and that would be all it would take. If he ran, it was entirely possible that they would come after him and then he would be equally doomed. So there he stood like a dumbstruck person as the man of the church leaned on the water pump and looked around at the gathered crowd with a sombre expression on his face.

"I know you are all worried, but know there is nothing you need to worry about, if you see anyone coming forth to rid this place of undesirables know that they are from the church and are harmless if you yourself have performed no wrong. You will know them from now on as we shall be among them as we are always among you. As for the reason why, we must all be vigilant, as there are stirrings outside our lands that wish to destroy our proud kingdom and the sanctity that we hold. There has been a need to act swiftly in recent times to stop this place becoming so warm from a warmth not created by understanding or belief in each other but from fire. They fear our noble light, the light that you all share, seeking to overthrow it with their scorching hands. So they come here to our towns and cities and live amongst us unawares. We will not allow that to come to pass in our lands. While the rest of the world turns to fire, we will turn it aside and remain unharmed."

There were murmurs from the crowd and Rin thought of the woman he had met some days ago. In truth, as the prince he was not sure of what to make of this person he had run into, but as Brodie he thought she was nice enough to be around. It was good that he wasn't alone and she seemed happy enough, as he was to have someone else to talk to and some of those that were talking could also spill secrets.

Best I do this snooping quietly in the shadows with as few people as possible. After all, someone who runs a home for orphans can't be too unhinged. What does that make me though? A liar, that's what it makes me but I'm doing all of this to keep the future of my kingdom in one piece. The church isn't saying anything wrong here yet I can't help the wringing of worry within me.

He watched as the crowd moved, leaving him be, all looking past him to follow the group of the church's men.

His relief was only momentary, as he watched those men enter a home then leave with a man dragged out to the streets to be carried away while the crowd itself had scattered without any sadness in their eyes, not wanting to be near this persecuted person.

The water man shrugged.

"There you go. Just let the people who protect us do their jobs. It's our responsibility to let them get on with it."

Rin stood in silence, trying to be just another person on the street. A thought came to him which made the task easier, but no less harder to bear. Right now it didn't matter who he was, there was nothing he could do for them in a way that mattered. He turned away and forced himself to focus on the small tasks other people gave him well into the afternoon.

Chapter Seventeen
The Wizard Comes to Churl

The wizard had come from other lands. He had travelled across run down, ill maintained roads and dark forests and fields that were not just fields. He had braved many things, although he would not brave the fire. Why then, he asked himself, did this place he looked upon fill him with such dread? The new capital was Churl and within it was the church of Churl that had once resided in a whole land called the same thing a long time ago, many ages ago, which now was a piece of Alegan.

The name would have faded away were it not for that which gave it such attention and such attention had not been enough over the years where a castle had been built and a town built around it, so small had it been but people had come and remained. This was the second chance it had to be more than a name.

That castle stood low before him, fortified and looming under the same murky sky that had covered his journey from its beginning. In that beginning Bernard had been so sure of himself yet as he was now, right where the dark lay, he would be in need of people who would listen. His mood was as dim as the sky above, from which a light spattering of rain fell down below.

That was it, in truth. That he could not find anyone of the most positive persuasion to help him sent him into a profound sadness of mind. The world was growing dark and people were looking in dark places or places blazing with the power of ruin and death. Neither were what would save the world from the end. People were being taught in this place to see those beyond as flawed and to shun those far away, yet a lack of knowledge should not have made people fight.

To say that one person was superior because of what was written in a book was preposterous. Well, that was what people wanted to hear, they wanted to be important and look important and have the words of what had been said to remind them. Here was a book saying how they could be what they wanted to be. By shunning the people of other lands and leaving them out in the cold. Oh but how cold this very place before him was.

He had a role to play in stopping the end of the world. There was a problem, which was that his betters had done such a thing already, many years before. Then what it made his own journey in his mind was one that felt more like an afterthought of fate, a mockery of success, to say that the ones who had been saved were not worthy of being saved quite yet. Or at least not their children's children. He had to pose a question to stop the doubt from creeping up in his mind. Would they really have risked it all if they had known that the world would have been in peril again so soon?

He himself would have hated to go through all the effort only for the world to be needing saving again such a short while later, with him to die in ignorance happy that the world had been turned aside from a great peril. So had his teacher gone content to her grave and on her passing there had been a time of celebration for a well spent life that only a few years later turned to woe when he thought back on it.

We live, hoping that we do not waste our lives in doing so, so that our successes are meaningful and that others can make the most of what we have done.

So he thought quietly to himself, knowing that he could not fault the future for accusing him of much the same. So much had been lost to history it was possible that no one would know of this one day and there would be none to wonder at how the world had fallen down.

He was mostly alone in his other goings on and had once been happy to have spent his life alone in peace, but with the return of the darkness he would have liked someone to be around so that someone could remember. This was not why he had turned to search out others for his cause and that such others were not vital to his success he was most thankful for, as he had failed spectacularly in bringing people together, with not one person having heeded his call for help. Too many selfish or bent on their own whims.

I'm right at the gate, where all things could come to pass and yet I am alone, with not one person standing beside me. How many might have been too many I do not know. Even one person to lean on and believe along with me would have been a mighty reassurance yet I alone must toil at this task.

This was no open war, he had no plans to let this become open war, that sickening black shimmer that came and went told of the dark to fall on the world without the need for such battles. It would surge to cover Auralin in misery while feeding off the animosity that those here held for the ones outside their lands. Unless the pyromancers got to the world first and burned it all down.

Bernard wondered how much it was they knew and when they would deem it be that they had to act, too late for anyone else to stop them. Risks of death or not they would come into this land and even their own bones would crack and smoulder in the fire that would follow.

At the very least the church was on guard for such behaviour, for when minds went to dark places the dark would come. There was no negotiation for him though, neither this church nor fire would be a wise choice to continue existing in the long run. For now he would settle for removing the one manipulating the population here.

The church feared the fire for what it might bring while directing the world to hate it and those who used it for whatever reason. People went along with what was said knowing that in their belief, there would be a future for themselves without fire. He could trust them to do that at least and save him some time while he dealt with the church itself.

He had to stem the source of the darkness, where first there were those who would only increase its reach. Despite that emphasis on light, people were being left in the dark to be swallowed whole and they would be sacrifices for others more twisted who would take advantage of them. Bernard wished he could focus his attention and energy on those people, but the walls here called for him to be bring them down and have this place lain out bare as it once had and to remain that way ever more.

Somewhere in all of that was a king and a leader of that dark church who presumed itself to sit amongst the light, as did all who worshipped it. If this place fell, the dark would lose a foothold, as the light they thought would save them was nothing more than a place for darkness to settle and too late would the realisation be for anyone to be able to do anything about it. He would rather they take this fall then be burnt alive in their foolishness.

That was why he was here when he would rather have been in so many other places. To save as many as he could, all by himself if he had to and in such a way so that he would not arouse suspicions to himself. Yet the thought of taking away so much from people going about their days did hurt him inside a little. He would have much preferred to have been the belief that people needed and instead he had to be the one who would bury them.

Bernard came to a tree at the top of a hill where he could get some shelter from the rain that was overlooking the city and from here he looked down to face the city's north side. The tree was not tall and spread out to create a canopy that nothing sat on while offering sparse shade from the overcast sky. Under the cover of its leaves he turned to it and examined the trunk.

"A'hoy I see the lands around here have long been forgetting the biting blade of their own conviction, or would that it be forgotten the people with such convictions that might have saved them from my own hand's intervention. Away, away all you people who look down as the world falls down around ye. For you shall not find it on the ground the pieces enough to rebuild as all will be swallowed in dark and fire. I do wonder which will take you first if not I."

The darkness of the deeds of the church had swallowed many people already from the places he had been and they had been taken and slain in a display not of malice or kindness but stern necessity. At the very least the dark of the outside was a threat to them and from what he had heard none knew the extent of the destruction in their own lands caused by zealous, blind fanaticism held firmly in the dark away from prying eyes. He didn't need to see it, even though he had seen the ruins to know enough about how Alegan was seeing itself. He was sure that if such actions were said to keep them safe then the people of Alegan would have waved away the horror of such sad, sorry acts in the name of the blind who could see.

It was not thoroughly unprecedented, as those who used fire in any way had been hunted down as his teacher had been, even though they had not been consumed by it and had studied such things along with countless other magical arts in a most scholarly fashion befitting of a witch who had sat at the magical wizard's tower. It did not matter to those hunters, the notion was that they were all too dangerous and in a way that was true.

"It is difficult to feel the magic in the world without fire, as the view through which we see around us can only get colder and more dim without a source of light. I can reduce houses to rubble and move rivers with my hands but fire I must not touch."

So said the wizard as he again looked at the view before him. He had to squint to try and see better, as due to the wet haze of rain he couldn't see clearly.

So this is Churl, the cold, stone city built from the belief of light. These new walls that ring the whole city ensure the safety of the king who resides within, where before people could approach from any direction but now there are only these gates around it from which you can make your way in, and those entrances can all be watched.

Beyond the castle and the first ring of the city were older houses, some that did not appear to be made from stone but old wood. Beyond that was one more ring, newer, larger and it was this wall that separated the whole place from the outside. Out the front of these gates were stone squares with the insides carved out to have what was a fire burning in each of these alcoves he could see. As such, if his memory served him correctly, people were supposed to be at church or somewhere they could remind themselves of the church's teachings. Whatever that was these days, the wizard did not know.

Making my way into the city while playing the role of an old harmless man should be easy enough without suspicious glances being sent my way. It is entirely possible that a message might have been sent along the road ahead of me to advise those here of my arrival. Not being stopped along my way here suggests otherwise. I should keep my wits about me regardless.

As he stared at the gates, a stillness fell about his senses and increased so that he had to stop and make sure he was not being sneaked up on. Once everything was clear he turned about to have another good look at where he would be walking into. The castle stood tall over the rest of the city, helped by the naturally upwards sloping land.

Did anyone look down at the people far below from there? Were royalty looking down playing to the fear of the all seeing king? Bernard could not shake the feeling that something was. Perhaps they would fall too when he toppled the church.

What a dark and terrible place to come live, all for a bit more power.

He noticed a few black dots, a trail of people coming up the road to the castle gates. Pilgrims, weren't they? Easy enough for him to pretend to be one, to be a man of belief and then be honest that he would be on his way home when all was done that needed to be.

The wizard thought about all the people who lived there, in that unmoving place.

Those walls just make it colder and harder to see from the inside.

It was a strong feeling that he had but there was something more on the tips of his mind. The place chilled him to look at it. Not because it oozed evil but because it did not. From out here there was no movement that could be seen from within. It was silent. He could imagine a final sunset falling over the place to be swallowed forever in a dark greater and more absolute than night. And it would go silently.

There were those who went about their days gladly without knowing, so while one might ask who he was to take all that away from them, he knew that he must. He also knew, of course, that it was not like this everywhere else in the world where one man's happiness could come at the cost of another's. Why should they be glad when the focus that gave them their strength was so misplaced? Arrogance, ignorance, whatever it might be called, they shut their land away and dark things now sat within.

In the north they blamed this king but those who had minds to look elsewhere for answers knew that the church was complicit as well, if not entirely responsible.

Some might not see it but that religious head has been much too glad to take control and even now the king is just a mouthpiece while they copied the power of ancient days, if our most brooding Knight is to be believed.

"I think it best for everyone that doesn't happen." Bernard said to no one in particular.

On hearing his own words, the wizard felt reaffirmed of purpose. It would have been easy for him to slip quietly into the life that was here, one slow and yet fervent of faith and hope that shone out all others, as long as there was belief in the church. Yet his mettle was with magic words and those words, not the ones in a church, were what directed his future.

The sky suddenly darkened above him, to be darker than night in the ill and sickened way it did while something darker still twisted in the clouds, but only for a second while he felt a world consumed in darkness.

"That very end is coming for you all and I doubt that any of you saw it." He talked to those down below, who could not hear him.

"But those of us who see magic know of it and the strength of the promised end becomes ever stronger. Oh for that foul pulse of a malign beating heart, what I would not give for the world to see its peril. Yet the burden must be on the few for the many can not be trusted with the direction of the wind that will come. All who live further along these Haralands to the east will know it and then everywhere else besides."

As he looked up he held a hand out to the rain, thinking of the pulsing blackness up above. Not for the first time he wondered if it effected the water that fell from the sky. A world where such a thing could effect the rain falling from the sky would make more people mad. But then, surely by now there would be a noticeable change in people or the world. That was if any of it was not just some vision of doom.

Bernard shook his head of such thoughts. Here he was and here he would do his best to combat that terrible end that was being cast over all lands. There was some dismay that the days were over where one such as he could simply march in with hands raised and bring the entire place crumbling down. Such force would strengthen their resolve and turn others to greater means and such terrible power, of which such records of ancient history scarcely mentioned the events in detail. Everyone would be grasping for a means to defend themselves with no consequences and what good would that be? It might even hasten the end and the coldness he felt coming from within those walls was in itself a warning.

Yet that coldness was not the worst thing that he could feel.

The light has gone out of this place and those who took up its mantle are lying to us all. They don't keep watch over who really believes, keen to just remove those who would shatter the illusion.

Bernard didn't doubt that there was a time where the blind had been made to see, but that time was long past. All that was left were words, to keep their people tightly held in their control, which one had longed for, and the other had known its place.

And what place was that in the world? The church had taken into themselves the king and along with it had swallowed up all his power, those last remaining scraps of it anyway. None of it mattered, as beyond Alegan none would treat with this king who had blocked his borders with the flowing blood of the lands besides and that of his own people by the very nature of how far on the ends of his land they lived, meaning that they could not have been trusted.

Bernard knew that he could not be trusted the moment he would step foot into the city. Now that he was here he felt no closer to upturning it. He had seen rain wash things away and wished that he could have been the person to trust in the weather to do this for him.

The church didn't care about the rain, or why it fell. But he did. That rain, the rain that fell regardless or not there was blackness in the sky, the rain that filled the rivers and the oceans, it would fall even when there was nothing left. It would always be there, even if none could see it. That was unless the fire burnt out the sky, as the pyromancers of long ago had promised they would. Quite deeply within, the wizard believed that it would not be a matter of which happened, one end or both, neither had to come to pass.

Despite the dull grey sky and the light rain the day was peaceful with barely a breeze, yet days like these were more common where what lay around them was just a cover for the world becoming ever colder without anyone noticing or caring. That posed the wizard a question. Was what they were seeing above coming and going, or were they simply afforded a glimpse every so often, to remind them that their peril was ever coming closer?

It may have already been too late if that was the case. It left him drawing an uneasy, shaking breath to calm himself. He spoke as he looked into the sky, even though nothing was there, even though nothing could hear him.

"Was the war just to wake you, whatever you are?"

Chapter Eighteen
A Wizard's Fears

The wizard walked through the front gate, where no one at the gate paid him any heed. Just a man walking in who could have been anybody, which was exactly what he wanted to be seen as. Beyond that, the castle now stood far above him and held the same uncertainty within it as it had from a distance.

Bernard longed for the old days again, where a man such as he would have been given such a fast and speedy audience with the king to have this whole concern resolved. He might have even been able to turn the king's mind to other people's other than his own and find his own strength not in words, but in deeds.

He had to concede that were these those old days, he would not have been the one to come here, the task having been passed to another, one more stalwart of presence. Yet for this task he was deemed as the one required and he could not muster the strength and following of the wizards of old. Too much he must have been the unassuming old man, and as was he, so were his peers so perhaps that was why he had been sent. Vanity running thick amongst those with talent was no far off, long forgotten myth and was deeply settled in who they were, even to this day.

There was no vanity in this place. A stone wall prevented access to mundane townhouses in all directions. Now that he was on the other side, he was greeted with an immediate block of such houses on the left and right with paths winding off between them in all directions, including one that sloped upwards fairly steeply before disappearing out of sight behind a curve. All of these were surrounding a wide circular space which was filled with grass. In the middle there was a signpost that told him the places he could go and not the names of the individual streets. Once this would have been a simpler place, but the wall behind him betrayed the purpose of it now as something abnormal.

Who would defend such buildings if what was up ahead was not important? And defend them from who, myself?

He had the feeling of a person when they knew they were somewhere they should not be, only because he knew that were his motivations to be discovered he would be in great and imminent danger. People were not staring at him and yet everywhere he looked there was a corner that should he turn his head, might then bring forth a pair of eyes with which to snoop him out. He had to quell that feeling and properly orientate himself, that included finding somewhere to stay. Even if he had enough coins for what he might need here, there were not enough that he could carelessly spend without ever worrying. There had to be enough for a return journey after all. Then again perhaps not and then he would make time after to pilfer from the coffers of the church if he could get away with doing so.

The wizard thought that most ideal. After all, the king hardly needed to line his own pockets with that wealth or show such gold in his belly. Best it be distributed to rebuild the kingdom if there was still to be a kingdom at all when he was done. He had to consider the possibility that the stability of the land would falter on his success, with the king becoming no one without the power of his words made divine, as those who appeared to have power scrabbled to pick up the pieces for themselves. A southern incursion might be entirely possible if they knew no one would be coming after them.

Those in the north west reaches would have to travel far and spread themselves thin to lay claim to these lands but he could see their king doing it too, if only to catch him or any of his escaped prisoners who might have been anywhere by now. Some would have fled north out of his reach but here in Alegan, despite the modestly longer distance he might just send someone if the coast was clear. That king was greatly jealous and protective of his own land though, certainly he himself would not leave it.

I should position myself within reach of the king of Alegan's ear, to support him as much as possible were it likely this would come to pass. I was not told to come here to break up a kingdom, merely halt the wretched darkness of within which he has found himself.

Of course it had crossed his mind that the king himself might be more directly responsible, he would not have been the first king having gone mad with power that a wizard had been tasked to put down, but this did not sit right with the man's pattern of behaviour previously exhibited. A king who hid themselves and their family away didn't seem to him to be one drunk on power unless he knew what he was doing and hid away due to the shame. Something Bernard was determined to find out all in good time, sooner rather than later.

He turned to a young man who was carrying water pans out to be washed.

"Young man, anywhere this old man might stay at all in your city would be most appreciated if you know of a place to rest."

The young man seemed a mite annoyed at being approached, eyeing him strangely with his scruffy ragged clothing and dark hair that was just the same, lending him the appearance of a young man who found his life full of work.

"Well, you don't have the look about you of a pilgrim, but if you were a pilgrim, I would suggest that you make your way to the inner city, where you will not find tents but actual proper lodgings that would have before been the homes of others which have before too long become places given freely by king and church to those on the road. If you are not such a person, then you might find yourself in need of somewhere around this outer circle, unless you wish to show your devotion properly and at all times. Just ask any place for lodging that you can find, it'll be as fine as anywhere else. It doesn't matter where you stay, people that cause trouble get taken away eventually, we can never be quite sure when."

"I'm not here to cause trouble." Bernard said.

This was true only as far as he meant it, to those here who held power they would be of the suggestion that he was absolutely here to cause trouble were his magic be revealed.

"Well regardless of your suspicions you're a good young man, helping your elders out. What is all this about people being taken away?"

The young man sighed.

"I'm only doing this to help out. I don't want any trouble yet you seem clueless enough to my eyes. Listen well, for here in this city, by the grace of the king's word do we take all measures to be free of heretics and those that would bring about the fire and the darkness in the mind's eye. People suspected of that are taken beyond the city, into the castle and are never seen again. If you can not restrain yourself, stay away from those inner walls or you might find yourself taken in among them. Never used to be this way, mind you."

"No, it did not." The wizard mused.

"Not to worry boy, I'm merely a lone traveller to this weary city. I come from the old capital to gaze upon this place."

"Is it true what has been said, that the place has fallen into disrepair?"

"Mightily so it is true. Nothing good comes from there now and many would be leaving across the rivers and bridges to the north. They will not make it in time and find only barren, barricaded places where once they themselves shunned all outsiders if you can believe it. Those travellers shall find their inhospitality returned to them were any to brave the lone journey past those mountainous slopes leading to passages into the north."

The young man was silent and Bernard found such a sudden turn in his mood strange.

"Don't look down boy, look only to yourself, for surely this is the best place to be in such a world on the edge of madness. You should agree that while that problem is only the making of your king and belief, you should be fine within these walls. Be happy where you are. Unless I am wrong, of course."

It was clear that these comments were being thought over, the young man having his brows knitted together.

"The rest of the world is turning to madness?"

"Yes, yes it is, to say more might make you look like a fool, so be careful boy."

"I...I'm really not that young any more."

But the lad had said so mostly to empty air, as since Bernard did not have anything else to say, he had begun to walk on, so Bernard had heard those words to his back.

Leaving the lad, he walked up the climbing road until he came to the main street where some of these buildings had several stories and were stacked close together. Above the door of one such place hung a wooden sign that told him of its use as a tavern and place of rest. He could see at the wooden floor where the boards at his feet was scuffed and well worn, where many had heaved themselves up to the inside warmth that could only be found off the streets. So it was he found himself joining the countless others over the years who had done as he now did.

"It is very cold outside, is there anything warm for someone to eat?" He asked to a man seated at the bar.

The man looked up with bags under his eyes and his features betrayed a lack of self care the wizard very much hoped he did not pass on to his customers.

"I could heat up something provided you'll pay for it. It might take a while to be ready though. We've all been forbidden from lighting too large a hearth because it attracts the dark presence that dwells in the fire."

"A dark presence dwelling within the fire. Are we talking about the war?"

The man behind the bar sighed.

"Don't get me wrong, I know how many years ago that was, but now it's a royal decree, has been for some time so must be adhered to."

And do you think your king is doing the same, or the church behind closed doors?

Such a thing Bernard would have liked to have said, but decided to keep that thought to himself. Having marched through chill castles as cold as death and ones so heated that it had made him sweat, he knew that there were those up in the castle having it exactly how they wanted it to be.

Instead he put on a warm smile to hide his feelings on the matter in a most diplomatic manner.

"Well it is a fair bit warmer in here than it is out there so I'm not complaining, I shall wait for you. Tell me about the two walls, while we wait."

The bar man told the wizard all about the two layers, that he could pass undisturbed into the city proper for access to the church but that did not mean he could get past the third wall into the castle.

So here is where all the farmers and peasants live, as I suspected.

He thought on this as the man set about getting him something to eat.

With the king's wealth he built a wall, not new houses for his people. What kind of a man is that who appears to command the church but builds up barriers, a giant fence to stake claim on all that he owns? If all the land encompassed by the city is holy land then it seems obvious that the church extends their reach. It should have been enough that the king regained control of his lands and the faith of the people. People are taking the words of a silent and invisible king with fear and that fear echoes throughout his kingdom even as it crumbles.

A plate of roasted meat was eventually put in front of him, that while smelling musty and unappetising he reminded himself that he had handed over three gold pieces so took it, along with a mug found to be of watered down ale.

"This looks like it would go nice with some bread." He said, but the man at the bar shook his head.

"We don't have that here any more, not since the baker was taken. You'll have to go to the church if you want to bake bread. We do have some tougher stuff in storage but we're storing that, aren't we?"

"I might do just that. And what was that about them being taken away?" Bernard asked.

The man winced.

"I don't want to talk about it. Nobody will take up the job because they were taken proclaiming their innocence for any wrongdoing and it sounded genuine. Perhaps they heard whispers within the fire that none but they and the church could hear."

After finishing his food and handing over several more gold pieces, Bernard was shown to a room upstairs that looked down to the streets below. There was no firewood in the room and besides, no fireplace with which to use any. If anyone came in and broke down the door they would find no roaring fire here. Too great a fire anywhere and the ones making use of it would be accused of pyromancy and whisked off to an early death. The tiny flame in his lantern was all he had.

As he looked at it he thought on how the dead were the lucky ones, for they would be spared the long death that would come from this world and all those who remained.

That would be only if he and others like him failed. There would be no future where he allowed the church to exist, that was simple. It strengthened the darkness that came ever closer to swallowing the world and breaking it apart was the only reason he was here in the first place. Some lived here, and some died. Still, as the wizard heard the screaming and saw the cart dragging two people away as they professed their innocence, he wondered at all those people who trusted in the church and that promise of a guiding light which was only for them.

This posed a problem for the wizard, as he could not simply remove every single person who might be a vessel for fire filled thoughts, because that might have been everybody, or no one at all. The church would still do as it did and this much further inland, people believed more in the church, so it was hardly surprising that they were effected by it. People might be being taken away but here was less death that would shock, such as that he had seen. As the sounds of sobbing and crying disappeared up the road, he knew that there were ways that the church had of keeping up their appearance of being for the people, all the while not saving anyone at all.

They would leave the world to its end, happy that they clung to authority and power for as long as they did, even when the world turned to darkness around them, which they could not possibly consider themselves the source of. Unless, that is, they did.

The king is fortunate that the world of mortal lives is not poised for conquest or war or he would undoubtedly see his kingdom overrun. The north among the Ruthlands is not much better, although I only know of the situation so far above. He will have a lot to answer for, if I even get my hands on him, which is doubtful to happen because there is so much else to do, dealing with the church, that hideous slab.

There were only two pieces of furniture in his room, a bed and a small drawer away in the corner. On top of it was the small black painted leather book that had given him so much trouble. It did not matter if not everyone could read it, most could, but the spread of such words was the real problem. Someone would be able to read it and when they did it would fill their heads with nonsense. With such a book in circulation, why did anyone decide they were safe here? There was no safety in biding your time until death. A guiding light? It was blinding them to the truth, not helping them see the way to their future. If you read and you believed then you would be safe, that was their promise to all who read or listened. Those who were not regarded well, they were not seen by the light. What a stroke of good fortune for him in that case for not having to throw himself into the maw yet. He picked up the book and began reading it.

As the rain continued to pour outside and the day began to fade, the wizard looked to his lantern for his only source of heat and light while his mood turned as dark as the night's sky.

Maybe all those people who remained here did not have a future. Maybe all those people were destined to die, for why should all others suffer just for these people who thought themselves better?

"Perhaps I got out of the wrong side of the bed that long gone morning." He murmured to himself.

His bed did not yet look approachable and there was a stretching itch along his back. And that, whatever it was, left him standing and rocking against the window sill for the remainder of the day and most of the night, despite the cold against the dirty glass.

When he awoke to swirling shadows in his mind and a chill he felt deeper than his bones, he felt that every corner he could not see must surely hold eyes that were red with hate and stared accusingly at him. In the early hours of the morning, he burst out of the front door of the lodging gasping for breath.

Back at the great library he had flicked through a copy of the Churl book but it had been old, faded. There were newer copies that he had seen. This new book, the words were all different, although he couldn't call them wrong because they had been wrong before and they we even more wrong now, worse, even. He supposed that the best place to go was the church itself for some answers, whether or not it was the last place for him to want to go, most strongly.

The darkness after the fire. I wonder if it has taken you, king Raylen, so that you came here for some change of heart, to remove the dark from your mind. And yet for what I have read, this might only make it worse, for these are your own words are they not, in this book? I am afraid to ask without revealing my lack on knowledge but I must read these for myself, somehow. I must find the words of the damned lest I be revealed as ignorant.

Bernard could not stand to be in the place for a moment longer and ran hastily to retreat out the gates. The morning air was biting cold but there were no clouds and the sun was coming up.

He had to find a place to rest and found himself walking into the farms. A farmer was sitting in his chair on his deck, getting the morning sun and had watched the wizard approach.

"Good sir, may I use your warm decking to rest myself on?" Asked the wizard.

The man squinted in his uneasiness but waved a hand to a sun soaked patch of wooden flooring.

"Be my guest, strange fellow."

Bernard collapsed in a heap while the farmer looked down at him from his chair.

"I would like to say that strange people don't come here but they certainly do. And a good morning there to you, by the way."

"Is it really? All these days look so similar that they just pass from one into the next."

The man put on a wry smile.

"Aye it is for me as a farming man, I've never had my stock in more demand. The yield is poor but the prices are high. You had any luck with any of that?" He enquired, regarding the book in Bernard's hands with an air of bemusement.

"I would have thought that one such as yourself would have had a bit more reverence for it, then to call it 'any of that'."

The farmer's face slackened and gestured at the buildings in front of them.

"There had been all farm houses in front of the actual city before the walls went up. Some of this is new though, you can tell, but me and my family among others used to live in that space, before it was swallowed up. There's less security out in the fields but here we are." He explained.

"The further in you go it becomes a rather narrow and cramped place until you get to the castle. There's a nice little space around it, for watchers, you know, but it isn't what it used to be."

"That is good to know."

They sat that way for a while until steam was rising from the fields below. The whole place began to steam, wispy white little threads floating off into the sky.

Bernard was looking out over to the city.

"I don't know what the walls are for." He said.

The farmer leaned back in his chair.

"Sometimes walls are just walls. People put them up for any number of reasons, doesn't matter who they're keeping out or what they're holding in, it marks the edge of something. Take a look at these fields. Some used to say those were ghosts coming up there now, but not any longer. I doubts ghosts would stay in this place. While some people can be fearful and strange of what they don't understand, we know they are not escaping spirits. Boundaries can change, you know, whether that's putting up or pulling down. In a space you can limit or expand what you know about something. I don't find it all so confusing. One day we might not need those walls, because they won't mean anything."

"I notice a house over in the fields yonder, do you all live out in these places? It would seem to me that the king would want his people all within the walls that he has doubtless spent a fortune building."

"That over there was where we used to keep the young ones with nowhere to go, they're happy in the city now and the place has been returned back over to the king. Don't trespass over there or you'll find yourself in trouble."

"I see."

The farmer rose to his feet.

"Well I best get started for the day, so you should leave."

A thought suddenly entered Bernard's head.

"Do you believe that the church can be changed?"

"Come now, there's no saving that place. I'm thrilled to have the king here, in name only if I must say for all we've seen of him, but that place is ridged, fixed."

He turned to the wizard, who had found his feet and warmth.

"I only hope that these fields don't change. Truth be told it's all that gets me up in the morning, seeing this. Now if you really do excuse me, I need to find that layabout of a neighbour's son, he's supposed to be helping me."

The wizard made his way back to the city proper, which felt a much longer walk back than he remembered actually getting out to the fields in the first place. The wizard walked back into the first circle, but he decided against going to see the castle. After all, that high building could be seen from many places and it didn't matter how close or far away he was, it was locked up tightly against all things as had the king been for many a year.

He would have quite liked to know what had happened to spark the king's mood towards hiding himself and his family away but the wizard had a sinking feeling that he knew what it was.

Bernard thought that people would have been tired of war, from the last one the world had not yet recovered in such a short space of time. And that could have been it, the final war, the world was slowly fading away after the fire, backing away from it as fast as they could. Yet a bitterness hung in the air and the church was telling people to ignore the problem and he knew that he would have to put it back into focus, no matter how painful it was, because the whispers in the world said that the dark was coming and no words of some king would prevent that from happening. That was why he was here, to stop the dark from rising and as he looked around he knew he was steadily running out of time.

He decided that he wanted to avoid people for the moment and the best way he could do that was by walking along the river, as anyone wanting to do so would be busy with their morning chores. There was only a little waterway here, one that would have been fed from a larger river somewhere, funnelled down so that if he didn't mind getting his feet wet he would have been able to make it to the other side. He did mind, though, so he went along the bank of it, as there were no buildings along the length of the waterway in the outer ring. Where the river had to travel up to the wall, it escaped through a grate.

The river led right out to the banks on the other side of the wall and along such banks he found himself wandering out alone along the grass. There wasn't much grass inside the city, nature seemed averse to the place, and he could not imagine the need for others to come here such as those druids, but he supposed that there was reason enough in the end. Perhaps they had wanted to plant some more trees.

He smiled at that, but at the same time knew that they had abandoned the place, off on their own quest. He didn't know what they were trying to do but if they knew that they could not succeed in this place then getting as far away as possible was the best idea. None would follow them on their trail and give up this city and he was thankful that those forest people had not been successful, but regardless of that they were most likely doing whatever they wanted, which wasn't a problem at all, for as he had found no help in them he very much doubted that the rest of the world would either.

Chapter Nineteen
Lessons for Druids

Out in the cold grey skies was a hawk, flying with their beady amber eyes set into the distance and the hawk could see for many leagues all around. The conditions in the sky had been clear recently, so even though the time spent flying during the day was becoming less and the time spent down on the ground in darkness much more, the rumbling days of thunder that made flying dangerous had for a short while appeared to have reduced and as such they did not mind the infrequent hours of flight. They made the most out of the time which they could take to the skies and had been needy in the wish to do so.

There had been long flights through wilderness, a sprawling place of green, yet now off in the distance was a sight that was not so, as in the distance lay what was a dark shape that cut into the world and stretched as far as they could see, over the horizon and possibly much further. Sticking out of the ground all throughout were structures not built by animals, the collapsed, tumbled ruins of which could have provided a spot to nest, were it not for a weariness that rose up when looking at that discoloured ground. It was too far away and too dark to spot prey but the sort of creatures that hid in those shadows were not ones that could be hunted.

Down below, where it was still green, the bird spotted some humans and spiralled slowly downwards out of sight of the sky, below to the canopy where the humans were at rest, not afraid in the least because they themselves were a human. With a whirl of feathers, the body grew and the bird disappeared as feathers became tied into worn clothes and Zelda became human in body again.

She staggered over to a tree, still feeling like a clumsy bird of prey using its legs on land, to stretch for a moment and rub her eyes, which were always nice to be able to feel moving freely inside her head.

Zelda had not been taking herself terribly far from everyone else, however she had gone up and taken flight herself enough that she knew they were steadily moving closer to their next goal which could not be spotted through the trees. Down here amongst the green that place felt very far away still, even though her eyes had told her otherwise. Flying by herself had been worrying at first, not wanting to lose where she had set off from, but she had learned to rely on the animal instinct given by the forms she inhabited and the feel of the world which felt strongest when she did so.

This was also why she found the dead land they had been getting closer towards to be so concerning. Simply looking at the darkness sapped her of the connection she felt with the land and from merely looking upon the shadows, they threatened to cling to her mind as she saw them in her mind's eye.

She shook her head free of the worry and focussed on looking at her body, as this was her body, who she was, not a vessel for darkness or dark thoughts. She could take the form of animals or strengthen the plants of the ground, but none of that mattered if she did not take care of herself. Or her clothes, which were variously important in her ability to do so.

Over time there had been many little lessons such as those. Looking down at the tatters of her clothes, she had to admit that they had taken the brunt of her exercises and training. Sometimes they got snagged on trees or thorns, other times the method of transformation would have her hear ripping or tearing and the only thing she then wanted to do was to resume her human form to see what needed fixing this time.

It was never so simple, though. She had used up all the stitching thread they held and had at one point gotten into an argument with Survel for taking up his tough fishing line for the purpose. Thinking on what lay ahead, of water best left alone, Zelda knew he wouldn't need it and after all, she had been the one to fetch it for him to begin with.

As she patted down her clothes, it seemed nothing had been ruined further this time, but she very much wanted to buy something a little more hardy the next chance she had, even if it was a leather vest string tied together, which would probably become tackle-tied when the string failed and she reused what she had. That also reminded her to buy some more, if she could, whenever that might be. There was no one to simply provide that for her, much like food, where she had learned to scavenge.

Whether or not the pain in her head could be attributed to a lack of good nutrients, sleep, or a constant worrying tug that something was not at all right about what they were walking into was to be a personal matter of debate for another day, if only anyone had the time to bother wondering which it might be on any particular day. Or it could be that over time her head had been expanding with all this worldly understanding and she needed some time to absorb it all. Not too fast, even if Zelda had been making quite the pace away from lands ruled by a cold and distant king, the further she went the more she took this as a change in herself that she could not keep forcing on herself without knowing what needed to be known.

Sitting alone, lost in thought with head in hands hoping their coolness would still the throbbing, it was easy enough to simply think of nothing at all and hope that would help to clear her head completely. But she knew that there were people who knew a great deal of things and their heads were quite intact, so perhaps it was idleness that caused her mind to slow on some days and feel sluggish. She needed time, that was all, which she would spend right here on the grass with a breeze blowing amongst the trees in the shade. After all, this might be the last grass she got to lay down on for some time, or close to the last. She didn't think much would grow in that dark, horrible place.

Ah, here she was going again, thinking of the doom and gloom. It would not do to dwell on such things while she was not there, for once they were set to walking on such ground they would face the doom and gloom with nowhere else to look. She needn't hurry her mind to the dismay that would come from taking in such sights when being surrounded by them. Best she didn't think that way at all.

Gunter had watched her come in to land and had sat watching the young woman settle herself. Nothing seemed terribly out of sorts with her today but there was a silence as she sat which was rather at odds with what he expected was going on inside her head and that irked him. If people were thinking he preferred that they did not keep their thoughts to themselves and so breached the silence not so directly, because asking someone what they were thinking implied that you did not already have an idea of sorts of what someone was thinking and he did not like being thought of as that type of person.

"Anything worth seeing up there?" He asked.

Zelda tiled her head to a shoulder in the closest thing to a shrug he would most likely ever get out of her for asking such a question.

"I'd like to think I got a good look around."

"And what did you find?"

"That closer now I can see the dark land we encroach upon and the foulness feels greater than before. I never thought I would see it myself let alone have to walk through such a place yet I suppose for us there is no way around if we must not go too far north. It reminds me of a bruise. I wonder if we ourselves going forth will be a source of pain for the world if we stand upon it?"

Gravely he nodded his head.

"Malleau. Yes, we have been getting close. I can not deny the possibility of disturbances, yet our journey will not be for looking and seeing, or even helping I'm afraid, for it is to be the way through we need to take in order to get ourselves to our much needed forest without heading into the maw of the king in the north west most reaches of this land. Doing so will make us lose our freedom as I once lost mine to that monster."

"And I will be back behind walls." Zelda said.

"After having been given freedom I didn't realise I needed. The world outside from home felt so cold and dark, yet the feeling has come and reversed itself from one side to the other. Now I can't imagine why I never felt the cold inside before."

"The world is going stale. It fades, slowly, but it fades. Those who live in it, but mostly us humans, have forgotten the truth found in the world of nature that they came from. Only we can restore this world to what it once was, one free of kings and their courts and such squabbles, for none deserve to be above nature. They take and do not replace, they devour the land and turn nature into a meaningless play thing for themselves, all for more power that causes foul shadows and drains Auralin of life. If we return the spirit to its rightful place we will be taking the first step to realising the old world again and the only darkness any would need worry about would be the night's sky itself."

"You mean to say that the darkness is caused by us?" Zelda said, thinking of dark nights and the shadows that fell on people's minds.

Gunter gestured to the east.

"Look around yourself, think on the people you have seen go about their lives without purpose or one most vile. Dark and sheltered are their minds. Where is the life and energy in their beings? Taken away by the need to be someone else's instrument with which to fill their own bellies with gold. A darkness in this world feeds on human misery, Zelda, but with the return of the old world it will have nowhere to hide, and we will destroy it."

"Then we will all be free?"

"Yes, then we will all be free."

She could not help but think again of the distance they had come, with the distance making up a space between who she was now and the person she had once been. How far they had gone from the city of Churl, to one where the more she had learned about the person she should be, the colder and more distant that world had appeared. At least now she was able to voice her concerns with people she felt she could trust.

I want those I left behind to be part of this new world. I want them to breathe and feel that they live in a place they deserve to be.

Gunter rose to his feet.

"You look very determined there. We need to stop the worrying and look beyond what could go wrong and look to our success which is all that matters. That's enough ruminating for today I do think and you should keep to your feet for a while. We will all need to stay together in Malleau as much as possible and I don't want you taking flight on habit or instinct as doing so might bring harm."

They wandered over to where others were sitting, where Findal himself was waking up from a nap.

While others might have looked at him and been envious of his vagabond life he knew they did not have reasons to be so. When you couldn't even be sure of a warm bed at the end of a day, that was when things didn't add up over time. All the little things that you have been put through were not outweighed by the crude little place where you lay your head to rest. Then upon waking you realise your back hurts and you slept restlessly throughout the night and that yesterday's problems are still today's problems to deal with.

Today he would again have a problem of a particular kind. That young one had been displaying talents of late that could take her far along the path of understanding, containing within her a concealed wisdom that was both quiet and sure of itself. Being too sure was a problem that he would have to discuss with the others at some time, for surely he could not be the only one with concerns.

For instance, in the manner of a hunter, the girl would follow certain tracks, these were tracks in her mind but like the foolish hunter would not stop to realise that they might have gone the wrong way, or off slightly. One needed to only misinterpret a sign slightly to cause ruin for themselves and others and it might take her a while to get to that point where she would have to make a decision. So she spent much of her time thinking of all the possible things that could happen, when she wasn't studying of course.

The only way he knew this was because he had asked her and she had told him, as if thinking too hard was something everyone did. He had known people who had spent a great deal of time making plans, then went about acting them out when the time was right, but when things did not go the way they had expected, it was at that moment where those people could falter.

Despite the girl's youth he could already see in her the one track mindedness that was so engrained in those who had left to find their own fortunes and some of those had come back as poor as beggars with nothing to show for the years spent trying make a place for themselves. Of course anything was better than nothing at all, having no idea what to do or being paralysed when you could have done something, that had almost gotten Zelda killed at least once that he knew of.

He wondered how she would feel if in the end Zelda failed in finding a place for herself. If the road she followed along with them led nowhere she wanted to be there could be problems. He had found distraction in such things as this, which was now his entire life, yet plucking someone out of their own life and leading them on this journey? To him the prospect of that felt absolutely dangerous for he did not know what kind of person that road would make.

If we succeed here I hope she finds not just a place but a voice for herself along with the place to settle. It would not do to have her wandering aimlessly on her own whims across a world with no law and only the ancient ways of nature, that of the strongest to stand between all of us. Lending the sound of her voice to those who would guide a whole and undivided world would be best and she would need to find her use in that.

He spoke to her, trying not to sound flat, also to keep the resigned dismay that he felt from edging into his voice.

"Good morning Zelda, you're well today I hope?"

"Very much so. Did I wake you?"

"Well you could say it is late enough in the morning already for that to be impossible. I simply have not had the chance to say hello to you today yet."

"Hello then. What's with the strained face?" She asked.

"What? Oh, I'm just debating amongst myself whether only other humans will listen to us when we come to speak or whether or not that would pass along to the other intelligent creatures and beasts of our world. Our study and journey will take us far but is it far enough for those who might outlive us in years or live in high nigh unreachable places?"

"If beasts live on mountains then they have to respect the call of the mountain that they rely on to live. So then they will rely on us." She said.

Findal hoped that he would be able to rely on her. That wasn't a done deal even if everyone was able to act about as if it were.

"Zelda we can't move mountains, but I know what you mean. Creatures that live in a place are beholden to that for their continued survival. On that point, we need to be careful walking into ruined lands such as we are, for those that live off it are certainly as ruined as the ground around them. For example, I know we are not going to find anyone with a shop for me to talk to, so I change my thinking and temper my expectations to better work with what we might be dealing with. There could be no one of any sort at all to talk to apart from each other. You should do the same and not expect the people or land to make things easy for you, for the land ahead of us is long lost to a point of no return and may not speak to any of us and of any who might speak I hope we come upon none."

Throughout the day various members of the party came and went while Zelda watched them all come and go, each in no doubt spending some time preparing themselves for what was to be up ahead in their own way as she had. When it was time to finally go both Survel and Peter picked up their things but Peter appeared distracted, keeping an ear to the ground as if he could hear something. That had appeared to be a bother for him over the day as if he were not quite sure if he was hearing anything or not.

"What is it?" She asked him.

There was a look akin to worry in the corner of his eyes, softening the usual snarl but it was not at all an improvement of expression. If anything it was disquieting and Zelda hoped whatever was bothering him in this manner would go away quickly.

"The closer we get the stronger a feeling gets beneath my feet. I am unsure of the meaning of it. Could it be some dull spell of Churl that we had left behind has come upon us again? Only some rite of magic or other odd spell could turn the world for me into such unease."

Gunter should his head.

"We've travelled far out of the entire kingdom's influence let alone that city. As much as they would wish they could lay claim to these lands I doubt any have the backbone to come and claim them. This far west there is hardly anyone here to enforce the laws of Alegan and we're soon to enter a place any would curse themselves for having as part of their lands. There's a reason why no one on this side so far from the mountains and wilderlands bothers and we have nearly come upon it. A curse resides on the center of this land and it covers all the ruin you will soon see before you."

Seeming to have made up his mind that whatever was bothering him wasn't important enough to dwell on any longer, Peter kept his head down and resumed busying himself with his packing. This made curiosity build up in Zelda's mind.

I wonder what it could be? It isn't like him to admit to a fault such as that, but if he means to say that he is having trouble with feeling the ground and his connection to it was such the case in Churl I must admit I can not feel any lessening yet that has not come from my eyes.

With everything packed and everyone ready, they made to move on to that dark place that made their legs feel heavy with reluctance walking towards, even if they knew that they must. They had come upon it sooner than they had expected, the party had been making very good time thanks more recently to full moons and cloudless nights, allowing them to walk for much longer than they usually would have been able were the sky dark and cloudy. This had the effect of cutting into the hours used for sleeping when one might desperately want to sleep and when they did stop at night to sleep it was slight, over much too quickly as they rose when the sun did to continue on their journey to make the most of their shortening moments of daylight.

They were coming to the end of the wild brush and trees, walking upon to where once would have been a bright and vibrant land. Knowing it was no longer had doused their spirits and all were quiet as they waited for the sight they knew they must come to see. Hours passed in such a manner and while she was as silent as the others, Zelda's mind was not resting.

Ever since wondering if something was amiss, she had been spending her time concentrating and eventually had felt a strangeness in the world about her. It was just beyond her touch, a barely noticeable air of difference that compelled her off to the side away from the others as she searched for that strangeness.

Was this what Peter was talking about? She wondered.

She wasn't looking where she was going, just following the sensation that told her something was out there. Just on the edge of her mind she could feel this shaking up through the ground, another pulse through the air. Even though where she needed to be had been in front of them, Zelda moved along through trees now sparse enough that sky was peeking through gaps in the trunks. Instead of wondering at this and feeling any sort of sadness at having the greenery around her be coming to an end, she sought where that feeling was, to a place not quite hidden but not out in the open, either.

There were two trees standing just as any others that looked out to the land beyond. They were no different from any other trees, it was what rested between them that made Zelda stop upon finding the source of the strangeness. Between them was a twisted bundle of tree roots shaped into that of a person, a man curled up in sleep. He was even wearing clothes that were old and dark and tattered, his head resting on a curled up coat.

Zelda could not tell if the tree had been grown around the clothes and for a moment she inspected the person's shape closely, in silence.

Even though she had not disturbed it, very slowly the tangle began to move and she jumped back. The tree man opened his bark eyes to blink slowly, then turn their head to look up at her. The tree man spoke with a voice of creaking branches.

"Well this *is* a surprise."

Zelda blinked, because the tree was speaking to her and she had no idea what she should say to it in return.

The tree man continued to talk.

"Thought I would lay here for a time quietly yet look what happened to come across me so long into my sleep. A surprise for us both, judging by the look on your face."

The tree man slowly uncurled himself and sat up out from between the trees with his feet in front of him, yawning and stretching out his arms which made the sound of branches blowing in the wind. He peered at her with his bark eyes, then looked past her as sounds of movement through the undergrowth and voices increased.

Gunter must have seen her back because even before turning around he was speaking to her.

"Never go off the path Zelda, the way we have set for ourselves and our journey must be held above all else."

Then he stopped, as he saw what was there before her, surprised as Zelda was but not at seeing a talking tree.

"Well then perhaps from time to time there are exceptions, indeed. I did not expect to see another one of us out here of all places one could be."

The tree man moved slowly as a great rushing wind sounded and the man dislodged himself completely from the trees around him. After he did so the bark of his body paled and softened, receding and smoothing over to become skin. The man had a long face and dark beard with short black hair on his head. He appeared in years about the late to middle age of Gunter but without the same naturally pleasant expression about him. He had rather keen eyes set into his paling features. He coughed and cleared his throat several times before speaking in a much more human voice.

"So tell me friends of the forest, what takes you through these parts, where it might be that you are poised so close to walk along the edge of such darkness that you find yourselves near? A place and time this world has become of such, and also of bleak ruin that I had set myself to rest and wait for it all to pass on by. Many years I had rested and thought to rest many more while coming in and out of this slumber. Yet it seems that was not to be, for all intents it looks to be you have a mission on your mind."

Gunter nodded.

"Indeed we do. It is fortunate for you to awaken and now would be nothing but a waste if you were to return yourself to such a sad slumber as you had put upon yourself. We search for the spirit that has fled with our power in hopes of returning them to the forest with strength and averting such a dark future as you have doubtlessly seen. First we must return to that same forest in time for solstice to review our direction of search."

The man alighted from his seated position, unfurling his rolled up jacket that was in even a worse condition than had first been apparent, being little more than a thinly stretched black rag with patches in various stages of deterioration. He slid his arms through it and checked it, thoroughly at ease.

"Then I shall come with you, for whether north or west you should need my help. My name is Nasker and as you are to me, I am pleased to have you amongst my acquaintances."

"We travel west, through Malleau."

A sad, thin smile stretched on Nasker's face on accepting what he must have already guessed.

"Well then fellow sir you shall definitely need my help. Even though it may be most preferable to be not needing any help at all along that dead road on which we shall walk, I can not but warn strongly of the possibility. One more such as myself may not do much but we can all look out for each other with one more pair of eyes as long as no one takes this as an opportunity to be lax. As your young miss must have been to find me, we all must be, that is to be on our toes all throughout the charred land, with a sky twisted warning or no."

"You have noticed that darkness?"

"How can I not have? Ever since it first appeared in the sky many years ago I have wondered about it because I have never seen nor heard of such a thing. Even in my slumber I could feel it."

His eyes looked to the sky but there was nothing above that threatened. Zelda knew of that fear and knew it was not a thing one should spend their time thinking about. To stop the possibility of concern she spoke.

"Well I am delighted to have found you, Nasker, so you now have the opportunity to see that all is not lost. We still have the time and the means to right this world even while the warning signs of darkness above do warn us of an awful fate."

"One that will reach us if we do not keep moving." Gunter said.

With that the party turned around to continue their way on west as a cold wind began to blow, with another in tow.

As they slowly walked through the trees, Nasker was fairly quiet as he was introduced to the others and was told of what had transpired, all with a knowing look on his face or a slight nod here and there while not asking any questions for anyone to clarify what they said. When everyone had filled him in on their journey as it stood, he appeared hesitant to ruminate on the facts and relaxed, seeming to prefer to listen in to the conversations going around him rather than spending time questioning until the topic came to himself.

"There isn't really much to say." He began.

"I learned everything I ever needed to far north away from all this, coming down a few times and going to the Great Tree myself, as I suppose everyone close enough should. Then it is as I said, I wished to spend my time sleeping and wait for better days but have been roused somewhat earlier than I had expected. That's not a concern though. I'm glad to be on the move again, I mean it."

When the topic of teaching the ways came up he appeared interested in those three who were newer to the ways of nature than he was.

"You are, after all extremely important for our continued survival. Each of you demonstrate what I see as a hardiness from different walks of life which is precisely what we need. Not everyone is born and bred as a druid, I would suspect not these days. Even having a basic grasp of the magic of the wild world among you proves that others can be made to listen, for you first had to listen, if not to your teachers but the whole world around you. Yet there are places and spaces and people who would choke out this knowledge so important for the world we have. And I find it strange, Zelda. I would not have guessed you were so new among us, as there is a feeling about you that is old, older than I. Or I should say rather that it is not something you see every day, for you did find me, after all."

Zelda shook her head.

"Oh I wasn't alone. Peter said he felt a feeling and that was the only reason I picked up anything at all. Would have gone right past me otherwise if I had not been looking for something, even if I didn't know what, because I wanted to know what that was."

"I see." He said politely.

Gunter was watching them and felt annoyed. At any other time he might have continued berating Zelda for where she had gone wrong so soon after his warning, but this new person was an acceptable distraction for all of them while further adding to his group those who might do as he said, or at least gave the impression to others that he was among those who did as he said.

This was fortunate for me, to come across another, but I have to wonder if I have gone too far in telling the girl to relax. It is much too unpredictable for her to be going off on her own way. I need those who are reliable, not those who I can not control or predict. Oh she listens well enough some times but other times such as this I worry for my efforts. They were talking about mountains earlier and I find such words apt, as I must ask myself what might be needed to bring down a mountain such as her mind. I'd rather not wait for us to get to the forest and find her out of sorts and against us with such certainty in her own ways.

He did not like to question his own decision making but perhaps she had been inspired just a bit too much by their presence. There was a certain primal instinct that pounced which she lacked, preferring to take a slow and methodical approach. Too slow. Too methodical. He had taken it onto himself to loosen those straw knots that took up space in her head and fill it with the world of nature beyond that of castles and kings but alas there was still straw amongst it all and through his lack of progress realised he was getting desperate.

I very much wish to not go ripping those straw knots out now, I do not wish to cause damage. Nor do I wish to set the whole thing on fire and start over but this mess is becoming intangible from the girl herself.

Indeed there was this stone wall that went up that he could not get through. He liked the comparison because a stone wall could be a natural obstacle or it could be crafted with human hands and he wasn't quite sure which this was. He felt the others did not share his concern as much but he knew they saw that some revelatory peace had descended on her once they had left the last remnant of civilisation behind and it had come from seemingly nowhere at that. Surely they had to see it and if they did why was he the only one thinking of taking action while the others waited until it would be far too late?

Perhaps this new arrival, Nasker, could tip the scales in his favour, another person for her to talk to, one who might ask of her a directness that he had been lax to enforce. Zelda would need to think quickly up ahead, there might be no time to contemplate the horrors that awaited them in the dark and shadows. There were no lessons to be learned after death.

His teacher had done much contemplation and in the end had come to his own wicked decision that had ended in death. That was what he feared about her above all, that she might follow in the footsteps of another, even her own, after deciding for herself what it was the world needed most. Or even without knowing the meaning behind her actions, history might repeat itself were she to be manipulated. Only he could ensure that his future was the only one that would come to pass, even though he knew teaching her the ways of the world to free her was important as well. She really could be something special, he knew, despite his growing reservations.

"She sees something new everyday." He murmured out loud, without realising that he had spoken.

Nasker had heard his faint words.

"Something that shall only continue from here, whenever it is that these days are."

No one responded as the black land of strange, coarse grit and ash spread out in front of them. Unable to be resting weary legs during the day, none of them could hope for sleep ahead or even the possibility of dozing off lightly while they remained on their feet. They were also running out of food that they could not ration and knew that it would be dried food they had rationed up ahead or nothing to eat at all.

The sound of a grumbling stomach at mid day told only of what else might come but none would complain for none wished to be the first to admit it. Then perhaps it was fortunate that the view ahead of them was one that made their hunger evaporate, the wind coming to a stop as they walked into a cold, dead land.

Chapter Twenty
Malleau

Walking through Malleau was awful. The sight was horrible, all blasted and weathered. The land had been buried in a grey mixture of dirt and coarse soot, heaped about in mounds as far as they could see. Such a place should not exist, or so Zelda thought, as to her eyes all this dead and wasted land stood in the face of what she had learned and defied the words she had been told. This was no land where anyone could live, free of the shackles of kings.

There was an awful smell all throughout of a burning wick or smelting metal that offended her nose greatly and clogged her senses. Picking up a handful and running it through her fingers had left them stained black and attempts to fully clean her hands of it had proved unsuccessful and had only caused to create black smears on her clothing.

Littered throughout the land, rising from the windswept slopes were the stone remains of buildings where people had once lived, where the stone itself had melted on the tallest ruined tops leaving sad trails as wax on a candle did. All else were low to the ground stones, ruins and rubble sticking out of the grit no matter where she turned.

So this is the place you would tell me of. A place so foul you could not forget it. Now I am the same, for I surely will never forget this either, this travesty of nature. You would have judged all this, remembering the view as something different, having known it in the days before the end. Wouldn't have you, Lara?

There was no grass sprouting, but skeletal trees clawed up white and thin much like bone from the ground in places. Feeding on the tainted soil they found themselves in appeared to have turned them twisted and ill.

"I almost see now why what was done to the elves and others happened as it did. Anyone would wish to prevent a fate such as this from spreading to their own lands." She said.

Zelda noticed that Gunter was looking out grimly to the distance, not admiring the view in the slightest and she felt as he did.

"Yes, this is what the war did. We only have the sad remains here and over there off in the furthest distance you can see it, that white blur, the ruins of the great castle. It had once been a shining light, high in the sky as a mountain so it is said, that covered all in its brilliance. Now all of that is gone and crumbled to the ground. When fire came upon such brilliance, borne in the hearts of the wicked, it blackened the land so that it cracked and dried so that nothing would live here any longer. Or should I say no living thing *should* reside amongst the wasted fields and ruins, for there are tales that beg to differ."

Nasker too was sharing Gunter's expression.

"We must be careful in these parts." He said.

"Who knows what is waiting for us as we travel through. I myself would rather we walk around it but having been caught up on the reasons why and where we are going, I admit we have little choice in the matter. Walking through Malleau is not going to be easy, what's left here is…distasteful."

"That's certainly to say the least of it." Findal said.

They made their way deeper into the desolate wastes, the colour draining further from the world as they did so. Even to look behind, the green of the forest was now pale and thin. The group walked single file, with Survel, Findal and Nasker in the front and Gunter, Peter and Zelda behind them.

Zelda walked up to a tree, finding herself fascinated by the shape of it that reached towards the sky in its twisted, grasping way, only to have Gunter's hand firmly on her shoulder.

"Stay away from those and do not touch them, they ingest the poison of this land. That goes the same to say of any water, all that we took on our way here will have to last us, there shall be no drinking out of puddles or any well you might find and don't touch the trees.

"You don't have to tell me twice." Peter said.

He still had his head to the ground from time to time and Zelda had tried to hear the trees as he did, still with no luck. She wasn't jealous, a part of her wondered if it even mattered. People could have different skills, only she was made to wonder just how much of that particular understanding would even be hers.

"I wish I could understand the trees as you do Peter. Animals I am beginning to understand but there are none here for me to talk to."

"Maybe you will get better at it." He said.

"But do not worry yourself, these ones are sick and silent, with few stories to tell in such a place. And yet there are whispers among them to which I find myself concerned, because I don't understand the words that creep out from them in quiet tones. They seem to weaken the connection I have with the ground, which while already faint has become only ever more so the further we walk. I fear for the connection we all share with the world in its entirety is being stifled by the evil of this place."

Gunter span around to face him.

"Then stop, stop what you are doing. If the noise of the trees turns the sound of the world mute to you then it is a sign you will lose your connection and then yourself entirely. That goes for all of you. Do not open yourself to those words you might hear from the ground. Besides, the words may be of elves and their words are not ours, so it could be that is what you hear. Regardless, let us all keep out wits about us."

Peter huffed.

"Well I didn't consider the elves to be so adverse to silence, for approaching each of these sorrowful trees there is much noise that I hear with barely a touch of my being against it."

"Do as I say and hold yourself back from it. There are no lessons the world can teach you here that can not be seen with the naked eye."

The sombre grey of day turned to late noon as the light began to dim and the land around them began to fade from view as all the greys and whites and shadows began to look the same. They could all rather easily imagine themselves getting lost in such a place, left to roam forever while chasing the sun, hoping for its warmth. As the night moved in and the moons rose the shadows that followed behind were not grey or black at all. Instead a deep blue that settled over the sky, along with everything else, turned the shadows which were not those of the deepest darkness to indigo blue, which seemed to creep ever closer as if waiting to ensnare any who stepped foot in them.

To keep those at bay, a torch was lit by Findal that was passed around, the orange glow clearing the darkness. The places they carried the light through that had been cleared of shadow by their passing however returned to it darker and more wicked of appearance than before as they walked on.

They had not travelled far with the crackling of the torch in their ears when they became aware of another noise, a whisper like the wind but there was no wind, one that grew with every passing step to that of a faint howling, a roaring that came from everywhere at once.

Zelda found herself admiring Peter for keeping his sanity if perhaps this sound was what he had been putting up with throughout the day. Now however, Peter had his hands clamped over his ears.

"The trees are yelling! Oh how they are yelling. Can't anyone else hear this? Can anyone hear me?"

They came to a halt and Survel began pulling at Peter's arms, trying to dislodge them from his head.

"Of course we can hear you and among it something else which we're ignoring, so you do the same."

But Peter still had his hands firmly clasped over his ears.

"I can't hear you over them."

"Then take your hands off your ears."

Peter did so, with a grimace on his face while Survel shook his head.

"There, stop making us all nervous that you've lost your head. Do as Gunter says and we're all making it out of here, so there'll be no more asking the trees for help, as much as it pains me to distance my own self from them. Eventually the feeling will return, you just have to wait, is all."

However, through them there came a sudden shudder, along with it the feeling of something approaching, an imminent doom that none could see from where was it coming. Left, right, above or below, none could tell but all could hear the thumping in their own chests as the desire to run filled them, for something felt very wrong indeed.

"What was that?" Zelda asked, wide eyed.

Peter's hands were crawling up the sides of of his head to his ears again.

"Oh no."

They were all backing up together into a bunch as Gunter commanded everyone to move. He took the lead and made sure to grab onto Peter, with one arm to stop him fleeing on his own while unsheathing his sword with the other.

"Stay together. We may have stumbled into some trap or alerted some foul host of evil and darkness. We must go forward from this place. Quickly now."

Everybody broke into a run as to whatever approached they did not know but they could feel it around them as much as they could a rumbling at their feet. Then the ground itself burst and from it spilled forth bones of people right out from under them and all around. As they emerged the ground surged up around those bones to clad them in a body of foul dirt and earth. Some others rose from nothing but the ground itself, twisting into the shape of a person so that they had arms and legs to use.

Whether bone or ground, their empty eye sockets stared while their hands reached out grasping at the group or holding weapons long bent, rusted in the elements.

Zelda pulled out her sword and turned to Gunter.

"There was a great battle here and I was going to ask whatever happened to those fighting. But now I know, they were never put to rest, they never moved on, they never left."

"Oh the people are quite gone, whatever residual command called forth the demons with their fire has brought forth all these dead. They take their orders from the behest of a dead master who is alive no more, one who has certainly even met the same fate while bound to their own words to rise with no rest or pause considered. This place truly is a stain on the world, to be a habitat for such things should never be."

"We need that spirit more than I thought, so that places such as these can be brought back to whatever they were before. I can't see us doing that alone."

"Quite so. Don't feel bad about cutting these ones down if you must but remember your whereabouts and do not waste your energy. We're not here to defeat these mindless shells compelled to rise on the remains of past orders. Now will you stop complaining?"

He had turned to talk to Peter, who was beginning to look ill. He had the shakes and there was sweat beading on his face.

"They are so angry." Peter said.

"What could they be angry about?" Zelda asked.

A clang of metal meant she did not get a response as to distract Peter any further or even herself might prove deadly. Everyone fought their way into a ditch that turned out to have been a road that they saw winding off into the distance.

Weary of being surrounded they all knew they could not stay for long as the dead moved in. In fact, now that she noticed, it appeared to be that they would move closer to whoever it was that had the torch.

Gunter too watched it being passed from person to person and suddenly came to a realisation.

"The fire, they come for the fire! Discard the torch, be done with it and carry on in the night."

So Survel threw away the torch away from the group, which drew away the attention of some of the dead, until the torch was taken and covered by many such hands of earth sprouting from the ground and piling on top of it.

Yet still there were others who pursued with empty eyes. Seeing this, Zelda tried calling upon the ground beneath her but found she could not, there was simply a pit of hunger in her stomach and a weakness as if suddenly she hadn't eaten for weeks. That sapped her of strength and made her stagger, being caught at her shoulders before she fell by Findal and Nasker who heaved her forward to keep her moving as strength in her legs returned.

The path ahead was blocked as more of those dead crawled out of the ground in front of them and they had to make a right turn up the remains of a staircase. The floor at the top of the staircase had fallen away to a pit ringed by the collapsed circular wall of the building. It stood above them while down below there was a way out, an arched exit being spied from the left side. Down into that hole they all went while Findal was the last to jump down and was battering their pursuers at bay even as more piled up the steps.

A small deluge of bodies piled into the room just as everyone had made it out and back to the road on the other side. This road they followed along for what felt like a very long time indeed, defending themselves from the occasional dead that had risen up in front them, including one that had quite rudely gotten a hold of Zelda's legs with a grip hard enough to rip into her calves until she had smashed the body in half with a crunch. She continued on through the pain, refusing to hobble as she felt blood trickle down to her ankles and eventually a dull throbbing settled in that she found she could manage.

No one stopped until off the left of the road a path twisted that led up to a crude area overlooking the road. There were warped remnants of a spiked metal fence around it and raised slabs of stone. On approaching the entrance the group found the area to be both gated and shut but they helped each other climb over.

Gunter was not happy that they had wandered into a graveyard of all places, despite it being one where there were no more of those fighting dead, who could still be seen out of the corner of everyone's eyes in the shadows beyond the gate.

"What a horrid place to rest. I see there is no choice as the horrible rites and rituals over this hill allow us safety. How terrible that we must rely upon them."

Nasker shook his head.

"Or to rely on anybody. I must say that I haven't said anything up to now, but I'm feeling quite out of sorts myself."

He collapsed on the ground and Survel and Zelda checked on him. He appeared apologetic and even more pale.

"Sorry, it seems to be that my own rest has made me rather susceptible to the evil here. My body wishes to simply keep drawing from the land and I've been struggling to make it stop. I did not suspect me sleeping for so long would turn out to be this problematic, however. At least some barrier does linger in this place, making it much more bearable. Hopefully it won't be too much time before I'm back to my usual sorts as long as some time is spent concentrating on not reaching out so much, at least not here."

Zelda left him and went to look further at the place they had stopped to rest. The twisted paths winding around the graves were ancient and paved in strange stone. There was a lone twisted tree on the furthest side that Gunter sat under and Peter stayed well away from, lingering near the entrance although smartly away from the gate itself.

There was a feeling of being watched from beyond it and no one wanted to have hands and arms grabbing them through the gaps in the bars. Nasker chose to sit on the ground propped up against the gravestones to sleep while Survel reclined on one without care.

Findal was seated on a gravestone overlooking the road they had come. Looking out at the winding road, his face was as emotionless and unmoving as what he sat on, but when approached he let out a sigh and his shoulders slumped.

"Well, I can say I've had hairier encounters with stubborn gatekeepers demanding more than their fair share of coin but this is certainly a first for me and I do not like it. Is anyone else having trouble feeling the world in this place?"

There were nods and murmurs of agreement and his own head joined them.

"That is so, then? It is not just me that feels smothered. What a terrible war it must have been to hinder even us. I detest feeling like a helpless trader again. Sure I have my sword, but a sword is just a sword, nothing more."

Zelda remained thoughtful in her attempt to lift his mood.

"Surely that will fade and we will get to be ourselves again. I felt worse than I thought I would have when I tried magic before and look what happened to poor Peter. The land itself is ill."

"We'll try find somewhere before the next nightfall to rest and perhaps not light a torch when we do so. We're not staying here a moment longer then when the sun comes up." Gunter said.

"An entire kingdom was burned from the world's reach, which need I remind you is that very same sad desolation we now tread through with some way to go."

Zelda was sure nobody seriously would have needed to be told that in order to get up and carry on in the morning. This was the land that a jealous king had sent his foul army of fire and demons to without warning, having his sights on Malleau. Now scattered and barren were his own lands, having suffered little at his own hands, but which belonged these days in small part to Kasynne, with Alegan having gobbled the rest. All so that no one else would have it in their own borders, leaving it as barren as it had been when they claimed it. As for Malleau, hearing the stories was one thing, experiencing the horror with her own eyes and body was something entirely different.

Zelda considered that she wasn't part of the problem of what she saw, yet was able to quite relate with those who had been driven out of the land. There was something else wrong back in Churl, a place she could not call home any more than call this place a part of the world for what it now was.

Gunter had his eyes shut and head bowed as if attempting to sleep. Despite this he continued to speak.

"I think most what was revealed by the devastating fighting here was that some places were waiting for excuses. Far away from this land there was even more fighting, more wars, worse than what you see here. Mountains scoured bare and oceans poisoned. The use of fire was just a convenience for evil, as evil will find a way regardless of the method, it is just one that comes so easy to those who hold the magical power of flame."

"If not for this I wonder if elves and others might be more well spread. With such terrible power could have the elves conquered us all?" Zelda asked.

"Perhaps long ago they did but they were better than those of us who live in the worlds of men with their towers and wealth, they relaxed their hold on the great wide world so that others could have a chance. I for one believe that they chose to give up most of their power and standing willingly, although I don't know why. As for not seeing them around in these times, it is known that Malleau was home to many elves and creatures that would otherwise call the forests and mountains their home. That was a long time ago and from where you have lived the church of Churl has had all the time it needed to purge all sources of them from their more populated places. So of course you would have seen little to no trace, though I must say you have tread too little of the world to be disappointed."

Zelda was glad she had not told any of the others about meeting the elf. She had read depictions of elves where they had seemed to be peaceful and happy folk in the homes that they made for themselves. Judging from the one she had met they did not seem to be bad folk, mischievous and self minded perhaps, but that was not enough to consider them all trouble, especially if they had wished to share in such a land gladly with others as the tales of Malleau had said they had been.

There was no longer any warmth inside her on remembering the pleasant happenings that she had been told or read, for as she looked around she could not help but be reminded of where she was, sitting in the proof that said all of that brilliant light was no more. The light had been stolen from those who had lived in it by its destruction, to be replaced for all people with a precautionary reminder of fire magic, along with one other, she realised, that the true light had only ever been of Churl. The meaning behind words she had once been carelessly apathetic to now cast viciously from her mind.

"Lara had told me that it had been a wonderful place to behold. Not all were guilty of what happened here. An army came to this place and destroyed it, not one full of its own people. It upsets me, wondering what the world could have been, had those who made it out alive been given a chance to speak. But no, they were all implicated and fled and not a single person could say a good word to defend them. Even if they wanted to, as it was a decision made by those pretending to be most high in the verses of the world. The very world itself, so they said, so they lied, demanding that they decide the fate of all things afterwards. However, I suppose Churl is not alone as the pyromancers didn't agree with everyone living together either." She said.

"No, they did not, which is the way it has always been among those who called themselves as such for the longest of times. Not all who have an affinity for fire count themselves among those wicked people, human, elf or otherwise, yet certainly you see what happens when such power that they hold is used in an evil manner. A near unstoppable raging fire, consuming all in its path. We are lucky to live in these times of seeming peace but the balance is tipping too far off the edge and darkness bleeds into the horizon most unwelcome. All things must be surrendered back to nature to keep the world turning with magic and the ways of the world must be a wedge between the senseless fighting in places near and far where they will be glad for our return. The age of greed will come next, otherwise, unless it is swallowed whole."

Findal did not appear to be convinced and he thought to himself of such.

I'm not so sure about that. I'd say it is already here. Even in the north people pick through the coffers of others searching for the gold and elvish ryhm while looking about with sliding eyes.

He looked out at the wastes and the moons up above.

"If that is so then tell me, if the world is destroyed such as this, what is the need for any of it? If I can be honest, that's one reason I'm here. A dead world is not one that cares for anything, but one of life that can have gold and rhym slip through one's fingers, although not perfect by the means and codes by which I now hold myself, is one that I would hold above the darkness. Even as we tear it all down, one piece at a time. I apologise for the grimness but this was just to affirm myself that I am no coward. Sometimes we all need to remind ourselves about what an ideal world might look like, even when we're facing down a future such as this, only one of many horrors."

"Yet it was greed that did this to Malleau, Findal, did this to the whole world which the moons shine down on and even the ones they do not."

"Yes, I know Gunter. But such acts were brought about by a greed of a very different kind than one of wealth. One that would swallow the world or take it all away. In truth I don't think anyone will ever know why the king did what he did, to proclaim himself a demon king, such was the blindness of his want. That is why we do what we must to bring about our vision for the world where we will teach all who live in it a lesson to reject such greed as it has seen, so that all may live in peace. But not peace like this. What one might give for a shovel in these times, or the command of the ground at their feet, to bury all those foul dead. Even if it would never be enough on its own to heal the land, it would be a start."

Indeed they could have had shovels and all the time in the world if all they had to do was put some bodies back in the ground to rest. Just because they could have attempted to do so didn't mean that they should have been expected to do it. All in all they knew it wasn't a problem they could remove from the world, no matter how much it pained them and would doubtlessly pain others after them. Some cursed places remained ever cursed.

If the druids failed in their mission, well, there might not be any particular people who would come after to speak of it. Each one of them could feel the peril, looking up at the turn of the sky above to know that the whole world was slowing and would stop turning eventually then fade away into darkness. The only thing to remain would be echoes of conflicts far greater than the one they found themselves facing as they were not carving their retribution on the world. Those who failed to save it would leave nothing behind. Even after so many years these ruins would outlast them all and it was possible some attempted to find sleep thinking about what it was they could leave behind.

Zelda found herself believing that others would be thankful for the sky above on clearer nights such as this. No one might know of her in the future but to just forget about the world for a moment and look up at the sky was enough. Despite how far she felt she had come, that part of her had not changed. She was still getting used to the sleepless nights and spent time wondering if she would ever, as for her the night was restless, particularly as moonlight shone into her eyes.

She had been unable to sleep a wink, so had spent the time by herself checking on her legs and those angry little wounds on them. While doing so she had discovered something rather strange while toying with the flat stone she had been given, back when everything had seemed idyllic and free of worry.

Blood that had been on her fingers had been disappearing into it. First she had thought it merely porous, yet when pressed against her wounds they had bled out from her all that messy dirt which she had come to worry, due to threat of some lingering curse. And the stone itself seemed unaffected.

She had gone through her wounds slowly because the process stung greatly while removing from her the foul, dark mess amongst the blood until it ran red. Partially in the middle of drawing out these nasties, she stopped and blinked, taking time for a moment to take a look around. It hadn't until then occurred to her that of course someone might be watching with interest. Fortunately no one was, not right now as nearly everyone was dozing or minding their own business so hopefully hadn't been alert when she had been so focussed on it so strongly to not be worried about watchers.

Did she have to worry though? She wondered. Surely someone would have said something about this stone before, or told her about what it was she might be able to do with it in times of need. It hadn't been the first time she had pulled the stone out just to look at it. Then Zelda remembered what the elf had told her some time ago.

An incomplete understanding. Could this be one of those things? Certainly they would say that this stone holds knowledge. Just as the mountains are ours to understand, so too are the streams that travel through them and the far off plains that turn into rushing rivers that lead straight to the great ocean. Which is another place I have not seen. What might this stone do if I threw it into the ocean, or one poisoned as I was told? Maybe it only works on blood, then if that is so I have many questions on the existence of such a thing and Kieke is too far away to answer if she could indeed answer anything at all. Who to ask of this then?

She felt ripples of concern in her belly, worried that if she broached the subject, she might be told off for doing something wrong, very wrong. This didn't feel wrong, there wasn't any evil or malice or darkness carrying in the air that surrounded her. After all the stone didn't seem to be helping her injuries, just getting rid of the blood. Perhaps that was simply the nature of the stone.

I think I should ask someone at a better time than this, when we're not all tired and in need of rest.

Because she did not wish to surrender the stone were she unknowingly doing something wrong, Zelda kept her actions to herself. She herself might come to an understanding of it one day and whenever that would be, she hoped the stone would still be a reminder of what lay ahead to do, not a reminder of what had been left behind.

Despite the vastness of the purple skies above and the stars amongst them, the land beneath it was one without the good murmurs of life, such was the hurt placed upon it. This land really was one with nothing returned to nature, nothing reclaimed by it, but she felt something about Malleau was just waiting for them to help it do so when they were ready.

The strength, the knowledge needed for what that might have been, was something none of them had found or learned as of yet from the words of the world, Zelda knew, or had come to an understanding of that at least. Even those who had lived their lives among such words the longest, Gunter, Survel and Nasker could not have reached within themselves to bring forth the power to do so.

That was because none of them really held anything at all, they just heard the world through the words of nature and the more she thought on it, the more she wondered how much she was actually hearing herself. She looked at the stone and ruminated on her own knowledge, on an understanding of the world incomplete. Which only made her feel sicker to think on it, really.

Chapter Twenty One
Concerns of Those Present

If the days were bright, they were only as so bright as they were grey and there was no warmth to the brightness of those days. Among expanses of grey did everything around the party of travellers fade into each other with uneven angles in the distance, little points of darkness that told of something sticking out of the landscape. Such objects could barely be seen, where once had been perhaps a home. None of them would have been able to tell for sure, as the further in they walked, any ruins they had come close to were the remains of what must have been only the mightiest of foundations.

Not all buildings had been built with foundations such as those so more often than not there was nothing that remained other than vague shapes appearing out of the ground at knee height or lower still, buried under grey dunes.

As they had gradually walked further in, the bleak mounds piled around had become larger and they were trudging through it up to their knees. Sometimes the road would be lost for hours or even days until they found it again, which they looked for only for solid ground and towards that path appearing out from the sloping mounds was where they headed only out of the need to know that their footing was sure.

Because of this the lot of them all too easily began to blend in with the landscape. It got into their clothes, into their hair and worse yet into their minds, as even on days where the light did shine down all they could see into the distance was more of the stuff. Even though each of them had gotten used to the smell, they knew they smelled like the land as well and kicking up settled ground sent forth a fine dust that made them all cough.

Wary of what might lay beneath, they had not made the mistake as they had before and nights had been spent in cold darkness, waiting for the sun to rise where the earliest to awaken would rouse the others and off they would go for the day, some days without food where the sound of unhappy stomachs gurgling would be the only sound from anyone, accompanying their footsteps only until they had walked for much of the day when Gunter would decide that they should stop.

Due to the lack of warmth none of them needed shade, yet here and there they found it in places and ahead of them stood the remains of a great castle and tower brought terribly low where only the base remained. Even with no roof or standing walls, the size of it defied belief as it appeared as a city all to itself, larger even, layers around layers seen within.

They were close enough that they could see through the collapsed walls to see the inner rings and foundation pillars, where at, its stone had melted and blackened. All else left had bleached white like bones of a dead creature. It poked out through the soot and dirt that buried it, a circular spine emerging from those uneven dunes that only a cursed wind would have dared to mould.

Even when the path turned in towards it they all kept themselves at a distance so they were far enough away to not have to fear anything hiding in such ruins, even when the path took them right along beside it so that the wear on the walls from the elements could be seen.

An eerie sight were those sad insides, so that none could have figured out beyond the crudest sense what the shape of it all would have been, such was the way it had been melted and malformed to leave only the barest reminder of a long gone greatness which none of them could do anything for.

Despite having seen it from a distance and having spent quite some time approaching it, getting so close made this a rather sad day, to see such things and on this day the sky had begun to become covered in strips of cloud high above. Those clouds seemed themselves to be on a journey, marching slowly across the sky, endlessly, just as dark and grey as the ground.

At the far north horizon, light shone off them to illuminate their edges in a crimson lining that did not reach to colour the sky above those who could see them so far away. There was no such red in the sky and apart from those clouds they were alone, save for a writhing darkness that hid amongst such clouds and had made itself known again from day to day as it ran across the sky.

That darkness was something they could all see and something they could all feel, but it wasn't as if it was talking to them or ridding them of the barrenness of the place and was gone as quick as it had come each time. It put each of them on edge and kept them to the path that promised to lead them out.

And although there were stories of others who had braved this path, there was no trace found of them or their passage. Considering exactly what it was the party had found, they had not thought it a challenge to understand what might have happened to any particular unfortunate individual who had left to make the trip, perhaps to head low across the mountains then make their way across the sea to the south.

Days had passed like this, with conversations scattered to a few short murmurs amongst two or a few, not whispering though, for there was enough of that when the wind picked up, for it had begun to come, something that might carry the spirits from the ground up to them again.

Some days were days of dourness that passed around from one person to the other. Only the road they walked on told them that they were not walking in circles whenever they had briefly lost sight of the castle ruins as everything began to look the same after a time when it disappeared from view. Days and nights faded into each other and Zelda wondered if such a scene would stretch on forever, until they ran out of food and water and joined the dead.

The world itself did not help them, reaching out to it did nothing but bring confusion and pain to the one who tried, for Zelda did desperately try. No one else voiced their concerns any longer, so neither did she, otherwise others might know that she was still attempting to feel the world. She saw herself in a dark place, after all that she had said herself and been told, the whispers if there were any might be telling her that she was no help at all. There was only the pit in her stomach that began to gnaw more than usual.

She had been taken further on this journey with the expectation that she would aid the people about her in their quest and while she did indeed have some skill at this, some magic she could draw, she felt saddened and moody by how plain she felt.

Where is that magic now? I feel terrible as if having been accused as a liar to be saying to myself that yes, I can feel the land. Instead what is left is me being judged by the land itself that keeps itself silent from me. That ease from before, feeling the turn of the world, has vanished and fled so now I'm left to consider my uselessness again and this knot in my chest does not help. I suppose what that feeling could be is nothing more than the world around me telling me what state it is in. But all I feel is thin and strained, something surely coming right from me and not the land.

Her thoughts were left unsaid and it was best that they were, really. She along with everyone else had been told of the danger and had seen it after all, where one might soak in the sickness of this place. Zelda was just making sure she still could feel. There was something else she could feel brooding among them all, so that she could make up her mind that further exploration on that particular subject of conversation would have been most unwise.

Eventually Survel let out a groan.

"Ah I am sick of wandering in the foul dimness of the day and darkness at night. Not the day nor the night here seem natural to me, as if a layer of the sky has been stripped back ridding this place of its colour while the sun shines, to only reveal the deepness of its tear in the absence of it. For have these not been nights of deepest blue and purple not seen elsewhere?"

Peter nodded.

"Indeed. Don't misunderstand me, for I have found no wondrous sights here, yet I am set to thinking where else I might see a sky such as this."

"I would hope nowhere as tortured as Malleau or anywhere at all of the sort. What I was going to suggest, as it has been rather some time, is that we should light a torch to lighten our spirits somewhat. The dullness hangs from my eyes otherwise and it is all that I see."

Gunter had his brows knitted together.

"Hmmm, you could create another problem I do not want to repeat, my friend. One that I am sure will come if we are not careful. But you make a good point, for my eyes themselves are tired, peering around while seeing nothing good and proper and all of it dull, as you say. Also, the wind blows here, so I suggest later, only when we can be sure of a night's sky that is clear, that we attempt this. For I do not wish to be running from more fiendish things into a night that is dark and overcast where we would certainly stumble about when not being able to see and potentially be taken."

With that settling into their minds and with some trepidation, preparations were made and as the blue began to appear in the sky an unlit torch was passed around. Everyone had a hand in inspecting it and holding it to check for anything untoward about the object which in the end they could not find. So it was judged that to raise the mood and hopefully not more of those terrible dead they would light the torch.

The skies were becoming more clouded but there peaking through were still the moons that began to shine down as the daylight dipped. They were all ready to sacrifice water if it was needed to douse the flames and run as Survel set about to striking stones and lit the torch as all waited and listened. The whispering stayed low, not rising to the heights that it had before. They all breathed a sigh of relief, Zelda especially. She did not want to be running at all.

"Are we in luck here?" She said.

Gunter appeared happy.

"We appear to be most fortunate. Or rather, where we were before must not have been the best place to light a torch. Maybe there is less of a problem with lighting our way here, as where before the spirits of the dead were restless, here not so much."

Nasker was eyeing off the torch, rubbing his jawline in an unease that creaked into his voice.

"We can't say that we're further away from the battlefield. So close to the castle tower ruins as we are we're quite in the thick of it, as all throughout was there much fighting, I was told. Here amongst the ruins more might have sheltered and gone to their peace but I'm worried they're not at rest just the same."

Ahead of them off the road there came an echoed laugh that came up from the ground. The voice sounded like an old man, old and cracked from long years.

"Oh yes, someone has the right idea to be cautious."

Coughing came from behind half buried bars of a dark cell, hidden in shadow and devoid of moonlight.

Gunter motioned for everyone to stop and took a step off the path.

"Is someone there? Speak, if you will."

He turned back to speak to the others in a low voice, although it still carried fairly far away.

"Such a clear voice could only be one of evil. I did warn you about what we might find here and this could be one such instance of trickery best avoided."

The voice laughed again.

"Evil? You would speak of evil as coming from me, Otis, as if I were the one to sunder this world and scar it deeper than you could possibly fathom?"

The voice laughed a little more then breathed in deeply to as if to take in the air.

"That burning I smell, unmistakable as the flame of Illit, is it truly among you?"

Gunter spoke gruffly.

"None here can speak of Illit, so I aught to say that you are mistaken. None of us are pyromancer slaves to either them or their Houses. We are druids, I say, not vessels for wretched power."

"Ohohoho, lovers of the land are we? Where do you run when the land spurns you? Tell tell, I must know, as there are those on the edges of this desolation who know the hardness, nay, the truth, of living off the land. No fanciful lure nor whimsical coaxing could improve the lustre of these here fields nor the ones that border with the north. And when they first failed, lo and behold, they ran from this land. As for druids being here, what can I say?"

His laughter drawled on the back of shaking breath.

"Ha! One could say that those of Illit are more welcome here then any druid! Keep yourselves to yourselves if it would suit you, if you would then pretend to be druids and not of that most open, most charitable House. If you would keep to your lie of your hearth born heritage then free me, to assure yourselves passage most *unaffected*."

His dripping voice, rolling into laughter that wheezed out in the dark rid them of any silence there might have been.

Findal was shaking his head.

"A difficult customer, one who does not know how to ask properly for what he wants. We're all covered in this dirt, perhaps that is what he means to say by the smell, although I find it strange that loyalty to fire would be recognisable by smell of all things."

"We could make use of one more lookout during the nights. Getting ambushed again would not be wise. Yet his sneer might draw them to us." Gunter said.

The voice calling himself Otis laughed at this.

"Oh yes, such wise thoughts are the hallmark of the druid. They must be maintained. And I can help, for I am very wise, although not enough perhaps to prevent my incarceration, but enough to prevent execution."

It was clear from his reply that Gunter was entertaining the thought of proving the voice wrong, for to provoke him was not a wise thing to do at all.

"I look for neither, you talkative fool. I tell you what, we shall let you loose, but that will be enough accursed talk. We still have swords and may be glad to accomplish what others could not if you irritate us so or dare to cross us."

Zelda stood in front of the bars.

"Can we not begin to threaten people? Freeing the man should have been a priority, regardless whether or not he calls us whatever it is he likes. There's some horrible people out there who would lock someone up and leave them to die in this place, wouldn't you agree? Besides, there are no others to listen to his words that he could convince saying we're anything other than who we ourselves say we are. Indeed we are all who we say we are."

"You seem rather keen to have him along."

"Well I-"

She stopped for a moment in thought. She didn't have a clear reason why, just that every other scenario that came into her head left with the old man dying and she didn't think he deserved that, no matter how harsh his tongue. In the end she shrugged.

"I just think it is important to have him along. Also think on what would happen if we freed him and he just followed along with us. Would we really stop him?"

Nobody answered her question but she had a sneaking suspicion that swords would be pointed.

Everyone came closer as one to the dark and shadowy cell and they saw that the voice did indeed belong to an old man. He was emaciated, wearing no more than rags and he had a beard and hair of a white stained black that were so long while he so short, both could have been used as clothing. He spoke casually while Gunter and Survel ripped out the ancient bars and moved on to checking his chains.

"Oh yes, from here on you will be fine if you venture west. From this side of the ruins of the great castle, people have come far down and found the places where ones such as myself are now locked up, with the key then thrown away along with their minds."

"Is that what happened to you?" Zelda asked.

"Yes, of course. Now, as you said, let me go freely so that I might help you all on your foolish task as thanks."

Peter had been watching everything unfold with a bad feeling about the lot of it. He knew he could not have met the man before but there was a familiarity in his voice that struck a cord. Or rather his mind was telling his something was familiar, but he wasn't sure what.

Maybe I'm hearing my own words back to me. I had better not turn into him when I'm older. Perhaps I should start watching what I think. When life starts to go the way I want will I be able to change my tune so quickly? I'm seeing a terrible mirror into a possible future here but oh let this place not mirror anything of the sort I might see in those future days. There must be a way of best avoiding all that and I shall work towards that end most rightly.

It then occurred to him that he was on a mission to do exactly that. Only because it wasn't his mission with him in the lead had he not given it any thought. Just because this was not of his making did not mean that he should discard it. In fact, on thinking on it, what he set out to do with the others was absolutely the best way of going about it, which was every reason to give it his all.

After striking at the chains binding the old man, Otis came free and was dragged out of the cell. He rubbed his wrists where the heavy iron manacles dug into them.

"Now should we all get moving? I tell you that this road is the right and true path which leads from one side of Malleau to the other. Not all the way but close to the forests. Is this where you might be going or dare I guess, further on?"

Gunter appeared to be annoyed with this new raspy figure tagging along, his hands on his hips.

"We go where we go and you just follow without causing a fuss."

"Of course, there's nothing else for me say against such words as your own. I've been caged for so long, all I wanted was to do was finally have a conversation."

Zelda eased him away from Gunter. She wasn't feeling guilty at releasing the old man but was weary of being the one who would be blamed for bringing this irritation upon them all.

"Then listen to your words and understand why you might be gagged. Learn to keep some silence about yourself, especially concerning pyromancy, where you should not joke or take lightly such things. Your words certainly begged to be silenced." She said.

Otis shrugged.

"Easy, girl. I know well my own faults and failings thank you very much. I'm sure you should focus on your own."

But there were doubts in the minds of the druids as to why he should be trusted as there had to have been a reason for him to be locked away and for others to make the journey solely to do so.

Nasker spoke to him as they made their way along the road, where the ruins rolled downwards and they could tell that the land was changing, becoming firmer and more packed in.

"Tell us about the people who locked you away old man."

"About them there is little to be said." He wheezed.

"They are as any folk with poor tempers and manners that you have likely ever known. A whisper of words passing around is all it can take for the many to persecute the few as they lack resolve. And listen as I say this. Despite my words, you must be thankful for what knowledge you have received that put resolve in your heads and not let the impulses or words of one take sway, no matter how they might try to convince you. Otherwise you will end up chasing glory for the rest of your life with nothing to show for it. Success is judged by others, you can convince yourself that it is not, but sometimes what you want is not the best for everyone else. Nor will it be what you shall be remembered for."

So it was that they went along as far as they could into the night before finding a spot to camp. Even with apparently no need to, they found a ruin they could barricade themselves in. Otis snorted upon seeing this.

"What use is my advice if you will not listen?"

I should explain this to him before he he causes trouble. Zelda thought.

"It is not that we do not listen to you, merely that this is the way we have been sleeping over the past few days and being so close to the other side we would very much like to keep ourselves alive and that includes not taking chances if they can be helped."

Zelda had found herself attached to Otis, because everyone else seemed to have decided that the best course of action was to simply ignore the old man's raving, where she was doing her best to be polite and keep paying attention to him. It was almost like dealing with a little child, so it wasn't such a hard task to keep him entertained with small talk or by answering his questions when no one else would.

He keeps questioning us, however. So it sounds as if he doesn't trust us either. Zelda thought.

And what was all that talk of pyromancers? All rather worrisome if I do say so. I wouldn't want to find myself caught up in that. Being around here now, I'm sure it won't come back to descend on us, there's nothing to burn here after all, nothing to hurt but ourselves. That might be enough for someone evil though.

She took a look around where they all rested. The remains of the walls were shallow but the floor on which they sat was a stone base with pillars sticking up from it and all of them could sleep together around them without worry, taking it in turns to watch as they usually did.

Zelda spent her time on watch looking down at the ground next to her while playing with her sword without a sound. She hoped to be done with this place and at least trust the ground at her feet again soon without having a vision of a skeletal hand rising from the depths to snatch her away, which the sword was helpful for but she knew it couldn't help her when she went to sleep.

She just had to imagine that enough so when she did sleep it would hopefully appear she was as useful in her dreams or nightmares. All rather childish by her own admittance because nothing really was the same in dreams. That being considered, she had to admit that the old Zelda never dreamed that she would have ever found herself on night guard duty practising any sort of enjoyable swordplay in a place such as this whatsoever.

Chapter Twenty Two
The Pyromancer

A single torch burned on the broken pillar to which it had been strapped. Even though it occasionally crackled, almost everyone was sound asleep, finding small shadows behind other pillars to sleep in or cover their heads from the moonlit glare. The torch had just been there in case it became dark, yet with the moons so high in the sky it did little other than cast shadows around them. Merely a single spot of orange in a sea of blue, so small and weak, where the moons would still remain even after that light was gone.

Nasker looked around the ruin in which they all sat to make sure that everyone was asleep. He was supposed to be on watch but did not doubt the old man's words saying they would be safe. Tonight of all nights this was most fortunate, as he had been getting closer to a familiar glow each day and did not want to miss his opportunity to wander off on a search while unobserved.

He quietly left the camp behind and stepped back onto the road. Crossing it to the other side, there was a brief incline which then dropped back down to give a view of the fields to the west of the castle ruins, stretching north and west far into the distance.

While the fields themselves were reasonably flat, in the moonlight there were plenty of places to hide in the shadows. There were ditches and buried trenches and holes to hide away in as well as the same rubble and remains everywhere littered about that cast all kinds of shadows, dark patches against the blue grey.

Carefully looking over the landscape, the glaring light shining off the stone ruins made it harder to see, but there was someone here. He knew because he could feel them, as that burning glow was now close, one faintly letting anyone who could tell know that they were there. Intentional or not, he thought it was foolish of whoever it was, because that meant he could find them.

If he stood where he was for too long he knew that someone might spot him, so Nasker set off down the other side of the slope leaving him out of sight from the road and focussed on that flicking flame of a person unseen.

Where are you and why are you here?

He asked this to whoever it might be, even though no one could answer him.

Why anyone would reside in this failed disaster or even just choose this as a place to hide, he couldn't fathom. There were far better places to do so, unless you couldn't trust yourself.

With no one in sight, he looked through ruins and explored the remains of archways, partially filled in holes and the downward sloping leftovers of hallways leading to nowhere. These places would have once been grand entrances to judge by their tiled pattern flooring, some of which were scattered about and shattered even if most of the floor and the pattern was buried.

The search led him on to what would have once been winding irrigation channels, all filled in and useless. So all they resembled now were rows of trenches, some with bits of rock or even metal sticking out of them that had been revealed over the years. If he was not careful about where he stood he might find his feet sinking down where something sharp might stab him.

He continued to follow the glow and found it was coming from somewhere around a mound close by, where a retaining wall in some small part remained and he approached quietly. Nasker knew he was getting closer and closer, but the feeling was not quite so exact as to know exactly where they would be. Some magics never were precise, flowing around people, not to them, and the source was just one small part of those magics that never stopped moving.

A sudden crumbling noise came from below and he quickly turned to look down as there, curled up in one of those ditches was a young woman covered head to toe in layers of dirt and not much else besides. They turned to look up at him and he looked down upon them with disdain.

"I didn't think I was going to find what I was after but I'm still disappointed."

At the very least she could speak a reply, her voice thin, parched and cracked.

"Disappointed with me, you mean? Didn't think I would come across another of us so soon. Well, who be you?"

"I? Yes, a clueless peasant would ask. I am Nasker, House Illit."

She trembled as she curled back into a ball.

"You name does not travel, Nasker, but have you come to kill me?"

He sneered.

"Not a chance. Look at you, you're pathetic. As you are now, getting rid of you would truly be a waste of my time. For that matter, get out of dirt and put some clothes on, you're a disgrace to your House."

"I can't."

He let out a sigh most exasperatedly and crouched down to offer his hand. He felt he had been displeased enough and he relaxed as he forcibly put aside his frustration so that he could concentrate, it wasn't like himself to stay that way for very long anyway.

Tentatively the woman took it and he pulled her out of the ditch, after which she simply stood stark naked, there dead eyed in her depression. Those eyes were light green and her hair might have been a significantly less dirty blonde but it was hard to tell with the state she was in.

He took off his cloak and threw it over her shoulders, which he then shook lightly.

"Dirt isn't clothing, so you're probably feeling better already. Let's just go sit over here together, look at the sky for a bit. I really would like to have a chat. Especially with that House Nalla smell on you. You're one of their girls."

He led her over to a hill where the two could sit with their backs against the few remaining stones the made up a piece of the retaining wall. The two watched the quiet night with the twin moons hanging in the sky. She sighed, her breath coming out as a white mist as the night became colder.

They were all being blamed for this. For them to be targeted was easy enough. People had not forgotten the war and each House had not forgotten the crimes of the others, so of course they had been picked apart and hid their practices in secret.

Places such as this hid many secrets and she had hoped that it would have hid herself. That hadn't worked out for her so well. She adjusted the jacket about herself and warmed her hands with a brief puff of flame.

Nasker gestured out into the distance.

"Done anything worth your time here?"

The woman shook her head.

"Not much. Just dreaming I suppose. Nothing like the real one though, where there will be a world where only we chosen to hold the fire will live to rule. A fire will rise and in the wake of the coals left behind from the discarded wastes of the old world will a new world be built, as all else crumbles into useless nothingness. The dream leaves me warm and fuzzy inside, but as you see me here, I falter."

"Why should any of us stand by in this retched place and let people go on with their ways? They won't even have to cry for what they've lost. You don't have to worry, no one will remember anything that you did. So why not be you? Stop being ashamed of yourself and show the world what you are."

She shuddered.

"I am *not* ashamed. I feel it too, of course. The fire is in every step I take and every waking moment, it's inescapable."

"You certainly can't run and hide from it. So don't try to."

Both gazed above as the sky convulsed and glazed over with blackness, the pulse sounding of a diseased heart, but that great black stain that was there and then gone was something neither wanted to worry about, even if they knew they had to do something and stand against it. The world beyond didn't seem to be ready to want to make that choice and it would be too late with all the infighting and the words of many a fearful council, kingdom or church to stand and attempt to convince the masses.

Saying what they said and doing what they did was not endearing themselves to many who thought to know the right ways of the world. In secret they all had to show what little good those ways were. Growth in their ranks was slow, so slow it was painful, but they would do what they must with what they had.

The woman broke the silence some time after the darkness had left, staring at the moons.

"All I needed- no. I only needed some time alone, however long that might be. But that can't be all I need. The fire is always here with me as you said so I need some outward focus or it will spill over. Now I'm no speaker for my House asking ancient House Illit for help but we made up our own rules and went off on our own. You know what it did to us wild bunch of blazing amateurs, who got what was coming for us for thinking we could handle it. I'm scared because I just don't know if I can handle it myself. We're so new but there's already not much of Nalla left."

"There weren't many of you to begin with. My advice would be to go take what you have and do something with it. Make use of your gift to destroy the world. This world that should not be is waiting for its death and we, all of us, most of us, shall rise above it and be the rightful rulers of Auralin when it is new. Don't waste your time sleeping now, or you might just miss your chance and die, or wake up with no standing in the new world whatsoever. Tell that to all your lost sisters. Isn't that what you all wanted?"

It should be. You all made a pretty big mess in the Ruthlands. Yes, that's the resolved look I want to see appearing back on your face. Much better. Much more pleasant to look at.

She certainly appeared to have calmed somewhat, checking her own breathing, her voice steadier as she stared up, eyes hardened yet still searching above for something even he didn't know. The sky above was a deep purple blue so clear beyond the clouds, a great polished stone with pieces of amber gold caught inside around those two silver moons, all reflected in her eyes as she spoke.

"I want to live. I want to live in a new world, to which the old one we shall have delivered death from the burning within our hearts. We all do. The only ones we have to trust in are ourselves after all, to pick up the pieces of whatever remains of the old world and make something of it new."

"We'll have the first spark of light and be moving before anyone else notices. They won't even have a chance to say a word against us before it will be too late. Then everything will be as we've all wanted. Now go play your part and put yourself to use."

"What part might that be? If you think you're going to drag me along with whatever little scheme Illit have going on the side then you can forget about it."

Nasker smiled.

"Who says I'm scheming, Nalla girl? Spread the word amongst the others to remind them all, not just your own, to ready themselves."

"I have a name, but who indeed. I also think that towards me the others may not be so cooperative."

"Maffer and Sharnal can fight amongst each other as much as they like but they will see it in themselves to come around or they will be left behind."

"Understood then."

Nasker watched over the dead landscape in silence, seeing the moons travel further across the sky. The land should have been at peace, but it was not. Here had come some horrible example of their power and with it, a darkness which they all refused to run from. Even if the responsibility should not have been their own, they had no choice as the world began to chill. A world that was alive, that was all he wanted.

He looked over at the other one, who seemed to be deep in thought.

As for this one, I'm just thankful that at least House Nalla seems to be in agreement. If the others must fight and lose themselves in their own bickering then we shall see what needs to be done after the new world is assured.

"I suppose you're wondering if the new world would look anything like this and I can't say that it will. I also can't say that it won't. Best not take guesses at the unknown. Everyone who does is either a liar or a fool and I should know, I'm surrounded by plenty of both."

"And yet you travel with such people. The mighty fall, don't they?"

"Hardly. I am aware others would suggest I end them all now and be done with it."

She giggled at that.

"You can include me in along with those others. I don't know what's gotten into the world but it really is a sad state becoming sadder by the day."

"I find myself curious about what those tree huggers are doing. There's something you all need to know. Their link to the world and the very core of their magic has vanished some years ago, leaving them crippled and weak. That is what they say they search for but I have a feeling I'm walking into something more than they are letting on to me. I carry on with them for as they search I too search for something our own plans may hinge on. It is more of a guess but if I fail or am too late all our power could be taken out right from under us even as our future is realised. I can't stand by and rely on others as darkness approaches and that possibility looms."

"What is it you seek?"

"I've told you enough valuable information already. If I tell you any more and you are captured whoever does so might torture the information out of you."

"You could always do away with me afterwards and save yourself the trouble if you need to get it off your chest, that is if you think I would simply reveal you to them." She smiled sadly.

Nasker remained tight lipped.

"No I will not tell you even though I could do both of those things. Leaving another one of us alive is more important. One of us is all we would need to avert the greater risk, letting everything fade away from the cold that creeps up in the dark."

"Best all is gotten over and done with in fire so we can go back to being where we should rightfully be, on top of the world. That was all well before my time. I wonder what being on top of the world will feel like?"

Nasker did not answer. He was probably running out of time before someone would wake up and did not have long before he needed to get back to the camp and that was more a pressing thought at this moment. He nodded and got up, leaving the woman where she sat to recoil in his sudden movement.

There were twinges of a hopeful smile on the edges of her face.

"So you're going to leave me alone and move on without telling me why you're here?"

"Consider it a gift in decency. So that you know what decency is, certainly not anywhere around this place. But think on how much you really hate this place, Nalla girl. I can't burn it to the ground, but you, now you might just have the feel for it were you to try. Do what you do best out there. Or not, it's up to you."

With that he left her there wondering only briefly how long she might stay, but he never looked back to check.

When he sneaked into camp he noticed Zelda's eyes looking up at him. Although they were peering without harsh suspiciousness he rather wished she wasn't curiously staring at him at all.

"Hmmm, that darkness in the sky woke me up. I do hope that I'll be able to get back to sleep as I thought I had tired myself out enough earlier in the night. Did you lose your jacket walking around?"

"I did lose it but don't worry about it, I was the one who lost it after all. There are still those that would rise from the ground out there. You must be careful not to let them grab you, so do not wander too far, if you must at all."

"Everyone is saying that."

"Because it is good advice. Even I should listen to such advice, as you can see."

"What about the advice that says people should rug up in the cold?"

"Don't worry about me getting cold, that's a funny thing to say. After all we'll be moving about soon enough and be quiet warm then. Don't you worry about a thing. I've got everything sorted out myself."

Chapter Twenty Three
The Ghosts of Malleau

The mornings were still rather early and they all did rise early, as all knew that they were closing in on the final days ahead and were waking earlier in anticipation of it. Because of that none had slept well recently, even were it so that the empty eyes and moaning which had previously been seen and heard had left ever since Otis joined them. Days had been made without distraction but despite that they were still careful of where they laid their feet, for shadows still clung to the dark recesses of ruins, calling for caution and sharpness of their senses.

None had spoken this particular morning, as while accustomed to waking and rousing at a pace, the disruption to the nights left them wanting more and wishing that they could fall back off to sleep. To rest in such a place for too long would doom all else, so a determined hurriedness possessed them long into each day as the shadows thinned out and faded, if only to reveal more of the dreaded scene that remained. Their vision drowned in the grey, one the rest of the world would become were they to fail although not from such fiery means.

They could not look into the sky for relief of it during the day, they could not even shut their eyes for the smell of it, of a fire being put out after having burnt something foul. All in all it was clear now much more for having experienced it why few would speak of what was found here. They could not turn back, so what else could they do but walk on and trust that the end was approaching where again they could be among a world of life?

Zelda was doing her best not to be distracted by the burning torches they carried, as from the time they showed the ground fire once again she had been anticipating more fighting.

So it was that she turned to the others with a question she felt had to be asked.

"Have any of you felt this way before coming here? Our magic is faint and near the fire I feel apprehensive. Yes the flame is warm yet still feel tired all the time and am becoming cold. This is a fair bit of solemn motivation of what the worst to come might look like. I just don't understand why it is effecting me this way if it is only me."

Much more could be learned if the ground opened itself to me, but still it is closed off, dreadfully. We might be fine where we stand together but I can't help but want to make sure I'm not falling behind.

Gunter stroked his beard.

"It should be all of us but you appeared to be taking this better than how it really must be, if you are having trouble. All the more reason for us to make more speed. Come, we must use these early daylight hours to cross what is left of this land quickly. That stain on it will otherwise stain ourselves yet in the end I shall hear no burdensome moaning for having come this way from any of you."

This left Zelda wondering if as a group they could have been more of use had they gone up north and around, where they might have found themselves in company of those needing their words and assistance. As it was she felt wasted in a place that in its current state had no use for them and what they could do. Of course there was the danger of being caught, the certainty of which she was not sure she could judge appropriately with what it was she knew.

However she could have done without feeling the way she did, having her usefulness being drained away from her in such a manner. Treated poorly by the land for using it, even. No disapproving words or gestures, just the silent, wordless judgement of the ground at her feet.

Then again, someone else had caused this to happen to Malleau and it had been that someone who had gone about destroying the land and those who lived on it, not her. Despite this, Zelda felt that she herself had been targeted while the land was judging those in the future by the actions of the past. It wasn't her fault, but she could feel the guilt inside, eating her up.

This was home for someone once. No longer is it so. I seem to just be afraid of such places. A home that no longer is. If we fail here how far would I have to go before finding somewhere else, or will all places know me as one who failed? Just like in Churl I'm running scared, even if I've done nothing wrong. It is as I thought, not being known I don't mind about. Me, I would be happy as long as my name is not known for taking away someone's home, or failing to bring one back, either. I wonder how many people there are who's names are forgotten once they have been locked away? And how many names might we not know because their lives were brought to nothing here in Malleau, to be forgotten and never spoken again?

From what she knew, all that had been desired from that king and his army of demons was the destruction of all things and much had been done to further turn the world down the path of a death which was all that remained here. The king had succeeded to tear at this land and people wanted to forget, so almost no one came and those who did regretted doing so very much.

The curse on this land almost felt designed to spite them, a deathly calm over everything with a desire to keep it that way and shut out those who were the keepers of the ground and stewards of the sky. If that king had known it would effect them so, what had they feared in the palm of a druid?

She wondered at this and it only made her resolve that much brighter against the silence that intended to choke her with its burning hands around her neck, so she imagined. Her own hands could have wrung the necks of those who would do such harm to the world and to others.

I certainly don't want my journey to end as a corpse doing the bidding of some dead master. As long as I've got these hands I'll use them to undo the suffering of others. Even if I have to forget about all of this for a bit, put it in the back of my mind and return to it later. There's nothing I can do now, that much has been made abundantly clear.

It suddenly occurred to Zelda that it seemed to be a suitable request to ask a spirit. If they could ask, that was, then surely it wouldn't be too much. If they could do such miraculous things when returned to its rightful place she could imagine asking for such a thing. She'd beg if she had to. Lara had told her never to beg for things but she had been unable to help it from time to time when she was younger.

Maybe she would think of other requests in the future that would be better, but for the moment this seemed not at all too selfish. A more selfish request could wait until after she understood more about the world. She found herself happy in knowing that each and every step forward in this dead land contributed to a world that wasn't dead and desolate at all.

There were still shadows and always would be and here in each and every one she imagined the same enemy that would face them, skeletons with flesh of grit that slid over bones. That was the end that came to those who had fallen so long ago where the ground would not allow them to rest. Tainted so it was that evil dripped from it, commanding the dead to rise on long gone words spoken to bring forth an army from the ground, they had to remember that it had all been coaxed into being by fire.

Survel listened to her concerns as she voiced them.

"The master to such foul beings has certainly fallen and out here amongst them he would share in their fate, joining his work without mind or purpose to shamble and ensnare those who might dare walk these lands, yet we must walk them. To stray from these lands into the north where those lands of torment and capture reside? No, we stay on this path and escape a fate worse than death ourselves."

Peter could only shake his head.

"Really now. I should think that joining these would be a fate far worse than death as at the least we may escape from such places. To become a foe to friends and a most awful one at that."

"Oh no, if we fall here we shall not rise, but die painfully and fall away forever from the world. So perhaps you are right but at the same time, many purposeless souls have lost their way along this road and I know that we are far from aimlessness or purposelessness and shall not so easily fall into despair here as long as we keep moving. Ridding this land of those who first commanded the dead to life would do little, for they no longer hold any sway over their magic."

"True, but suddenly knowing that doesn't make me feel any better."

Zelda was listening to them talk.

Peter has a point but he didn't have to make his own opinion in the way he does. Well then I suppose he wouldn't be Peter then. At least he seems to be back to normal. As much as I would like to see him change I don't think he would have deserved it come at the cost of being scarred by this place. But then I don't know what's going on in his head.

"I had always thought it to be bad memories as to why none went through these lands." She said.

"And ghosts, but it is much more than that. It is a shame that this land is so corrupted and foul as a war should not stop the survivors from living in their own lands."

Gunter seemed to unstick his jaw to speak, unless it had clenched up due to the sound of Peter's voice, which wouldn't have surprised her.

"Of those who remained, many went north and perhaps east into those lands beyond Churl, but even that is a small number of people as you can imagine. It is almost too much space for so few. Almost makes me wonder what would have happened were others to fight over the land were it not so cursed nor had fallen so far. Then again, those who fought the demonic creatures scraped up from the land itself did not truly come home, so it is said. Those few who held lines while the Demon King was taken care of were never the same."

"There were never many who spoke about it back in Churl." Zelda said.

Peter would not be silenced.

"I wonder why? Ah, I know, most likely because most of those brought up to serve were not from Churl to begin with, they were the ones who only sent their dogs afterwards to pick up as much as they could. I wonder what they did with all those towns along the mountains they claimed up to the north? We were going to head that way before we got detoured."

Zelda decided it best she say nothing on that particular reminder.

Are you still going on about that Peter? Am I that much of a problem to you?

Zelda didn't terribly mind being the focus of Peter's moods because the whole thing was rather silly to her.

"Aren't any of you going to help me out here?" She gestured at Peter.

Findal shrugged.

"If I don't see him I don't have to think about him."

She pulled a frown and pouted, trying to copy that sad man's behaviour down to the slouch.

"But it almost seems as if he doesn't want me here."

Peter shook his head.

"I don't mind you being here." He said.

Zelda broke her act and laughed, which hurt as her empty stomach hated the movement.

"Well, we should all be happy you're completely back to normal. That's all that matters."

I wonder why he doesn't mind? Oh well, I don't think now is the best time for me to press him on that, either.

Everyone seemed to be ignoring her silliness, which was fine by her. Everyone but the old man, that was, who was peering at her rather irritably.

Old people sure can have an odd sense of humour. I don't see the harm in lifting the mood, or at least trying to do so. It is best we knew if one of us was out of sorts on the inside, after all.

Over a hill they all went and there on the horizon they could see a line, left to right, that carried as far as they could see. The very land ahead of them was sunken and here again were more of these white trees, twisted and many stone ruins snaked their way throughout them.

Zelda looked to Peter but found his face to be emotionless, trying not to look at the trees, instead looking far into the distance. She wondered if he could hear anything, or if these ones really were silent and was hoping that when they came to the forest and left this place, that those trees would not be silent, as she wanted very much to be able to get better at hearing them herself.

Off into that distance Peter looked, it might have been green if they were closer but from this distance she could not be sure. It did however look an awful lot like a line of trees and every body spent some time admiring the view, even the old man.

Zelda looked behind her.

Behind in the far distance where the land sloped downwards, a ring of white, broken ruined seemed to glisten.

Gunter turned back and he appeared sad.

"So there it lay, where the elves and many of those who were peaceful lived. You wanted to learn and know more about the world, now you know what the war did as you have seen it. There once it was, the great land and city. Not as great as that other city in the north for which the elves are known, mind you, but great none the less as its sister. Being so close made it easy prey for twisted minds back then, now it's left alone to just fade away. I can't think of how close we are to seeing off the world with such a similar fate. Indeed I do not wish to think on it."

He sighed.

"Well let us move on and soon we will be in the presence of better sights that are not surrounded by evil and greed."

Otis pushed his way between the two of them.

"Now now, don't get your words and thoughts all muddled. All about you here is a testament not to greed but the folly that comes from power, similar in the way you cling to yours. You seem to be doing well without it, for it appears that all it gives you is suffering. There would have been no jealousy from that demon summoning king without it."

Zelda spoke again before Gunter had a chance to do so.

"But surely the king saw and wanted what others had and was jealous?"

Otis shrugged.

"If all he wanted was more power, then why didn't he stop after getting it? Why come here and do all this?"

He gestured around himself.

"For that matter why did he travel east after doing so, not west? Answers from him I will never have. Now shiver at the thought of what could have become of your forest home. I know the answer even without him to tell me. There's nothing in the forest, meaning there's nothing he could have wanted from there. Ahh that it could still be the case, who's to know, who's to know?"

They kept walking along the road and in the distance spied little blue dots which were like light blue flames that steadily moved around. Getting closer they took on much more familiar shapes.

"I see people." Zelda said.

"Ghosts." Gunter said thoughtfully.

Zelda was happy to not have to see any more of those ground creeping dead. Her legs still ached and did not want to go through that again.

"These look much more pleasant then what we've been dealing with. I wonder if we can talk to them?" She said.

Otis shook his shaggy head.

"These are the souls that linger on, whereas before might have been only puppets, here we have proof that some are not at rest."

Gunter nodded in agreement.

"Yes and we shall do our best to leave them alone. Linger too long in places like this and it does things to you, to say nothing of surrounding yourself with ghosts. Those with nowhere to go don't wind up as starving pilgrims at some church, they come to places like this and do not leave it. Maybe not here exactly but you understand what I mean. Lost people are drawn to lost places and in the end both die together. We must not fail. We will stop this fate from falling on all people along with the world and both will live on."

As their path turned them closer to the ghosts, they came upon a round, gently sloping dish made of blue stone indented lightly into the land that stretched out in front of them perhaps one hundred meters in size. Due to its appearance, Zelda wondered if it had once been a shallow pool where people could have come to spend the warmer days, but the strange curved markings and lines in it made her think of other more magical things. Ghosts were moving around and through it rather aimlessly.

"Have we come off the road again to instead be led astray?" She asked.

"This is a rather strange object to come across and suddenly I have realised another thing that sets my hair on end. There is no dirt in this thing."

She looked down at her feet. There was certainly a path leading to this place and that was where it ended as from the circle there was no continuation of the path to lead them on. She suspected that there was indeed another road somewhere out there buried that they could have taken. It did not matter too much, as they knew where they had to go by looking ahead, but she had imagined walking out on a road back onto greener land and it appeared that was not going to be the case.

Despite the oddness of the thing, Otis didn't seen phased in the slightest and walked right into it, nor did the ghosts seem bothered by him, who moved slow and sombre, ignoring the old man entirely.

As they stepped closer to the dish, a wind picked up to whistle through the broken rubble of the ruins and the trees and among them there were noises that could have been whispers. She tried to imagine what the surrounding area would have looked like as she, along with the others, stepped over to the dish.

As if on that very same wind, colour seeped back into the world with dark blues smeared over a purple sky overhead, stars twinkling through dark lines of cloud as if day had suddenly turned to night. The world became shades of dark blue then a burning purple blue, as light of this false night covered the land, lit by the moons. The light was not that of the sun, which had disappeared from the sky, making the temperature plunge and the wind chill.

Zelda looked about and thankfully found those others around her equally as aware of this sudden change. All except one, as despite her own trepidations, she saw that Nasker appeared to be enjoying himself. He sauntered over at a casual stroll with a grin on his face.

"What's with the looks on all your faces? There's almost too much wrong with this place to even pretend I could be cautious."

"Your grin seems a little out of place all things considering." She said.

"Only because I have to wonder if this could be nothing more than a strange illusion. I'm just trying to lift the mood." He added, replying to everyone's serious faces.

He then went about lighting a torch that illuminated the surrounding area in light.

"Much better. Anybody cold?"

He offered the torch and when no one went to take it he kept it for himself and walked to the front of the line.

"If we intended to sneak through without angering the ghosts should we have lit that torch?" Zelda said.

"What's to say they can be angry? I don't think they can feel anything at all." He replied.

Survel was not happy looking up at the sky.

"I do not like these days and I do not like these nights. Nor do I like days that suddenly turn into nights or were it even the reverse, such things do not happen unless the effects of the magic of trickery are present, which I realise might not have been all that uncommon in such a place but everything is so dead and without mind. It should be a simple matter of leaving this circle to free us of the illusion. This thing I am sure we can take the time to walk around, not through."

He walked back a few paces and stepped out of the dish. As soon as he did he shuddered, collapsing back into the circle. He was dragged back over by Gunter but appeared responsive after a moment.

"Ah this is not good Gunter."

Nasker wasn't smiling now.

"Not an illusion perhaps? Do we move on?"

Otis was ahead of them.

"Yes, yes, of course. There is no other way but to move on."

The air in the basin was chilly and cold, the further they went approaching the middle of it, the more a mist crept through to surround them. As did the sound of a faint sorrowful moaning.

Zelda was trying but could not find the source of the noise.

"Oh I hear something now. I wish I hadn't heard such things but I do hear this. It sounds more like people, not trees."

Otis cackled, seeing her discomfort.

"Don't worry. You see, what is here in Malleau is rather different to anywhere else. A long sweeping death brought by foul burning magic that has sunk into the ground and the minds of all who have come here. You have seen it, you have knowledge of it and have trod through the worst of it. Yet there it is! In the distance the end is in sight so that you may go and do whatever else it is you think you can. Being druids there are things I am sure you can do."

Findal spoke.

"Again with your sarcasm. Here I was becoming happy that we were leaving the horror of this place behind so that we could finally remind ourselves that there's a world out there not yet ruined. Yet I wonder if one with you in it would be such a glad place at all."

The old man was rubbing his hands together.

"Oh not yet ruined, not yet indeed, but certainly on its way. Whether or not you leave this place you will not succeed, your plans have been made for you. Do you not see what the fire has done, bringing forth a world full of lies and misery?"

"That is why we are going on our way, so that we can change all of this and make people see the truth." Zelda said.

"Wrong, your understanding is wrong. What you seek to do will turn out to be nothing more than playing the fool in a world that has moved beyond needing any of you."

Zelda was not sure how to respond to this.

What can I say to him? He seems to be more than just a grumpy old man. The things he is saying, playing the fool, that's not right at all.

"Well then how about we find you a home where you can see us at work?"

Otis was shaking his head.

"Enough. I have played your games and am now done with them. You mock me, slaves of fire, pretending to be what you are not. My home was destroyed a long time ago, now all I do is wander this place while I watch people walk the world who would do the same to all of it."

He spat and turned to face them all.

"Our land was full of people who were gone in an instant and could not fight back despite my own duty, where it too burned away unfulfilled. How many of those could have been the ones to stand firm against the end that came for us I will never know. In the calling darkness I found myself trapped in this world and that is a fate worse than any death. I have taken you far enough so that you might see your freedom, but you'll never see any more than this glimpse of it. My only regret is that I would be bringing you to your ends and not anything far worse such as my own. I have stopped many from crossing these lands and you shall be among them too."

The ground groaned and shimmered and a chorus of many ghostly shapes rose up from the ground, howling as one in anguish, reliving that last bitter moment of their lives in despair.

"You think me an old man but I am no old man. The human body of this fool would have served me well after the loss of my own at the end of better days but now I see no use for it. The fire separated our minds from our bodies and assured us that we could not rest, doomed to roam this land while any who lived for a short while had their remains do the bidding of others."

Gunter unsheathed his sword.

"Who are you really? Identify yourself properly."

"I tell the truth. I am who I said I am and we all are the lost of Malleau, those who died with hope in our eyes and lives unfulfilled, those who dreamed to defend the world most precious to us above all else. I ask you to look with your eyes and see how our lives have been remembered and honoured. The existence of the world that changes into one of darkness makes it right that we are remembered little more than ghosts and filth as that is all any see of the world this day."

"It is up to us to break the darkness that is falling on this world, you lingering here does nothing to aid the place you once lived and died for. Now you exist only to strengthen the darkness you stood against, causing woe and heartache to all who would seek to use these roads. You can stop yourselves from doing vile and vicious things when it suits you. Let us pass beyond these lands and you shall find the world better than you had left it at your deaths on the success of our mission."

Zelda cleared her throat.

"I myself would seek a way to restore this place as much as possible. If indeed that is possible. All of us here want a chance to prove that there's more to come, that the world isn't over yet. And this place might be the only example anyone should need to say that they have to do something against the dark that is coming for us all. We can't let the world turn out like this. If you show us an endless night above our heads I say we will keep the cycle moving, in spite of you if we must. As a matter of fact everyone should spite you and how could they not when you have become such wicked things?"

The old man raised his hands as his body steadily turned to dust, what remained was a blue, ghostly mass that did not hold a form as the others did.

The wight cackled, but the voice was far lighter, free of a body with which to speak.

"There was darkness enough after all was done. The world burned, girl. The ground and sky were on fire that day. Be it whatever you say to yourself, but there was no darkness here that caused this, only a terrible burning flame. Oh the dead crept in behind them from what was left, but make no mistake what caused this place to fall. This darkness you seek to end will not come from this place but we see no other end than that. All will fall as we did, there's no reason for us to care in the face of such darkness."

Nasker stepped forward.

"Then look beyond the dark, there's more of a world than what you think there is out there but it will not be for you. You would doom many others if the intent is to bar our way and I am thinking it is because of the anger of knowing what it is you can no longer have. You are who you say you are and yet can you truly say that standing as you are on this awful soil makes you the same being who died all those years ago who had a task to defend it? I doubt it, you're nothing alike what you were. Having changed, shared too much of yourselves with this place, you risk becoming a further more despicable creature wallowing in pain, for these are early years you know of yet."

The wight hissed.

"What could you possibly know of our pain when everything was taken from us? Our sacrifices meant nothing."

"Then change again, this time stray from your dark path or stay as you are and watch the world change without you. No matter your choice it's all the same to me because we shall proceed with or without your good graces. The dead shall not stop the cycle that brings strength and purpose to the living."

Ghostly figures began to come closer. Survel turned to the others.

"I feel the sameness on these as was around me when I failed to breach the circle. We will be lost forever if they reach out to take hold of us."

Gunter took his shoulder.

"The ground is dead so we must trust in the sky. Look at what is ahead and focus strongly upon it, using what hope you each have to your advantage and do not stop. I know it will be hard but think not of the ground but the sky and the forests you will see underneath."

He stared ahead to the forests and turned into a black hawk that made for the skies. The land did not speak to Zelda and she found it difficult to change. Tired, hungry, surrounded by angry ghosts, she did as she was told and looked ahead to imagine how much better she would feel once in the land of the living again.

There was one other thing Zelda had to note, as she changed to follow the others and her vision shrank as she took flight, flying through gaps in a white blue wispy substance that were similar to clouds. She did not like flying through clouds.

They could be nice and fluffy at a distance but there was something about getting her feathers damp along with being unable to see that absolutely, with complete certainty she could say she did not enjoy in the slightest. This sensation was rather similar to flying through clouds, only these ones chilled without the dampness. This did not change her opinion of her surroundings.

For one moment she considered attacking the ghosts, but inside her mind she laughed because that was the most ridiculous thing she had thought of for some time. That guided her like a shield out of the ghostly mist that could no longer chill her and soon she could tell that the world was brighter and her spirits soared as high as she did. Then she was out to fields that were green and seeing five other birds around only made her feel even more happy.

Eventually she came to green trees and down to where others had already landed in various stages of collapse she went.

She had barely hit the ground before resuming herself as a human. Everything was so green it was truly wonderful, even if it hurt her eyes because it was so bright. But the best part for her was the weight that she felt of every patch of ground. She couldn't help hugging it and feeling the grass between her fingers.

It still turns, it still turns. I feel it, that great motion of the world.

She checked the others and found that Gunter and Nasker were in conversation. It was a little bit difficult to hear Nasker as he was laying face down and had shoved his face into the grass.

"Next time I am thinking we go around."

Gunter was laying with his back to the ground.

"We will make the north king bow to us first, then walk freely through his lands, not before, so we will not have to do this again. It is nice to know that you have picked up the pace so quickly."

"I think I might be sick again but yes, we are all in this together. No one should be leaving themselves by the wayside, especially if they have the ability to do something. So soon it was those dead forgot their purpose of life and were content with pulling us under with them. It chills me to think of what manner of world would be left if what they say was to come to pass. All the more reason for us not to fail against those who would willingly tip the balance."

While Peter wandered, Findal and Survel were checking their belongings. Both seemed to be more paranoid that usual about their things not regaining proper form once human again. Zelda didn't understand them for this, it was a small price to pay to become an animal at all if it did happen, as long as any of the items you needed to help you change weren't damaged. There were a few crooked feathers on her clothes as she inspected them but those she could replace. Looking into the dense trees, she didn't think she'd need to worry about that for a while.

Peter eventually returned from his walk scratching his head.

"There's a road close to here. Is this the old south road? If so it would lead to the Great Tree, wouldn't it?"

Survel nodded.

"Yes it would and that is the road we were planning to take. In better days by our reckoning it led all who would listen to us to the Great Tree. Now it does not, as none take the road. The king who's land we are now in on this side of Malleau has no liking for us druids, as you well know."

"The king of Kasynne doesn't have much of a liking for his own people either."

"Indeed. I'm going to be honest and say that I would rather go through the forest than travel along the road. This isn't about getting caught as it has been long abandoned with no reason to go south or come up alongside that mess we scraped out of. I just want to feel the world in my bones again."

Zelda put her head up.

"We're right alongside the forest and we were going to walk along a road?"

Peter too seemed surprised.

"We're going through the forest. There can't possibly be any other way. I just wanted to make sure there wasn't any other road I was missing."

Findal shook his head.

"There's no other road. If this is the fastest way to the Great Tree we should take it, I'm eager to see it for the first time and meet others such as myself."

Gunter sat up.

"We can't afford to falter now. The plan was always to take the road north."

Nasker too sat up kneeling but his head was still facing the ground, eyes distant.

"We need this. We need to feel the world turning deeper. We *have* to. I can't get that along another road, the world is out there so close to us and you would say that we ignore it? That can't be possible. We've all suffered and I don't mean to say for us to get lost in the forest, but I could think of nothing better to recover our senses faster then to spend some time walking through it."

Survel appeared downcast.

"Well a lot of it is just brush and scrub, but I'm sure there are paths we can find."

"If you need me to, I'll help you find your way to the Great Tree."

Gunter stood up, arms crossed.

"I hear all of you, but know that we are cutting our time rather thin to reach the Great Tree by solstice. However I have no desire to argue my point or split up, so we shall go through the forest presently then."

If Zelda could have powered the cycle to spin for the rest of eternity from the giddy relief she felt at that moment alone she would have done so. More than that, she felt with each step she was coming closer to answers she hoped would help not just the world, but herself.

There might be other ghosts or creatures out there and instead of running away she wanted to be able to tackle them head on. As they entered the forest and she was feeling her heart swell to bursting in her chest, Zelda wondered on what animal might be the sort to do just that.

Chapter Twenty Four
The Black Knight

The room was empty of people who lived, all but one, that was. That lone one was in a room full of the newly dead where outside of it there were hallways, gardens, open chambers just the same. And stained those places were just the same as his sword, with crimson red and ruby drops that fell from it as he made his way to the streets in the dawning light of morning with the heavy, thudding sound of his steps the only sound apart from the dripping.

The Black Knight knew of this, that the streets too were just the same, where there was silence among those who had before been on the cusp of their madness and delusion. No one would bury them, they had all been left where they lay.

It would have been troubling, once. Such a sight to see, to behold all that remained of the madness of people gone to the darkest of places, asking for a blind bliss to save them from the world. Those here had wanted to be saved and so he had brought death to this place that was full of selfish belief. Indeed this whole land of Alegan was rife with it through a war they had taken advantage of, yet had made nothing to show for it themselves.

They might ask why their lives were not better. Despite all they had, especially all they thought they had to hold over others, it was not enough for them. The mingling of the desperate believers who remained dipped their hands into such a pot to test its temperature to make sure it was to their liking. It had not been and never would be exactly how they wanted.

Others would take the blame, he had seen it before. Armies marched out of great gates into the lands of their foes, while those here who thought themselves forgotten would be feverish to find that they would be remembered. All of them would take their justice and zealotry as they marched, leaving ruin in their wake.

The wall to the north he would block off, with no better way to do so than making sure no one reached it in the first place. For he was a gatekeeper purposed with keeping all such evils confined to their own lands. It was a job impossible. After all there were external forces he could not control or counter, but this land he held away from the rest of the world at least from the north. If they had wanted to do something they would have to get through more than long mountain trails. He had been at that north wall and had seen the state of it. Not too different from here, not that he had torn down some walls and put barricades over others which no one would need.

If such people as had been here took themselves over the wall their foul words would crawl up the world like a tree growing with twisted and evil intent, roots feeding off foul nourishment that would strengthen it. A tree such as that might be grown with thick branches so they could hang all their dead from it as a warning for all who might look upon it and stand against them. And those laughing among the shadows would still do nothing until the dark was upon them, he could feel it. None laughed here now, he had made sure of it. Others who moved in, they would see this place and take heed, as first and foremost it was not those who preached that he had on his mind but the ones in between them.

As such here he had been, searching for those who would be not for any good cause but for the ruin of the world. Under such a tree that the preachers would grow, this other kind would have the world burn from their hands where they would laugh and dance. That too he had seen before. To leave this city to them would go against the ideals set down in place with his body long ago. To deny them all that fire which they would hold with their hand out was his task, long and old, given to him by a person he could not remember, nor even their words. He had made a choice to do as they had asked, setting him on this long path, stained in blood.

That had been in a time when the world was younger and fuller, where the sounds of all the peoples in it were familiar and well spread, where madness and insanity were for none but a scant few sent to a pyre, a river, or a gallows death and the people watching on would laugh, sometimes cry, but always remind themselves not to be like those ill fated ones.

A man had once looked upon such a scene, when he had eyes and a body to hold them in. What a strange, grim firmness in his chest there had been on seeing this punishment meted out. For that had been the just and right thing to do at the time. And even now some might.

Now there was no such feeling, only a red river made by his sword to walk through. Even if his means were the same as those executions, none would look on this justly, he knew, only with a horror in their hearts. Those who did would not know the whole picture. Just as he had not, with drowned witches and hung men being accused for all sorts of false reasons, some he only got by pulling bodies out of the river and having them speak to him. Those were the days he wished to see again. To bear no ill on witches or other sorts falsely condemned, but to feel a world bright and full of life.

To achieve that goal he only did what he believed to be right. He could go where he wanted and do as he wished. Some times, many times across ages that had been to do nothing at all, without involving himself in the world where all he would do was watch. He had been most careful in his deliberations to keep it that way for many long years, yet there were those who knew of him in stories, so he was always cautious of being remembered as a monster. Yet here he was surrounded by all this death of his own making in the knowledge that none were left to speak of who did this. Had the people here got what they wanted, no one would be remembered anyway.

The world had turned far, far beyond his own expectations and was now slowing to the point where it almost wasn't moving at all. Then it would end. He wasn't sure what would happened when it came, but knew that as the land failed to provide and the seas themselves became rancid the end would only be worse. A great fading, where only silence would remain.

The armoured helmet stared at the dawn sky. Of those who lived until then, would they see the end or would it come in gracious night? A final dawn or a final dusk he could not care to guess. Such romanticism of fate escaped him, to which he did not mind. His own exile from the fate of the world was his own choice to make and as long as those he sought did not escape him, nothing else mattered.

Whether the world was alive or not was not for him to debate, but he had known that in hopeful days of gladness the world buzzed and hummed with a potent energy all to its own that all could live off.

Living with hate, jealousy, scorn or forcing others to live in fear, while here and there such individuals would always exist and some people had bad days, when made for the basis of one's entire existence or reason for kingdoms full of people to thrive, such dark thoughts made the world very ill indeed. They didn't care, as all were chasing days of old glory. Such days had long accompanied kingdoms gone from history itself.

He wondered if those who had waited for their king to return had even known what it was they had been waiting for. The king had left Autumn to grasp at the last absolute, remaining indication of his authority that he should have inherited at birth as proof of his right to rule over these lands, a light which was not his own.

A long time ago before he had worn, needed or set his eyes on his armour, the Black Knight had heard a story quite new, where blind men had been made to see, a thing that happened from time to time. It was an occurrence he certainly had not given too much thought of back then. In those days there had been many tales of magical fountains and wondrous cups, cursed books and swords with minds of their own, all of which had passed on mighty boons to those who had held them.

Yet for some reason or another over the many others, this had stuck throughout the ages while many of those others were now gone. Be that as it had been, whatever had returned the blind their sight was not shielded from the passage of time and no longer existed, not here. So while the king had left to regain what he believed to be his power and dignity, in truth they would be inheriting no such thing. Indeed the Black Knight could not think of any magical object he had seen for many a recent year apart from the one in front of him. His own hands, his own body, his sword.

He didn't need to be in possession of any magical object to know what this king was doing, however. The king would dive back into public life with power absolute or he would not come out from hiding at all. Wanting to appear the ruler to those that believed in Churl was the path he had chosen to take. Even though there were other paths to power, he had chosen the one most familiar to his subjects that they could gather around, such as in the manner of a banner bearer on a battlefield.

When the Black Knight had gone to the north Alegan wall, he had found no one with their banners flying as there should have been at that barrier, that northern point where once many would have come to ask each other if all was clear for them to pass into each other's lands. In such a state of ruin he guessed the damage had come from the southern side, however it could have been most possible that the north lands beyond had already fallen into nothing, with not a word or single messenger to call out a final doom. If it were instead the case that the Ruthlands and the north were fine in their own ignorance and one of them did make their way so far south to see before them the ruined walls he doubted they would journey further in.

Perhaps when this was all over and all being well, he'd take up place at the gate as he had done with another gate and another person many ages ago, himself being the one who would tell of the colour of the lands they walked through.

As for now, he would not be warning off those who came down from the north and as he was not at the gate he could not stop them entering. Any who might would find the recluse who ruled these lands doing nothing even if they came to him. That man's banner was not yet ready, the knight felt.

Ah, but would not such a thing, supposed to be so white and clean be stained with blood? Those who were left of the king's people might do as he said, but far and wide the Black Knight knew, he could feel the lessening of life as people were called up and taken away. Their blood would be on that banner.

Such a banner would be waving in a breeze, surrounded by those who had gone off to war underneath it. Whether anyone would be left to see it or be able to fight under it he did not know. Those who did would not have much time as each step would march the world closer to the end. That banner would burn under a red sky of fire, burning out until it was no more and the flaming threads and trails of it would float into the sky to join its peers. Only fire would be there to greet the end of the world, no long dark that they all feared. All would then be reduced to ashes, with none left to live in the dark.

Certainly Autumn had taken up those words with either a grave seriousness or villainous gusto, either was something he found his sword could not abide by. So here he was, in a city he himself had made red, to be added to the fields, entire lands of red of his making spanning over the many, many long years in which he had walked. Each could hold within them the darkness of blind zeal or the bright, burning rebellion of fire. It did not matter to him that they were both against each other. Neither were pleasing to him, so both would get his sword.

What a woeful sight to behold it would have been once. From place to place he had gone, silencing them all with his giant blade that no man could hold. From the dark he could feel the eyes watching him, almost waiting for him to end them all, for that would be the surest way to stop the fire. By cutting down the madness most completely while searching for someone to blame would give them fuel for their delusion.

There was no one to chide him in this silence. A demise such as what he brought here could consume the world, some might say, yet that same world was responsible for bearing the selfishness of those who lived in it and that was a burden it could not hold. Unbalanced, it would slow to a demise far colder than any his sword could mete.

The Black Knight did what he could to ease its pain, but knew that in the end all would be for nothing without the loss that would have to come from all of those who hobbled along with the faith they clung on to as a crutch. All forms of death and darkness gathered at signs of weakness and he knew a seeking darkness that ran across the sky in the clouds was watching for such weakness.

Despite the light Churl flaunted he knew they were powerless men mincing their jowls to make words without a scrap of magic in their being. They nor those to who they preached could see the thing as he or others could, nor that which it left behind in its wake, a blackness of a sort that was cast as a malign smear across the sky.

He had heard the mad speak of it, but not those who might go about their days fantasising about the king's return who held no special talent themselves. Another time, another place and those people instead of being sent to rot would have been honoured, but not here and now, where they were imprisoned and made of only to be liars and mad when they were not the truly mad ones. The ones who could see had potential, which this kingdom had squandered and flattened, strained out and left to die if not executed outright, which could almost explain the desolate places he had found that had once been full of people. There was an old world in the distant past longing to become new again and that which would deny that world would find his blade.

Then there it was, that darkness watching in the sky. If he knew he could fling his sword into it to stop its malevolent observation then he would, but alas he could not be sure that such a throw would do anything at all.

Such mystery the irritable witches and wizards might know the answers to. He could not travel north to visit them, wishing to remain in these lands for the time being, so wondered on the whereabouts of the wizard he had met. The man could be anywhere, he could even be dead, however such a man was his best lead to answering the question that now sat in his mind and irritated him with the lack of an answer.

The Black Knight was choosing a direction to travel in when a sensation, of a prickling that could not be ignored, made him turn his head to the south and the grip on his sword did tighten.

What was that other dark shadow he now saw on the horizon? Out there was a darkness he could feel from far away, an aura emanating from the south. A supposedly bright beacon of hope was wrapped in a corona of darkness. He could feel it in the sky signalling the corruption of life and the loss of hope.

The sky, while cold, would have been bright in the dawn for all who could see it. But for him it was brighter still against this darkness that left a stain only he could see that smeared the way grease did. Whether or not he did anything else he knew that the dark would spread. As he looked out to the south, he knew each scheme he had silenced in Autumn would be nothing compared to it. Whatever kind of fate was awaiting to overcome them could not be a pleasant one, that he knew completely. That was something he had felt before.

Slowly he began walking into the day, to where he might make himself alone in the world if it came to that. As for this place he would leave it to the dead, it was set to fade anyway. The vermin creatures of the ground would eat and wallow in the bodies of the fallen yet what time there would be for any of them to make use of such food he did not know.

Then again, animals did have a rather different perception of the world around them and the passage of time, much like himself. While he walked on he did think again of what it was he would have to do. Eternity was a rather long time, after all.

Chapter Twenty Five
Into the Trees

As they had walked deeper and deeper into the forest, Zelda could say that this was without a doubt the largest mass of trees in one place she had ever walked through, at least the most dense for sure. Even though she had walked through the wild and untamed lands on the outer reaches of Alegan, those places had also been where she had seen rocky planes and wide open lakes.

The first stream they had come across was clean and no matter how cold the water was, they all filled their water bags, then became otters to swim and test their limbs and limits. In those forms they caught fish, and brought them all to the bank where later that night they cooked and ate them over the first proper fire in a very long time.

And so came something else as they journeyed through the forest, proper clouds and rain, to smother the sky and their fire. But filled with fish and with fresh water, there was a thrum of happiness throughout the gathered ones as they sat under trees in the rain.

Simply knowing that the trees stretched off to the horizon in all directions was enough in itself to cause a bubble of giddiness that Zelda suppressed, with the reason for doing so being a troubling matter with which she tempered her feelings. It was dark in the forest, a rumbling of warning she could hear if she stopped and tilted her head to the sound that did not come from the sky above but the ground below.

In the most recent of days it had become harder to see the sky and she suspected that it too rumbled and crashed overhead. In the days where the skies had become obscured the weather had turned poorly and while not against their march as it could be said for some, the clouds were moving in and did not relent with winter marching ever on.

On days where it rained and the clouds above were dark her mind had been drawn to the blue nights looking up in the skies of Malleau. She felt conflict within herself as what a strange feeling it was to have her most recent memories of a nice open sky be of a place so horrid. Despite the cold, she was content to know that it was from the rain that fell and the chill that came from winter and not from anything else. That grey hell was becoming ever distant in her mind and distant was where it should have been, or at least where it was wanted, the furthest thought away from all of them.

Now they were all following a forest trail quite invisible to her eyes that had been chosen to lead them the appropriate way north to the Great Tree. Zelda did not know what she would find there, but from all she had been told she imagined it to be a place of significance, one that had held more significance when people far and wide had cared of such a thing and where a spirit had sat in rest before being frightened away.

Perhaps if she looked upon the Great Tree herself she might understand better what it was they were looking for in such a spirit. Simply being told that she would know it when she saw it did not completely sit right with her, so she had decided that it would not take the shape of what she saw but how she felt. There were tales of shape shifters and tricky forest creatures that took on appearances based on the eyes of the beholder. If no one was looking who knew what shapes they might take to amuse themselves.

As it was now, surrounded by all the trees, the heady smell of them and the mist that came from her breath as well as that which settled around the trees of the real, not ghostly kind, she found herself able to cast aside any worry concerning what it was she could not see.

It was much nicer to focus on what she could see, as it was clear to see on the faces of those who had needed to recover, that they were making good progress in their state of mind. A few days in the forest had done them all well. Zelda had happily passed the time resuming her lessons where everyone gave their advice or their own thoughts on the matter at hand. She had not fully appreciated it before but had since come to realise that everyone else alongside her in some ways had still been learning themselves.

Zelda found herself wondering how much it was any of them really knew. It did seem that Gunter was as usual doing most of the talking to all the others, as he did know the most about being a druid. At least he was able to say which way or that someone should take their understanding and put aside their uncertainty.

Maybe there is hope for the rest of them, just as there is hope for me. I really do need to take a step back, or am I in too far to have my understanding adjusted? If it comes to it I will save myself and work on doing the same for all of them as thanks for everything they have done.

It was easy to be uncertain, for these trees spoke to them, not with words but a humming, vibrant tune even when they were mostly dormant in this colder weather. This was what she could hear now which she could not hear before. So it wasn't as if she was learning nothing at all, in fact there was a lot that she could now pick up on, even if something inside still did not feel quite right. The feeling was a buzzing that was growing in her that was drowning out all the other sounds, slowly but surely.

Then instead of feeling it she heard it. They all did. There was a sound that buzzed and she looked for it among the trees. She tried reaching out but could feel nothing animal from around her, so it must not have been an animal. Quite the strange sound it was, not a harsh, deep buzzing or even an annoying buzz. The sound that came from above sounded the same way hail did on the ground or bouncing off buckets when the rain had been cold enough to freeze which had been a rare sight even in the colder days she had known where there had been rain.

The trees were not buffeted by any storm winds or rain, quite the opposite. Aside from the growing noise, there was not even a whisper of a breeze that would have told them that anything was on its way to where they were.

"I'm worried that we are going to be attacked by a horde of flying beasts far up in the sky that they we can not see." Zelda said.

Perhaps these creatures were invisible to their eyes and senses, if that was the case then there would be trouble coming their way.

Gunter nodded at this.

"We are being approached, everyone. Let me do the talking here. No harm should come to us but just to be safe allow me to speak with these creatures that come before us."

A high pitched chiming voice came from above.

"Creatures? We are no creatures, if anything you all are the slow, lumbering creatures making such a racket through the forest so that far and wide the trees joke about you."

Down from the trees came rather small creatures, small enough to fit into the palm of one's hand, so it was strange that their voices carried so far. They were not elves but the appearance was uncanny. These smaller brown elf like creatures differed in that they had wings along their backs like those of a dragonfly of a light green that was vivid against their brown bark moulded skin. Each wore a cloak made of leaves and pine needles which made them well hidden against the trees. One did appear to be leading the way but not one of them could be told from another as they were all so similar in appearance.

The one at the head of the group settled in a tree and the others of its kin dispersed around where they could not all be kept track of at once, some high in branches above while some seemed more curious and could be seen lower to the ground.

It put its tiny hands on their hips and with a disgruntled look spoke down to the group below.

"So how is it that those of yours would be here? Speak human, for while we pixies might be small we are mighty and do not tolerate lumbering fools in this forest."

Gunter did not move from where he stood.

"Here you see these around me, they are others I have gathered for the search we must undertake that you know of. From all over the land and beyond I have been and now return with people I have met along the way. They are proof that within this land there are those who heed the call that has been cast by foolish others from their own ears. The world lives still in the hope I have found and although we have tried in our journey we have not found the spirit. Now we come at the instruction given to us of the druids as we approach solstice. I take it the spirit has not yet been found by others?"

The pixies chattered their wings in agitation.

"No, not yet. Still they have not been found and still you all journey on outwards hoping that you will. Many long years it has been as the world becomes ever colder and this forest ever darker. Even since you have been away there has been a darkening deep within that even we fear to approach. It makes me wonder about the other places in the world."

"How they all fair now matters not, as we will change all places when we have the strength to do so. Then you can wonder and even may find a place for yourselves outside of this forest."

The pixie bowed.

"How gracious of you. For the moment I then turn my head and continue to look inwards for that is where all our attention must honestly be. There are things in this forest that should not be there and frequently a darkness surges overhead in the sky. It frightens us and keeps us far from the sky so that we dare not break above the trees."

All the other pixies began to chatter their own wings nervously again in response and as they did, talked to each other in voices that were mere whispers.

The pixie in charge of speaking cleared its throat and continued.

"Not everyone holds the same opinion. Some places where the forest is dark there are those who are not frightened at all. This place is divided, even when it is whole so I would exercise caution as in some places the ground itself might be treacherous to you. You smell as if you have had enough of that, for we can tell where you have been. Bravery and familiarity with this place you find yourselves in will not be enough, as even the world itself is changing. Those of us who have spied the kingdom north of the forest have seen the weariness of those humans increase ever more as time passes so we know something is upon us."

"We are all running out of time to find the spirit." Gunter admitted.

"You have your own way of seeing the world but for us we must look outside of the forest as we can not wait for the darkness to come to us and hide in this place. Not while the rest of the world waits and for what end they believe they wait I do not know, but we must do what we can for all the world. I do not know if you are able to see why we do such things but as for ourselves, we can not wait."

"We can not judge you for what you try to do, regardless of what little we think about you attempting it. On that matter, an endeavour such as yours calls for haste. You travel on the wrong path and we would be happy to put your travels on the right one for I would imagine that you seek the Great Tree."

The pixies all began chittering to themselves. It seemed they liked the idea of escorting people through the forest. The eagerness was not lost on the group but particularly not on Gunter, who did not look amused by the suggestion. The pixies were too willing and eager to assist, by not only what he could gather, but by what he knew, first hand.

"We know the right way." He said.

"You are tricky creatures whose words we must be cautious of. Yes by that I mean thank you for your offer but we will not be thanking ourselves for going along with your mischief."

The pixie hummed.

"Are you sure? You might get lost if you keep following along this way. We are offering you this and you would decline so rudely."

"This is only common sense, coming from one you have already tricked. I need none of what you have, truthfully I can not stand it. We will trust in ourselves and walk on alone."

"Very well."

The pixies turned to confide in each other in their soft whispers. After a moment, they all flew away, filling the air with buzzing.

A look of strained tension left Gunter's face and he seemed pleased.

"Now that they are out of the way, we can move forward without further misfortune. I hope you will not come across the misfortune of being tricked by the pixies, as it is a terrible thing to be caught up in their amusement."

Findal was squinting into the sky.

"I've never met them before. Are they evil creatures? If so they did not look it. Perhaps we should have taken them up on their offer."

Nasker shook his head.

"No, but they are a troublesome lot. Best to save any sort of gathering for when we are surrounded by others that might attract their attention rather than us. Who knows what they might have decided for us on the way to the Great Tree were they to guide us. Anyway, we should really keep moving. Don't want to keep anyone waiting now."

With that meeting having been concluded they all moved forward so that they could come to the second one which had always been their first intention. Soon after resuming their walk, they came across a stone pillar with a small metal ring attached, similar to a distance marker which was only about a meter in height.

"Such a thing is new here." Said Gunter to the rest.

It certainly had the look of newness about it. Even if the building blocks for it were old, it looked newly constructed. The reason for why it was there at all eluded them and there was no writing or symbols on the marker to say what for. None of them were able to inspect the pillar too thoroughly however, as the bushes and trees around them suddenly bristled and out appeared men with spears and swords and bows that had not been there before. It was as if the party had become surrounded by people who had shimmered out of the shadows.

Those who approached the druids saw little more than a shabby group who had been making their way through the trees, yet nonetheless those who saw them were relieved that they were just people, not anything strange or any creature of the forest. Calling out would have done nothing to confirm who or what they were, as such creatures could very well mimic human voices, as these men well knew.

So it was that the gathering of humans met together, surprised by another group of their kind with one side who cautiously kept the other at a distance but still had their bows and spears trained onto them. Their forest armour was metal in spots but had been covered in mud to conceal themselves more appropriately.

"What are you people doing in this forest?" Gunter asked.

"Well what are you doing in this forest?" One of the forest men responded.

"We are simply returning to the Great Tree." Gunter said.

One man alighted forward, rubbing his hands together.

"Ah, druids are we? Well that's a believable story but what are your reasons for returning? Could it be that this vile feeling that makes us chill even during the morning light might finally be put to rest?"

Gunter nodded slowly.

"We are aware of such darkness but there is something that must be done first, to ensure it stays that way if we are to defeat it. We would move on."

In a cautionary way did the man hold out his hand.

"Not so fast. Things have not been going so well down here in the forest. There are rumours from the north that the king's army is on the move into Atwixie, or to say the least are stirring at the edges. We were supposed to be hidden, this ground on which you now walk should not have been found by you here. You could be spies for the king. To release yourselves of that suspicion you now must come with us. Refusal or resistance will be met with our bows and blades. I ask again. You are heading through the forest to some place but what might you be doing in it?"

Gunter stroked his beard.

"If you are asking that question then I know that you do not share our understanding or goals and that we are all here for different reasons. I do believe that the forest belongs to no one, more or less."

"No, like it or not it belongs to our king. Even though we disagree with the harshness of his rule, we know that all his lands are his absolutely. Now must I keep asking you to explain what might you be doing in his forest? Might any others among this man relieve him of his stupidity at snubbing us so?"

Gunter spoke again before anyone else had a chance.

"We come to it from afar to protect it, but most importantly we protect all lands and would come here to meet with others of our kind that as I have already made myself so inclined to suggest, you are not among and have no good reason to stop us."

"I think the point of my spear would prove otherwise. You'll be coming with us and don't try any of that magical stuff, you're through the barrier now so you'll have a hard time making it do what you want. As for your true intentions, others can find that out from you."

Gunter turned to the rest and kept his voice down, not appearing apologetic in the least, merely a little annoyed.

"It seems we are too late already to flee with speed from these inhabitants and now must join them in their march. All the hurriedness should have been ours yet here it is we crawl. I am however intrigued to speak with those who built whatever place we are being taken to as they have no business in this forest."

With the points of blades so close and watchful eyes with arrows notched at the ready, there was nothing else they could do but walk along with these forest men.

Eventually they came to a cleared out road of dirt and as they walked along it they came across a break in the trees and a settlement came into view.

The town was more of a glorified fort, built up with moss covered stone blocks to create pieces of wall unfinished, mixed with thick stakes locked together, sharpened into points as if preparing a barricade for a coming battle. The buildings themselves were a mixture of that moss covered stone and wood with most of them having wooden roofing. There was a fair bit of space cleared out for the town, around five hundred meters at the diameter. There were more of those stone pillars standing around the outside edges of the buildings and some were standing closer inside too.

Nasker was looking at the sky, for the sky appeared strange, as if they were looking at it through a haze.

"This place had been well hidden. For what purpose I-"

He had turned his gaze back to the ground as something shimmering to his right had caught his attention. There was a girl standing in the distance, chained at a pillar by their neck. He squinted and noticed the pasty dead complexion of their skin with empty, charred veins and blackened sockets that were directed right at him without emotion.

Then before his eyes all the pillars suddenly had attached to them a different person chained just the same and all had heads facing him.

He halted in his tracks but as he did so the lot of them disappeared in a foul black vapour and were gone as fast as he could blink.

Nasker shook his head. There were no chains on those pillars or people standing by them at all.

Zelda nearly bumped into him.

"Nasker, is everything alright? You're looking a little pale again."

He took a deep breath.

"I didn't expect to see what I'm seeing here, that is all."

"It is all going to be well and fine, I'm sure these people will let us go when they find out what we're trying to do."

"I hope so indeed." He said.

More of the town could be seen poking over those low walls. Almost all of the buildings were crude, one story houses, with a small patch of dirt next to each taken up with rows of plants that had become dormant for the winter.

They were marched further in up to a house with closed shutters and two stories. Next to that house was a larger field than all the others. Standing before it was a man with a small, pointy brown beard, wearing a red hat with a wide brim and flat top. He had a matching coat covering his common brown leathers and despite the cleanliness of most of his clothing, in particular his hat and his coat, his boots were muddy as he had clearly been working through a small patch where he had attempted to plant something. In his hand he held a pitchfork.

With limited sunlight and also having them currently being in the middle of winter, there was nothing growing there behind him. Indeed his efforts appeared quite fruitless, more so than the other patches of dirt they had passed.

Peter was looking at the sad rows of dirt.

"What are you trying to do, planting at this time of year?" So he said, despite being poked at by spears.

"Nothing you do will make growth happen. Do you not have any sense?"

The man under the hat waved the pitchfork at him and eyed off the men escorting the druids.

"Who are these that come here and ruin the peace? Do not tell me you caught spies, I do not wish to hear it, the possibility that the king has come."

A man stepped forward.

"I apologise. We found these ones at the north shield stone, inside the barrier. They say they are on their way to the Great Tree but how they got through I don't know, so we've brought them here for questioning. Certainly we can't let them leave otherwise, without knowing how it was they did it."

The man with the red hat leaned on the pitchfork.

"So we've got ourselves some druids then? I find it suspicious you would come here now of all times. You can look around and see the darkness in this forest that you let creep in. Until it became so noticeable that it could no longer be ignored, even by you. Isn't that why you have returned?"

Peter was not please by these words.

"Please don't skewer us, you have no idea from which we have escaped."

The man sniffed.

"I might just have to. Your clothes stink of that place of death from over yonder, maybe even coming further from where foul phantoms rise from shallow graves. No one comes out from that direction unless mad or with malign intent."

Gunter shook his head.

"Well then he was wrong, you have some idea as to what we have been up against. But we are tired and could very well do with some rest if not free passage completely. If you insist that we stay shortly might you leave us in peace? I would like to learn more about this place you have made here. If that can not be made possible I would rather then not stay the night while waiting for you to make up your mind as to our intentions. For what it is worth we only did cross through with great haste in order to be saving us a northbound journey that would have taken us far off course and into the clutches of the king it seems you have trouble with. As you are probably aware, we too have trouble with the king."

"You think you know of our trouble? *You have no idea from which we have escaped.* To throw your own words back at you. Allowing you to rest here would only have you rob my house and home, to which I think not, that is my ruling."

Zelda huffed.

"I don't agree with this at all but I do agree with some peace and quiet. I would very much like the next king I come across to not have problems with me and there be no need for any rulings if it could be helped."

The man's eyes peered at her from under his hat.

"Oh it that so? Then I should keep my eye on you, girl. But enough. I have a challenge for you all. If you really are druids and not magical spies then call on your ways of the world and make my garden grow."

He gestured to the dirt next to him.

Gunter continued to look unhappy, his face rigid when he spoke, holding back other meaner words.

"You certainly share nothing in common with the king, who would care nothing for a single display, called for or otherwise. Yet you are so very much alike in demanding acts of us. We do not answer to the whims of you nor the likes of yours who would hold a court over the powers of nature. We have travelled through a land full of creatures that make a mockery of nature without asking and I am not about to do the same when asked."

The man in red threw a disgusted look at the armed men.

"You're bringing us trouble and this is just what I needed right now. Oh to have crazies in my yard, in my home."

From inside the house, a young girl's voice came down, causing the man in red to jump.

"Despite what he says, there are no such creatures. Instead it is that old souls, many old souls, rested in that place, or lived on the cusp of fading away. To some it would be a mercy to give them peace but their existences are nothing more than just that, peaceful. You needn't worry or feel concern, as many might see themselves quietly passing on the same way."

Peter could not hide what he thought of such words and called out.

"Well you can put me in the ground and make mulch from me before I turn out like one of them that I saw. If the whole world becomes as I have seen it there'll be nothing left for me here anyway. Who are you, whoever you are that thinks to know our wants and travels?"

The voice did not respond and the man brought his attention back to the druids.

"So will you do it?"

Gunter shook his head.

"No."

Zelda pushed her way past to the group.

"I shall do it and you may scold me afterwards when we are on our way as I am sick of not knowing what it is anyone wants. But I know what I want."

She knelt down and stuck her hands into the dirt of the man's fields. There were little tiny creatures in the soil but they were all sleeping. It would be rude to wake them up but she would apologise to them properly and explain why she had done what she had.

There was movement she could feel in the little creatures. No, what was this? It was not movement but the feeling of shadows cast by each of them under the ground yet such a thing could not have been possible. Each little creature had a wavering presence of darkness next to it in the soil that wriggled and turned from a shadow cast behind the light of life of each one to move in front of them to eclipse the light, with a deep darkness that bore holes in her mind that grew larger and she found she could not let go.

Zelda collapsed in front of the group to the alarm and dismay of the others but to the pleased happiness of the man.

"Ha, she could not do it, so I was right. Take them away to the gaol, where they shall await my verdict on their fates. I have surmised them to be fiendish entities of poor repute but I must consider this further before they receive what is due to them. It is only right that I do so. I shall not ask again, take them away."

Findal picked Zelda up.

"She is not stirring but she seems alive. What is this?"

He nearly dropped her on remembering what he had on him.

"Wait, I have gold on me. Perhaps if I make a deal we can come to an agreement which makes all of this unnecessary."

He failed to see the eyes of all the soldiers and the man light up, predatory animals that had each caught a whiff of blood, of wolves surrounding a fallen herd animal outside of the protection of the others. All their eyes shone with greed but all were waiting on the man in red, who sneaked in a wary glance back at his house before speaking.

"Do you now? We'll take it, all of it. Here I was thinking druids did not care for such things. Further proof that none of you really are who you claim. We'll take anything else we can find of value from you. Do not resist, for while I place no value on your lives we will take those too if need be. Now get on with it, take them to the gaol then search them."

A heavy bag was retrieved from Findal, who could not do anything as he did not want to drop the poor unconscious girl or get a spear in his throat.

The man in red eyed it eagerly.

"Maybe this wasn't so troubling a capture. Bring anything else you find to me and I'll share the gold around once you do."

As they were marched off, his voice carried into the distance.

"Heed this you fools being taken away. If you did truly worship nature then you aught to know how lucky you are at being given this chance, for with nature there would have been none."

Chapter Twenty Six
The Hidden Village Seer

The druids were lined up outside a small, low building with walls made of stone rocks. There was a wood overhang over the front and wood planks were fitted together at the edges to create a partially enclosed space against the front. The only door inside was made of thick planks of wood with a metal handle that surely did more than simply lend to the appearance of being heavy. In the top of the door was a square cut away with metal bars built into it.

A man was seated on a chair out in front resting against the wooden wall. He was wearing similar dirty armour as the others but offered nothing but a tired, amused expression to those around him. He blinked up at the druids like a man just waking up, heavy shadows due to lack of sleep under his eyes.

"It's my job to deal with anyone we need to keep away from anyone else here. Can't just let people go and have the forest take them, they might escape and let others know about us you see. Not that you can go anywhere now. Scouts say they saw you coming in and others could even smell you. What business was there for you in those dead lands or even further on? The fools that rule those lands would have us be ruled the same, to say nothing of the king we fled from, unwanted and alone. You seem honest, that's why I'm asking you. What have you been doing? Shame you lost all that gold, it would have been nice to have been part of the group that'll get a bit of it as long as that old man doesn't keep it all for himself. I wonder what else there is for you to lose?"

Gunter remained calm despite the blades pointing at him. One had cut the left side of his face and he was bleeding, so spoke around the wound as best he could.

"Is it really so unbelievable for us to be telling the truth? I will say the same thing. We're headed into the forest to meet with those like us. Once there we will discuss many things, the dark beyond this place among them I'm sure. I wouldn't have believed it without seeing it myself as the darkness in the sky really does feel wicked and having felt that darkness grow it makes my skin crawl in a way more than you could know."

The seated man sighed.

"Druids and their feelings. If you could just tell the sky to stop that would be great and take a load off the king's shoulders which might keep him off our backs. I'm sure you'll all just have a little meeting around a campfire and then everything will be fine again in your minds. That'd be wrong. Nothing will change for you heedless fools. The world will move on as you people say, huh? All part of some great cycle but I don't recall being told about any of this going on in these times. I'm not even an old man but why do I feel that my best days are behind me? To say nothing of all the people out there living off hope and not much else. The world is growing old, so it is nice to be somewhere new such as this. That isn't just me, other people feel it, that we're just waiting to be told that we can stop, lay down and give it all up as the days pass us by ever slower. None of you are doing anything about it, you oh so worldly people."

All the druids were gradually relieved of their possessions, which of value the searchers only found their weapons and any bags that contained food or leather sacks used for water. The weapons were bundled together and taken away with the provisions left at their feet for sorting. Their things were treated with respect and of course they would have to be if they were, soon to be passed around or auctioned off to new owners.

Another man came out of the gaol to look around at the group lined up. He shook his head.

"There's not enough room for six people, we've stacked too much wood trying to keep the moisture off."

"Then we'll throw half of them in there while we interrogate one lot and swap them over later." The seated man said and pointed at the unconscious Zelda in Findal's arms.

"You, hand her over and I'll pick you other two to go in with her."

He then pointed to Gunter and Survel, who were both prodded into the room. Zelda was taken from Findal and thrown in after the two men. Both of them were forced to catch her when she was thrown inside and the door then slammed behind them. Those who had caught the druids then dispersed around the settlement, leaving Peter, Findal and Nasker in front of the seated man.

Now that he was alone with the other three he sat up in the chair.

"Not even that woke her up. I think she might be dead, don't you? So now that we've got all that sorted and that man is out of the way, tell me what your reason is for being here. We've known for a long time that your kind has been here in this forest but this trouble we're seeing in every shadow and behind every turned back can't be you. Something is going on and I want to know what."

The man busied himself with a pipe while waiting of an answer. When none came, he took it from his mouth and gestured around.

"Well the old man Miller wants to know so we'll find out sooner or later. You don't have to go anywhere, I don't care, just want a little mutual understanding between us so you know one of you will have to talk. Do you want to know what I believe is the matter with this forest? You have done something, you with your reaching, grasping hands trying to play animal instead of using your heads like civilised people. There are other forests and other cliques I'm sure but this one you have spoiled. For too long has the forest begun to turn into a dark and dangerous place, one which we can not venture in with small bands of men safely."

Now that his body was free from the danger of being impaled, Peter was able to take a breath that he felt down to his feet.

What really was what you attempted to try and do Zelda? You've put us in this mess, even if it is the truth that I suppose you didn't get us here exactly on your own. I could be equally to blame for that. I don't like that I don't know what is happening but at least I'm not the only one without all the answers.

He stared past his feet to the soil.

"It is not for the likes of you to know what we do, but hear this. The sky fills with a darkness we have not seen before, all the while the people of this world are content to let it spread and effect each neighbour. This stinks of a land being misused by those who have forgotten its worth."

"I agree that it stinks. It stinks that you seem to be distancing yourselves from the blame here. If anything we as a people have been good at only misusing each other. It is true that lands to the east and north have been refusing travellers. Alegan is in a spot, hmm?"

"We travelled from there and that land is lost. You should be thankful we choose to do what we can here."

"And you're doing nothing that I can see to improve the situation for anyone. Now feel free to roam around, unless either of you other two have anything else to say."

Findal's face was creased with unhappiness.

"You're letting us go?"

The guard shrugged.

"You won't be able to escape as the ward on this place is strong but feel free to test it as much as you like. There's no use standing here talking nothings to me, go do your own thing but don't make a ruckas."

Nasker leaned forward to interrupt.

"I thought we were going to be put into the gaol and have the others let out in our place. They may need it more than we do."

The man blew out some smoke.

"That will be later. I was expecting to be here for a while but you've all clammed up apart from this young one. So now I've got nothing better to do and neither do you. Miller is going to want a report of all the wonderfully useless information you've given me. He's not going to take it well when he finds out all it is I've got to tell him."

"Don't mind if I do, if I'm free to go for a stroll." Nasker said.

He stretched and began walking off, tapping Peter on his shoulder as he went.

"I'm going to go look around. You saw the strange man in the large house, maybe go see if you can find out more about him before he finds out more about us. Make yourself useful."

So while Findal was left looking at the gaol, Peter had gone to take a look around for himself. No longer being forced to walk at a disagreeable pace he was able to slowly take everything in.

What use could he be now? He wondered at that while looking up at a firm but quite invisible layer above in the sky. It was something he had not felt before but surely it was the ward hiding them from view.

He could not touch it and there was nothing wrong he could feel that would prevent him from seeing the world and turning along with it. He would become a bird to see how far he could get.

Peter felt his temples throb and a blackness surrounded his eyes causing him to stagger and snap the reach of his mind back.

He now had a headache, but at least his mind was clear of that sudden alarming blackness.

"Is there something wrong young man?"

He turned to see the old man with the red hat. He did not look on Peter with the kindly concern of an old man, but of one twisted with suspicion.

"Nothing." Peter lied.

Is this what happened to Zelda? Wasn't that something else? After all I'm still here.

"Just sick and tired of being put in these places. Are you Miller?"

The old man called Miller nodded.

"Indeed I am. And you, you worked to avoid places such as this, did you? Or was it unavoidable? Quite the difference there. We ourselves do not enjoy the cage we put ourselves in but we had to do it for our safety. Sometimes telling ourselves that there was no choice is what we do when we don't want to admit that we didn't work hard enough to get the things we wanted."

"So is that why you're here where you shouldn't be? You're some noble or whoever that didn't get what you wanted and think it comes down to effort. I was wrong about you. It wasn't that you were all a different type of corrupt, you simply weren't corrupt enough. That's what you get for expecting anything to come out of hard work among walls and supposedly civilised ways."

"Be careful, I can make your life temporary, you know." The old man snapped.

Peter would have very much liked to remind the man that life was temporary enough already, but did not want to make his headache worse. Instead he spent his energy on walking away. The last thing he wanted was for this person, who appeared to be in charge, to lose what little patience he had for them. Peter also noticed that he hadn't appeared disappointed in the least when Zelda had failed to create a crop for his garden. He would not have attempted it himself but he would have expected anyone being offered free produce to be saddened to then not receive it. Unless Miller had enough for himself already.

So Peter took his time checking on the fruit trees that had been planted, ones that while quiet for now, would eventually emerge and would have been expected to produce fruit for everyone. He strolled amongst the soil barefoot to get a feeling for the ground that left the same trepidation within him. Yes, he felt after some time this could be good soil for planting but as it was he was worried for whatever might grow. He thought about tunnelling underneath.

If I were to become a digging creature, perhaps a hole could be dug underneath where the others have been held. Ah but then, what if there are bricks laid between us? Then it would not work and I would have my energy and time wasted. Also I had better find out more about why I have been seeing dark things approach my mind before I try anything else.

It turned out that there was little in the way of answers to be had. The three men were left roaming around for days, as days did pass without any other word of when they would be able to leave. The man in red was taking his days slowly and that caused them all to worry that they would be trapped here for a great amount of time that they did not have. Attempts had been made to leave but the forest would always lead them back to the village. It did not matter where they left from or how they moved through the trees, they would always come back.

Worse still was if they stayed in the forest outside of the village and chose not to leave. What would fall over them was an unsettling feeling, the darkness in every shadow that had been described to them as if by such shadows they were being watched. None of them could tolerate such darkness for long and by some means they did not know the look outs always found them.

Zelda had eventually woken up but from what they were able to share through the gaol door she was the only one not chained up. Both Gunter and Survel had been found in a similar state to herself and Peter had a suspicion that old man Miller had guessed from watching his own faltering attempt that they had tried to slip out of the gaol. The chains would help to prevent them changing, especially if they were tight, but the connection they had with the world was deeper and it was that which he worried for the most.

On one walk he spied the man in the red hat, who appeared to be sorting out some disagreement or other problem between two people in the village. If Miller was not at his home, that most likely meant that no one was there. So Peter decided to do some snooping around, as long as he could get into his house without being spotted.

Despite its position in the rough center of the village, Peter was able to sneak along the sides of the house and found himself undisturbed while doing so. There were certainly people about as he could hear them but was able to take himself around the front and make his way to the door without any incident.

To his surprise he could easily get inside without breaching the door as there was no lock on it. He walked inside to darkness that took his eyes a few moments to adjust. The home was nearly empty of possessions, merely a single table, chair and candle holder in the first room. What surprised him just as much was that he found that there was no second story, the building had just been built with a rather high roof and there were ladders allowing for the shutters out of reach to be opened.

The house was split into four rooms and in two others he found the home empty of possessions apart from a bed, a pitcher and a hat stand. There were cabinets and drawers helping to secure ladders on many of the walls but none contained anything more than some clothes.

Who are these people? Little more than runaways who have near only the clothes on their backs, most likely. He thought grimly.

From the last room came the voice he had previously heard when outside the house.

"Even if the door had a lock I would have opened it and let you in."

Quietly Peter walked into the fourth room. There was a girl who sat in the middle of the room on top of a tall pile of blankets, wearing a single sleeping top made for someone much older. He would have thought that she was asleep by the way her head was lulling over with her body slumped forward. Due to the gloom he could not see her face but could not have seen behind the long black hair she had that nearly reached the floor anyway.

She did not move when he entered but he could hear her breathing.

"You do smell of a long, drawn out death. It seeps out from deep within yet it is not from within yourselves that it is found. We've never had any of them come so far out from there."

She raised her head to face him and Peter had to stop himself taking a step back as even in the gloom he could see that her eyes were white with blindness.

"Nor will we. They can not move beyond where it was they fell. Even though we are still alongside Malleau in this forest they can not get close to us. Even if the rest of this world joins them they shall remain there until it is their time to fade. The people here will instead find other reasons to distrust you. I may be blind but there are things even I can see."

"I am not blind and there are things I can't see, such as yourself, terribly clearly. Does the room have to be so dark with you hidden away?"

"It doesn't matter to me. It is what it is and I do not live in filth, so be at ease. It does matter to other people, however. Some in the village you might see were forced to make the journey here alongside me all because they helped me. They left much behind so as you can imagine some see their crossing paths with me to be the worst mistake of their lives. So here it is I stay out of sight for my own good."

She sat up straight and stretched out her bent neck.

"But where are my manners? You have come into my mansion so I must be hospitable. My name is Bort and you have come upon me for some reason, not one of your mind but one of heart. For yours is not a treacherous heart."

There was a light humour to her words, so while Peter did not quite know how to tell her that the house was bare, he did not discount the possibility that Bort knew all too well how she lived.

"You don't know anything about me. Or any of us for that matter."

"That's why I don't mind so much that you all somehow found a way through my barrier. So I can finally meet new people."

"Your barrier? Well we didn't find our way through anything, your people found us as we walked on most normally. And as for your other words, you'd meet a lot more people if you were outside. Have you thought about how nice that would be? As it is, no one can see the person they threw away their lives to help. Do not feel as if you have to become indebted to them just because you might have caused them suffering. Instead show them that you can go on and live because of their actions. I am sure they will appreciate it, especially if you help them further."

Bort rested a hand on her chin.

"It would have been nice to flee north, but that way was closed to us. Perhaps I could have found myself among those who could have helped me with my talents but it wasn't to be. Preferably I'd rather be there than here but I get what you're saying."

"Then do not thank them by hiding away. There are times when we cross paths with people we never see again, but one way or another we are glad that we did, even if we can not see them getting on with their lives. What you do here is live in darkness. Unless that old man forces you to hide away I see no good reason for it."

Peter was feeling a little awkward standing, he particularly was not happy standing over someone to talk. As there was nothing to sit on he sat on the floor instead. Bort's head drifted over to where he sat down just to be a courtesy, as he was sure she could not actually see him while they were talking.

Bort idly played with her hair while she spoke.

"You think it is simple, going out and meeting others. They think they know the world in ways you never will so have certain expectations of you. Even if that's not quite how it all is some people will never be convinced. I hear that you have somewhere to be and people to see. There is only so much I can do. Of course I can drop the barrier and allow you to escape but then that causes problems for everybody. The way things are here must be followed and life must be maintained. I am sure whoever you would meet at the Great Tree would agree."

Peter sighed.

"I honestly dread the meeting. I have too many bits to pick with enough old people already and scant want to have an increase in that number."

"Then maybe you should practice understanding your elders."

"They're not always right, trying to tell me what to do."

"But *I* might be right and I'm much younger than you. Thinking as you do might leave you cold and indecisive your whole life, unsure on who to rely on unless you only rely on your own advice. It could be that you wish to merely become old and senile so that you can not tell the difference in meaning from one word to another."

"People are not so old and senile out there that they will know the meaning of your words regardless. By the sounds of it, I'm going to guess that when you fled you were hidden away from everyone else here."

If she's right why can't she see that she's just one more unknown that everyone in the village is afraid of? It only makes things worse. Hiding from the things you're afraid of doesn't mean they aren't still there.

Bort nodded.

"We pretended to be traders going south and I was hidden even then. As the road lead nowhere and there were further words being said of a shadow overhead we moved into the forest. We did not want to get caught out in the open and that darkness was especially troubling which hung over the forest, for while we knew that druids were not doing much there had been talk that they had finally lost their place or given up."

"Well some of us are here and we're determined to put an end to the troubles and that darkness troubles us too. I've never been here myself but such dark clouds are not meant to be. None of us are able to do anything currently not just because of yourself, but because a darkness takes away our ability to feel the world. We would rather not think that it comes from the barrier, meaning that it would come from you, it turns out."

"It is because nothing is there. You can not take something that is not there and use it. That's what you're feeling as that is what I see in my mind for myself. When you take the time to reach out and find yourself without the sustenance you were looking for you end up that way."

"I wouldn't think of how we connect to the world of nature in terms such as that."

"Is that so? I am at a loss for words. That's not in the least part convincing."

She brought her blank gaze up from her lap.

"This world is a vessel for life. Be careful not to fill it with dark and terrible things yourself, as there is no other way to empty it than to tip it all out, which means to start again. And I say this because there are many who would fill the world with dark and terrible things, already have."

The girl became solemn.

"In fact it has already begun and you're all far too late. Something beyond fear has already found this world in an age ripe for using. Whispers and words are on the wind just as they are in the darkness all around. Might that we find those words and write them down they could be to you as words of a greater power. Words that would make the world quake in fear. No one can live on in such darkness and nothing will survive it."

"Then what is the point in continuing on?"

Bort looked to the roof.

"You ask what's the point? There have been many times and ages when the end has seemed near in one way or another and indeed for some it has come for them. Even if the world itself has moved on, it moved on without them regardless. Indeed one day it will move on without any of us, so ever will it be. You do things not for the tomorrow you will see but the one you will not. Until that day comes you should live as if you are going to see it. So do not leave the world in such a state as you have seen it. May that it be you leave your work unfinished on your final day, the world will find a way to have it carried on. But for that to happen there needs to be a world at all. As such there is a task I feel I must dedicate my life towards while you go about doing yours. So I must ask you for help, no matter how strange it must seem."

"You can't tell us our future."

"No, but I can see directions all the same. Such a gift could be used to taunt others who wonder if they are doing the right things in their lives or demand to always be making the best choices for themselves. But who is to know what that is? Not I."

Peter left the house and out the front was Nasker and the man in the red hat, who didn't seem in the least surprised to see him exiting his home.

"Find any answers?" Nasker said.

Peter shrugged.

"Some. I am however more surprised at her willingness to be kept hidden if she can feel out the future."

Nasker turned to the man in the red hat.

"So what is the reason for all this? You have a strange person hidden here. Hiding not just her from everyone here but all of you from everyone else. It used to be that those who could predict the future weren't too uncommon."

The man shrugged.

"I had to come out here, far away. They wanted to hang the girl and do further things for speaking the truth one such as her could see with their eyes while being blind so we took her with us but have been hunted by the king's men ever since."

"I can understand that."

"Of course, people don't like being told that things can not be changed and instead take it out on the messenger. Poor old me."

"You believe her then?"

"Of course."

"Have you thought of letting her go to the forest and train as a seer amongst us? Her gift could be valuable when honed correctly."

Miller shook his head.

"No, I shall take her further south if I must, even further away from all of this where she can live a normal life without being shut away, her mind undiluted by fantasies."

"Such as what?"

"You're asking an awful lot of questions."

"You are the one giving them to me." Nasker said.

The man shook his head and made his way inside the house. As they had decided not to follow him, Peter and Nasker began to walk through the middle of the village.

Peter shrugged to himself.

I really don't want to tell anyone else that this person thinks we're too late. I just can't believe that. Whatever Bort thinks she is she's not going to be right about that. My future is mine, not one guided or predicted by anyone else.

He turned to Nasker.

"I don't think she would want to come with us and be a seer. She said as much herself, preferring to have gone far into the north of all places but that would have been difficult. Plenty of space for them to be cut off and trapped. She also asked for something of which I can't believe."

"What did she want?" Nasker asked curiously.

Peter nearly laughed and shook his head.

"A book. The blind girl asked for a book. There are things she wishes to record, so it could be that she merely wishes for paper for another to write on."

"Did somebody take out her eyes?"

"No no, they are covered in a haze. For how long she has been that way I did not ask."

"Then a wizard could mend her eyes, so I see why she would want to go north. A book does seem to be a strange request at the moment. As for that we still have our duty so I hope you didn't promise her anything."

Peter was silent, but Nasker did not push him further.

Later that night, Nasker remained awake around a fire as the three of them had been given a fire pit to sleep around on the edge of the village where it was rather dark as most who lived here were shut away within their homes next to their fireplaces. While Peter slept and Findal was off somewhere else, he was left thinking to himself.

Here, through a gap in the stones barricaded up by an angled wall of wooden stakes they could see outside. The wall itself was not terribly high, not even as tall as he was and the trees with their needles reached far above it into the sky.

That man was giving me many useful questions indeed, telling me what it was he didn't know. She's already a seer, living in a forest that lives and breathes like a person, quite the spectacle to think about. I wonder if she could tell the forest its fate?

He looked beyond the walls to the trees around them.

Rather, it is made up of many creatures that live and those creatures have an aversion to being tricked and that trait is passed onto the forest. The magic in Atwixie makes it so. Not the best to keep thinking about the darkness yet it must be faced head on. If a dark influence afflicted the forest then a darkness will become all of it and will twist all that live in it. How troublesome if we were to fail that this darkness would surely spread beyond the reaches of the land surrounding it.

Then he frowned.

And as for you, you're not here either. I knew almost straight away, even if I feel I am getting closer. Now I waste my time looking at these trees as I can not simply do away with the one who holds us here. And if she would like something to read I'll have to come back and give her something that will open her eyes that much wider.

Then out of the corner of his eye there was something that had not been there a moment before. There was a person, standing just outside of range of the fire. She wore no clothes and was covered in grey ash over skin that was cracked and burnt. Long hair of the same colour was parted to reveal an expressionless face with shadowy sockets.

His eyes snapped back to the fire where he could see only her feet out of the corner of his eye. He blinked and the phantom was gone. His heart hammered loudly in his ears enough that he thought anyone close by must surely wake up to the sound.

I did not see that. He thought as he relaxed.

I did not see that at all.

He spent the rest of the night by the fire, keeping it alight until the first light came through the trees.

Chapter Twenty Seven
Bright Intentions

Findal was unable to sleep and he had spent many nights in somewhat of a restless manner. Ensuring during the day that the guards were treating the others fairly did not put his mind at ease so sometimes he would go without sleep. The days had kept passing them by and he was keeping count.

This should have been a place most at home for him he thought, compared to the rest of those he travelled with, but instead he was being reminded just why he was leaving it all behind to begin with.

Taking my gold, sticking to suspicion and ignorance. We'll be better off without any of it but this awful darkness in the ground here, I can't do anything without feeling bleary eyed and faint. It certainly will be that there are those who would rather hold onto everything with their last gasps than allow those of us who wish to fight for something new to make it happen. At least nature abhors all of that. We step in, we do what we want, we step back, having taught those watching their own coffers a lesson along the way.

It would be a permanent lesson, one he hoped most would not need anyone to later remind them of, as they would take heed from what was said, not like the people here that had made themselves a place in the forest where they should not be.

He wasn't sure how long this place would last if they did not branch out or at least try and go south. Perhaps they could be the ones to live in the ruins of the south along the sea, giving him somewhere to return to on his own travels as somewhere people respected the natural world.

If any of them were to return north it could well end up leading to a swift death. Staying here could be just as fatal, if they would forget what it was that brought them here and what a waste that would be considering all the trouble they were putting him through.

Late in the night though it was he made his way to the gaol. There was a torch outside the door but he didn't mind. It would stop him falling asleep. The guard was next to the torch, dozing under what little warmth it gave him. Findal moved past him and approached the door.

"It's just me." He said quietly.

"Is anyone awake?"

From behind the door, Zelda responded quietly.

"I am. You didn't wake me. The cold woke me up while Gunter and Survel both sleep soundly. I think it is all this waiting while not wanting to admit that they are trapped inside. Waking seems to be like falling into a nightmare for them. How are Peter and Nasker at the moment?"

He sat up against the door.

"They're out and about, both are still fine. As fine as we could be expected to be. Apparently Peter met with a seer in the village today. I remind you these people came from Kasynne, beside the forest, so do not hate them for what they have done here."

"So they say. However, can we not ask these people for help if we are in the same circumstances regarding their king?" She asked.

Zelda sounded tired and Findal had to rub his eyes to relieve his own tiredness. The torch on the wall was bright and the light hurt his eyes that wanted sleep.

"Just because their king is trouble doesn't mean they have to look kindly on us. I fear an army would have to march on their walls for them to take up arms and still they would ignore the forest and blame their neighbour, cousin or uncle. Isn't that how the rulers of lands sort out their problems? We are nothing to them. Leadership successions and squabbles over land bore me to pieces."

"I've never met that king so I can't know what he might be like. If that place is anything like this then it is best we keep ourselves away. That being said I'd rather not have that mean being trapped in here while everything gets darker and darker ever more. Is there nothing else that can be done?"

"We're doing what we can, which isn't much I will admit. Hopefully we can come to an understanding with the people living here. We should be allowed to leave but others are in no such hurry."

"I am going to try to get back to sleep." Zelda said.

On the way out, he noticed the guard on the stool was now awake, looking lonesomely out at the darkness in front of him.

"Did you get what you wanted?" He asked abruptly, as Findal passed him.

Findal turned to the man.

"It's never just one thing I want. The line has to be drawn somewhere for the day or night, else I'd go mad. Maybe I'll never reach my goals and get what I want but that's life. You just go back to thinking you understand us, be blind to the world and let the rest of us take care of the problems you create. People often accuse us of having our heads in the ground yet that's nothing such as the trouble you're giving us."

"Does it not occur to you in your boundless consideration that I myself may have my own wants?"

"And I can see you're doing a lot about it. Don't mind me, I've got people I know to be concerned about."

"As do I. Let me tell you something, if you are keen on leaving."

So the man told Findal his story. He had gambled all his money and left his family with nothing. His daughter ran away and to escape his debt he ran away too down here but was not actually making any money and would have none until he returned home, meaning that nothing was going home to his wife. As such it was highly likely that there would not be a home to return to. He did not like where he was but was weighing up his options of returning at all.

Findal hummed.

"Well we can't help you leave. I suppose you found yourself stuck as we did. There is a girl in the middle of the village, I am sure that you know of her. She's the one creating the ward around this place in case you didn't know. You might have to talk to her if you're keen on returning. Only you can decide if you want to return empty handed however. We can only do so much to help the world, you must do some things yourself and accept the times in which you can not. I've had to remind myself of that from time to time. Goodnight."

With that he left to go back to the fire pit and even though the conversation had just been between the two of them, Zelda had heard everything as well.

The room was still cold the next morning and she was busy tracing dust in the floor in the light that shone down through the barred hole in the door.

A fine place we find ourselves in. So close yet so far is hardly what I would call comforting, but it is better than being dead.

They had been fed sparsely with bread so old and dry she had to soak it in her bowl of water so that she would not break her teeth on it. Her stomach had protested greatly to being fed something so out of sorts, but there was nothing else so she often spent her mornings in further solitude keeping it down. And she would keep it down. On occasion the guards would be provided with something warm and the smell would always bring on to her what she thought to be madness for a while.

This was not one such morning, one where the little piles of dust that she disturbed floated about the floor and were illuminated in the light.

She had once been told that other people could make signs and symbols to use in their magic but she wondered how any of that would help if she could not use any of it. Especially since the patterns had no meaning and such mindless work saved only to pass the time.

Zelda hadn't the faintest idea how one would start learning magic based on symbols. There was certainly more to it than drawing out what you wanted, she had not delved far enough it know more than that. So here it was that she simply drew animals on the ground, amusing herself that maybe they could come and save them from this cage that animals might be kept in.

"I'm sick of being trapped." She said.

Gunter's voice scraped up from the floor below, trying the raise itself above sounds of people moving outside.

"We are not the only ones. I should have known from the start that as these people are all from Kasynne, not survivors of any concern, mind you, but seekers searching for new land. I have tried to suggest they all travel further but we are obviously too late to unburden them from the fate of the forest within which now they are trapped. Trapping us then is them simply repeating all the pain they know on others. They have set up these walls and buildings and have ploughed the fields earlier in the year and set them ready for warmer weather that might not come. Whether we accept them or not does not matter any longer, we can only hope that they come to an understanding of the forest and allow us our freedom to do what we must."

"Perhaps one of us, if not us ourselves, another druid, should be stationed here to help them do just that."

Survel was not so enthused.

"If only our senses were not so dulled. No one can come soon in the poor conditions that we're all in for and I can say that we will not be the only ones feeling the effects. I do not like the way in which our magic fades and we lose our own understandings. This only aids others in their ignorance if they are to suspect that we were always to be so weak. We can't just say what is on our minds, even if it is the right thing to say."

"From what we have all felt it is safe to say that something dark lingers in the forest. What a terrible fate this is for all involved and as it is now, no right way is being made towards a remedy. Our remedy." Zelda said.

Gunter's voice came from the ground.

"That is all I can think of but I'm feeling much better now. As long as I shut my eyes I don't have to be reminded about where I am."

"That man Miller only wants to judge us from what he has heard so far. He could merely be worried that your words would sway him too much. Our words should sway after all, just as they used to as you all have said."

It is best I not tell him just how little I myself have spoken my mind on a great many things to do with him and other issues. I might not be able to stop talking were I to voice my concerns on every little thing that happened to give me cause to speak. I would go hoarse and then lose my voice completely, which wouldn't be such a problem if the plants and animals could still understand me. The people would still be a problem.

The sound of the door lock unlatching made her sweep away her aimless scrawling and look up, regretting it as the full blast of the sun made her cover her eyes from the overwhelming glare.

She spoke to the person she could not see.

"Please hear us out. We must be gone from this place before the middle of winter finds us. There is a place where we must find ourselves first and it is not here held inside these walls without escape."

The voice of the man who had sat near the door spoke from beyond the doorway.

"So there's really nothing you can do now that we've got you here. How fascinating. Still, a word's a word and you'll find soon enough how things will go, one way or another. It would seem that you are not wizards and a witch, but druids after all. To some people that is all the same but most of us who live in these lands know to tell the difference, even if no one told me to care either way."

"I would not have thought that we would be so hard to tell apart." Zelda said.

"Have you ever met a dark, evil, slithering witch or wizard before? You too would be cautious in their presence."

"No but it is well that we have our eyes and priorities set on saving this world from the likes of all who would ruin it and I very much gather that would not only be witches and wizards of malign intent such as you say but a list that would include even more besides. I'm not saying we're always right, however there are forces out there that need no suspicion attached to them and that would be us."

Gunter stood in his chains.

"Are you saying that we are free to leave? That we have been truthful and that it has taken this long to be decided? I'm sure we have not been judged on our words when we said why we were here to begin with."

"As I understand it, you have a job to do and a mess to clean up. You had better do so."

They were escorted outside. With the others nowhere in sight they walked slowly to the way out. People stared at them as they went but no one held in their faces any familiarity, emotion, or concern at all.

The guard pointed outside the village.

"The ward has been released for you. You may now leave."

Zelda turned to look at Gunter.

"We're not going to leave the others are we? If they are still here?"

"Even if we can leave we are not moving on without them, for I detest cages of all kinds. To arrive at the Great Tree with only half of those I had intended to show does not sit well with me. We were so very close to being safely away too, but alas this place sprung up in the absence of me and other eyes looking down here, I am thinking. As such we were trapped. What else might they sneak down here from the north I do not want them to be subject to, with their evil prisons and all manner of tools used to pry secrets from the hearts of men and women alike. I do not look to grant those that follow me death, so to stay them that fate were it to be approachable, we must ensure they come with us. Or is it only that after all this time we are now to trade places?"

The men around them were moving uneasily in their armour and the guard spoke.

"With all your complaining I thought you would want to hurry away."

"On top of that, other things are missing." Survel said.

"We will leave having reclaimed everything that has been taken from us. Maybe not the gold. How about you keep that."

"Oh I bet you think you'll reclaim the world, too? Don't you understand that the world changes? I understand, you say there's a cycle to all things and that our world is one that endlessly turns but it never turns the same way more than once. That is what you do not see."

Yet they were wondering if these men would not see that they would not leave without the others, for that would have been quite a poor display of manners, even if they would have been able to find their own way to the Great Tree.

***

Peter had not seen Findal for some time and while this had not been uncommon of late was wondering to himself if he had been rounded up. He went looking and while searching found Nasker up a tree.

"I can't seem to find Findal anywhere and he didn't show up at camp last night.

Could he have been taken in?" Peter said.

"Well I don't know about that. I'd rather be safe than sorry though, so how about we just ask around? I have not seen him myself." Replied Nasker.

"I've been seeing people carrying pots about. Someone needs to go ask what those are for. So maybe it is entirely possible that I have seen Findal, or at least bits of him, from a distance."

"That's not funny. I suppose this will be up to me as I can't see you doing any of the asking from where you are."

Nasker yawned.

"That is the point. Not only that but I am tired. That's also because I believe in the people of this place. I may not know them, or the extent of their, shall I say generous hospitality, however placed as it is to the forest I expect a part of nature and by extent us to rub off on them. It is inescapable this close to nature. Have a little heart in our captors and don't waste your breath."

Peter found himself unable to steady his concern, so went to those who were gathering some alarmingly large black pots, now that he saw them.

Upon asking what the pots were for, he was advised that it was for a stew that would be made up for everyone. This did little to calm his growing worry so had to ask them to elaborate.

"What'll be in it isn't up to us. You had best talk to the storekeeper, he's the one in charge of what we can use. Not everything stays edible throughout the winter so we're going to cook it all up."

They had better not be trying to stew us. He thought.

With that, Peter made his way to the building where all the goods were kept. Outside, a bored guard sat on a stool with his chin in his palm and did not move when he made to enter the storeroom.

The storekeeper was in charge of keeping all the dried and cured goods in one place. The room Peter found himself in had nothing stored in it at all, being small with one man seated at a bench surrounded with books. Not surprisingly, the door to the next room itself had two guards by the sides of it.

"Just thought I'd ask of what would be in the pots in the coming days." Peter said.

The man raised himself from his books, his face twisting into a smile.

"Oh, come to suggest something have we? Well we'll be having no funny business while you're here. Don't think you can add anything suspicious to the pots to turn us all silly."

"So you're not going to boil our friends up?" He asked firmly, but as politely as he could muster himself to be.

The guards began wheezing and he turned to see if they were having difficulty breathing but it turned out to be that both were trying to stifle laughter.

"Do you doubt my concern?"

The storekeeper responded as the guards continued to chuckle and guff together.

"It would seem that we're not people eaters any more than you are."

"We are all in some deep shadow filled trouble. Do none of you care what happens to the world?" Peter said.

"I care a lot less after having to speak with you, now be off with you and your concerns."

So he was made to leave as both the guards had regained their postures and were eyeing him in a menacing way that would have made him back out of the room had he encountered such glares on entering it.

On returning outside he found himself face to face with the man in the red hat and some armed men that were beside him.

"You are to come with us now." Said Miller.

So it was that Zelda, Gunter and Survel, who had refused to leave and had spent some time sitting out the front of the wall on the grass were wondering what to do when they were interrupted by the old man, who had come with the other three prisoners, along with a blind girl holding onto his arm.

The old man did appear slightly irritated.

"Yes, so here I was expecting merely to deal with the three of you when I'm told here that such an act will not do. I would have liked three druids for my personal curiosity but that can not happen apparently." He eyed off the girl, who shrugged without caring that eyes were on her.

"All of them have to go, as even though there are things I can do it is nothing out of the ordinary and we are walking in times far from that, even if to others these times are most ordinary indeed. Who is to know how the future will judge us? In order for there to be one there can be no one held captured to curiosities here. Had I said nothing or had my words held no weight I would have suggested that the three of you be best on your way, yet because that is something I hold dear then you should too, even if you might not see it for the brightest of intentions."

"Who's to say we'll do that?" Survel said.

"Me of course. All your intentions are quite like that of ignorant animals who can't see the world beyond that which you perceive, which is all I can imagine when I think of you."

"Maybe we should leave faster." Peter said.

Surprisingly, Gunter shook his head.

"Listen, Miller. You know you could have just asked me earlier for as much information as you would have ever needed but still you put us in this position and you endanger the world in which you yourself live."

The man in the red hat shook his own head.

"That is not my name, I must admit. I used to be a miller who wanted better for his town and the people who lived in it. Due to scheming I was made the focus of hostility and chased out, you see. Once a man of some low yet growing standing who was hoping to get the king's ear, it now doesn't matter who I am as long as I am someone to all these people. I don't seek renown or remembrance for myself, that everyone lives on is the most important thing. Know me as no man other than one who helped others. Such should be the fate of a man who does not get what he wants in life."

He gestured back to the village.

"It is clear you will not make yourselves to the Great Tree by tonight, as solstice will be over, I am sure you realise. So stay, for one last night I am saying. As surely one more will not make the difference to you and you have been poorly fed so far and have been met with the hospitality suited to far more wicked men. We do not want to inherit the wickedness from the king yet you see how we have allowed it to become part of us."

"And perhaps the people here could show their generosity by returning what has been taken from us. While we ask politely." Gunter said.

They all spent the rest of the day attempting to reclaim all the things that had been taken from them with success. It was an act that did take them all day and there was little of the day left by the time all their weapons had been retrieved. Zelda didn't bother searching for lost tools or implements, she should not have taken them to begin with and here was a good place where they might get some use.

For those who had found themselves searching the longest, there was unfortunately no way that they could reclaim what had been taken from them fast, as what had been taken was scattered about the place. While there was some debate over whether or not to even try, they ran into the problem of convincing people that the things that they had suddenly found themselves in possession of were actually belongings to be returned.

And yet they could not be rude or crude about it, for they all had to take Gunter's words to heart. They were visible representations of nature, and that they were aware of the dark times they were in and that it was their responsibility to not be as what Bort said they would be.

Night fell and people came out of their homes. Even with plenty enough houses, there were more people here than it had first appeared. Even though they were crowded in, all those people were able to have an enjoyable time as they danced and sang songs around a large fire in a space large enough to have one built.

The druids had preferred their spot, out of the way from all the crowding and noise. Occasionally one would wander off then come back but Zelda found herself detached, happy to watch these people that she could not feel anything towards. She turned to Gunter.

"Shouldn't we sneak out now that we have been set free?"

"Yes but to be honest that man is right, the solstice will pass us by tonight. In ways such as this can we hope to turn people around to us, by accepting hospitality. They have listened to our words and while we stand on shaky ground and all could soon turn to darkness, this little victory must learned from, where we can see people turned from their fear. I would have liked to be with all the other druids by now but that isn't going to happen, meaning there's no use complaining about it as we must make the best of what we have now. We will not be alone when we reach the Great Tree so we'll take the time here to relax. And eat."

He handed her a pie then disappeared into the crowds, perhaps leaving her alone for a time, unless she would decide to get up and stop watching by herself the crowds, the noise, the happy people who could put aside their problems when the world was ending. Not that they knew.

I don't want to be distracted by everything going on. If I go out there amongst the people, doesn't that mean that I'm just people too? Every moment we spend here is just another that passes and we could end up just like them. Worse, because with what we know about the world, the darkness is that much harder to ignore.

Zelda had to admit that she also found the smell of food hard to ignore. There was also drink to go along with the food and before she knew it Zelda found herself stuffing her face with both until she lost her legs and found herself resting up alone. Then after a moment she found herself somewhere else in the village. Then it happened again, in one place one moment and then another the next. As it suddenly dawned on her that she had gained the magical ability of instantaneous travel, she realised that she had to tell someone. Because this all along could have gotten them out of their problems, she knew.

But how to control this new found magic? She did not know, until quite abruptly she found herself now away from the crowds, sitting under a tree being watched by Nasker. He had relieved her of her bottle and was now helping himself to it, although he soon put the bottle away from his mouth to hold it out of the reach of her grabbing hands.

"Looks like you've never had a good day of fun in your life." He lamented without a hint of a smile on his face.

Zelda tried a few times to speak then found she couldn't make her mouth open to form words, so she just pointed at him and waved an arm to the crowds in place of saying *'then why aren't you there?'* And then from side to side as to say *'look, I'm over here now'*, which was just as important.

Nasker appeared disinterested but seemed to understand.

"Who, me? I don't enjoy all these crowds, but I do enjoy watching them, I'm sure you do too. We can't lose sight of the real problem here, remember. All of this could be lost, so it helps to put things into perspective."

She shook her head. This was urgent news she had to tell but still her voice failed her.

"I mean it, really. Tomorrow will come and it will just be like any other day. But for how long if not then, you must ask yourself. How long this can possibly go on for? We celebrate a cycle but it coils for only so long without anyone considering the possibility that there is an end for it. The key it is grab it by the tail before that end comes."

Zelda just stared at him. How could he be so serious at a time like this?

Being stared at, Nasker's face creased into a frown.

"You really think we can keep all this going on forever?"

"Yes!" She finally said.

Nasker's seriousness evaporated and he burst out laughing.

Zelda went to respond but felt a strange, creeping feeling in her stomach, that generously reintroduced its contents to her mouth and she turned over to throw up. Nasker heartily laughed himself to tears.

She shot him a stare and wiped her mouth clean with the back of her hand as she looked up at him. Even though she felt she had humiliated herself in some way she couldn't come up with a response to his laughter at her expense as she felt tired, so was forced to listen to it as her body bid the world goodnight for an alcohol induced sleep.

The next day did come, as he had said it would and Zelda felt that it was no different from any other where the ashes of a fire still burned and smouldered in the middle of town but the dark of the early morning was silent and cold. There was one difference, as she had woken up with her head in a splitting pain. There was no time to complain as eventually everyone was awake and moving before soon enough.

There were no goodbyes, they all slipped out bleary eyed, determined to make for the Great Tree with no further delay.

Peter was yawning.

"So will we be having another fine year? I hope this was worth it."

Gunter sighed.

"Of course. Now that we can be on our way there is nothing that can stop us. There is no such trouble that can't be dealt with by believing in the natural way of things and the understanding that we are all part of the ever repeating cycle that governs this world. We do as we do to retain the world's balance and ensure that it will even be so. All we do is usher in the dawn and give thanks that we may view the world ever more. Even if those such as these folk are hesitant, it is proof that we can still make all as it should be once more."

They could move through the trees and far past the points that before would have turned them around. All of them were uneasy, however, as soon after passing beyond where they could go, they felt steadily about them a creeping movement that hurried them along.

Nasker lit a torch and none of them strayed far from it.

Only Findal was truly unhappy, having been relieved of much of his baggage which had not been recovered.

"I say when we're all done I'll come back here and buy everything I can. Here of all places they can't make use of my gold yet I had not once piece of it returned to me."

Zelda stared at him out of the corner of her eyes.

"I always thought it funny that you needed the coins."

"We are most likely going to need something to bargain with once we are past the forest for I suppose we might have to keep going north when we are done here. Gold is something everyone understands. Now it is just us and not even our words, pleading to be understood. We can't even pay people to heed us."

So further into the forest they walked for a few more days, where it seemed that some knew the way they were headed, as paths that twisted and flattened disappeared in many directions but Gunter, Survel and Nasker walked with confidence in their steps.

Gunter seemed rather pleased indeed, turning to the others to explain little tells in the forest in particular places.

"We'll be passing by the Great Tree where we hope to return the spirit to. It does not matter that our reason for going there has lost meaning, I won't blame others if they would rather be searching than returning to it themselves. We are close enough that we should make the effort for the journey instead of turning about as there will certainly be information left that we can make use of and a much more friendly place to rest. That is clearly a rest we will need as this forest bound darkness is becoming increasingly strenuous to keep on top of. To which I have something to say, despite my earlier positive outlook when we left that village."

He sighed.

"This darkness in the forest which is growing is not what is taking away the connection we have with nature. The spirit leaving their place at the Great Tree did that and we have been losing our magic ever since. If we do not do something soon it will be gone for good. More than anything else for ourselves, that is what is running out. It is as Findal said, we will have nothing. To have this forest effected so that it effects us in this way can only mean that there is a dark heart in it somewhere or near it as well. I worry for what we might find at the Great Tree but as the north kingdom is settled alongside it I can think of nowhere else that wretchedness comes from so close. That is why searching for the spirit is so important. The world will lose a voice and it shall not return. We may have to confront that north kingdom but even that may not buy us time."

"Could it be that they took the spirit away from us?" Peter said.

"In order to destabilise the world and get back at the rest of the world that spurns them, even as they spurn elsewhere and all other things? It is possible."

Zelda was building up a rather worrying picture of that kingdom in her head. As to her understanding, they still had to journey further into the forest, yet here they were, having failed in what they had been asked to do such as that crazy old creature still somewhere in Malleau had. But she knew they all had a difference. They had each new day at least, but how many more then that they had going forward she was unable to guess.

And just as how she would have felt dread had she known they were going to miss their gathering by watching the days get closer, she would have been no better knowing how far away that last day might be. As long as on that day she would be able to make the most of the time that she had then all else would turn out fine.

PART THREE

Belonging

Chapter Twenty Eight
Watching and Waiting

The city was changing again. Just as when the walls went up, there was a shift in the mood of the people as more of them went missing. She could feel it, could see it in the quiet eyes of those coming and going about their days as the cold further crept in.

This cold was not just the weather, it was much more than that. A house would find itself suddenly abandoned, those from the inner walls might have found their home repossessed, but it was hard to feel sorry for them, as they still had some wealth. Even if they found themselves outside searching for places to live, often taking the homes that were now empty in the outer ring, because people had lived in those once too.

A scant few chose to leave Churl entirely and of those Kieke was careful to watch them go and pick off stragglers at her master's request, their family no doubt thinking that they changed their minds or ran away, but in reality they had not gone far at all. Bodies were sometimes needed, or rather the stuff in them was needed for all sorts of important things. She wasn't one to be afraid of getting her hands dirty, not when she was bidden to or when she wanted to feel that face flushed rush of the last fleeting moments of life.

Often, the midnight wailing could be heard of a family being relieved of one of their own, being taken away, lost as it were. Where would they go? Where else but into the castle, past the gates and inner walls. Kieke was almost jealous. Almost, as she could not be allowed to give in to such a thing as jealousy. There was far too much at stake for her to be carted off in shackles and then swiftly disposed of. Far too much preparation had gone into her mission now, although if she had the chance to make the one kill she needed she would jump at it.

She could not reveal herself, not let a rumour spread about herself, for it did not take much at all to be accused these days, as was likely for those most unfortunate ones already gone. By doing something of the sort in spreading rumours she would be throwing her life away, along with it everyone else's.

The sky heaved, with blackness bleeding into it in wet streaks that vanished from one heartbeat to the next. Kieke watched the sky for a few more seconds, scanning it, but the darkness did not show itself again.

You had better stay watching up there.

There was a distance to it, but she could almost smell something in the air whenever it passed, hidden amongst the shadows and the clouds. It made a most terrible sensation that just barely brushed the mind. She knew the minds of others could not feel it or see it, for they were lame in a way. It could not be helped, if people were unable to feel and see such things there was no reason to look down on them for that.

What a loss some of that was, when all could be known if their eyes were truly open, but even that wasn't the best way to go looking at things. Magic being split into the haves and have nots did not make a world much better if at all than the one found right here. That created fear and a sense that having power created security, which it did not, at least not in these days. Here in Churl was such a man hiding away with no such power yet with all the security he needed to keep himself safe.

Kieke wondered at what use she would have found for herself were it not for her mission and the drawn out length of it. Had she roamed the world she could have hardly been better off. Wanderers would have scarce reasons to come to a place such as this, so far away where people thought so differently. Surely as one of them she would not have come here. Now that she was, she knew that she found herself amongst a people proud to have their eyes open, knowing herself that their reliance on what they believed sealed them shut instead.

Still, waking up a whole population to that sort to magical potential was not wise. While some might not learn or refuse, others would not even try properly to understand it at all fundamentally. With the king dead and the people directionless she might attempt it, if only to have the place be further scattered and the left overs set free from their king's remaining, echoing words. But if they picked up the magic and took it far, who knew who would stand against them? Such a thing had happened before, years ago when out of nowhere an army of single minded zealots sprung up to tear a hole in the world. Kieke did not know the answer so it was best to take things slowly, keeping your own head about you and watching the sky while thinking about that possible future later.

After all, there was another future which needed to be avoided first. And she knew she had tried at first, walking up to those gates and not being let in, having walked those inner grounds before it was all shut away and she had a rather good idea about what would happen to her if she was caught close to the other side in these times. Especially now, with whatever had happened to keep the king and his family sheltered away, leaving them out of her reach.

What a terribly cold winter this is. She thought.

We've got so much to worry about, I just hope that we all make the warmer days, those of us who need to. I can't keep waiting forever, when the snow begins to fall there must be some chances that I will make myself. Yet where else would any king be in such weather than deep inside his castle shut up tight?

Her mind strayed briefly to that silly girl, wondering where she had gotten herself to with those flea ridden tree huggers. Some place out in the cold most likely. But Kieke shook her head free of such thoughts. There was nothing she could do for her. Maybe when all this was over she would go set off and look for Zelda and hoped very much to find her in a better place than she had when she had first gone to find and comfort a girl who had hidden herself in a corner of the city to be alone.

Now why has that same thing become such a problem for me? People are living and dying on the words of a mad man that has also hidden away in his city. However the ripples of his existence are far more destructive.

It would have been simple one day to solve such a problem with magic but simplicity was the realm of old days and accepting that they were gone. There would have been a time where a little show here or there of what she could do would not have bothered anyone and might have even brought out a king to look and see with his own eyes.

Now such a thing would condemn her to death. Granted she could do nothing wrong, be discovered and still be condemned to death. She wouldn't blame them for that, for as far as she could tell the belief that all magic was the same path down to evil things was steadily creeping beyond these lands if the rumours could be trusted. But these were no triumphant rumours that were openly shared and the Northlands were quiet. She shook her head out again, stronger this time. That would be enough of that.

Silently she went about her ways, as she should appear to do so. The morning had come with a headache attached to it, so she sat out in the sun, even though there was no heat in it, around a communal fire pit where there was some warmth. One of the church preachers was there with a fire poker and would ensure each log that was put on the fire was meant to be there, otherwise there would be no fire without him to keep that weak flame safe.

People around the circle said the names of the blind who were given the light in the those old, long gone times, the very ones who had discovered the light. In this place long ago had a group of blind people come. Through the clouds they had seen rays of light which allowed them to see again and because of such a miracle was a holy city built up around it. The people speaking those names, to her sounded like pleas to take them back to those better days when the kingdom and people were strong.

Back then it had not been these days that were here now, but many seemed happy to forget that in favour of a world where they themselves were bright, even if another had shone brighter.

The wind changed and the smoke started blowing in her direction, stinging her eyes, so Kieke got up and moved out of the way. After rubbing her eyes she found that there was no space any longer for her to sit around the fire, as that place had already been taken leaving no room for herself to wriggle back in. Someone happily sat where she had been, looking pleased with the stinging pain in their own eyes.

Maybe the way the wind blew would get the king moving. All she had to do was bring enough smoke to throw in his face so that he would have no choice but to move, while she would stand to the side in hiding, waiting for him to come out.

Oh but to think that one of those people who would cause real smoke might be here in this city, she did not want to think of it. An easy enough problem for her to deal with but it was not her intention to bring forth evil, merely pull the wool down over the faces of all those here long enough to do what she needed to do, to prevent most from suffering far worse a fate.

She toyed with the ashes with her feet that had blown out of the firepit.

The man poking the fire took notice.

"My lady are you all right?"

"What do you think is all right about any of this, holy brother? The world outside this basin is stone cold and I now have nine children to look after."

She slapped the stone basin around the fire that was outside its range and indeed, it was cold. As cold and dead as the stone walls and buildings around her, as cold and dead as the minds of those around her that were freezing to death in their own homes, carted off either out of the city, which was a rarity these days or further into its bowels, which was far more common.

She wiped her hands of the soot on them.

"I would ask what else I can do to keep them warm and believing in the things you and the Minister say. It is hard for anyone to say where the carts will go next, where the guards will come and off to where people will be carried. This place is losing its warmth and these warm lumps of coal are all we have to look forward to."

The preaching man hummed for a moment.

"Coal can be a powerful artefact for pyromancers. Some say that they keep a clump of it chained up around their necks."

"Says who?"

"Says I." Said the Minister's voice from behind her.

Kieke jumped a little. She had not heard him approach and had not realised that he had been standing behind her but he seemed not to care. He gestured around to the buildings and surrounding walls.

"But says that one too I suppose, as they should. It shall as such be written as when I now speak, that none may take burning lumps of coal or keep them in their homes, for I have seen it, what can be done with such artefacts in the hands of evil. Such uses must be disallowed from occurring. It is however such a thing, I must admit, that all these useless editions of the book are piling up and up and up. Far too many of these are still in circulation which could prove to be the doings of heretics, who will be treated accordingly."

He stretched on the tips of his toes and sighed.

"But that is an easy case to judge, some other things not so much, wouldn't you say?"

She felt her gaze could have dug holes into the dirt at her feet.

What have I done?

Those seated around moved as the Minister spoke to the man tending to the flame.

"We shall start right now, there's nothing wrong with getting ahead and putting ourselves to good use bright and early. Put the fire out. People sitting still are at risk, while if you get up and move about you will find new energy in your bones that you did not have before. So rise all of you people to go about your days gladly in this holy city I say, and tell your peers about the dangers of coal or it might seem that their faith is lacking."

As he was obeyed, the Minister strolled away, a man the same as any other on a leisurely walk in the cold morning air, now even colder as the fire was put out and people and went about their ways no less gladly than they had before. All but one.

Kieke was still blaming herself as she watched preachers make it harder or nary at all possible for people to keep fires going through the day and into the night, as those of the church with fire pokers went about to people's homes to crush down the coal of their fires into powder and doused with water from the river so they would not be used for other purposes.

On those nights it was becoming cold and dark indeed, where families huddled in their homes and hated that fire which precautions were being taken against, not the church through the king who demanded that they do as such.

Kieke had rearranged the beds several times to get all the children as close as possible in the single upstairs space, even moving some together and advising that they huddle if they needed to.

When she had put them all to bed, tonight she would go to a tavern she did not usually frequent. It was a long way to walk just for tonight and between the lamp lights she made her way carefully into the inner city ring. On some nights there had been people patrolling the streets and while there was no expectation that she remain inside even if that was where common sense in this cold said she should be, Kieke still kept her eyes alert in case someone had thought to stop her.

From where she was on the street she could see that there were no lamps at the tavern entrance and only a light coming from under the closed door to tell her that it was open at all. Further down the street was the only lantern, everything else beyond it was in darkness. The sounds of her feet against the ground suddenly seemed rather loud and she hesitated, wary of any who might be watching where she would go.

The sudden, deep voice of her master in her head made her flinch.

'Do not delay yourself.'

She took a breath.

Really, first before now again here. I shouldn't be this jumpy.

Without anything untoward happening at all, she managed to get inside the tavern where there were other folk inside, among them was Brodie. The months had not been kind to him and more often than not he would simply not turn up when they had thought of sharing information or talk about their days. But today here he was, looking as haggard as any other person in Churl with a steely look in his eyes as he peered at the walls, the floor, such strange things to scrutinise.

"I almost didn't know it was you." Kieke said.

"That's not funny, no matter how many times you say it." He shot back.

"With all the cold weather of which this is the season, I thought everyone would be better off in church, where there are fires, warm and glowing rather than here."

"Why not here?" Kieke shrugged.

Both looked over the room, where there was a fire going, albeit a rather small one.

This tavern owner had his own fire poker and sat on a stool in front of the heat, seeming to ignore all conversation. They continued quietly.

"What do you mean?" Brodie said.

"Not everyone can get to church and besides, none can stay there after all the preaching is done. That won't change. A place like this should be fine for anyone to preach under, provided the warmth of the place matches the hospitality of the church."

"Are you joking?"

"A little." She admitted.

The tavern owner stabbed the fire with his poker.

"Here now, in my tavern you would suggest such a thing as a gathering? What little I could do for a mob of people clamouring for the road to truth I don't know. I'm not a heretic, the people who can go to church go and I'll tell you all such. This is not a fit fine place for any congregation that doesn't want for food or drink and I must say both are in ever a short supply, more so that I have seen before."

Kieke shook her head.

"Who are they to judge? You are taking it upon yourself to cause no trouble with that fire poker I see, at the ready to crush all those coals that set to do us harm. I take issue with the words that say it is an offence, for it was my words that seemingly spurred the Minister into action. Perhaps it was a sick coincidence of my demeanour at the time that I just so happened to be playing in the fire pit like a child."

Brodie frowned.

"You, acting like a child?"

"Indeed much like a child in the way that I wouldn't know the first thing about using the fire that has set us on this sorry course but I still wonder what he saw in me."

She shuddered.

"But in this place? Let us humour ourselves of the Minister if all would be well. What would he see and who here knows that the church is a place locked up at night where none can access that warm heat? Everybody. So where else can we go and get closer to those words than here?"

"I do have a copy of the book." The tavern master said.

"Then with it in this place we can be pointed to a future where we are warm and happy. For I am only one person here with young ones to look after."

"Well you can't bring them all here." Brodie said.

"And some not so young ones." Kieke said.

He huffed at this.

"Don't go having jokes at my expense, for I am tired like the rest, wishing for these days to end peacefully and move over into something more agreeable."

"We're all just trying to find meaning in this place. This city we call home, is being battered with a storm and we must see it through."

"Then I think it is good that you are willing to do what you can for this place."

She only felt a little unease at his words, even if in a way he was just the same as all the rest.

It may not come to this though, after all we're not even there yet. I for one don't intend to let the rain come down, I should banish it all away with the king's head in hand. Then we will have our shining days, full of promise.

So it buoyed her a little when in fact, everyone in the room was in favour of such an act, one where they could demonstrate what it is that they believed in while also staying warm and safe. Believing did not stop when the church doors closed and the bell knelled its last for the evening, no, there were those who were warm and glad to be so listening to such words of wisdom that came from the Minister, direct from the king.

Let us see if we can not lure out of the king from an act where we might cause a commotion enough to leave this place in chaos.

How fascinating it was for her to see the world in such a state. All these people hanging off the words of a fool dooming them all, all the while that arrogant mouthpiece strolled around, telling tall tales and making everyone's life more miserable.

It did confuse her as to why there would be such an emphasis on making everyone's lives so much worse and she wondered on who the target might land for taking the blame. There was no army marching against them, no pyromancer or anyone else. Were that to change, she expected to be cautioned by her master.

For the moment, here Kieke was gathering up the fools so desperate to believe in something when really, what they had to believe in was nothing at all. It was a stranglehold over the weak willed, telling them they could be strong if they gave up their eyes and put their trust in what they were told. She could show everyone just how foolish their beliefs really were as the source disappeared into nothing. Yet so would everything else and that would be a terribly late time for her to act. Who would save them then? She would have to try. For now, she would try get enough people to act on their own and get them used to the idea of doing so.

She thought on the magic that had made Churl possible long ago. Would the people here rely on a new miracle, or would they descend into madness when proven to be powerless? She hadn't discarded the possibility of recruiting more people into her particular ways but until the time came where she could be certain, she knew she couldn't turn them all. People might then come with their pitchforks, tools and other implements to do away with the lot of them with most likely some torture beforehand. Because that was what people did to strange people they didn't understand.

All they understood was what they were being told was the truth, through the words of those who could say it. Well, here were the buildings that proved it, some might say. Here are the people saying those words and protecting the people of the land with their commands. The decree of the king was a ray of light itself. Living proof that was followed, hardy and unshakable like a great fortress of old.

But oh how it cracked at the edges! How the very world itself was turning dark as if to spite it, where the king moved to a new seat of power to remind everyone from where he spoke. Yet the other lands had doubts. One did not have to go far to lose that voice entirely, but those who stayed and saw only savagery and death beyond the horizon of Alegan's furthest reaches still believed. Those doubts made those lands the enemy of the king, she knew.

While gathered around a fire here it was clear for Kieke to see, that while they believed words of a book of light, the belief itself only left everyone in darkness and they were already blind because none could see the dark, they wouldn't even feel the cold all things considered. This light was not the light that would make the blind see. The light was false, there was no light other than the fires being snuffed out.

All together with all the rest they made plans to go around and spread the suggestion of preaching in warmer places and other darker spaces, now that people could do little to rely on the fires that burned in their own homes. This the king could not deny his people, surely, if all they were doing was as he wished, for them to read or listen to his words.

While Kieke knew that she wasn't really enthralled she did have to wonder at everyone else. She was sure that eventually they would all come to tread on the king's toes and if enough people complained, well she would have a mob on her hands. Both her and Brodie would do what they could knowing that they couldn't be everywhere, at least she hoped she could find him reliable where it mattered.

They might get accosted for setting this up to begin with but then others would have to admit to being among them too. This relied on those who were present trying to encourage those around them to do the same thing, to get as many people as possible having these little night time gatherings that might aggravate a certain someone and get written out of the king's good graces most suddenly.

With this first grouping up a success, people were leaving either individually or in smaller numbers as not quite yet was anyone willing to risk being seen in larger ones walking out and about. Kieke bid an early morning to Brodie and made her way out.

Hopefully the king will have his anger thrown right in his face, if they do come to anger. Nothing angers people more than doing the right thing and still being punished for it. With that someone's belief might be shaken.

As she stepped out into the cold darkness of the morning she felt a query in her mind and she chuckled.

No, not you Master. I'm doing all this for you anyway, because you're the one doing everything for all of us.

In her mind burned the fire that she would use to smoke out the king and with that thought along with the pleased flush from her master's approval she was able to keep herself warm.

Even though she had been keeping up appearances for a long time, it didn't matter how it was she really felt regarding matters and day to day things, life went on and for some it did not. People would get sick, they would get cold and some would die. As long as everyone stayed away from those who were sick there would be no trouble.

But how could that be possible when this entire city, entire kingdom was trouble? Never mind herself, she knew that there were others, out and about making life a problem for people. The lands beyond were something else entirely, even if right now she could see so little of it and she doubted they could see much if they were to look in.

The nights of Churl were all encroaching and the chill just as crushing as her breath steamed out in front of her while she walked alone, underneath the wall before the castle. She was aware that she would be in sight had anyone been stationed on top of the walls looking down to the burning torches sitting chained to their sconces along it. These were too high up to reach, so that a person could not steal that fire even if they needed it. Each one of these with its burning, flickering flame was mocking her on her way, as if to say *'look, look what you can not have. Let it only light your way and show you this wall but do nothing else'.*

Kieke knew what to expect this morning and unfortunately found herself right as she had any other time she had been unable to sleep and had decided to take the walk here. Nothing had been pinned to the message board that was placed on the wall, so there were no indications of just what might be provided to certain people these coming days.

Nor had she ever come upon anyone adjusting the notices, even though the habit had become to put them up in the middle of the night and she had spent past nights waiting to watch the notices go up. The nightly postings were likely to avoid the poster of such a message and others from being crowded as it was most possible that some would be asking why they could not have more than someone else, or why they were overlooked entirely in favour of another.

There was always one lot of people rarely mentioned, so it seemed nobody thought of the orphans, at least openly these days. That, more than the cold was making her feel ill. Of course she was having her discussions behind church doors about what she needed but as it was, all the work that went into caring for them was put in danger by the church itself and she dared not try and hold their little minds in her grip to shrug off the cold.

She could pull on their leashes if she needed to but found no need and the results would have been obvious for any to see in their blank faces. If anything it was best that they were looked after properly, rather than keeping them tied to her master's magic until they were older, to not get lost in it. And for that she would need the church to be a little more helpful.

She had once leaned more heavily on those around her for help, but since then many years had passed and Kieke had given up the appearance of being a beggar of a girl. Still, she would consider going to the church hall itself to beg if she had to. Yet this early in the morning, who would be there at those great doors that were barred shut? Who watched for any early risers? No one. Just as there was no one here to offer up a word as to why the king's decrees gave with one hand and took away with the other.

It is possible that someone is trying to do the right thing for the people but they're fighting a losing battle. Or maybe there really is some insanity behind these walls. I can't tell.

In front of the gate that led into the castle, she held onto the dark, heavy iron grill and tugged at it in vain. The castle stood beyond it and the gate did not open, another thing she had not expected to change, yet again. Of course it did not come apart or open. It would not be that simple or it would have led her into the castle years ago, to slit the throat of evil in this place and move on. But here she remained while the gates were shut, trapped in this circle of hoping that the day having just passed by was not the last for them all.

What would she have to do to get through? Even if she could force her way in, there was most likely a sizable garrison of guards inside and that wasn't something she could deal with all at once. She languished in the dark for a moment, again considering the possibility of doing something stupid and deliberately getting caught. But possibilities were just that, nothing might come of it other than her drawing attention to herself.

Not useful stupidity, useless stupidity.

Just beyond these walls, cooped up away from the world was the one she needed to kill. Of course, she might need to be rid of his family too if they lived and would deal with them if they were a problem, yet she would not lose sight of why she was here. Her mission was the king's death, no side member of the family or any other pitiful mouthpiece would do to quell the darkness alone. Although bombastic and loud, the Minister was all hot air. Hot air that she could not help but notice had been steadily going to his head over the years.

Even though she was sure that the king could speak for himself, it seemed that the king had a use for such a man and so everyone suffered through those words because the king could not come out and say them himself. Perhaps some had been curious and had willingly left their lives behind to get through those walls if only to hear those words with his voice.

She did not know if those people would have got what they wanted, her master had told her and had warned her from ever attempting to send in a single person that was not herself and she dared not defy him. So she had told those youngsters to look by all means but never go forth had a way in been found. It had to be her to proceed.

Before the king had arrived it had been much simpler. Instead of being stopped from passing through those cold stone walls for years on end where people went in and did not come out, it had used to be that they could walk the grounds in a warmer, sunnier time when the grass was green and people might meet and talk with other neighbours and catch up on old times. Now people went missing behind those walls and were dragged in and many of those were the old faithful who had lived here their whole lives.

As such the city was becoming quiet with the voices of those who had been here the longest disappearing. Pilgrims coming in found places to stay and the houses of the missing were filling up slowly with the pious and the righteous and that was not many in number. And even they were not safe from being taken away. Would everyone go missing between these city walls where she now stood?

The world had been running out of time for a very long time, but even though she had to rest, Kieke was well aware that her duty to the world and her master did not. Despite the tiredness that had begun to cling to her, ebbed on by the hours spent awake, this was one of these nights where if the opportunity had presented itself right in front of her to succeed she would not have minded. Not in the slightest.

***

Brodie was by himself and having left the tavern, was walking near aimlessly through the streets, hoping that the matter he had with the person he was looking for would be sorted out quickly, so that he would be able continue on his way back to the castle a little faster, to retreat for the remainder of the morning, wherein it was at least warm if not musty.

However, he always had to be careful on the way back to avoid being spotted, inspecting the houses that he passed. Often he would find homes and other buildings painted with a red X on the door, not due to any sickness that had to be avoided, simply as a sign to say that the house had been taken in by the king. On some doors the paint was fading and yet the houses themselves unoccupied and decrepit.

Over many nights he had come to prowl amongst many such streets only to see the numbers of them grow. Someone was still ensuring that torches were lit every little way but this barely helped when the light was so small and low, barely enough to stop someone tripping over their feet and in some places one did have to be careful to avoid that.

As such in the dark it was quiet. It would have been quiet anyway but those painted doors added to the silence, as knowledge that there was no one inside those homes played in his mind.

There was someone who had not been at the meeting with them and Brodie had decided to see what reason there might have been for them not coming. The man could have just been a coward, that was possible, however he wanted to hear the reason why from the man himself. Understanding his people's unwillingness to participate in gatherings was important.

He approached a house and the door opened just barely a crack without needing for him to knock at all, as if he had been watched all along. Only a single eye looked out and as Brodie put his face up to the door the eye narrowed.

"I know what you're here for, to ask me why I wasn't out tonight. The answer is that I had things on my mind, and those stayed me from going out into the night."

So the man recognised him, not that there was anything wrong with this man recognising his false identity at least.

"I was wondering if you had simply gone to another one but at least you are being honest. I find it odd that you would rather stay at home, where it must be cold while we stayed in taverns and places of the same make where it was warmer. Unless the church opens its great doors after dark to allow us all inside we'll be forced to congregate in places such as these to stay alive. Why not come out of the dark next time?"

"Well you don't convince me. Don't know what you're saying. We don't have any of those people around here in this town."

Brodie nodded.

"Those people? Of course not. You wouldn't be looking to getting in the king's good books by doing the wrong thing by telling someone what we're doing here, would you? It really isn't a problem if you do."

Let him go after all. Let him tell the king or as get as far as those words would allow him to. I'm interested to see if they will at all.

The door closed then opened again just the smallest amount.

"Look, I know I've got the king's ear through his church lackeys some of the time but what's going on isn't right. Don't be worried, you're not going to hear a word out of me even if you might think otherwise."

Brodie shrugged.

"Whatever you say. But we're all desperate here. I was more worried about you than I was for what reasons you might have had for staying away. At least you've told me now that you're having doubts. That's important to know."

The man stammered behind the door and his voice came from within.

"I don't like being thought of as a some sort of liar, I'm not that person but you're making me feel like I'm being accused of something. I don't like it. Clear off and leave me alone, you're not like the nice lass who tried to convince me to come along in the first place. I suppose I don't have to stare her down now and say that I'm sorry. As for you I thought you'd be different but there would have been a time when you would have been chased out of this town."

Before Brodie could say anything in response to this, the man's footsteps had already retreated further back inside, leaving him alone and scratching the back of his head. He made his way home, thinking of what the man had said.

Chased out of town was it?

He liked that idea very much, even if there was so little he could do. He considered getting someone to drag the man to the next meeting but he didn't want to get their suspicions up any more than they were.

I think I'm doing pretty well but I can't keep thinking that all is right.

It wasn't as though he had been given a chance to do anything as prince. Maybe if his father wasn't alive things would have been different. Or maybe not.

That got him tensing his shoulders. Some possibilities weren't worth thinking about just because the gloom took your mood in a certain direction and the winter was just making everyone a little bit out of sorts. That was all.

Then again, sneaking out early could do that, wandering the streets in the mornings perhaps made people turn to darker things by spending time in the dark. Not even he knew what the church was doing and the thought was frustrating because that lack of knowing was the reason he found himself spending this time out in the dark in the first place. All these people disappearing and life went on just the same. His life was meant to be one of solitude, above all these people. These little escapades were what he lived for to rid him of that and he had to admit just how grim it all looked out here.

In the distance up the main street he saw a light from a window on the second story of a building. Quietly up the paved street he went. While all else was dark, the light shining out through the window looked like the rising of the morning sun on the horizon. That one window, surrounded by darkness, where one little light was the only thing that was willing to come, each morning.

He stood transfixed, watching this false morning and as he did he found a strange feeling in his chest, a worry coming quite unbidden that tied his chest in a knot.

Would the day come where this would be all everyone had to look out for? A dawn made real not by the light of the coming day but by such false means as human hands? And this light was such a fragile and tender thing, he thought.

The darkness around it suddenly became all encompassing and threatened to overwhelm the world around him. He wanted to hold the light in his hands and shield that morning from the suffocating darkness. That could be his purpose. The people didn't matter if all the world went dark.

He fell to his knees as his chest burned. Not for the safety of people, who's minds were fickle and twisted, but this gentle, beautiful orange glow that made his chest heave and abdomen knot up as he reached for the light from the window above.

Everything I work towards is that light, for everyone, even if they don't yet care. Something I must safeguard and protect. Can't it be so?

Up above, Bernard the wizard was busy in his room. Despite it being early in the morning he had stayed awake and lit a small candle to read and prepare for the days ahead. The nights were long recently and little was the light he had to work with throughout the day.

The candle flickered and his eyes looked above to the ceiling. Up there he was sure that darkness had flashed and squirmed. He could not see it, but he knew it was there. It had watched him and others who could use magic and followed them from one place to the next. A reminder and a warning, or perhaps a thing that was gloating. He desperately did not want to think about the possibility of such a thing simply being everywhere.

I shall turn in for the night then, even if the covers of this place would offer me no protection in the slightest.

He slammed the book shut and the flame went out. In that moment he thought he heard a young man cry out from the street below. Of course, he had probably just imagined it.

Chapter Twenty Nine
A Wizard's Self Reflection

Bernard was seated alone in the graveyard, sitting on a bench in the overcast and grey chill of mid day. The graveyard resided on a hill that peaked above the wall, allowing those who looked out to see the plains all around it but the wizard was not enjoying the view.

"It is just me or is this land of stone cold belief readying itself to have the lid of the crypt scraped over it? Oh how I detest the noise, the sound of it. Slowly, steadily the scraping comes. Surely it is heard by those in the furthest reaches of this land, while those off in their kingdoms and high castles beyond look upon Alegan and laugh at its fate."

He spoke to no one in particular and indeed it would have been rather alarming had anyone responded, for he had come here to this secluded place with the singular purpose of being alone with his thoughts.

The graveyard itself had been left unattended for some time, for no matter wherever it was the people of Churl were going to at the times of their deaths, and he was certain that they were being sent to their deaths, he knew they were not being placed here for their last rest. That seemed increasingly less to matter, he felt, as he stared solemnly up to the cloud covered sky above.

"Soon it will be dark, the stone slab having crept over the top of the world to then seal the tomb shut. What words are engraved on that lid, the one that should seal this place for eternity I do not know. Only the one with the chisel and tools knows of that."

The sky twisted and writhed in its ill and dark way and Bernard watched with his face downturned in displeasure.

"More frequently it comes, yet is this nothing more than what awaits all who look upon such a sky and a warning to those who would read upon it the words to persist beyond the awaiting doom? Should the lid ever still be lifted what gravedigger for that matter might risk doing so without care, uncovering a darkness and expecting us to be whole when they do? How long would we wait in the dark? The answer is far too long, too late for us cursed below these skies as we may be. So I am here and on my own find myself waiting for the moment to bring forth the undermine of this place, to save all beyond here even if all in this world are so careless to that end that follows us now. We sit on the lid of no other crypt and Auralin shall not become one."

He held his arms out to the cold grey sky, breathing in the air of death and stagnation that he could feel in the wind which was picking up, whipping those clouds faster, to bring rain and gloom. From where he was he could not feel the sky, he could not feel the rain, but he could see them approach.

And as the dark approached them the lid was slowly being shut over them all. Churl was a beacon of blackness, a vortex of grey moods and fear. Some might suggest that if it came to it, he would point and show people. But ah, the images in his mind showed his body held up broken, in chains, as the darkness descended on them all regardless. That would not do. That would not be what he needed.

This world that was dying, it was on the cusp of being swept away to oblivion not by the cruel march of time but by being swallowed by a blackness with no end. Only hinted at in a world of madness, one was made aware to something beyond the sight of learned and reasonable people who could not comprehend the piercing sight of something terrible and dark. That thing was lured to this place, waiting maybe, yet if Churl had turned beyond despair then such a dark power would hopefully fade and be cast back to where ever it had come. This would be no place for evil to feed off of if all were dead.

"Who else among us in this world shall come and make it right again? Should it come to this, that we in our high towers, who walk all lands must put ourselves in the place of the ordinary ones and stand alone against all this doom and gloom? All for what, in the end?"

Some might look upon what he could see and already see death. The fields were still and silent, being left dead in the winter cold. The view to the far horizon contained no battle, no bristling or turbulence of motion. A shivering stagnation of form was passing through and sinking into the bones of all who lived. And so it would be, with the world careless and fading, where borders would break down and men at their watchtowers would abandon their posts and go home to look for their families and ask themselves why the world was getting cold.

Who had cared to come to this place where the dark cold funnelled to? A stone slab in the middle of the world that was alone and slowly fading, no place for wanderers and yet people came to pay their respects. Not one of them had come to the realisation that they were holding up their hands for their deaths. That stone slab, on which the world was to be sacrificed, was an alter held aloft by people fit to worship the blind, where there was a respect for the cold death and none of those beyond their land.

Churl's worshippers were more than happy to just fade away with the design of fate that had been placed in front of them, as long as those from beyond did not interfere and it was that which brought the lid scraping over them and all far beyond, to trap them in a dead world where all there was to do was wait for the end. It was so aggravating, for in the book all such read and told those around them, it never promised any such end. Those who believed accepted what was written, believing that no other possible end would ever come.

Then the ones who left Churl's reach spread such lameness to the rest of the land, spreading the words anew, that what would be provided to them all would be done so without any modicum of effort.

Behold the land of the lax and the sky that comes to wipe away all manner of foulness and suffering through the plunging of a blackness that would erase all to nothing. I must bring down the walls, the ground, the flooring, which must be shattered and the sound must resonate throughout the world so that all may hear of its demise. What release would then come from such an unguided pathetic bunch of naysayers I can't fathom but I feel sick in the very pit of my stomach, no, further into the depths of me to see such a place standing firm and indifferent in the light of the destruction that would surely follow were I to do nothing and I say to the world 'who is with me? Who?'

If he had brought followers along, he probably would not have decided to find himself in a graveyard of all places, as that would be most suspicious for a group to find themselves in, doing nothing but plotting and planning, if indeed any plotting and planning needed to happen at all. Quite an awful place for anyone to spend their time if they didn't need reminding of what to avoid, this was.

As for my own words, what do I hear back? I hear nothing from anyone right of mind and now I must increasingly look elsewhere in my planning and workings to find the means to break the ones handing down this old and broken belief. How shall I do this myself while running short of time? There is this feeling of being smothered that must be heeded or I might consider myself choked when I least expect it.

The sky held no answers for him while he sat on the bench. The dead would hold no answers either, he knew, nor did he want them to tell him anything at all. The dead could stay that way forever and give the living the chance to speak. Of course those gone could pass on their knowledge by speaking and writing things down but never should someone be forced or dragged along with things no longer provable. Churl's magic was long gone, yet still people believed. There was nothing wrong with believing the past, there was however everything wrong with burying yourself in it to the point that you barred yourself from letting the future take its course.

"What sign are they looking for? The sky will not rain down with fire to signal the end. It will be quiet, perhaps with a shiver as they look around for the cold deep inside them, trying to separate it from the cold now in their homes, the cold in the air descending from the sky and bursting up from the ground."

My voice can be loud but to think that none who hear it would be lastingly persuaded. Must I doom us all of magical kind and inclination just to get this place to open its eyes? Do I tear the sky asunder and call down the devastation not seen in several ages and bring armies to the door of this ruined place to fight over its remains?

He did not have to think long on such an act.

No, that would only make it all worse. I don't want happening to us what happened to those who were most innocent yet had their ways with fire, however that was surely well deserved for so self called pyromancers and had been a long time coming. Indeed I do feel troubled by all those who otherwise might have been caught up in that mess. You can't just shake the pot but aren't we at the base of that now? Stirring the mix. What would creep out to feast on the mayhem I would leave? None shall be excused who might, certainly not those of the fire and flame taking all this in their most dismal reach for power.

"The heights, oh the heights are too far to reach, the gaping holes of fire that rip into this world shall be a poor match for the times to come, much too far away and powerful in its raging. There was once a world that stood strong and proud against such a beast and we are not to lose the sacrifices of all those who stood up and were burned."

A burning travesty awaits where bodies burnt to ash would fall on the ground like snow, in a storm as in a blizzard where the edges, just on the edges of those flakes would they burn on until either the world would be alighted or it would fade away into obscurity, turned to ash all the same.

Such it was that those of the fire could not be relied on. They would reach out their burning hands all too late and those who would grasp them to be saved would find only a world burned utterly at its end.

Indeed, all it seemed he could rely on was the long, stretching plains that pushed out to the furthest horizons which were still and calm, to have them remain so. He stared out to those plains that were unmoving and shook his fists.

Change, you. Change.

Yet no change came. He could not even summon the dead from these graves to march on the people to cripple their faith. There would be death on top of death all too soon, the sinking feeling was in his bones that the sky, while so high above, would descend on them and make good on a dark, promised end which the mages in their towers were all too preoccupied with lifting themselves above.

He expected no help while they prepared what they needed to prepare. He would not be left behind, with the great tower gates closed, no not at all, but there was an expectation to at least try to keep the dark from descending, rather than hold their own world aloft from the shadows.

How then, with all this stagnation, could he proceed? What a fine place he found himself in to watch the world turn over. It was all one giant grave and he could see in his mind's eye places turning to white dust and collapsing, with great stones surging up from the ground to mark the great many deaths before them but no such slabs would hold up the sky, one that wriggled and writhed with dark musings and anticipation for the end to come. The wizard did not know which end would be worse and there were ends worse than death, he knew.

As much as some had tried, the dead were dead, the living were living, for how much longer he could not say. The knuckles white in his fists, with skin stretched over them, he imagined that the living would look like the dead. They would have to forgive him here for his indecision, as a man yelling doom and gloom in the streets would be put to the sword in any of the lands and no sword would find him shouting such words, even if they were true.

There might have been expectations once for him to do so. All would fall if he would fail, he could see it in his mind, the world crumbling from the inside out with the last few survivors pushed to the ends of it in a futile attempt to stave off what had already come.

To put it another way in which he could think of it, the world was as worn out as an old map, closed and reopened hundreds or times over countless years, every crack and crease and spill further ruining it until it was no longer readable, covered with such wear that faded its very features.

If there were gods, surely they would discard such a map which was no longer important, no longer useful, to be tossed aside and forgotten.

But there were no gods, he reminded himself. Every time kingdoms went off to war things changed and there was a new map that was remade over and over. That was where they were at, at a stage where they needed a new map. Churl could go, to be replaced with whatever new might come.

It had to come and he would do everything he could, as too many people were looking at this old map, trampling it even while they cradled it, as if they themselves were gods. But there were no gods, only the snatching, grasping hands of lies that would not let that old map go.

Holding onto power, how awful that the ones to suffer the worst were those with no understanding of the trouble they were in. Yes he had tried to gather people and get help, but he had not wished to whip up a frenzy beyond the borders and have an army march into these lands. As much as that would change some things, it would not ultimately effect a thing and bring the darkness closer.

How could he make them believe that their belief was not worth this place, this church, anything at all he did not know. And yet they still clung to it, wearing it as a shabby cloak that they would not remove, even if it was old and smelly and foul. Sometimes people burned old clothes of the sick and diseased. If only he could use that magic he would have done so.

As he thought, he realised that the world would see enough of fire if he failed and it was not for him to place the blame of destruction onto them, or even his own kind. Nobody wanted to march to war with wizards at their helm any more, for the worst had come and had been shown to cause grief.

Not even that would be left. There would be no emotion or any goodbyes. But then, that was the point. He would have to cause them grief, or otherwise a grief would come to them after which there would be nothing. If they could reassess their own understandings, throw off the shackles of the church, then they would be saved. The king did not matter. Such a lonely and cowardly old man who hid himself and his family away trusted in the one thing that he thought bound his kingdom together, ever present worship and preaching, hiding behind a wall of servants.

The dead in the graves did not care. Once you died, your worshipping was over. None of the dead cared who was king. And nor would they even as the living became the dead and the sky itself became the crypt wherein which the grave of this world would be where all people resided. A certain motivation, then, would be required.

I have to make the living care about the end because the dead will not. This is little different to how it would be anyway. Silently, with no one left to heed the end of the world, or a questioner that might ask, 'is that it?'

Sitting alone in the graveyard in silence, he realised further preparations needed to be made. If there was going to be any hope for this world, he needed to think that it might be one without magic, one where he could see all the burned bodies and the ruins of the wizard tower. To do so he would fill in this empty grave and despoil the perceived sanctity of this city, while placing a sign in front of it that said, *'Cast yourself away from this place but do not look away'*. Then the mage hunting would begin.

Far away, he knew, people screamed and died because of the church, the fact that they could not be allowed to live, even a little, was a problem for those staunch believers. He could have spent his efforts there, doing those things, helping those people. But the dark would have kept coming and he wondered if he would have gone mad like those who had been locked away, unable to do anything. He had talked to them and they could also see the darkness in the sky that no others could. All attuned to magic could see it, yet he had succeeded little in bolstering his chances.

Actions of the church would bring the darkness, as would people wallowing in their despair or hopelessness. He would have done much on his travels to raise the chins of the downtrodden, were it not for the knowledge that change had to come from within for an acceptance and a willingness to change. Kind hearted words were a soft fix and if someone could not find those same words within themselves then they would again falter.

After all, it was not his role to stamp out all sadness, as there were times to be sad. It was a possibility that the darkness simply fed off it and so that church had to go. It was a world away, down here, where the church took up all your guilt and all your pain and made it perfectly acceptable if directed to the appropriate person. All for one thing. Illumination. That was what the people believed the church would give them, but the wizard knew that it would plunge them into the deepest and darkest night, one that nothing could escape from. He didn't want to be eaten, or left in the dark to rot, but he would not entrust the future to pyromancers either and their ideas no matter how much they would leave of his body to prevent it from being defiled.

If I must trust in other people, I can't entrust the future to a mob. Armies don't just liberate, I wouldn't want to be at the head of one. He thought.

It would be the same actions, all over again where the whole of magical knowledge might suffer when the word would spread of what he had done. Sympathy for the church would grow and his hopes would be undone. He shook his head clear of such thoughts of gloom.

I'm not that kind of person and I didn't end up making that choice. I am merely upset with the possibility that I need help and have not been able to find it.

Long ago people would have been aglow with a wizard walking into their town asking for their aid. Those days were long gone, people were suspicious of such calls and rightly so. Only the king's men could call people to arms and now that they were with the church, such open words asking for assistance would filter back to them and accusations of heresy would spew forth from its gaping maw and he would be carted off to his demise where he might not witness the end of the world.

Enough! I should very well slap some sense into myself. I am not the builder of sad tales, building myself into the wall of my own home of misery to die in stagnation. I shall move beyond these walls of mine, put down the tools of self contempt called overthinking and worry, to walk on.

He looked around, forcing himself to take in the scenery.

There's got to be someone around here I can rely on. Tricking a pyromancer into raising the place to the ground would have been nice but that's out of the question now I fear. 'Illumination?' I have to make people see the truth, open their eyes. But how?

The problem with joining king and church was that it stopped the church from being without fault, as those faults could be put on the king but still be attributed to the church. So much then for the divine right to rule. If the people reacted strongly enough to a problem, or issue, they could turn against the very church itself and see no difference between it and the king, who the people wanted to believe in, but were growing distant of due to his inwards focus, his shirking of the outside world for his family. That would be a problem for the king himself that Bernard did not care for.

If Bernard had gone out to the city proper where there were some people, making himself and his intentions known, he would be blamed for opening their eyes and scattering their tears across the world. He would be the one they would rail against and pour their hatred into but not as part of their belief, as ordinary people, with nothing special about them whatsoever. At the least of it, those tears would put out any fires that might approach claiming to be a rescuer from death.

That once would have been rather rare but not so in these days or seemingly this place. Any person of magical potential would have been here, right here alongside him to help, snuggling up with a plan together to destroy and ruin the cause of the coming darkness.

What if he had been too late to save any of them? Of course people were being carted off but there was a fair sight of less mad people here than anywhere else. That came with the territory of the residing king, surely, but there was no madness on the streets.

Of course no one was here to help him, they were already lost to this place. The madness in other cities meant that anyone else had not fared much better, some being truly insane, but the wizard wondered if there were truly any others, the ones smart enough to keep their heads down and their mouths shut.

Perhaps he should have gone further into the country and branched out his search into the northernmost hills and checked all the valleyhouses and spots for those living out amongst the streams. Ah but he had been so sure that others would come. Where were they, the ones who were supposed to save this world? Now in this terrible time he had to put others like him at risk, if they existed at all.

And it was most likely that the wizards had been all too arrogant, watching, waiting in their tower. That place where many a young aspirant of the magical ways came were judged as lacking and had been left locked out in the forests alone, far below the tower, to find their own way home.

How he wished that he had someone like that with him, that he had sat out in front of the gate for the next sad failure to find themselves lost on the outside with no way in. But no such person had there been as he had not done such a thing. Indeed, on beginning his journey he would have snorted at the prospect of accepting such a failed pupil with which potential had failed to resonate inside them. He supposed that such a person would be hiding out in the world, unsure of what to do with their magic. He knew that many simply disappeared, refusing to return home to a dull life, not as a mage or as a failure of any kind.

So that made him wonder how many of them would have willingly sought out a life in this place. Crossing the south into lands unknown through countries and across borders no less. None that had felt the embrace of such potential could scarcely believe in such kingly ordained power that once found itself here. That old tower too, one day might be nothing more than a relic, one where the leftovers of a better past clung to it, because that was what people had always done.

Some might one day wonder to whom they owed the reason of a new future to while being thankful, others would be shaking their fists as he had, asking for an answer as to why this bad luck descended upon them and what that reason was. Would they know? Or would the answer be lost to time?

Whatever it would be he pictured this place a blasted ruin on the ground, rubble overtaken by a thick and ravenous wilderness, not unlike those which he travelled through to get here, even if he did note that the plants and trees were different this far south.

Bernard was staggering about as he tried to get feeling back into his feet. The slower it took him to get to the church the better for all those currently within it. He would animate the church building itself so that it would run amok about the place and would sink the outer ring into a stinking bog, so that all who escaped would be stuck in it and know of some form of shame. Or perhaps he would not, not today.

Would that darkness watch on or would it be gone from the world? He hoped that it would be gone with the howling of a wind free of dark tides.

Bernard spoke again into the sky when rightly on his feet.

"What is such a sign to come upon this world and give fear to only those who can see you? If your reach extends beyond this land and that others might see this would they too heed the sounds I hear and speak of them?"

The sky was as grey as it had ever been, clouds rolling across the great expanse above, covering it completely. Beyond them he could see no sight of the thing that had him so rattled. He thought that perhaps the elf had gone south in an attempt to stray far from this madness, seeing clearer and deeper than he, but then she was no longer around for him to ask.

"And I would hope that they do."

Flickers of rain fell from above, so he wrapped his cloak about him and made to leave while thunder boomed behind him. Clearly it was going to get worse, but he turned around anyway just to spy above him again, those black streaks, they couldn't hide from his watching eyes. Whatever it meant, whatever the warning, it encroached and to stop such a thing was not for one person to do alone.

Then before his eyes it twisted and bled into nothing, leaving him alone in the rain.

"Run then." He said to the sky, but even though he spoke, it was unlikely that anyone nearby could have heard his words. The wind was beginning to pick up along with the rain, after all.

Chapter Thirty
To the Great Tree

Zelda found herself waking up to the faint daylight, where the air was incredibly still on these mornings and sometimes cold with misty morning dampness soaking into her clothes and drops of dew hanging off her hair.

After a few days of that happening she found her nose runny. More material was stripped off her cloak to make wraps for her hands to keep them warm and protect her arms from thorny brush and branches.

For her nose she scrounged up the roots of some forest plant that was when chewed on produced a hot, burning sensation which only seemed to make the problem worse, but none the less found that she could breathe easier as they walked on.

I'm seeing and tasting a lot of plants I haven't come across before. She thought.

Survel had been watching her over the last few days, sometimes giving her advice if it wasn't given by someone else first.

"You seem interested in what you've found. Some plants that have helpful properties only do grow in this forest, or forests such as this one. A lot of these plants don't like open spaces and prefer wet, leafy ground. Some plants can't be too old, you need to pull up the young ones and use them or the effect isn't as potent."

"I've learned about animals and their shapes, how to feel the rain and the ground around me, but I have not learned as much about plants as I would have liked."

"There's too much to learn without stopping and we have little time available to sit around. None in fact. So it is better that you learn small things on your feet, rather than you learning all about herbs and plants and running off to be a witch."

Zelda shook her head.

"But while I like my animal shapes and being able to talk with others of the wilds, which I wouldn't give that up for anything, I'd also rather not be poisoned at the same time. I wouldn't have known to find those roots and eat them. I would probably cook them first."

"If you were to do that, then you would get a poison. Just to humans however so you would find within yourself an easy remedy."

Indeed she knew that switching to an animal form would have been her ideal way to fix her problems relying on her further deteriorating clothes and her chill, but all of them were feeling the dark strangeness which held them all fast to their human shapes.

It was odd getting a taste for something only to have it be slowly taken away from her. Zelda did not tell the others that she found herself with a certain hunger, anticipation for finding the spirit so their magic would no longer be stifled. That had been building inside, as was the thought of just what exactly she could get up to when she was free to do as she wished, as that interested her greatly.

If she couldn't have that, she would settle for a nice wide view where she could oversee many things, as she had decided that the forest had gradually come to not be to her liking. Zelda had always pictured a green and vibrant place but the trees here were a dull green that brought with it a dark that soaked up all the light so there was next to nothing to see but shadows where inside could be the darkness that had smothered her before.

"This place is dark and damp. Tell me why we are here in this particular place, it's not what I thought."

"You were perhaps thinking of some cleared out hamlet on a hill that meant you could see the sky and gather in the rays of daylight. Aye, climb a tree and you might see it if a branch were not to break and have you falling to your death, where your body would be made short work of by the animals you will find. There is much of that in this forest that you will call your home and yet the darkness was not always of this kind. You see it, do you not? Why we went away. It was that dark the spirit held at bay until it vanished without a trace of its whereabouts and it had to be found."

Gunter had been listening with his arms crossed.

"That is why we are here. To return the forest to its glory and place the spirit back to where it aught to be for the good of all things, that is the purpose of our search that has brought us all home. Zelda I can not promise you your sunny hamlet when we succeed or the rays of morning light, only a tomorrow under the canopy."

Zelda did not mind.

"Well I was never in this for myself. I didn't want to be a burden with no purpose and you saw something in me I did not know I possessed. I shall do my part for this forest, not in the least because it could be a place to hide. You've given me something and I shall give something back to the place you have spoken so fondly about, regardless of my own personal shortcomings upon actually seeing the state of it."

Nasker stepped back to be in line with their conversation.

"I believe the point is that the dark is still to be expected but that it's not meant to be quite so bad. There are many other places in the world that may hold brighter sights of a wonderful future yet are none too advisable to tread on account of one's safety. For what you fled from and what you look to for yourself as you are now there's no finer place you should wish to be or want to get to at a greater pace. I myself am tired of all this walking around and can't be alone here."

A clear squeaky voice echoed from the dark gloom.

"You are not alone for were you alone there would be a great need to worry. A forest without life and light and the beating heart of that life would be one taken over fully by the dark we all so fear."

The creature that approached them was small. Humanoid though it was, with two sets of beating wings on its back. Unlike other pixies they had seen, this one had upon its head a crown of shining amber.

"Or am I wrong?" It asked, finishing its words with an air of smugly regal importance.

Gunter was the first to quickly before anyone else.

"Everyone mind your manners, for the king of pixies is upon us."

The pixie king had its arms crossed.

"You're late. And that comes from those of us who have a most relaxed sense of timekeeping indeed. To say nearly none at all."

"We were trapped and imprisoned by those who would cling to a world that would abhor the natural way of all things. It could not be helped." Gunter explained.

"Oh so you say, instead of taking my vassal's advice and being done with that trap all together? But sure, tell them that you feared being tricked. It seems to be one mistake tumbled into after another, yet quite on form for you in particular I must say."

At this the druid sighed.

"Begone from hassling us, harassing us or being any other sort of vexatious pest."

Yet as he frowned he still went along the line of the other druids, correcting their postures, something that put a twinkle in the pixie king's eyes.

"Ha! Those words are a laugh coming from you, though I shall not deign to do as you so suggest, for what I shall part take in is a decision for myself alone to make, even though I could just as easily be done with my attempts at unpixieish seriousness. Humans need to be treated with a certain pained seriousness, otherwise they'll never believe what you have to say and you'll never get your point across." The pixie king said.

"My ancestors and kin have a certain whimsical nature about them, do they not? One spoken of as helpers and makers of maladies, at the same time we all are. Well in these grim days I say to you that it is all in the past for us. Only a dark tragedy remains, one that you are here to avert, I do feel. So let us do away with these past trodden irritations we both find ourselves in as we are both in need of the other."

The pixie king certainly sounded very serious indeed. Even if it was all an act and they did not feel the way they spoke, all in all both parties understood in all seriousness what would be lost were nothing to be done.

Gunter replied in a mild tone.

"When the spirit fled, we knew we had to act and I myself have gathered about me these here people to aid in the efforts of the search. We will do what we can but first, with no more delays, take us to the Great Tree so that we may see it with our own eyes."

The pixie king found his own turn to sigh.

"Very well. We do not bar your way nor block your path, certainly not in a way more than you have done for yourselves already. Further northwards we go."

The day stretched on and despite those short daylight hours, time was made during them to make the most of those hours where they could see, without resorting to torches or other means, for there were creatures in the forest that would not take kindly to those sort of fires, while others would use them to keep track of their prey, such were they warned by the pixie king, this close to the Great Tree.

The concern wasn't even entirely that of animals, as Zelda had sustained many little snicks and cuts from thorny branches and razor sharp leaves and had to keep an eye on the forest below for creeping vines that might trip her.

How would they know when they got to where they needed to be? They would know when they came upon it and that was the only answer she had been given. They plodded along in silence, until while humming to herself found she had caused all the others to start humming and murmuring some incomprehensible tune to themselves, perhaps to drown each other out, or maybe they were all joining in. She dared not interrupt whatever curious bout of behaviour she had elicited from them herself in case it had any real significance but it could have been that it really was just a bunch of men humming to themselves. Zelda couldn't feel any sort of growing magic power around them, no matter how much she concentrated.

Because she was concentrating, it took her a little while to realise just how far down they were descending, until she had to stop with a lurch as a creeping vine had wrapped itself around her leg.

"Stop that. Shame on you." She scolded the vine. So told, it hastily retreated. Looking back up where it had come she could see the sharpness of the slope that was carrying them down below.

The further they went down, the more Zelda began to sense that something was different about where they were. The ground was still the same firm dark brown dirt beneath her feet, but there was a change that carried on the air. It wasn't a smell, it wasn't a sound, but strangely enough to her both those senses were aware of something, some other change, some signal or sign that she just couldn't grasp.

She wondered if she needed to feel the sign with her hands, a thing she needed to hold tangibly to be rid of her hearing and smell playing a trick on her and she was very close to asking if anyone else felt the same way when they broke through the trees to find another tree. Not just any tree. This was the single biggest tree Zelda had ever seen.

She had not even imagined that a tree could be so tall so that she could not begin to see the top by looking up, or so wide that an entire neighbourhood could have been swallowed up within and there were ripples up and down her back as she stood before it.

Gunter sighed when he saw the sight before him.

"There it is, the Great Tree."

"This is quite a sight." Zelda said.

"It has been a long journey to get back here." Gunter said.

Findal couldn't even wrap his arms around it all from where they were standing.

"I have so much to be thankful of this place for. This means a great deal to me to be here."

While the others chatted to each other, Peter alone was silent, even though there was a strange, distant look in his eye that Zelda had not seen before.

They resumed walking down the curved path that spiralled around the tree, all the way to the bottom of a great split in the ground. Trees stood up tall on all sides, with the walls of dirt to the outside showing roots and bugs that crawled among them.

Even though they were descending deeper, there was a brightly glowing ambience down below and orbs glowing with golden light floated around some of the trees on the path as they passed them, so while there was darkness above, they were walking down into a brightly lit place. Zelda wondered if they were ever going to reach the bottom or just circle down to the bottom of the world itself and then go even deeper.

Getting as close to the edge as she dared, Zelda looked down over the edge below, where the base of the great tree could be seen.

Nestled around the tree and between the gigantic roots were scattered groups of huts, absolutely minuscule by comparison underneath the tree, raised off the ground and made with mud and wood, all with thatched roofing overgrown with creeping vines and moss so that some looked to be part of the forest floor itself. Little lines that appeared to be wooden walkways connected all the huts together.

Eventually they did reach the bottom and on doing so the pixie king hovered before them.

"I must go and make sure that others know of your arrival, so that you do not encounter those who would not wish to meet with you. You too should be wary of what you find."

Peter had a smug, rather amused look on his face.

"I never realised you were so troublesome Gunter. What in all the lands have you been grizzled about by my behaviour when it seems your own on home soil is itself much to be desired?"

Gunter rubbed his temples.

"If you want to see it later you might get it. Be careful of the questions you ask, the answers might not be received in a manner quite to your liking."

Zelda could not help but laugh.

"I had hoped this place would not have done anything to cause untoward conversations about ourselves but look, not even ten steps inside such a place and we're already at that point. If we can forget our pointless poking, such as you did between yourself and the pixie king then surely that sameness can surround ourselves as well? I would hate for a wrong turn to be taken in our journey at this point, all because some of you could not contain yourselves."

The Great Tree looked even more giant down below when they made their way to the forest floor itself. From down at the base of the tree was a soft grass and moss that covered the entire space around it. The party all stuck to the twisting wooden walkways that ran off in all directions and as they passed by the huts, could see that they were little more than one room buildings with gaps in the walls and no doors, so that the insides could be seen that were plain and bare.

Out the front of these huts were the everyday objects that one might have, one's cooking tools and utensils, an axe, a shield and a water bag. Just to leave things out like that in some parts of some towns would be madness for thieves would surely take them, but here it was clear there seemed to be no care for such issues.

Even down here there were trees, the leaves of these ones glowed gold, providing an illumination to clear the dark that came from light not being able to reach them so far down and the light was soft enough not to be harsh to look at. Findal was trying in a most unconvincing way to not appear interested in those trees but he caught Zelda staring at him, so broke his attention from them.

I don't think leaves from these trees will have any value to those beyond this forest, Findal. Why is it that gold still turns your head so?

That golden light glowed around them but Zelda knew that up above it was dark and wondered if most people would be asleep.

"Should we be apologising for the lateness of the hour? Our arrival is at a time most late where people should be sleeping."

Gunter turned about to gesture at the space they were in.

"No one cares about the exactness of the hours we find ourselves in here. Lose those city ideas that have come back to you all so suddenly and be one with the natural turning of the world. There are times to sleep and times to rise but regardless of all of that someone shall be waiting. I shan't think that the pixie king would wake up anyone to tell of our coming, however as a pixie maybe he would. The behaviour of those creatures is not easy to predict."

As they walked further along the boards that made up the walkways, Zelda began to wonder where everyone else was if not in those huts that they passed. The creaking under their feet surely should have brought some attention to themselves. Whether it did or did not, she soon found that they were not alone.

Along the walkway ahead of them came two people, an old man and woman, both who were hooded and cloaked in brown. The old man leaned on a twisted and gnarled staff, his fingers grasping around it just as twisted and gnarled with age. Underneath the hood was a long grey beard and long, matted hair. Over the hood he wore a crown, one with horns strapped to it all around, sticking above.

The old woman did not require the use of a staff and wore a simpler reed circlet under her hood that kept her own grey hair out of her face, woven down behind her back.

The old man spoke in a cracked voice, the years clear to hear as he talked from underneath the hood.

"Ah, Gunter. Might it have been that the days were better and time moved slower, but now is not that time when it seems to do so, whenever that shall be. The ground cracks and weeps silently for these better days that have been promised, the tree waits for the vessel to return to it, that strengthens our understanding of the world."

He looked graven faced around to all present. The old woman then spoke, her voice just as aged as that of the one beside her.

"By that he says you have missed the solstice, however for what efforts you made I do spy a few new faces. Aside from that it is good to see you again Survel. And you too Nasker, it has been a while."

Gunter nodded and gestured to the new comers in turn.

"Of course I must introduce the new faces of those among us. With me I have Findal, who was once a trading man who hails from the north yet below the Ruthlands he tells me and can trace his family far back to the days of the south coast. Peter, who has been following me for some time and who I have trained in spite of his upbringing in the kingdom beside us. And lastly here we have Zelda, who was quite an unexpected find when I went to Churl looking instead for an old friend."

The pair looked over the new comers with a critical eye each and the old man nodded.

"I am sure you would like good news but know that darkness encroaches evermore across the world from the bellies of all civilisation. Such darkness emboldens the growth of twisted things to thrive in our own forest, so that the forest itself struggles to keep those forces at bay. While we become ever more helpless we must redouble our efforts across Auralin to find the spirit and make this world whole once more. In the face of the arrogance of those who take from the land to make their metal with which they only use to slay one another and subjugate the truth of who their true allegiance should be to, there should be no ceasing of effort on your part. To remind them what is the power that governs the world and the one we rightfully take heed to, the cycle."

The old woman sighed an age old sigh of sadness.

"We were once teachers to the world beyond, now we have been shunned as the old and the useless. Man is fickle and choosy with his knowledge and picks only from the trees of knowledge which he wishes to while he cuts down the rest. We must regain the ears of those around us world over and can not do so as frail as we are so now. Many who came to solstice on time claimed they would have trouble returning to their homes and some even spoke of the likelihood of not being welcome to such lands on their return, which is most troubling indeed. The cycle is in danger of being broken as the turning of the world slows evermore. Any further delay should be slight."

"To the Great Tree. To the Great Tree." The old man hissed.

The old woman ushered the group to follow her along.

"Ah yes. Those new of you here must see that which must be spoken of."

As they walked they came across a man with a blonde beard wearing a bear pelt. He was resting back on a tree stump with his arms crossed, eyes under the bear's jaws silently watching them approach.

The old man shook his head and sighed.

"And yet I wonder why there are always so many less of us as the years pass and what reasons they might have for not travelling the path that aught be travelled."

The man within the bear pelt spoke up in a clear voice, a voice which told of a man holding brooding thoughts presently in his mind.

"Perhaps they'd rather stay at home, as I have said to you."

Zelda didn't think that anyone should want to stay at home if they knew about something so serious as the world ending.

"How many of us were here this year?" She asked.

Bear Pelt slowly responded.

"Oh? Less than ever before, even if I was still surprised by the large number that turned out, it did happen. No more than twelve of us were present that you shall not find here."

That was a shock rightly to her and while she found her voice, had been close to being nearly stunned into speechlessness.

"No more than twelve? So thirteen? I had imagined a fair few more would have come. There are enough huts here for a small village."

Bear Pelt's voice was tired and a little strained.

"Well, keep that in your imagination, as none of them are any here longer and it is a good and fair place for such things to reside. What I said was not entirely the truth, for a fair few of whom I spoke to on the way here refused to leave their places even though they no longer had homes. For a full year I thought that I would be the only one coming down to tell the tale of the north east and wouldn't you know it, I was. Those others, they can stay in the lands where they wish to be and keep searching if they want but as we were called here then here we should be, if not to remain only to see such a sorry sight as this, of *latecomers*."

Zelda was still looking about.

"But the pixie king had said that they were going to warn off those who might not want to see us so someone should be here."

The old woman appeared saddened.

"The warning was for forest creatures, as some do not take kindly to us being here as humans, no matter what it is that we do. If he is calling off some of those creatures from making themselves known in this place then that is a thankful respite for the moment. It used to be that we would approach this haven as animals, such was what had to be done to earn the trust of the denizens of the forest but such a way has not been so for some time. To enact such a thing would be death for anyone who attempts it, especially deeper into the forest."

With Bear Pelt following them, they continued on their way and came upon a woman sitting above some wooden stairs made to reach one of the more higher stilted huts. She was covered with a cloak of black feathers and nodded from behind a beaked mask that hid her face. From up on not terribly high it was that she called down to them, an edge of sage amusement in her voice.

"Well well, I'd say I was surprised to see that the closest to here took the longest to arrive but you're not alone, I find. However, it amuses me that you could not even make your travel barely a few more days for solstice in a hurry, for it has been some days since most have departed."

Gunter frowned.

"No, we were held at bay until allowed to leave by some captors, which we did the morning after. I am not happy to have missed the solstice but of those around me, I have not dragged them here at least and each will speak for themselves, if at all. Aside from them there have been no others, yet there could be those later still following along."

"Hardly. And besides, what would Ban's pupil know about that?"

Zelda turned to him.

"Ban was one of those who helped defeat the Demon King in the war. You never told me your teacher was the same person."

The old woman raised her chin.

"That monstrosity of a man got the last laugh on Ban, for he turned to the very thing he had stood against and let it consume him. You aught to be careful girl, to make sure that none of that rubs off on you."

Zelda shook her head strongly, so strong her neck cricked audibly and she winced. Massaging out the pain, she replied.

"Ah, well it will not. Fire is awful and from what I have seen on this journey so far there is nothing to worry about for Gunter, as he has been clear on where he stands and what we all intend to do. After all, he taught me and gave me lessons. If he was willing to teach me something so badly of course he believes in it. I'm proof of that and so is everyone else. If you still won't believe in him then look no further than me."

Bird Woman tilted her head.

"Very well then girl, this will be a test for all of us, to see how much of your words we can tolerate."

Zelda found the comment puzzling. Peter was his usual silent self but there was still a different look in his eyes as he peered around that was less scornful and she could not tell what those eyes saw.

Bear Pelt spoke up to Bird Woman.

"One attempts to excuse himself from all the rest, how fascinating. Anyway, we're going to the Great Tree now, are you coming along?"

Bird Woman did not say anything else but stood up and followed them.

Along the way they were joined by some pixies who descended from the trees above, as they were to join in the meeting it would seem but their king was not with them.

They were all led through a winding path to the base of the tree where outside an archway stood a further person. This man too wore robes with a hood but the robes were green with moss and his beard was not quite as long but was still going grey from light brown.

He spoke as they approached, words curled from an accent who's home was far away.

"I am the seer of the forests, who sees far and wide many things. I can also direct people in many things and had thought my audience had dried up but here comes upon me some more that I had so hoped for earlier."

The old man bowed his head.

"We are here to see the resting place for the world's core."

"Very well, you may all proceed along with me." Said the seer.

Underneath the archway they walked and from a tunnel came into a large rounded chamber of smooth white bark that would have been many stories high.

Even though they were inside the tree, there was in the middle the remains of another tree. This tree was dead and pale, yet the pallor whiteness of it was stained and the tree was rent with a great split in the center. From within there was a blackness staining it and the floor around it. The air felt strange to all present, such it was as if all the light, life and colour had been sucked out from the world around it.

Zelda felt rather uneasy staring at it.

"This is such a solemn place. Since I have been travelling we have walked along the lands of the dead that have seen the worst of the war that ravaged these nearest lands and sadly do I recognise this dark feeling."

Bird Woman turned to her.

"You would not be alone in hoping to be wrong but you are not wrong. You should be thankful in some sad way that as humans we're all too small and hard of learning compared to some of the creatures in the forest who must face the darkness with every waking moment. Says this one at least. Some darkness is certainly taking advantage of the fact that the spirit, the core of the world, has gone missing. No matter how it hinders us we must uphold the cycle and not allow the world to stop turning."

Bear Pelt grumbled.

"I don't know why the dark wasn't stamped out to begin with at the first whiff of it."

"We can certainly give it a try, but I'd rather not tangle with something dark when our goal is the same. To retrieve the spirit that holds our magic, a task that may be in the lands utterly beyond our own."

"No sightings in the north then?" The old man asked, to which Bear Pelt let out a disappointed sigh, almost a groan.

"Not even one. Not a fleeting feeling of it either and it is quite the same here. This feeling of separation from nature has been disconcerting for us all. I will head back north and advise the others of what we have learned and the state of these lands. They may have been right in staying behind."

"What is the north like so far away?" Zelda asked.

Bear Pelt looked at the ground.

"The far north is dark and bitter, a place where all people bicker openly and amongst themselves. Elf people are fairly common in the north and are sheltered from their mistakes, not so much around here where the devastation that included the fault of elves can be clearly seen. In the north there are few who care for these lands after all the effort that was made to push elves out. Some of those of that church got stuck far on the other side of that wall to the east. It is rather interesting to see what happened to them."

The old woman turned to him.

"Best we not speak of such rumours, no matter how pleasing it is that such foul words are being ripped out on the hearing of them."

Bear Pelt shrugged.

"At any rate there is a burning heartbeat in the north you won't find in these lands save for in the darkest hearts of fools."

Bird Woman nodded in agreement.

"The far east is little better than here, by the way, but when our magic began to falter, the ones we held in our thrall and who offered nature reverence began to rebel and as such it is one such place we would not be welcome back I fear. It has been too long since I have been into the north and would like to see it again. I feel we must hurry on or lose ourselves entirely. We who can take shapes are finding it more difficult and I suspect the dark in this forest is taking advantage of our plight to stop us all together."

The seer was thoughtfully stroking his beard.

"We are standing first in line should anything happen. We must be prepared to restore the spirit so that the world may live on. Still, the darkness in this forest worries me."

Bear Pelt nodded.

"While we are away from home, twisted things grow in power and creep in. Taking advantage of us as such is cruel. Should we find anything we would let it feel our fangs if at all possible."

"So where is it we should go to next?" Findal asked.

"The darkness in this forest could be coming from all sorts of places such as the kingdom of Kasynne nearby. Shall we resume our search there?"

To this the old man shook his head.

"No. You shall not be going into that place, as you are late you shall be going away from these lands you have spent your time in. You shall go beyond the forest towards the west, travelling through it and beyond."

Survel had a frown on his face.

"You want us to go through the forest, out of these lands entirely?"

"The search must resume, but be weary of the darkness that lurks in this forest. You must not let it stop you on your path, as it would surely seek to do so."

"That would take us well outside of even Kasynne. We do not know what we might find." Gunter said.

"And yet you must press forward." The old man insisted.

Findal was rather pleased with this news.

"Well I still find this excellent. Though I am sure the journey might not be easy, I am intrigued about what the lands beyond are like. Isn't anyone else at least excited?"

Nasker spoke up.

"Dark shapes have been seen around the creatures of the forest, what of further from here? Have there been any sightings of foul or darker things deeper within? I can only imagine that the further we go the worse this might become."

The old woman inclined her head.

"Then when you leave I would suggest that all manner of haste is the speed with which you should make to leave the forest. Yet if you come across that darkness, all of you must do your part to quell it if you can." She said.

The pixies were keeping their mouths shut, mouths grim and quiet, but their wings chittered in nervousness. The old woman paid them no heed.

"I suggest you rest up more, for there will be those who will drum into you fear in a greater way than you think possible. Go all of you and meditate on that, I do not wish to keep you longer if you are that exhausted in mind."

So they were sent to huts where they could sleep, each being offered any hut they wished to sleep in, as long as the went there and did just that. With heavy steps they all went on their way, for the words of the two elders were to be respected amongst them. Such guiding words that they were, they were however nothing more than that, even if between all of them some took those words far more to heart.

Chapter Thirty One
Around the Great Tree

There was an undercurrent of worry and fear throughout that night. Almost everyone was asleep but Gunter was not sleeping at this time. It was bad enough that he had to deal with those who did not, would not, understand the world quite the way he did, but dealing with the consequences of finding himself to be late, yet not past the hour of no return? He was unwilling to find himself as a part of that. Such a problem should not have been for him, not after all he had done and certainly after all he had yet to do.

Still, he realised that there was little choice in the matter. Almost everyone else had already come and gone from the fragile, last lingering glow of safety under the protection of the Great Tree and on doing so had spread back out to their more familiar sights. That left him at the mercy of those who could direct him where they willed and he could scant afford to appear rebellious against the elders while in front of those around him. Survel would understand but the rest? He had grave fears for their loyalty, one that could be passed from him, to be stolen by those two old crones in an instant.

There was one small fact he did agree with.

It is possible that the spirit could be beyond these lands.

Admitting this to himself further dulled his mood as he made his way alone to the hut which was the home of the two elders.

He wasn't expecting to change their minds, merely get some more answers from them. At least with these two he could be sure of their cooperation, others not so much. There were those that could not be counted on to do as he asked and for them, while it was irritating to him, he knew that those others could not change the way that they were nor for the moment could he impress any change upon them. Not even the threat of violence would shake some people. In that case, the world he would make would not be for them.

From what little he could still feel the world, he could tell that one of them was watching him, that woman in the bird's guise. There she was, sitting atop a hut a little way back from the roof's overhang so that with his eyes he had nearly missed her. What was her name again? Cybelle...or was it Simma? He couldn't care to remember or even ask her which it was, if it was even either of them at all. She wouldn't be alive, hopefully before too long anyway. All he had to do was succeed where so far none had.

Gunter could not see her face underneath the mask, but the amusement was thick in her voice so that he could not imagine that rounded, scar cut face to be showing an expression that was anything other than smugness.

"So you come to throw yourself down in front of your betters yet again." She began.

"After all this time you should know better than to merely try. Indeed you seem to be forgetting the lessons of the past that gave you your more poignant victories."

"The only thing we can do is find the spirit. I would ask that you leave to search as well." Gunter said flatly.

I will not be drawn into the traps and wiles of this damn woman.

The chuckle was deep behind the mask.

"I only do what I need to do." She said.

"None seemed too keen on travelling with you to the west if their restless sleep is to be believed. Watching them all wrestle and tussle in their dreams is quite relaxing as it is a relief to see that you have not dimmed the wits of those around you as not even they are safe from these misgivings we find ourselves surrounded by. And why should they be? Indeed, that darkness crawling in the shadows and the one flying far above our heads are not the same. We're surrounded by more enemies than any of you realise here."

He watched her fade into the night.

More than you could know. He thought.

I hope you get torn to shreds out there when you're forced to face a world that cares nothing for your words and everything for the meat on your bones.

Not even the bones might be left, but then he couldn't be too hopeful, as long as some people who were seen were no longer heard again by anyone. There were plenty that could fit that description, he knew. More than a single person but whole swaths of people, lands of it. To think that he might not be there to see them falter after all the false words and lies from those places fell to uselessness seemed unjust in his eyes.

I can't be everywhere to see everything, but to be close enough to see something of a world torn asunder and reborn with a new life, just to see a little of that will have to be enough for me.

He could not say anything more to her, she who had left him alone, so continued on his way to the elders while wondering if she was still watching.

As he walked on he could feel the steps he took becoming shrouded and the light becoming dim before opening out again past the mud hut of the elders who were too aged to go out into the wider world. None who looked upon this place could have seen anyone walking in unless they themselves were walking alongside it.

Neither were surprised to see him when he arrived and in a way he knew that they would have known to be expecting him at this hour when he could have hoped to be alone. Both were waiting for him so he knew what it was that he had to first say.

"Why are you sending me so far away?" He asked.

"I thought that you would have needed me here, in these lands to watch over not only this place but the plan. The rite with the spirit itself when it is found was to be entrusted to me. Those here can not be trusted to safely hold the new world in their hands and surely you know it."

The old man shrugged his ancient shoulders.

"We can perform the rites without you if need be. Take with you those who would go and travel to those far off lands."

"I understand what you are saying, that the spirit could be elsewhere, but at what point should the travelling cease?"

"Whenever that time comes where you find the spirit or another does." Came the reply.

"Indeed your travels will be long, but I hope that you will hurry up about it. You have little fear within you of failing in your own lifetime yet it should not be yours but ours in which you will come into contact with what we seek and otherwise feel the fear of failure. The new world must come before we are rendered utterly useless or die, so that we may live again."

"And if I should fail in time for your bodies to become dust? Do not say that you would send your ghosts out to haunt me as that would be something others would not allow and even if you were able to do so, the new world would be clear of such haunting phantoms such as you would be."

The old woman held her face downturned in disgust.

"You won't, because we're all well aware just how much it is you long for that new world. We gave you this freedom, to make for us all a new world which we so aged can not go out and make for ourselves. Do not be so foolish to think that we would resort to decrepit actions full of folly. There really is no knowing like having the spirit here, to come to a better understanding of the world which can then be sent out to guard nature and the cycle. The spirit has to be found. Only it can wipe away this ruined world and bring us into the new world of savagery and strength. Then the only use for gold might be to melt it down and cast our enemies in it."

"By which method we could further prune the masses by finding out those who are weak and would wish to worship visions of gold. Of themselves as gold." The old man concluded.

He stared at Gunter.

That man is quite the fool. He thought.

But we need him for our new world as he an asset we cannot afford to lose. Otherwise we might be left with those who would prefer a cold, dead world in the face of sacrificing all that they see. Yet who should not revel at the chance to bring about this most pristine vision of our way of life? I suppose that makes him the least fool amongst all other fools.

He looked to the other elder, knowing that she would be having similar thoughts. And indeed she was.

As she looked at this person in front of them that they were supposed to be relying on, the old woman could not help but wonder if he really could carry it all on his shoulders.

Those others should really be keeping a look out to maintain their own sense of self but do they? Well that all works out in our favour, so I should not complain about those I entrust the future to, yet for that they must be on our side. I do not know if it is right to say that they are all perfectly mailable in our hands but there's no harm in believing that they can be just a little, regardless of what they feel is right and wrong. Such small inconveniences as someone's belief in what is right and wrong are however all so tiring, something that the spirit shall fix for us.

***

During that same night, Peter was resting alone. He found he could not sleep so had wandered until he had found a patch of ground that had suited him, a mossy patch where he attempted to find the rest that had escaped him thus far. Rather unfortunately his mind was not letting that happen, so he had to sit back and let his mind think up thoughts that had no answer. It was possible that there were answers if he thought about them, but all he wanted to do was sleep. Yet sleep would not come, so when it did not, there was a thought that had entered his head. There had been no elf people at the late night gathering.

That to him had felt rather strange, although not entirely unexpected as the only elf people that Peter had seen so far were rather nomadic and secretive. Still, they were of the forests as much as themselves, despite the understanding that elves had found in other places. Of those who were not nomadic and secretive, how many would have wanted to return to their old lands and risk capture can't have been many in number.

There should have been creatures of all types here, all pitching in to help them in this endeavour but there were none aside from the pixies, where their king had likely made sure of that, he suspected. Peter tried to figure out why this bothered him, after all, he had never been told what to expect or even to expect that there would be anything more than humans here. He finally figured out why.

I don't like people.

He had spent much of his time with the trees and the animals away from other people because of this and here of all places it would have been nice to have someone other than a human to speak to.

So I don't consider them people? He realised.

Or maybe that was wrong, as he had not met enough of them to see how human those other creatures of the forest might be. He could take pixies as an example. They were similar enough and smart enough to understand the ways of the world despite not being human, as humans too clung to the world that they lived off.

Whenever he saw an elf, pixie, or be it any other animal or creature, he saw how they fit much more into the flow of the ground and sky than a human who was simply residing in those same places. Even with such an understanding of their world as their own he knew that humans fit in no more than anyone else. Unless, that was, that the people in question were deluded in their ways, waiting for mystics or kings to save them. Thinking on this gave him a headache.

He thought on the vibe that the pixies gave, as well as his own vibe, which was different to that of a human just going about their ignorant life. There was a smell not dissimilar to that of animals or trees or elves about them all, but something was missing and while he was too tired to ponder, the thoughts cut into what little spare space of his alertness remained.

He knew that underneath that moss which he had decided to spend the night was dirt, and likened it to all the people in the gathering. It could have been layers and layers of dirt, or perhaps that not enough dirt had been layered on them, and the moss of the world had yet to grow over them and into their hearts truly.

Unless the dirt was hard and lacking in goodness with which to make anything suitable from. That was it. The dirt of humans was hard and crusty, preventing the moss what was needed to grow over it, where instead they would bake bricks and dig it all up in a quarry to find stones, gems and metals. They who had their minds well watered could grow moss.

Something was still amiss, seemed wrong somehow. If that was not the answer then what was this vibe that resonated inside of the creatures all around?

Peter came to an answer that was simple. None of the other creatures were the equivalent of moss, they were the tall trees that held deep roots in the ground and stretched so much higher and further than he would ever see. Even if humans were once part of the same ground that could hold trees, now they could only hold moss. He could plant a tree, but for that he would have to dig up the ground around which he sat and perhaps that ground was not best suited for a tree to grow healthily. Peter didn't want to be moss, he wanted to be a tree, or more rather, around trees, not where the moss was.

Everyone is being given their instructions and carrying them out with little a thought for themselves, but there has got to be more than this in life, as there is no life in being instructed, told to do all sorts of things all for the sake of what has come before, hoping that we will find the cure to what ails us along the way.

He rubbed his eyes.

But we're not learning, only repeating the same mistakes that have led us down this path. What then might become of the world if the same mistakes were the ones we needed to fix all along? Why is it we're so alone here with everyone else attempting to divide us? Why does no one trust us or our words any more even though we can see the world in a way others cannot? We would help those who don't understand do as such and yet no one can look to see where that has gotten us and say that we have at all been successful. We were too trusting to believe we would always have the ears of those around us. Such a thing is nothing personal, not a skill for each of us to possess, but only something given to us of that most magical nature where even those who were thin of their speech and words could be given the attention of an entire crowd full of eager eyed people.

He knew he had to stand tall like the trees and not trust that he had the ear of those on the ground around him.

"Just repeating the same mistakes." He said to no one, or at least he meant to, because he wasn't alone at all. He was being watched and listened to, by one of those creatures of the smaller variety that had turned up, a pixie.

"What are you thinking about?" It asked in its particular pixie voice.

Seeing he was unlikely to get back to sleep, Peter sat up, while the pixie continued to buzz around his head.

"People." Said Peter.

The pixie snorted.

"Well isn't that a waste of energy? Those people around you are not very nice."

"If I really don't understand what they are going through, perhaps I should spend more time thinking about them so that I can understand them better."

The pixie tapped its chin.

"It sounds as if your life is stuck. I heard every word they were saying. It's impossible to fully understand another being. The more you attempt to do so, the less of an individual you become."

"And here I thought all you pixies lived together."

"We do, but we also live apart in our minds. Except that we are all connected to the spirit through our king. That is how we know the spirit lives, as we live. What connects you to your fellows?"

Peter had to think at this for a moment. While he was thinking, the pixie could not help but to talk further to interrupt the flow of his thoughts.

"All I'm saying is this. If you do not wish to do something for your other humans, do something for yourself. Then maybe you will help another, if not intentionally then it could always be by accident."

"Do people come sparingly to this place? While the Great Tree is a place without walls or any barriers, we are within a deep pit so am wondering whether others find this forest to their liking."

"Here? Quite sparingly these days although I would have thought that you would not have wanted it to be so."

"I would not mind it not being so, as long as I was not so disrupted."

"There are many places you could go if you desire seclusion. This forest is among them I will admit yet it is the dark workings inside of this forest where I would hesitate to recommend you linger."

"You refer to the ones your king went and bade away?"

"Hmmm, not all, not all. But I think you might need to see things for yourself, which would be quite the waste. I would worry for you, meeting those who are in the forest."

He peered at her, suddenly troubled.

"What do you know?"

The pixie shrugged.

"Not more than anyone else such as your peers who purport to know so much."

"Well I've seen and felt what is in the forest so they are none too far off from what must truly be out there in the dark. Even above us in the sky there can be no escape."

Peter was reminded of the tales he had heard. Pixie folk are cunning little creatures of the world that some might see while others might not. There had been a time where they served to carry messages between this world and the worlds beyond where spirits first resided before making this world their home, filling it with light and life, a ball that many rumours had it they chased endlessly though the sky each day.

What they thought of this blackness that covered the sky was why they were at this meeting of druids, for it might have been that one day it had been a pixie that traded knowledge with a human to become the first druid, a long time ago. What the trade was, who could say? But that was not the moral of that tale, to say that you had to be careful with which you gave away, indeed there was no such moral to the tale at all, it was after all just a story. At the very least, a very, very old story.

So it was that this pixie that happened upon a young druid all by himself, who was unsure of himself and the way forward, heard those words and could understand just where it was he was coming from.

"It must be so tough being what you are, knowing that you should reach for further and greater things when all you see is people holding your hands down or trying to teach you how to properly beg. And they're not even holding them up in the air in triumph at what you've learned, merely down at your side, a parent dragging their child off to where they want them to be."

Peter eyed it further suspiciously.

"Why come to me and say all this to tease me?"

"You are interesting." It said simply.

"Not at all like the others, or most of them, if I am to be blunt. To hear the things you say intrigues me greatly, as I wonder what gives you the notions that you have. We're older than most, can see the patterns short lived ones miss, so when one seems to be following a good path we take notice. Why don't you tell me what it is that has you so...correct?"

"Correct?" Said Peter.

The pixie hummed affirmatively.

"A human of self honesty is a rare one indeed, who knows what they want and can go about getting that thing without a care in the world. To get that thing without hurting other people or wanting to cause harm. You are so nearly there, so very close to getting what you want."

"Should you really be doing something about fixing the other people about you if this is how you see them? Why it is you do not advise us on what to do when we should be doing it I can't understand."

The pixie bowed its head in exhausted solemness.

"Oh and then he turns back into a right and proper druid by his people's own reckoning, with all questions to be asked and answers expected when they do ask."

He shook his head.

"Not at all. I'm not like the others, it feels like I'm following a scent trail to nowhere. We're no better than the simpler animals than can be tricked and trapped."

It clapped its little hands together.

"Exactly. And see? You did know the answer after all, no need for me. Why don't you just tell them back there what you've worked out yourself?"

"They won't listen to me."

It giggled.

"I forgot. They won't listen to you at all. Moreso the worst for being the first too, to raise his head and look like a fool. Oh if only you could do something that would make you look big and strong, that would get their attention."

"And yet never once has my wit failed me, creature, at least in my head. You should think on that."

The pixie tutted.

"Now you're just being rude, that never gets you where you want to be, you know."

"Oh it's getting me where I want to be. Because I can't be the strongest, not to the point that anyone would commend my effort or care, but with my own means I can be left alone."

Peter was left alone in a bright blink of light, which while it proved that he did have the skill to get people to do that which he did want, it suddenly occurred to him what it must be like that have a world full of talent, yet no one to show it off to.

What does connect me to this place? Can I rely on a new world to show me the way or will this be more the same for me? A world where what I do won't matter and the actions of those who would look down at me won't make sense.

Tiredness suddenly gripped him and his head bobbed as thoughts entered his head with sleep swiftly on their heels.

The pixie was right, I do need to figure out my own way free of this nightmare. I want a new world but with the weighty words of the world or not, I need something it won't give me, that is if I'm to be completely honest with myself.

Chapter Thirty Two
What They Left Behind

The next morning, Peter found himself almost alone in the chamber with the remains of where the spirit had once sat. Almost because despite his mood the previous night he had a pixie hovering around him again. He wasn't quite sure if it was the same one as they did all look rather similar.

"Well you're awfully quiet today." Said the pixie.

Peter's mouth became a straight line on his face.

"That would be a poor joke even if I were by myself. As I am by myself, what need would I have to speak aloud when all my thoughts are in my head?"

The pixie looked him over.

"Ahh but there's more to it than that. I can see, you know. You're alone but you're still thinking of all the others. Again. So in a way you're not alone at all."

Peter nodded.

"I am afraid of being just like them, reminding myself about how different we all are."

That wasn't a lie. Peter had wanted to distance himself from those around him, a feeling which was only becoming more pronounced, at least in his mind. The pixie did not seem so sure.

"But aren't you already like them?"

"If our magic fades further, then I will have nothing over them that I can hold to myself and make myself feel special."

"Oh look at this, the human thinks that he's special. Such short lives you lead, it means you can not do much at all, even dedicating your entire life to a cause. I must be honest though, you've chosen the right one. Rather noble of you and your intentions."

"You know nothing of my intentions." He shot back to the pixie.

The pixie shrugged.

"Oh no? Well how about this. You just told me exactly what it is you want. And you're seeing yourself slip away from who you want to be and there's nothing you can do about it. You may be right, you may be wrong. But you deserve to give yourself so much more than just the thought that you can do nothing about it. You would like to continue making the right choice, wouldn't you?"

Of course I would and I can do something about it. He thought.

Everyone here was talking about the need to complete their search but as for how long that would take it was possible that he would have to get used to a world where the sky was dark and the ground was dark and neither would give up their secrets any longer. All the while, the world that had been at the mercy of human hands, the world of nature, would be laughing at even them as an age of darkness crashed about their heads. Most of all he knew that all these people would lose their heads if it came to them one day that they could no longer hear or communicate with the world.

It is so faint already, but if that day comes it will come and destroy us all as we will be nothing more than people and I don't want to be that. I don't want to have myself brought down to those others when it is clear that I have something they do not, and they tease me for it, or ignore me. None of then respect me, the only reason I'm here is because Gunter wanted to show off who he could drag along with him to prove that he can play leader. Zelda doesn't know what she's walking into in that regard but it's ok for her as she was known from a friend. I suppose Gunter believes he owes her a debt, or rather that one day she will owe him a favour in return.

"What are you thinking about?" The pixie asked.

"Wondering about what one who cares for no one else other than himself would want as a favour."

The pixie's face put on a knowing expression.

"We're good with favours. However the things we would take for one might not be found by you and may not even exist in this land any longer. If that is the case then it is all too bad."

"Not me, I mean another person and if you can't figure that one out it's your own problem."

Peter spent a rather large amount of time off on his own with the pixie, who was curious to hear of life outside of the forest. As humans travelled far, there were boundless stories to tell and Peter told them as matter of factly as any other thing he might say. But still, this was food for the pixie, who could not understand why he was still so unhappy as one who had gone on all these adventures and went about knowing secrets of the world that others did not.

Peter wasn't interested in secrets. He only wanted a place for himself in the world and all this moving about did not endear the land to him at all. The world was a ruin outside of this forest and was becoming as such within, being overshadowed by a dark cloud that choked out the sun and caused all manner of unease if looked upon. While talking about the forest itself, Peter told the pixie of the settlers some way in the forest that had recently come to be.

"Are they trying to hide from their king?" The pixie asked.

"Yes, and they thought to cage us there. Eventually we were let loose but they did so having learned no lessons so far of why they need to live more as we do, at least not by proving it, for letting us go is not proof alone enough for me. They have walls that no matter how low clog and stifle the mind as they live in the way they do purely because they know of no other."

Peter ran his fingers through his hair.

"All the while the darkness that hangs to this forest is trouble. It is not being ignored any longer but everyone still clings to wanting to get the spirit back when we don't even know where it is. Survel was right, the dark cloud should be a concern for everyone in the forest. The others can go off after the spirit, but who among them would take it upon themselves to find the source of the dark cloud I don't know. As for me, this fading magic is enough to make me want to stay in the forest and not become some lonely, wandering beggar who claimed he had once been something he no longer was."

If the worst was to come then he would spend it searching for that cloud, to show that no matter what he was, he could still defend a place he wanted to call his home. After all, his feet were tired and this was somewhere he could rest. All those others could go beyond the forest but that was their choice to make.

The pixie now put on a thoughtful face and stroked its chin.

"So in other words, what you're saying is that you want more than what you have, because what you've been searching for all this time isn't enough. And now you want to go searching for something that could be dangerous, to further put yourself at risk."

"Exactly my thinking. If I don't then no one will."

"Are you so sure no one has already?"

Peter was not sure. In fact there was rather a lot he didn't know and quite a bit more he had decided he knew without asking. He had made up his mind of those things, so that he could believe what he liked.

"No, but that's why, so that I can be sure, absolutely without me just deciding how it should be, that I should seek for the answers in the sky. I'll make up my own mind but I still need the basics to help me understand, otherwise my actions will be a form of arrogance that isn't me. I'm sick of honestly not knowing what's going to happen, pushing forward to some great ideal that might not even be reached while telling myself I know what will happen, which is a lie."

And I'm not going to forgive myself if I leave this place and find it's not here when I get back. It is best to live without so many questions on my mind. I was always asking questions when I was younger, then after being taken off the streets and being promised answers to life, it turned out the best thing to do was to not ask a question in the first place, then there'll be no need for those pesky answers.

The pixie wasn't so sure of his answer.

"It'll all come naturally if you consider the answer yourself. There's no need to ask questions of everyone, although it seems you haven't been that person in a long time."

"Well aren't you perceptive? I don't want to be uncertain again. That's why I'm doing this."

Being led around by everyone else was not part of life one should have to take part in. Especially if you're meant to be all grown up or at least appear to be that way. Others were going through life happy to just follow the leader and not question what it was they were being told. Peter himself had been told that this was the way the world worked and how it was expected to be. But on getting older, he had found that it was not quite as he had been told. His own answers to the world around him were insufficient and the questions he had were not for him to say, or he would shatter the illusion of being all grown up that others would readily pounce on with glee.

So he had made a choice where he could make his own answers not from what others had told him but from his own experiences and he would take his plan one step at a time. He would go to find the darkness in this forest. The rest of the world could be falling around him but this forest would be his home and he would make up for lost years spent travelling alongside others who had done nothing but watch while the world fell apart around them.

Now on the cusp of doubting what he had been told Peter looked inside himself and felt only shame for being fooled as he had. That whatever he had been led through, regardless of where it had taken him, was not what must have snared so many in its grasp, one well meaning but ultimately suited to those who revelled in the way in which they could exercise the grip of power given to them.

That was the worst part. He had not been freed from civilisation. Peter only hoped he wasn't too late and that he had not wasted his life already. Well, those people could continue searching and the ones doing nothing would continue doing nothing, but he would find his own answers and remove the darkness that not only covered the forest, but his own mind as well.

***

Just how long should one take when planning a walk through the forest?

The question was on Zelda's mind as she walked along the boards, making her way over to the chamber under the Great Tree. That room where she had been was still a picture she could see within her mind, an unsettling place if only because what she had seen had been so unexpected.

She had decided not to spend more time there herself if she could help it, if only to keep the image out of her head and while those around her had come and gone from there she had preferred to stay away and let them all carry on with their business.

There were other things she could fill her mind with that was not the remains of that tree. So much could have been different if the spirit had not been scared away, such as being able to do wondrous things. The reason for the journey of her peers may not have happened but the possibility remained that maybe one would have come upon the walls of Churl and from there she would have found her way out. Or maybe she would be dead.

As she listlessly walked on, it did occur to her that this was not at all how she should be conducting herself in such a place, it was only because she found herself with more free time to think in such a place than she had anticipated that she dawdled. Now was not the time for her to be distracting herself from her current concerns with further ones in the past. It was the time where she had to force herself to face her problem as that tree would keep bothering her otherwise until the day the spirit could be returned to it and have the world turn strongly once again.

They had to be careful, she knew they had to be careful, as there was to be no more straying off the path ahead. It really wasn't so hard to start moving once you knew how, you just put one foot in front of the other, which was easier when you knew where you might end up but as they were to be walking through the forest then there was to be no problems.

After all, it should have been clear that there was only one way for them to go to find their hope to regain what had been lost. As for why the spirit had run away was something she wanted to ask them very much, as they had caused harm to the whole world beyond any worth just by being afraid. Just as people could be careless, she suspected that other creatures could be too and she dearly hoped that whatever they found if they found anything at all was not one of that disposition. That would be disappointing.

Best then it be that all places in which they looked were accounted for as they travelled so as not to be overlooked or understudied lest they miss the spirit or some heinous trap. Or even stumble on some other calamity or be forced to flee in disgrace as whatever great darkness had scared away the spirit was most likely the one now deep in the forest.

Certainly she knew that in a way the spirit would be known when her eyes were set upon it, but to set them upon anything at all that might have stopped her dreams and the world left her wondering what it was she could say to one such as them. She supposed she could simply forgive them for that.

While walking along she came upon someone who might help give her an answer. Zelda was sure that there were many answers in the forest ahead, but she was also sure that a pixie might be able to give her the answers.

I have to remind myself not to be needlessly cruel to these little creatures of the forest. I know they can be all kinds of mischief and have heard tales where they have brought great misfortune and woe onto generations of families who have slighted them, but none of those tales should stop me in my proper attitude when asking others for help.

"Oh pixie? Might you listen to what I ask? I must ask you something with intentions that could help the land in which we all live." She said.

One of a few pixies that were fluttering around came down to her head so that it could look her in the eyes.

"You'll get no special treatment from us using those words." It said, not unkindly.

It stuck up its index finger.

"First, one thing. You need to understand that were you no one at all you would not be able to call out to us thus and bring us down. Yet do not mistake your call for any grand test or summoning that requires a demand be met from us."

"I am not from the kingdom of Kasynne to the north of us, who demands a show of that which they hate most for no other reason then to demand you do. I ask all in good reason and that you choose yourselves whether you should come down and listen to what I might ask of you." She said.

"Would you not become annoyed if we were to ignore you?" It asked.

"Perhaps, but do not test me on that yourselves now. There is no need."

At this the pixie grinned far too wide and mischievously to be trusted, Zelda thought, but she moved ahead with her question regardless.

"Tell me pixie, what manner of creatures in the forest are there that could cause the spirit to flee so, and if they are foul and unpleasant, what could one such as I do to arm myself against them? I know that we should be able to overcome them when our words have returned to us and we could rightly tell them what to do. However as it is I am worried that what we have left will not be enough."

"As far as I am aware there's nothing so fearful than the humans that might come into the forest to chop down the trees and thin the edges of the forest. Most recently however, because of the darkness, they have been scared away. Only if you venture out of the forest into the land they claim is theirs should you meet them." Said the pixie.

"Also, of that northmost kingdom aside the forest, what would you do if it turns out that they will be ignoring you?"

"What we plan to do when we have returned to our strength where we should not fear the ground at our feet. We shall return to them and tear the kingdom down."

The pixie hummed in thought.

"A land beyond the forest holding such ire of yours is truly the enemy of all nature. We can't comprehend of such a land beyond, being of this forest ourselves. Although this forest is not where we began, for it is just one of many forests I'm sure you know, it is however where we find ourselves placed in this age most prevalently staring down what could be our own destruction. Let me tell you something, where we are now was once close to the middle of the world but now we find ourselves on the edge, out of the way waiting for this dismal world to come to life again. If it dies, so shall we, see?"

It cleared its throat.

"As I was saying. The forest is not to be idly thought of. Forget about the outside of it where beyond are those that quake at the sight of our trees while scoffing at the darkness they spurn onto us. I have no idea where you humans come from if your reaction to a group of trees is to be afraid of them and to fear the words and wisdom within. This is of no wilful ignorance on my part or the part of my kind, it is simply how we are. You are lucky to see beyond the forest, but cursed to know how far the darkness spreads I will admit. In that I sincerely hope for more allies."

"So might you give me some advice that could guard our travel through the forest?"

"That can only come from our king."

Zelda put her hands on her hips.

"Then why isn't your king here?"

"To ask for a favour from our king requires that which you do not have. Furthermore, if you must ask then you do not possess the need to do so."

"That doesn't sound reasonable."

The pixie shrugged.

"Don't care in the slightest. Our goals here are the same and you who can comprehend the land outside the forest must do as you can to help in stopping this foul darkness that threatens many things beyond the world and understanding of us pixies and other forest folk. Our king has asked this of you I recall. As the spirit has yet to be found, if it is your intention to search then I say go out into the lands and search. Do not overburden yourselves with answers or you will find your feet walking with reluctance at forever considering yourselves unprepared."

She nodded somewhat sullenly, even if she did accept their words as nothing she could change, the knowing of that was bitter. Inside she felt that there were answers left to be told but these pixies wanted her to learn on her own. That was completely understandable but danger was best avoided if at all possible and they were not helping as much as she suspected they could have.

Regardless, Zelda cleared her mind as she came upon the archway, where the pixies waited outside. No reason for her to have a further glum face over small things such as pixies, she perked her head up and more when to her surprise she heard two angry voices caught in argument and she stopped short of walking further into the passage, leaning against the wall instead of continuing to where she would be spotted.

She could recognise Findal's voice, which sounded angry and frustrated.

"I got myself somewhere Peter. I kept my head up and I worked for what I wanted and would have never gotten here had I been like you. You, someone who just kept getting what you wanted, what you needed, all with your thankless mood."

Peter's voice sounded as it almost always did, careless and dull at the edges.

"You're saying I didn't work for what I have?"

"I'm not saying that. I'm saying that now you're giving up, *now* of all times. Why was this as far as you could go? I'm still making something of myself because life never stops, you'll never suddenly have everything you want because the thing is, even if you find yourself where you want you have to keep up the effort to keep it. That's life."

"A better world should be enough. Who cares about what I do afterwards?"

"It's funny, you remind me of all those spoiled noble brats in the north with their parent's money who have never worked a day in their life. I came here to learn more, discover peace and found a dream that can only come from a better world that I can help make real. One without greed and selfishness where all are in tune together as long as people work for it. And who do I find among us? Someone who doesn't understand what that means."

"Really? I would like to think that I know more than you think."

"At your age I was out there making something for myself, not waiting for my life to suddenly happen where everything would be exactly as I wanted it. Or are you worried that when we succeed you won't be able to sit down and do nothing? That you still have to get out there and work, because that's what we will all be doing. A whole world being saved with our words and we will have to spread that with our own voices. That was to be your life. But instead you've turned your back."

Peter's voice was steady.

"I'm not leaving. I don't want to leave this forest, a place I have decided to make my home. Yes we are close to those retched lands that I had wished to leave behind but soon they shall fall and safely here shall be my home. Even if I went with you deeper into the forest you would not convince me to leave further with you and yet the possibility remains that you might force me to. In all honestly I never intended to leave as soon as I laid eyes upon it. Now we're being told that we could be going to other lands. Do they expect us to go on a boat, travel the seas until we end up in poisoned waters? This was never why I was learning and doing what I was."

Zelda was left thinking about her own choices.

I really need to do what is in the benefit of me, and while I'm certainly not one for sneaking around, at the very least I should know when I'm not supposed to be around at all. Then again, can they really blame other people who might be listening in for doing so? If what they wanted was to let each other know how they felt I'm sure each have had plenty of time before now.

Peter was still talking.

"If you look around you can see all that should be worth caring about. Having the means to help this place by being right here. Nothing else matters and the rest of the world can fall down around me for all I care of it, as long as someone else goes out there and picks up the pieces and tells whoever still lives what is right from wrong. But that shall not be me. I'll keep searching on my own time and do all I can do, regardless what little it is you and all the others think of me for handling my life so. If I find the spirit don't expect me to be running to tell you and above all I'll get my wish first."

Zelda decided it best to say nothing. It wasn't really her place to break up a discussion that she felt might have been waiting to happen between those two before she had even known either of them. She walked back outside to sit around the trees, a much better place to do so than where in her thoughts she might be found and worse be forced to state her side in the matter.

It really isn't up to Findal to decide what Peter wants to do with his life, nor is it for me to decide, for that matter. Even though I've made up my mind that what he's doing is foolish and wrong, as to give up on his dream I thought we all shared in order to be alone does seem foolish at that. Sometimes one can not help but be thankful to be rid of the fools around them or else they might drag you down too. So in a way I am thankful if he does not come along, for if he has made a decision that would hinder us then it is for all the better that he stays behind.

Chapter Thirty Three
From the Meeting

So it was that the party left their place of refuge to locate the spirit, one that had left the world in a dark and cold time where those who relied upon it could have most needed the boons it would bring. Not for themselves but to bring the world out of the darkness. There was no fanfare in their leaving of that place of glowing respite, leaving to the destination shackled to them beyond the forest and there was no one to tell those who left that they should have good luck on their journey. Had they volunteered to go such a way perhaps someone might have wished them well.

Zelda, Gunter, Survel, Findal and Nasker left the Great Tree and were ascending past the light of the trees around them and then above, those orbs lighting their path until they gradually faded in number, leaving the trees about them to be merely trees in the cold of winter, nothing more. They had all supposed it to be the middle of the day but the sky far above them beyond the canopy of those trees which did not shed their leaves left little light to come down as the day itself was grey, shaded and cold.

Without the golden glow that had surrounded them, Zelda quite felt that cold, yet she had to remind herself that there was nothing untoward in this forest that had not been there before. Only the minds of such creatures deeper in the forest might have changed to be different. This made her wonder about the ones she had met on her journey most recently.

"I have had little luck getting the pixies to answer questions I could not know myself. Perhaps when our minds were sharper I might have known the answer but that is not what we face ourselves with now. The further we walk the more around us comes the darkness and as it does I worry for our eyes and ears."

Gunter nodded.

"The forest was not always the great dark and unknowable land you see drawn out before you, well as far as you can see, that is. There was once a time where we dwelt within it and laughed as it gave all that was ever wished for and more, we learned its secrets while we kept the cycle moving, the world in balance. It was traversed and known to all who would enter."

He looked around sadly.

"But that was at its peak when all kingdoms were a single great land under one king far more tolerant for all the mysteries of the world. Today we are fractured into pieces, ignorant and frightened of each other, as you have seen. Far to the east and far to the south all was well and good, yet all such as that seems to last but for a short time in the eyes of the world. We remember though, those days of yore, even if walking through here the world could be in any state, were it not for the foulness that pervades this place to remind us. One of the best pleasures of life, that of being able to close your eyes and let time pass you by while being happily ignorant, banished by evil who would hurry us on to our destruction."

Zelda hummed.

"Indeed, those of the world should not be hurried from place to place. Then perhaps it is sad, not only because we walk from such a place as we have been, the Great Tree, but to walk on in such a way means that the fate of the world could pass us by and we might be none the wiser, fading away to be like all others."

"I would think in all honestly that we would see it, for the nights are cold and the world shall be colder ever more but above and beyond we should be able to hear the world cry out in its final moment, may that never come to pass. In the case that it did, providing we were not instantly banished from the world, I doubt some of us might show our faces and eyes outside of this forest ever again. All manner of shame and woe upon us, that this forest would be a fine place to be exiled in our failure. But that is enough time spent on such dark murmurings, for that enough will be plain enough to see ahead, those of us who move ahead, don't you think?"

"Peter is not here to help us get through them as he chose to stay behind. I wonder if there was any reason why he wanted to stay? I do not want to find such an act alarming but I hope none of us turn on our own heels as fast."

Findal was shaking his head.

"He's been giving up for a while now, this wasn't anything sudden on his part."

Gunter nodded.

"Indeed. But it can not be helped, even if the ends we seek are not the same."

Zelda shrugged her shoulders.

"Well I might miss him for a time. Ah, yet it is no matter at all. We have chosen our path and he his, even if in the end all things we work towards will be for the same goal. Yet you say that we do not seek the same end?"

Gunter paused for a moment, a pause she was curious on as it lasted to her thinking just a little too long.

"Oh the cycle always continues. I'm sure we will meet again some day triumphant. If not us then one of the others, hopefully, will succeed."

Survel groaned.

"Bah, to be honest, I did not like him. Too centred on his own journey, that one. People should not be such as stones in a stream to others, to be walked on or thrown for entertainment. They should be the person next to you, laughing and enjoying your company along such a stream while you tell tales and fish."

Zelda was surprised by this and raised her eyebrows.

"I have not so much as seen or heard you tell of any tales or laugh while you fish. Aren't you yourself what you say he is?"

The man snorted.

"I tell myself tales and be happy, even if I might not look it. As for Peter, it was in his eyes that I saw something untoward to all others. The suspicion, the lack of care, of thought beyond whatever was in front of his face was plain for me to see. I could see that we were all nothing to him. So let him sit on his backside and sharpen his senses however he sees fit. I'm glad for one less pair of eyes staring into the back of my head for no good reason."

"Well you might have one more now that you've got me curious about those tales of yours."

"Maybe I'll tell you of them some day."

Zelda found herself doubting that she could ever sit down and get used to Survel talking at length, although it would interest her to see how long he could talk before giving up.

Deeper into the forest they all went where the light left them behind. The days were dark with the nights especially so indeed, for little filtered down into the trees far below, not happiness of all things. Seeking a distraction on one of these days where the wind whistled far above with chilly flakes of white threatening to fall upon their heads, Zelda looked towards the days to follow.

"What is in the lands beyond this forest?" Zelda asked.

She thought that in this time of year that there could be ice floating in the seas and burly buildings thatched thickly, hardy would be their walls and warm their insides, where smoke would be rising from chimneys that promised cosy warmth within. That at least was what she hoped for, as they could not even make their skin become like trees to stave off the cold chill without the threatening darkness clinging to them most dangerously.

Findal's face lit up at this chance to talk.

"My ancestors traded with a great sea empire up the coast in the far north west. Some say they went to war with an old kingdom far in the north and lost decisively. I'm not sure how they will take to us coming out from the forest, if indeed they take any measure of us at all. None have travelled up from the south for obvious reasons, it having been abandoned and we have not heard of them encroaching on this kingdom along the north border either. The Northlands itself is at peace, there has been no word of war in these times so it is safe for some to say that perhaps they have mellowed in their ways somewhat but I do not believe it."

"You think they are all gone?"

His face fell slightly.

"While there is land on the other side of this forest, that is something maps have shown if not stories told. I was thinking that there was no sea empire in this land and that they existed not here but across the sea itself. If some remained then we have heard nothing of them for over one hundred years."

"I see. I certainly don't want to go missing just as they have, it all sounds rather bleak without thinking of myself or the current predicament we find ourselves in. I like this world as it is, we just need to remove the darkness from it so everyone can see it with new eyes just as I did and maybe that will open some closed people up, at least I hope. Maybe they live closer to the ocean and are then closer to nature because of it. That would be nice, coming to see people with a mutual understanding rather than sneaking around or with swords drawn."

Zelda had read stories about pirates, they seemed to be seafaring bandits but she had never been able to think of what they might be like as people. Then she realised something with her eyes wide.

"But if there was a seafaring people and they captured the spirit, it could be across the ocean!"

Nasker stalled up ahead.

"Oh I hope not. That would account for our reduced influence though, wouldn't it? If the spirit was not in this land at all. First let us see what we find beyond the forest before we begin to worry about needing a boat." He said.

Gunter nodded.

"We must search everywhere and remove every shadow where the spirit could be.

You need to be prepared for the world to not look the same in your eyes when all the shadows are gone."

It honestly might be better to have her removed all together than find myself opposed but I shan't risk such a move now. He thought.

"If someone else cast a light that caused you to jump at your own shadow, would you see things as they see it or go to war against them with foul intentions?"

These words perplexed Zelda as much as Gunter's silence had, but she found she could not focus on what to say. There was little distance that could be seen through the dense trees until shadows swallowed them whole and none of them knew what was in those shadows, so she found herself wanting to be careful.

"I don't see why one should get angry at the casting of a shadow to begin with, after all it is just a shadow."

"But a shadow is an outline, and people get afraid when all they see is an outline. After all, what if the shadow was real and could move on its own? It wouldn't really be you but it would still be an image of you. Perhaps what they see is only the darkest outlines of your being but a shadow is still a part of you. But do not confuse that darkness for night, for many creatures sleep in the day and live at night. That is something unnatural and the beasts of nature know it is so and fear it. That doesn't mean that they would be standing with us. Not at all. In fact, we might find the opposite. Some ridicule us for trying to understand nature the way they do, we can only follow in their paths and learn from their teachings after all."

Zelda could not shake what the elf had told her, but she kept her thoughts to herself.

If really what we are being taught is not the whole truth, then there are answers out there beyond what I will learn here. Even if we return the spirit to its rightful place, will more need to be done to understand why this world is sick and will I really spend my whole life on this path? I had ideas of what I could be doing with myself and where my life would lead me but now, tied up in all of this, is a future getting to be something I should just put aside, letting it fade away in the back of my mind while I live out this journey? A part of me certainly says 'no'.

She could remain troubled and go off in her own direction searching for that future, one that may not last or even appear, or she could do something now, be a part of something, however incomplete it was.

It's not just about me. This is so much more than me, and I can make a difference. I just have to find the missing pieces and put them back into place, only then will the picture make sense. One thing at a time though, I should not be seen to disregard or have admonishing thoughts about the way things are right now. I need to listen and pay attention to advice given, after all, that's all it is, and advice rarely encompasses everything needed to make sense of a situation.

They were going out of the lands, leaving them behind and to Zelda it felt rather like abandoning a place she had only just begun to appreciate and being around those already with such an appreciation she knew their experiences would help her when she needed it most. Not only because they would all be walking into the unknown, she felt envious of those who got to roam the places they had known, who had found a place amongst the world to which they could return to.

To walk along the lands less travelled, she could then look back the way they had come to be reminded of who it was they were on this journey for, and it amused her to think how she would feel if beyond the forest they found a burgeoning home for themselves where the key to a new world lay beyond.

It all sounded rather easy in her head, the most preferable outcome which was agreeable to her giddy heart. She honestly found herself more sure of them finding nothing but a bunch of humble fisherfolk having no clue who they were or what it was they were after, some few years too late to do anything.

Once, all had been one, Lara had said, and Gunter and Findal had suggested as much. Once was not now, and it was pointless looking back with that rapidly shrinking future staring ahead. They would have to keep searching, maybe take a boat across the ocean to other lands unknown if they existed at all. It was a bother how little anyone knew from beyond the forest, but again, the reminder that this would be a question they would solve themselves came into her head and helped loosen the knot of worry in her stomach.

After all, those druids returning to common ground would be doing just that, looking over places that they had seen to previously for years, often many years, at a time. If those ones had not found the spirit then perhaps the ones among her would, pushing out beyond the world, away from that place which she had learned was home in more than just name but in the very ground itself. A place that had lost the world's anchor to something mysterious and beyond the understanding of most.

Or maybe it was something that could not be understood even by them to be used to sway people into an understanding until it was right where it needed to be.

Unlike Findal, she doubted that gold could be used to sway any who they might happen to talk to. Some said that gold made the world go round, but what would they do without it? Zelda figured much the same as what they were doing, searching for that lost something that would bring them purpose in life and the world would still go on without them.

However, without the spirit to guide them, Zelda realised all they were doing was repeating the cycle without telling people of its importance. When all had been better she had felt the rain in the clouds and heard the heartbeats of the animals around her and could feel when things were not aligned as they should be, but who would listen to her now if she was to walk out into the world of wealth and money and tell them what they were doing was disrupting the world?

Well, she knew that money could be used to pay people to make problems disappear. Without any herself, those she sought to sway might ignore her or call her a farce, perhaps both of those things. So she needed that magic, that understanding in her heart so she could explain just what it was that was making everything so sick and ill in the world right about now and what they could all do to stop it. Maybe the spirit would have the answer to that question but until she asked then her guess was as good as any, so that following along with someone else's plan was the best she could do. And if that was the best she could do herself then so be it.

Not everyone was doing exactly what she thought of as her best. Despite the doomsaying words of the two at the Great Tree, surely there were many druids far beyond the forest who wanted to help and lend their aid to the world, merely the way life was for some put them out of reach of lending assistance yet in their own way were doing all they could. As for others, a long time ago the elves would have dealt with this woeful time but now, with them all up and scattered elsewhere to be mostly in hiding, what could they possibly do about the dark that wouldn't come too late? They would have to journey through lands fearful of fire and of those they once held and Zelda understood just what that would mean for someone who did not want to risk capture and death.

Still, those thoughts lingered in her head and she spoke.

"I should think that those of elven kind should come here and face their own shadows that I feel they have beside them. However that would require a most bitter journey south or otherwise abroad I would guess none would care to take. Perhaps they aught to be chased out of their seclusion, they would see more of the world that way."

Gunter laughed humourlessly.

"Oh they see plenty besides. You are sounding confident in your reasoning, but why would you expect them to follow the path of your own circumstances? Many have the means to stand and fight and many might, just to die where they stand rather than to face with eyes wide open a ruined life of their own making."

Zelda was looking at the forest around them.

"I would not have even imagined a forest this large, nor seen it with my eyes had something not come and forced me to leave. Life, I thought, was idyllic at one time, and despite quite the fright for fear of death I would do the whole thing again if I had to."

"And if you came across such people again?"

Zelda crossed her arms and huffed.

"Then I would maul them with my bear paws and strength. Not a kind use of such magic admittedly but if only to show them that I'm no longer afraid."

"So are you afraid of them now that you can not use our magic safely?" Nasker asked.

"Furthermore, you are more than whatever talents you possess, as it doesn't matter what you have for not everyone will see you as you are, nor should you be expected to use your magic just because you can. It is easy to attach your worth to what you can do, but attach it to who you are instead, as that is something you will never lose. I just felt that you needed to hear that, that is all."

Gunter spent some time nodding to this.

"Well what Zelda says she has decided to do would not be what an elf might do, most certainly. As long as we get our magic back she would be stepping in the right direction if that is what she wishes for. I admit that she surprised me when I found that she was able to learn the druidic ways, yet it is not so strange when one hears her speak and the earnest words that come from within. Your conviction is strong." He said to her.

Zelda tried not to feel too pleased with herself over old efforts.

"I don't always think when I do things, but that's part of the secret. Just doing what is required. Lara had no time for timid, aimless wanderings of a person's own spirit. You have to trust yourself to get out of the situations you put yourself in. I guess Peter could not trust himself."

Survel rolled his eyes.

"Of all the times you could have chosen, are you telling us now that you resent having been rescued and carted off as you had not done so freely, chosen of your own wiles? Do be yourself and appear to be grateful for that which you wandered into, for the world seeks those such as yourself as its defenders. Those who listen and act."

"Another lesson she taught me is that you also have to trust those you put your faith in to get you out of trouble if not yourself. I wonder what she would have thought of the spirit having up and gone so suddenly. Did the spirit of nature have no one to trust?"

Gunter sighed.

"What need does a spirit have to trust? After all it knows all things and can see into all hearts and minds, can hear every whisper in the breeze. The spirit would know all it needs to know merely by seeing you and by that alone would know what needed to be done from there."

After some days passed they came to a small clearing made up of a break between the trees. In the center of which there was a surprise. Some stone ruins sat about, remains of what had once been a tower, where only one wall remained, that reached only a little over head height. Scattered about the ground was a floor of white tiles mostly overgrown and reclaimed by nature, also covering the ground aside from tree roots were vines that had crept along the ground and had trapped all manner of leaf litter that had rotted over time.

Most uselessly, there was a stone fountain built into the remaining standing wall. It was sticking out from the wall, sculpted in such a way that it appeared to be a sleeping, giant face. It had leafy vines for a beard and straggly hair that was also covered with real vines.

Staring down at the forest floor, Zelda noticed that although much of it was grown over and the tiles misplaced, there were paths in many directions from the ruins, travelling off into the forest.

"Which of these should we take?" Zelda wondered.

"We could take none at all but I am sure that these paths lead somewhere and one might lead us to where we need to go, roughly speaking."

There was a rumbling and a loud voice spoke out through the trees, an echoing, scraping sound of stones and falling rocks.

"That would be unwise." Said the voice.

It took them all a moment to realise that the fountain was speaking to them, the sound of its voice coming from all around.

"To follow those paths could lead you quite astray. Indeed, do not attempt to move the stones by your feet or make the paths anew, for doing so could send you anywhere, to where even I could not say, as would be your fate were you to tread those steps."

Findal hastily took a foot off the tiles.

"What do you mean by such a thing?" He said.

The fountain laughed most wistfully at his words.

"As a guardian left by the dwarves, allow me to say to you that these paths were no ordinary ones. The very stones themselves once directed all who walked upon them on their way and will take you to places most unknown to you."

"That sounds the same as any old forgotten road to me." Zelda said.

"Look around you and you might see the difference." The guardian replied.

Zelda was puzzled, looking from tree to tree. Doing so made her notice quite a difference then before, but not with her eyes.

"The creatures in this part of the forest, I can't hear them with my ears. Whereas before there had been sounds, here there are none. Or rather, there are no creatures here that I can feel even slightly."

Gunter was frowning.

"Neither can I or any of us I should think. It is a sign of further things to come and has nothing to do with where we find ourselves now. This place is a marker and whether or not darkness is drawn to it I can not say."

At this a voice came, one with a slight bleat from beyond the trees.

"All just as well, for I think that you should not hear me, human."

The voice was followed by a creature that came out from the furred trees that held their winter's growth and blended in around it. The bizarre horned beast had the lean body of a man at a little under double the height. They were covered in clumpy black fur and walked on two cloven feet and had the head of a goat, although flattened somewhat, which twisted this way and that, to better keep track of each of them. In one hand it held a supple black bow and over its shoulder was a ruck sack with another bow, some plain looking arrows and a bulge that appeared to be that of a lyre. With the other hand it thumped its chest and huffed, stomping up and down on its hooves in an appalling din for a single being to make.

"I am a beast of this forest and I stand on my own here without any help. What are you here for in this forest, humans of nature?"

"I should think that is obvious." Grumbled the guardian.

The beast sounded exhausted as it sighed.

"Oh no, you woke up the fountain? Now isn't that just grand? Look what you've gone and got us all into."

To this the guardian yawned, the air around it vibrating as it did.

"Would it not be that you should wish them to see into your mind so that time would not be wasted explaining to them why you think that way?" It said.

"My mind is mine alone. One free of insects or other troubles that bite and irritate."

Snapped the beast.

"I was just telling these humans about the bounds of these steps." Said the guardian.

"Ah, so that is why they have come to such a useless place. Or, as they have not answered me, perhaps there is another reason?"

His tone was curious but one of a quiet demand for his question to be attended to. All stood sturdy and Gunter put up himself forward and the creature whipped its head around to meet him. In a clear voice the druid spoke.

"We search the forest for the one who has gone missing that connects us all. The spirit of nature."

He turned then to his fellows and spoke in a quieter voice.

"Again I must remind you all to behave yourselves, there are many like he in the forest and it would not be pleasant to make enemies or otherwise make them disgruntled due to any conversation here."

The beast crossed his arms.

"Well we have not seen it. And you people cloistered it up and away so that none might have seen it barring yourselves, of which seems to have done you little good. The forest has no walls, yet you say you are like us while walling away the very thing that would make us the same. Whoever can blame the spirit for running from you into hiding it is not I."

"All were free to come if they wished for such was to keep the world as it was. Do you see about you the darkness? I disagree with what you have to say, the spirit did not run from us as you say. The darkness about is more than we have thought, and while you may look at us and laugh as your kind always has, we are determined to move on."

"I'm not laughing." Said the beast.

"Nor am I." Said the guardian.

Gunter cleared his throat.

"Never the less, have either of you seen any others like us searching? We do not wish to retrace their steps and would wish to use our time wisely."

The beast pointed further north into the forest.

"Then deeper is all I can suggest, for nothing else is far darker than that and I smell your kind everywhere but there. Do not ask the guardian, or you will be forever ensnared by its riddles, as my people have been to others."

"It would certainly make sense to stay away from the darkest parts as we would not want to fall foul of whatever creeps and lurks in such places turned to darkness. No matter how far we must go my hope is clear, that the spirit is still in this land somewhere." Gunter said.

The beast seemed unimpressed by the way he flicked his ears.

"It could be nowhere within a thousand miles of where you now tread, or perhaps it has been captured by the darkness. Because you humans know of it so well, surely you can ward off such influence, but even we fear to tread terribly deeper into the dark, where our feeling to the world falters and we lose all senses and become blind."

"It could have returned to the world, then their journey would be rather fruitless, as none from any tree however gold, or from any clan." The guardian said.

The beast shook his head.

"There are no more clans beneath the sky you foolish construct. And besides, the king of the pixies feels the spirit, as do others more closely intertwined with it. Not that I trust a pixie, yet some words must be taken as they are."

"That means nothing. All are connected to the world, including that which is being sought."

"Well some of us come from a time before its appearance and that description aptly fits us both although not myself personally. I think you're just an ancient construct made to lie to people."

"Yet I too am a part of nature, a stone spirit if you will. Created long ago by the dwarf people who scarcely inhabit this world any more if at all for I can not feel their presence. Long ago they joined with nature for their own means and ends, which is how I am here. A giver of warnings was my task, yet I have none for you."

"A giver of headaches more likely. I might find myself ensnared in your riddles if I linger too long yet look here, I have found myself in an argument."

"No sound shall come forth from me for your benefit. I wait for those who are true to the way left behind by those who put me here. No light or dark are needed for me. My makers did not care and nature does not care. What you call nature has thrived due to the way things are now. If a new cycle arises then what nature is will change, but it will still be nature."

The two continued to rabble among themselves and the druids quietly made their way away from the squabbling duo. Zelda kept looking back in confusion, so Gunter had to do some explaining for her.

"The guardian does not understand that there will be nothing left for anything to grow. The dark stifles all and his truth is all he can see. He might speak honestly but little of the world that it sees is the truth. I could say that there are rocks in his head but that of course goes without saying. The world they see is an incomplete picture of a greater whole, that being said it is possible that this was made in the purpose of dwarfish humour, as a monument that once told riddles. Those are some far gone years, blindingly far, so that we can not ask them, but evidently whatever magic holds up that wall is not what was afforded to the rest of the structure. The guardian is stuck, only able to comprehend what it has been told when it was made. It is so old that it clings to old experiences and isn't able to change."

Gunter stopped in thought for a moment.

"That is rather similar to the world around it and there is no hope for such a thing, which while it may outlast us in years may one day find itself alone unable to comprehend the skies above it. I don't even know if it could see them to be honest and I'm not about to turn about and go ask. That is the same for many places where darkness lurks. It might be wise for us to keep our distance, unless coming upon such darkness we feel compelled to take a closer look."

"Then why didn't we begin in the old town overlooking the valley all those months ago? There were plenty of shadows down the bottom of that place, even I felt them, although at the time I admit it would have been a difficult choice to get me down there. But could it not be that the spirit was captured by a dark force and rushed away to a place such as that?" Zelda asked.

"So you felt it, even back then did you? Well you are right to say that there were shadows and darkness there, but first we need to find ourselves a direction, a purpose, and stick to it, not jump at any old shadow, for there are many. Others were watching over the shadows down there in the deep, dark valley. That is for the purposes of those watchers to seek or find, but from what had been told to me that darkness is something born into this world, which has been tempted and swayed by foul reachings for power. We needn't worry, unless we are routed then told to go back ourselves and seek it out of course. We were not sent there so all is well and if that had been the case I feel the world would have been in a more dire place sooner. With such strength at your grasp you would aught to use it."

"But our strength bleeds from us with each week. Whatever shall we do if we find ourselves as regular people, with none to listen to our words of wisdom for by then we will have no words? No insight or art otherwise to convince people that our concerns are true?"

"The spirit will listen to us regardless of how we appear, as I have said, so there's no need to worry. It is true enough that there would have been a time, when we had more time, boundless amounts of it, where such a detour or excursion would have rightly made sense, but now we must place our trust in others who are there and all other places besides that we can not reach. We can be beside them, just with our minds. It is not up to us to be everywhere at once."

So he said, but Zelda found it unreasonable to expect that simply thinking about others could bring them any strength at all, as comfort was what that brought and it was not usable at all, especially when in trouble or where they could be in trouble. She thought of Malleau and even Gandagar, a city a king had forgotten and how little it mattered if others thought about those places at all. A thought was always nice of course, knowing that you were remembered and considered, but all in all those facing a dilemma or catastrophe would have been best served by having someone else beside them as the greatest help of all.

She did not wish to be alone, or drag others with her into peril, yet there were places in the world already clinging to the edge of it with people in the same way. Zelda thought of her old home and what she had not seen before while living there she saw quite clearly now. She would return to it to save them if she could, because she knew that her thoughts alone, while strong enough to make her heart ache, amounted to very little, ultimately.

Chapter Thirty Four
A Scheme in Motion

Kieke looked out over the fields on the wall, eyes searching for nothing but looking all the same. Today the sky was a calm blanket with clouds as far as they could see. There was someone missing that she had been thinking about lately. It wasn't a large bother, just a small disappointment that events had turned out the way that they did.

In her hand was a little red pebble, its twin she had given to that person who had been full of inner brightness. Kieke hadn't anything else to give and even that would have been a stepping stone to learning something more along the way but that had not been allowed to happen.

I wonder where she went?

Tilting her head back Kieke could see the thick stone walls and the castle off in the distance. This place had scared that person and they had run away, perhaps rightfully so to be away from this place where walls and towers did not keep one's mind at ease.

Kieke could not blame her now, because she could not see how that brightness would have been left alone here in this place which had changed with the turn of the weather in a way she hadn't seen before, darker and colder, the days barely keeping the light in the sky.

Of course she herself was bitter that she had not been able have Zelda stay, to find the leverage needed to do so, for as her master's words went, Zelda should have made her mission easier. If anything being unable to stop her leaving had broken the truth of those words and she had been punished for her misdeeds. Not only her but everyone else in these cold months that might have not had to exist but for her failure, where they found themselves trapped in the cowl of darkness that had covered Churl that had been growing for a long time. A darkness ordered by the king that fell on the ears of his subjects telling them to fall themselves to their knees in gladness. All people should want to be free of such darkness in the world.

Surely when it was all over she would have no need of someone who ran away from home, where such a place might be in a right state by then too. The thought was amusing, but if the girl did not like the result well then she had been given her chance to do something. If there was to be any change at all to Churl then Kieke would grasp at the opportunity herself. After all, she could look and see at what past kings had done to this place, how a stated significance had been twisted over the years so that they could grab at that importance and by holding it tightly, smother all who would doubt them.

It was only right that she leave her mark, however displeasing to those blind fools here. And didn't most kings and rulers work that way? She had known ones who were not so bad on her travels, however here was one making his people live in the dark while telling them to look to the light and as such that light could appear brighter and blind people who hung to their old ways, who took up swords against those who made their own ways in the world.

How long such blindness would be allowed to persist was supposed to be up to her and should have been gone already. Yet here she was, mulling over a past that did not happen and a future that would not happen just the same, one where no one would see.

It was possible that a few of the people of who's bits and pieces she had been making use of were some of those people the king despised but she wasn't doing him a favour that way. She was not one of the king's butchers, culling those who stood in her way. Some people were needed for fuel, nothing more, but there was nothing more personal than that hidden man who's life had sent her far away, where she ended up here watching him come so close before hiding himself away.

This world is thinning further out, what little light there is has been stretched as much as it can to keep the sky alight, but for how much longer? I dare not wish to fathom at the answer, or what else may need to be overcome might not be confronted if I consider the sudden impossibility of my task, yet I have stared down such before and refused to let those thoughts haunt me further during those moments.

Defences and fortifications and overly enthusiastic guards had made things very difficult for not only her but anyone indeed, not at all something she could overcome with such defences cast in iron. By the time such guards were to become idle and complacent it would be too late. With such an expendable supply of men willing to show their devotion, there was no point slowly whittling away at the mind of one when they would be simply be replaced, the tired with the keen who were waiting on all the dark to pass them by.

What am I supposed to do? Wait until the hinges fall off due to disuse and rust, then sneak in as they are being repaired?

Kieke was feeling a little frustrated and yet, here she found herself stuck in such a land, one of disuse and rust as it were. She counted herself as not the only one, for those fools themselves were stuck in the lands in which they made, unable to push out because they alone held the sanctity to belong in Alegan. There were no armies to force themselves beyond and hold their holy words above all others and make those heretical people obey. This king truly was a king of the people, they mirrored him so exactly, hiding away in their own land, perhaps now thinking that others could not be saved. Even then it must have been a shallow, fabled thing to see, a world full of people to see to your every whim, even if it was a world that was empty all the same.

Who could tell anyway when trapped behind those walls? Unless that was the point, to see nothing and wait for it all to just fade away. Any who might be left, well those were yours to rule over, you would know. Better to have a world in ruin and you holding onto the barest scraps of what once was absolutely yours than never being able to hold it all in your hands again. That would be a common course of action for a successor, she knew. Maybe to stop all of that nonsense from resurging the prince needed to die, if nothing more than as an after precautionary measure.

I wonder what the prince might be thinking if he is indeed still alive. Would he be a person to stand for such wispy a world in lands that might be his and march out one day as a foolish boy, desperate to reclaim the lost power he must have heard so much of in his youth? Or has he already been done away with, perhaps saving me the trouble if he is to be so lost in those dark ways as those have around him?

How much that would matter in the end was not a worry, for Kieke only had to think of the sky above to know that it would not matter. Far above waited one watching with great interest and in fear of that descending Kieke knew that others would have to do all manner of things over her dead body and at that kill her first. Not a hard task by any means admittedly but to let herself be killed, now that wasn't going to happen. To pass on her mission to another, just as unlikely.

Perhaps Zelda would be dead by then if she was not already, or she would die with the hurt inside to see a world so malign and vicious, trampled and burned if she suckered up fully to those fools. Kieke had expected great things from the girl but in the end perhaps the whole thing was just a fortuitous chance encounter between the two that she had taken too far and gotten too close, or hopeful. Yet to have that one slip through her fingers as a lure, it would have been worse if she had never tried and had been left wondering if the king could have been dead sooner rather than not.

A thought struck her. While intentional or not, the king had sent out a band of people to remove a dangerous person to them, but how had they thought of Zelda to be dangerous? Surely there hadn't been another who had felt her importance and Kieke realised that the king had given himself more time, saved from an earlier death. That couldn't do to happen again. How everything would be if there was no change was not worth putting her mind towards. That way led people to madness, she knew.

'Madness?'

The feeling of her master's presence shook into her mind.

'The girl would have succeeded, yet if that hadn't opened the gate you'd still be looking over your shoulder. Bloated are the ideas of a fool king too cowardly to show his face, who hides behind his walls, as are the ideals of those who follow him.'

He was right. So many people gushed to the king and once the number would have been even more. In those years he would have had to show his face but these were not those years. None would bother to send their armies to take this place, she was sure that looking in they could see the land wasting away, if their own lands were not the same.

Kieke closed her eyes.

That could very well be. How long will this winter last for in this cold darkness? People succumb to the cold yet there are no dead piling up in the streets as all who complain about the cold must find comfort in death. Too late some might realise that there will be no spring to allow for growth and this land will become dark and blacken like the corpse it is for all to see. Ahh but to believe it, now that is another matter entirely.

Her master was brief.

'You believe it.'

Kieke nodded.

I do believe it.

She really did and had for years. There was no reason for her to turn about or demand the end come so she could see it with her own eyes, for in the end there would be nothing to see, that she believed wholeheartedly. As the presence of her master receded, the echo of his power ebbed and flowed away as it was always bound to do against her mind, which she knew as a great shore on which her master tread. His presence was not the feet on that sandy shore but the water itself that let purpose and strength come forth for all who it was home to.

Other footsteps, such as those of a young man behind her, she could hear stopping several paces behind with her ears. Like all the others, this one too could only see so far ahead.

"I've been looking for you." Brodie said.

He looked around the top of the wall.

"This place is quiet."

"Well it was." Kieke said.

He smiled.

"Sorry then."

"No, that's not what I meant. Can't you hear all the voices of all the different people that have come and gone from this place? It gets quieter and quieter with the further passage of warmth. The wind, it's all that keeps the memories alive because it's always there with us, reminding us of our times with others."

His mouth drooped into concern that his eyes were not showing.

"I can't say I hear them at all. They're just gone one day from the world never to be seen again. I'm thinking more of the people who are carted off, after having only spoken to them once, or not at all. Some days I wonder if they are worth my memories. I don't want my mind to be filled with ghosts of the dead I have no need to be apologising to or to be feeling guilty for the way things turned out. Most of all I don't want this to be a city of ghosts after all these years, all that royal, kingly prestige, wasted on the place, on a cage."

"You can leave a city of ghosts."

Brodie smiled to further take the dark edge off what he had said but Kieke was still looking out with her eyes, searching beyond for any message in the sky she could glean for one last moment before turning as if to scan the city and the castle walls beyond.

It was cold and grey by the same eye, yet the way it stood indifferent to the turmoil around it cresting at the edges of the world told that the city would not care if it was swallowed whole. It did not have a personality, not without the people to make it appear to have some.

There was a certain atmosphere that came in abandoned places, old caves and abandoned, grand castle houses in the middle of nowhere. Walking joyfully through them as she once had done was not the same as looking upon this, spoiled by the feeling of dissatisfaction inside her. It could always be abandoned after her mission was complete, but she could not help feel as if something was amiss. One thing would be if people were leaving in droves but here they all came, to be treated the same by their king, holding a whip that coiled around them to drag those not trusted inside.

The people were not speaking for themselves as the king knew best. But death wasn't being saved, being dragged away wasn't being saved, all the crying eyes meant nothing when they were all so enraptured to whatever old ways held onto them in a grip that would not let them go. Or perhaps death was releasing them from such a grip, she did not know.

The quiet and the stillness reached out to her as if alive, as if to remind her of all the places she used to know and how they used to make her feel. But she would feel no joy stalking those halls and rooms above knowing that the rest of the city beneath her was guttered through means that were not her own.

Kieke sighed.

"What does all this say about our city? We'll all disappear before too long ourselves, the longer we stay here. I feel it. There will be no time for apologies then."

Brodie cleared his throat.

"Oh yes, that's what I'm here for, people from the church are asking for you. I came to give you a warning I guess, in case you get rounded up."

"I'm not going anywhere. After all they could just need me for something regarding the kids. I should go see them now, but I won't go running."

Kieke did good on her word until she remembered that she had walked out to clear her head, leaving one of the kids in the tub and a pot of food over the fire, making her run and stumble as fast as she could in a quite different direction to get back home.

Fortunately for her, the oldest pair had taken charge and had made sure that everything was in order, that nothing had burned and no one had drowned. Right after a late breakfast they were all restless in that most predictable way that kids could be and only so much that two eyes could handle.

Kieke dragged one of the older ones to a stop and another came to a halt beside her.

"Did you make sure that everyone had enough to eat?" She asked the boy in her hands.

"There was barely enough as it is, we tried leaving you some but someone snatched it."

"Probably without realising you hadn't had any." The girl beside him said.

"Well isn't that the usual every once in a while." Kieke sighed.

"You two don't need to worry, I'm going out anyway, I'll need to wash this baked in pot then go find out what the church wanted and plead for some bread from the church baker and I'll eat there when I do."

The two left her with their apologies and she made her way over to the cast iron pot and found that indeed it had already been emptied. She hoisted it up by the handle to take with her. She would have to go past the river at some point to get this cleaned out properly.

Other young ones were sweeping around the house, looking firmly down at the ground in a way Kieke found adorable in their innocently transparent attempts to avoid her attention.

"I'm going out again." She said.

"No worries." Said one.

"We'll keep a look out." Said another.

Hmm, maybe someone had seconds or thirds and maybe they did have second thoughts, or third thoughts about whether I would like some of what they pigged out on. I could always check their heads because I will know who did if I take a look. Best to curb that greedy behaviour while they're still young.

In the end she decided not to needlessly pry, there'd be time enough for that when a real need arose. There was a lot more for her to be concerned about than which one to pull in line, especially when it seemed that there had been some hint of sharing or cooperation in their selfishness among the nine she now had. It was best to enjoy all that stuff when you were younger anyway, before you were given wider responsibilities to take care of yourself.

Really though. She thought.

They do need it more than I do.

She took the pot with her and made her way out into the winding streets. On her way it was easy to reflect on just how quiet Churl had become, more so than standing out on a wall. Then again, these were all recent memories retreaded with her feet as she walked along places that had once held the sounds of life. Easy enough to excuse when people would rather be inside for winter but this was something else.

If there was wind, then she would hear the wind, that would push under doors and make them creak or whistle though side streets. A lamp chained to the wall would make sounds as the wind picked up and tossed those chains back and forth. There seemed to be traces of life around her so this particular street, hemmed in by stone houses that rose up and left itself in shadow with a strip of pale sky above was not as abandoned as other streets she had walked.

Those ones had been colder than the wind. She was thankful in some small way that she had never really needed to explain to the children why it was that this place was becoming quiet, most of them had always known the feeling of abandonment and had seen their own worlds shrink and become cold. So this wasn't so much of a change, just a continuation of all they had known, even with her being there for them, even with her master, one day theirs too.

A sight familiar enough to see brought no warmth even though the warmth of bodies were present when she walked off a step to a wider road, mostly flat from the left to the right across the city so she could see for a little while either way along it with an intersecting road sloping down.

Two people were being taken away, tied down on a cart loaded with sacks that would have once been brown but were staining dark, deep red, the colour leaking out of the sacks and staining too the clothing of the pair.

Someone had gone out hunting and this cart had likely been taken by the church for use. Of course whoever it belonged to could not have said no. Unless they were the ones in the back of the cart, but neither the man or the woman looked to her to be the sort that would go out and hunt.

Both were crying while professing their innocence for their crime that by the sounds of it they did not know of what they had been accused. Kieke could not play dumb to get information out of who was carting them away, after all she knew to play the part, that if people were caught then they had to have been doing something wrong of one sort or another, and not say a thing.

Before the king had come it was a sight sometimes possible, that a person had been dragged off by the guards. Then the walls had gone up and while they had remained for a time there were now no guards. Just those that did the rounds and often brought someone in, she thought, just because they could.

She had never heard of anyone being falsely accused being around to talk about it later and at least the bodies of these two would not be put up for display, but then again rulers south of where she had come never had been ones for such things. But perhaps the church had done that to the kingdom, a sense of not needing to use such measures due to loyalty to them or to rulers such as the king. This could be considered a sight enough, however if it did not deter her then Kieke doubted it would deter those others that might actually be doing something wrong.

Ahh these poor people, about to find themselves lost down a road where the only end is most likely a dark and cold road tread by many who are no longer among us. There's really nothing I can do for them, nor anyone else who might then be hauled up along with them.

Again the thought crossed her mind of simply giving herself up, but the thought of being thrown into a pit and forgotten, not given at all a chance to escape, that could not be risked. She might even be killed immediately and knowing what that would mean for the children always stopped her.

For them to be alone, I can't risk this yet. I need to be there for them to grow.

Then movement in the cart caught her attention. The sacks stirred and heads turned to face her from within and she could see them as the dead faces of children peering out at her.

In shock did Kieke fall backwards onto the street. The pot clanged to the ground and people scrambled up not to help her but to look into the pot to see if there was anything inside. Another person took the pot and ran off with it, but Kieke's mind was on other things.

She shook out her head and the illusion was gone, there were dead animals in the sacks, goats, pigs, sheep, but not children.

She remained on the street dumbfounded.

What was the point of showing me that?

A guard who stood by the cart looked back to her.

"What do you think you're doing?"

"I thought there were children in the cart."

He looked down at her sadly.

"Oh, the orphanage lass. Now listen here, if what was in that cart was as such as you thought, don't you think we'd have reasons for such? You know that, surely. And don't go saying such mad things, words of character don't mean much when the church or other folk get suspicious."

"So they can just tell us to up and go? Well that's not nice. I just hope these two find their ends quickly. It never used to be this way though, so I can't hold out too much hope that anything has at all changed behind closed doors."

A shadow then moved from the front of the cart and strolled over to her, a man in black robes with a rounded black hat now looming over her. It was the Minister and the Minister peered down at her. He was frowning slightly and holding the pot.

"Is everything is all right? I would be more worried if you did indeed see these slain animals as your children, as such a thing is rather barbaric to consider, for that matter should we all not? We are messengers, child, you know this. There have been some truly disturbing happenings which we are trying to pinpoint the culprits of, which is not the work of messengers yet such work is thrust upon us and as such we must do our dutiful part. Despite my comforting words I see something still troubles you child, you should tell me what that is."

Kieke stood up. She was sore from falling over but nothing felt broken, not that such a thing would be a problem for any long amount of time she could spend alone with one of her catches. She certainly was not alone now with the Minister's eyes staring at her while appearing tired and focussed all at once. She had never known eyes that could stare as such as his, but she spoke not because of them, but because he had asked.

"In a person I once knew I saw a fear of this holy city, only by chance was I there to meet them when they held such a fear and by then it was too late for me to help. That weighs on my mind, long after they have gone."

"Help might be quite beyond those who guide themselves by fear and not my words. Quite the thing to say for one in charge of so many of our forgotten little ones, or should I say that it is your role to ensure that they are not simply overlooked and forgotten. You should focus on looking up or otherwise they might pick up your downtrodden mood."

She straightened the hems of her skirt.

"You are quite right, of course. All this moping certainly isn't like myself, not to behave this way in the least."

The Minister handed her the pot and walked back to the front of the cart. He began making his way along the path then stopped and turned around to face her, taking his round black hat off his head to be grasped in his hands.

"You should come by the church some times with the younger children. Let them not lose their light due to the shadows under your eyes or have them drown in your tears. The sooner they hear my words again the sooner they can be saved. We all need that sometimes, and the church is waiting reliable throughout the day. But for the night the church relies on you."

He doffed his hat, tapping the front in a knowing fashion and the cart continued steadily up on its way.

The two people in the back had ceased their crying and were resting together. As the cart made further off into the distance, the Minister watched them as they went. He did not raise his voice to follow them but still, he seemed to be speaking to the pair.

"Stopped crying have we? Know that your child is safe in the light and has not been fouled by your deeds."

Kieke's face twitched. They had a child?

"I do not know these people. Where was their home?" She enquired, to anybody who might hear her.

A man by the side of the road had been watching the commotion. As he shuffled over he was nodding his head, held low, perhaps trying to hide the reluctance in his face from showing, although his hesitation was clear for Kieke to see.

"I'll show you where that is."

This one knows something and is hiding it, I want to drag that hidden thing out of him but I really shouldn't break this one. She thought.

The man led her to a house and there could be heard crying within. A young girl, six, maybe seven was being embraced by a woman, who was attempting to calm her, something that did not appear to be working. The woman's eyes darted to each of the people in the home as they entered.

"Michael, you're back. Oh, Kieke, I know why you're here."

Then why aren't you pleased to see me? Kieke wondered.

"I want my mother and father back." The girl cried.

The woman turned back to the child.

"I'm sorry but there's nothing we can do about that."

Kieke frowned as the child choked and cried.

True, but for the moment that wasn't the best thing for her to say. What is she thinking?

Kieke shook her head.

"There is, which is why I'm here. The child needs to be somewhere they can be looked after. We're not stretched too thin down at the orphanage."

The child was not happy.

"You're going to take me away, where I can't be with my family any more."

The woman nodded.

"Yes, that's what she's going to do. Come with us and we'll leave all this behind."

There was fear in the child's eyes now.

"I'm not leaving!"

The girl wrestled herself free from the woman's grasp and ran out of the house. Kieke went to the door, turning back to leer at the pair who had not moved before but were now shrinking back against her glaring eyes.

"What a thing to say in front of an upset child."

Kieke walked out the door in pursuit of the child for only a few paces when she could hear both people already arguing.

"What did you bring that wretched foreigner here for?"

"So the girl could see what the other option was! This is better. We're better. And the damn woman asked about her so if I had said nothing other people would have become suspicious, *because we're right next door* and now is not the best time to be suspicious. If the girl simply vanished then maybe we'd be blamed."

"But now she knows!"

"Yes, *because you told her as much to her face!*"

Kieke left them alone and followed where she had seen the young one run off to. She hadn't gone very far, choosing a dark corner to hide in.

Oh this is so familiar.

The girl had her head in her arms, so Kieke stopped a short distance away and crouched down. That wasn't always the best thing to do for kids but she suspected that this one had had enough of all these adults standing over her.

She called out softly enough, she didn't want to scare the girl any more than she already was.

"Hey. Do you know who I am?"

There was no response but the girl began shaking. Kieke continued to speak in a quiet voice.

"I look after lots of other kids who have lost their parents or have been abandoned here or along the roads either way, so they'll understand you too. It doesn't have to be forever, we can go find out about your parents. We just need a little bit of time then we will go see what we can do. We can go get some answers then. How about you tell me your name first?"

The girl did still seem inconsolable and was now shaking her head.

"I know what happens next, they're going to kill my parents, they'll be dead by then, I won't be able to do anything. What have they done, what have I done for the Light to hate us so? I always said my prayers and I tried to do the right thing."

"You haven't done anything yet, and you can do so much more than crying if you get up and come with me. You can tell me your name later and while I could go back and ask one of those other people I don't think they have your best interests at heart. I understand that you might be afraid, but don't be fearful and just listen to what I have to say. For your parents we can start looking into seeing them soon, I promise. I don't think you will be let into the castle to see them but we can try and I might just know a way how that doesn't involve anyone else."

Gradually, the girl got up and Kieke took them and placed her among the two eldest in her care while she went to fetch a few things. Those were a few short knives, a handful of musty paper out from the mountain of the stuff that had come with the house which she had some time ago sketched over in blood, some stones and shells. She was merely going on a little late afternoon excursion, at least that is what she told the kids, but a small part of them would know what it is she really meant.

Ideally she would have liked to wait until she had more than one to put under her eye before getting the required blood, because the blood of one dead person was enough for more than several of such kids.

She reflexively looked up at the sky, but there was nothing in it black and dark. Kieke didn't have the luxury to wait for more now. It could very well be that whatever unfortunate beggar she found alone first would be the one to use.

That was her thinking after a few hours of searching for an opportunity when night had fallen and she found a man alone in a dark alleyway. She had no idea who he was and that just made the whole thing so much better. Less guilt. Still, there really was no time for guilt when the world was ending.

Someone would likely find the man's leftovers but she had his eyes, enough of his blood and meat to not worry about that, so the rest went to her master which only added to her good mood.

Hopefully the girl is settling in nicely.

Kieke didn't want to lie to her, so would soon take them to the gates and give them what they wanted as best she could, but first there had to be a certain amount of housekeeping to be done.

When she returned to the house, hauling those useful parts of her most recent catch, she knew she would need to be rather focussed about all of this if she wanted to bind the girl's mind to her own. If she absolutely had to she could have tried to instantly wrestle it for some amount of control but that had produced poor results in the past and fixing the minds she damaged in this way was not something she knew how to do.

Of course the child was asleep, exhausted from grief, awkwardly alone on the bottom floor in the back room that she had made by taking wood that had been used to board up houses to create her own two little additional walls.

Kieke brought a candle over and woke the girl up.

"You can sleep in here if you want away from all the others if you don't want to mix for the moment. Show me your teeth first."

"You woke me up just for that? Why?" They asked.

"I've got a mat and a cover here for you to sleep on, but first let me check your mouth. Bad teeth cause big problems so I need to know."

I suppose this saves me having to stab her to get some of her blood.

The child's gums were bleeding from growing teeth at her age so that made her restless lifting up one side of her mouth so Kieke could inspect them. There was a little bit of blood and that was what Kieke needed so she poked about to get some on her finger and then sent the girl to the mat to rest.

The girl was most likely close to returning to sleep when Kieke flipped over a worn slate of pavement and set about marking out what she needed with the blood and a pitcher of old, salty well water. Then came her own blood to complete the bloody smeared mess.

When she felt her master's presence connecting all three she knew she could gently could wrap her mind around the sleeping girl and braced herself to fight sleep. Blackness descended on the sides of her vision, but she fought it off and maintained her awakened state. Then there was silence.

Success then.

It took her some few seconds to lift her head but Kieke couldn't help but smile. To her at least, it never stopped being strange looking at yourself from another perspective, especially if you weren't in control, merely looking in. You could only prompt the people you put your hooks into but if one day she had to give herself up entirely for a new little body then she would. It was always worth remembering however that it would only be the body of a child and she greatly preferred to keep the body she had been born with.

Kieke beckoned for the child to kneel next to her and those eyes looked suspiciously on the cusp of worry at the scene with the blood and the mess but she knew they weren't truly seeing. Kieke leaned in and whispered in her ear because while the eyes might lie, the ears could still hear.

"You'll get to meet your parents soon. I promised that, didn't I?"

The head nodded.

"Well you're about to go out and do something for me and something for you, to get you that much closer."

Kieke held out a large knife. It was dull and did not glint but it would do the job she wanted done with it.

"Those people tried taking you from your mother, remember? They tried taking you from your father. They're going to come back for you. But I won't let that happen and you've got all you need right here."

Kieke pressed the knife into her little hands.

"You know where they live, those people. You know what you want to do, because they made your parents get taken away. Now you can take them away, like a tide that will always be there to remove anything that isn't supposed to be."

Without a word, the girl hid the knife in her clothes and left the room, left the house. Kieke waited a moment, listened to the heartbeat of the girl in her mind.

The second part to control was easing off the reins while still holding onto them. Ideally she would drop the reins entirely but still have them within grabbing distance in her mind. When she gently dropped them and felt no change in the child's movements at all she was able to grin.

I don't know why I worry myself sometimes.

Kieke grabbed the tub and scrubbing brush and while chuckling gleefully, began removing the traces of her foul night's work.

The deeds of that night led to her having a very good morning. All the kids, all of them, were behaving and getting on with the new girl just fine and were making their own plans without Kieke needing to do anything, being good little industrious people. While they all munched on bread from the day before for their breakfast, she herself had to go and finally get this damn pot cleaned.

There was a group of women who worked mechanically to wash all manner of things from people who would pay them. Looking at the piles already set aside from cleaning and the pile of what still needed to be done, Kieke only felt a little bad about dumping one more object in front of them. Then again, maybe she would join in herself, after all she had done such work before when she herself had staggered into town as a young woman, to earn a coin here or there before her target had come down to meet her.

Today there was a half dozen of them set to work, talking amongst themselves. On occasion there would be boys and girls assisting them but Kieke preferred it when they weren't around, so they could talk about more serious happenings, such as today and as she settled down next to the trough she listened in to the conversation.

Apparently, two people had been viciously murdered the night before. Rumours were flowing around the work station about the dead pair. She hadn't heard the bell from home, but many had been awoken when an alarm was raised at the discovery.

Of course it only seemed as if someone was on the loose. While they were not wrong about what happened, there was nothing to worry about, because Kieke had the little killer right under her control if needed. See? Not loose at all.

One woman further up the line was talking quickly in a way that wasn't trying to be too loud.

"Maybe they killed each other. Can you believe that they lived right next to that poor girl? Could be another person out for all of them."

The one next to Kieke tutted while shaking her head.

"Really, there are better ways to get land, someone should know to just ask for it these days from the king, but that's greed for you."

While attacking the grime inside the pot, Kieke grimaced.

"I'm just thankful I took her. Whoever killed them most likely would have killed the girl too. I have no reason to believe otherwise."

"So how *is* the girl coping?"

"Haven't told her yet that her old neighbours are dead but I don't think that's a high priority for her right now. It'll take a while for her to get over her parent's deaths. Because they are dead, don't we know, even the girl herself knows it deep down."

"Surely you didn't tell her that?"

Kieke shook her head.

"Not yet and I never had it like this before, one old enough to see their parents go like that, so she desperately wishes to see them. I have a plan to bring her to the gates to ask to see them. They may say no and be done with it, they may bring the bodies out, I'm not sure as to which but she's not going to be getting what she wants, I feel. It'll probably turn her into a bitter young girl but I'm ready for that."

A third woman turned up her nose.

"That's cruel. Getting a girl's hopes up just to dash them so."

"I'd rather not have her live her early years hanging onto a fantasy that will never come true."

Kieke rubbed her eyes.

"After all, things might not be going so well for us all."

The other woman's eyes narrowed in suspicion.

"What do you mean by that?"

"Nothing that's new. Although you could say that the fear of even lighting a half decent fire enough to cook food let alone warm yourself has something to do with it."

"Do you need more blankets for the kids?"

Kieke did not look at her and instead was gazing up at the sky, searching for something.

"No, we'll be fine. The world keeps moving on, so we'll be just fine."

Chapter Thirty Five
The Gate Opens

With the night's events having transpired, so it was that a large group of many dozens stood by the inner gate, as close as they could get to the castle. Here was a common place for people to congregate, read notices, discuss their worries and otherwise complain to the guards who still stood in front of the palace about mundane things as it was unlikely that anyone ever had any problems that were not petty and selfish.

Even so, people had more recently been lining up when there had been some complaining to do about the lack of bread. That had been waved away due to the time of year and the fact that the church could more easily control and give out what was needed while keeping an eye on their grain.

This new problem was not one that could be excused so easily, for who was to say that adding more armed men to wander around silently would do anything at all?

More likely they would jump at any shadow which they might find or any hopeful glow of warmth that wasn't blind and truly faithful. If anything, you couldn't come down too harshly on those with a problem to say, for everyone had problems and many of those here all grouped together wanted to know if they would be safe, for there were two who had not been safe and no one knew who could be next.

People being taken away to protect everyone else was a perfectly fine endeavour, yet letting the harmless die who had done no wrong, well that was something else entirely. For they all saw themselves as the harmless being shielded from a harmful world. In some places shields could be used as weapons and it was a thankful thought that here it seemed a hand had been stayed from such outside travelling.

That was to keep the knowledge of what would save them all to themselves, the outside being too dirty and unclean unless you proved it by coming to Churl yourself. The last of those from far off lands had been some years past, but there were still people crawling in from the south and east, since they knew that they could come. None cared that such a place was quiet, for they were quiet and were glad to find a home in the home of their faith.

What they sought and what they thought of people lining up, to call out their pleas for what answers the church could give dwindling numbers of people, Kieke did not know. Perhaps to them all those people seemed like the faithless or the heretical, to speak a single word in worry or fear where there should be none.

Kieke had brought the girl, who was again stubbornly in her sadness to the gate, as she had said she would. A group came out from the high gates, men in silver armour and one man from the church that she had seen from time to time with a white hat. At their appearance the crowd began to make a din so loud that it forced the man, who looked rather tired without having done anything else to hold up his hands in order to silence the bustling throng of voices.

His face was drawn thin but he addressed the crowd with a loud voice.

"I will be the one to hear your fears today. On behalf of the church to be the voice of the king. Now, I know you wish to talk on this most recent tragedy."

The man's eyes knitted together in anger.

"Honestly I don't have time for any of this and neither should you. If you believe that this was anything out of the ordinary you are mistaken. We search for evil to keep glory in order for us all. By extension we are an arm of his majesty. We do not go about cutting people down as is done elsewhere. A little dispute between neighbours must be sorted out between them."

Kieke was watching the crowd's reaction, a mixture of acceptance and sadness. Some were even matching the man's anger. What did they really have to be angry about if they had been so happily living a lie up until now?

Perhaps I should have killed more often and not cleaned up. In my aim to be cautious I seem to have missed a realisation up until yesterday by doing my job too well.

This wasn't something much heard of, the blood on the street type of talk. It made her think.

These people aren't going to cause a riot, yet when did killing one another stop being a problem to begin with?

That's all any of this was, the feeling of comfort and safety being pushed a little too far away for their liking. No one thought they were going to be next, but here they could be cut down by the knife of a killer, not a person with the Light bound right to do so.

People went missing from time to time thanks to me but there was never any cause for concern, or not at least any that I encountered.

It hadn't occurred to Kieke previously that there could have been a problem with actual heresy or traitorous happenings. Well there was herself but she didn't count and if there had been any risk then her master would have said something to tip her in the right direction, to go stumbling over to appease him some way or another. It was no good making wild guesses and taking matters into her own hands either, that was a waste of time and energy, so in a way she understood why her master had remained silent and not prompted her further.

All throughout the afternoon and into the early night this went on and the crowd thinned out as demands were heard and then most likely forgotten and lights were lit so that they would not be talking in darkness. The girl had predictably become restless and bored but she had stayed put, thankfully. Kieke had to crouch down so the child could hear her over the din.

"We'll see what anyone else has to say then you can ask your question. I know you want answers but it is rude to push ahead of those in front of you."

The girl only half seemed to listen and before Kieke could do anything, the girl slipped through the crowd and went about her way to walk in front of the people who were there.

Well I don't expect her to be listening to me yet. She thought.

As she pushed her own way through the crowd, there there was a small scuffle that made her frown. In better days there would have been no need for such rudeness and if the mood was becoming this rowdy then she hoped someone would take notice of all this rude behaviour, or at the very least not have the girl subject to any of it.

But sometimes, things in life do not work out the way you want them to or even at all turn out the way you expect. Such as when the voice is heard of a girl asking honestly about her family not being given the answer she expected. For the girl had not found the illuminating light of understanding words to help in her acceptance of the ups and downs of life. She had found only the cold unforgiving darkness of steel in their chest instead. Then there was no more need for answers.

Kieke reeled for a moment as nine little minds snapped to alarm in her head and she held herself in place, taking in the scene before her. It wasn't that her eyes missed what she saw, as she had been moving through the crush of people and heard young words then saw a blade stained red in a guard's hand as people surged back behind her, a living wall of wide eyes and warmth which was not the same to be said as what was before her. That scene was rather cold. Everyone here knew, even the nine others who were not here to see it, who could instead feel the life having fled from the world, even if they did not know why, only that they knew it was gone.

What is this in front of me?

As she moved away from the people behind her to the girl it did occur that moving closer and reaching out to her might have put herself within reach of that sword were she to be the next for the eager executioner, but there was no blade on her neck when she knelt beside the body, those eyes lifeless and dead.

I hope you're with them truly, little one, your mother and father. As for the one holding that steel, why were they so scared of you? No no, I can't have them hide away again, stay right here so we can all see what kind of ruler you really are.

Around her there were voices from the crowd, that now had the sounds and emotions that had been missing. Of revulsion and also fear, that most important missing piece as far as she thought. Others were speaking their thoughts out loud, now moved beyond whatever thoughts they kept in their heads. Compelled to speak by what? Someone having gone too far that they saw their own reflections in the blood or perhaps their own faces on the ground and the voices all grew and tangled together, one madness replaced with another.

"They killed that girl."

"Why is she dead?"

"She pushed past me."

"She was only trying to help."

"They killed that girl!"

"She's dead, there's blood all over."

The people responsible were standing still and voices were raised louder so Kieke raised her own voice.

"Oh stop your rabbling the lot of you. Somebody take her from me, to the graveyard and bury her. Do not let others take her body away or cast her yourself in some ditch. There's no point waiting for her family, who will not come and see her put into the ground. Indeed they may have been waiting for her all along."

Without seeing who, someone took the girl from her. Kieke heaved and breathed in a breath to compose herself and there was a further dark murmur of voices to which she nodded.

"Agree with me or feed my neck to the sword, it does not matter what I say. The king certainly does not care. Use your eyes and look, look and see at what they have done and stained me with, not blood but this burden of guilt that should not be mine."

A dark shape appeared behind the bars in the gate and there was the Minister, just taking in the view as one might with any other scenic walk.

"Hmm, what is going on here?"

Kieke nodded.

"Aye yeah I hear you. Indeed what is going on here? Do listen when I ask you to think, what have we heard from the king these last many years? Are you to say that the words would vomit from his mouth to call for a young girl, where one is still innocent after having already lost so much, to be taken by the sword and put to death? If that is so then before you do and before you talk you should not talk about putting her out of her misery or other such noble intentions for how many amongst all of us would be culled by such a notion of sadness? I would have been one to say 'not I' but tonight I would be the very beacon of misery."

The Minister spoke as he always had, as if he had not just walked upon on such a scene.

"Do not look to yourself, look to others and see how they live so well."

"They live with their eyes shut but even if they were open there would be nothing but blackness around them. You will not find me to be solemn, not to be quiet, but to blaze with a fire that needs no light or direction. To you this may make me nothing more than a monster wanting to see in the dark where we are surrounded by such days but the monster is not me but the king, speaking through you. If you were to have me be put to the sword for such words then I say so be it and tell you to think about what you are doing. But I also say, take me in and be done with all of this. I can't take any more of a world that hangs from the power of old glory where real light would show you all just what a terrible world you've left for yourselves."

"That's quite enough from you." The Minister said, but she kept going.

"Shut up. Why am I here if I can't protect a world I would have for all the young ones?"

She could see the Minister through the bars of the gates, shaking his head.

"We only have one world and we must defend it from all influence that would change it. It wouldn't be our world then, would it? Beyond this land there is a darkness that threatens to swallow all that you know. These are not my words, all must surely understand that. To think you would spread your own words that carry the words from outside here is inconsolable."

"I am not the one spreading death." She spat.

"And how right you are." He replied.

There was a rumbling sound and the gate opened in front of her eyes. The gate! The castle!

The gate was open and the castle stood beyond and Kieke was right there in front of it. Her eyes went wide as the Minister stood back and she saw no empty space in which to proceed. In the way, out from the castle grounds could be seen that there marched knights, armoured head to toe in dark brown metal painted with a line of white from top left to bottom right, but in the dark they appeared as black as night. Thick swords and heavy shields of metal were by their sides and there was no sound from these knights other than the heavy steps with which they walked that shook the ground. These all looked ready to go out and journey far and wide for some battle. As they reached the gate the Minister spoke, arm outstretched, hand open over the throng of people.

"You who heard those foul words must not spread them. Stand still and accept what you must, come forth to your death that the faithful understands must be right."

All the knights drew their swords as one and then the panic began as the remaining mob of people ran. Kieke spent no more time considering if she would have been able to just walk straight past them into the open castle and ran with everyone else. She did turn to look back and by doing so she did manage to catch a view of the Minister shaking his head that was soon obscured by those knights marching past him and a spray of blood from those silver knights and that man from the church as they all were cut down before those brown knights with the white painted sash.

Yet the gate was open and it took much of her effort to fully turn her back to it once again, even against the procession of steel that was playing out the sounds of death into the night and all could hear its sound.

Far above the moons glistened in the sky as observers to all of this. But they could not tell her the answers she now looked for in the chaos that flowed out into the streets. Where was the king now? Would he show himself? Well, this could be when he might. Any good king who wanted to appear to be would do what his people would have expected. At least she was sure this was so, because for a place built on faith, it was cracking at the edges with steel, blood and fire.

Kieke would not have been surprised if he strolled down with his knights and began slaughtering everyone in the streets. Now that the words had failed them, that mouthpiece would have to be replaced and who better than the king himself to do his own work? He might as well have been behind every raised sword himself but she had encountered no one on her way back up, having looped around as close as she dared to get back to the gate and she was feeling giddy with hope that it might still be open.

From time to time you had to put a foot forward and say that what you lived your life believing wasn't the same as what it really was. You would have to be willingly blind to turn away from all things and yet some had and were only now seeing what they had wasted and she didn't feel gladness at this, people had to stop looking at themselves as objects. At least with all this fire burning as buildings were turned upside down they could keep their eyes open and see that the world was full of disappointment and madness and she would do her part here where all the rest of the world could watch and see.

Or maybe none would even know, it didn't matter to her what happened after honestly. Auralin would however be put on notice, that there was hope for lands so far gone such as this. But didn't the rest of the world know that already? Of course, in a sense, that was what made this a real tragedy to her at least. All these years and all these dead to make a point to a stubborn kingdom that would rather the world, not their kingdom, fade away.

Hopefully some had realised that old kings should not rule so absolutely that they put a stranglehold on the purpose found in life itself. It was that promising future that got people up in the morning. Day by day, year by year the means and the methods of wants and the reasons for wanting would change, but there still could be change, even if it meant that sacrifices had to be made, steel had to be made and used against one another, or that all had to be demolished and rebuilt to start again.

Kieke had to admit that she was poised, that if she were ever called upon to bring forth and suggest a new creed, she would have it made. Truthfully, the people here were about to become rather wary and suspicious to anything that would seek to rule them. She couldn't sweet talk her way through an entire city, anyway. But a place based not on old kings, instead her master and that deep ocean servitude, she almost wished it could be so, just so she could see it.

That was the difference between her and all these hapless people running about going rogue and now burning down their own homes, who were only now realising the difference and were doing all sorts of things to make up for it. Seeing was believing, and this chaos all about her was the true belief of the people of Churl. This was the tangible, gritty act that she could taste and smell in the air. A rebellious mark saying that they could see and were waiting to be seen themselves.

Yet who would come and see them enact such a future? Who would stop by the slain and say that they had seen the will of that person or peer up at the flames and the ruins therein and say it was anything other than reckless destruction? Would the king dare peek out? If not him then she would be that person, for all she saw was the will of people. But that was what happened when you cut people down in the street.

'The king lives. Go to him and slay him. Do not wait for cowards to show themselves. Hurry.'

Her master's voice in her head reminded her but she knew that she could not rely on the people to fulfil their own wishes. Of course she had been punished plenty of times, but this wasn't a sign to say that she was to be slowing down. She would find a way through the gates or over the wall and with such a distraction she would do it tonight. One part of her felt ill that she had quickly walked and then run from where she most wanted to be, but the other part of her was happy that she was still alive to be brought to the task at hand.

To do this she would have liked to stay as close to the gate as she could, but a part of her suspected that it would have been closed behind the wave of butchers now roaming the city. Some, of course, might have been roaming a bit closer to the gate and to walk into one of them, that was not going to end well for her and was a possibility best avoided. It had been a metal flood of soldiers that poured into the streets and they were indiscriminate with their blades.

The sounds of those so unfortunate rang through the night, still following Kieke as she ran full pelt off the street onto a main road. She was still in the middle of the trading district but there were sounds up and down that told her all she needed to know about the fates of those people. The trouble now came from deciding where the lack of sound meant people had chosen not to run rather than running into a death trap herself.

She came across a group of people who appeared to be throwing drink into an already burning building to make it burn more. Bottles and barrels were being spilled, adding to the blaze which only worsened when a liquor shed exploded that blew out the taller stories above it, sending debris flying into the air and other buildings burned along with it.

"What's going on? She said to them.

Hopefully that was stupidly innocent enough. I'd like to see what someone thinks about all this.

One man with a torch nodded.

"We came up from the outer ring to take revenge on people from the inner ring coming out from within with armour and swinging their swords. A lot of people are fleeing but there are those of us who want to fight for our homes but there's even more of them than we thought. This place belongs to us, no one is going to scare us away and we'll build it all back up if we have to. I'm not sure what I'm doing this for myself, why

I'm feeling so angry. Everyone's just following along and here I am too."

Without waiting for an answer the mob raced off in the direction of some of the sounds of violence, which surprised her.

Kieke found herself thrilled with the view of such a mob terrified of what to do. She likened it to a kid with a knife just realising that they could use it to hurt people and seeing their little mind try and work out what to do with that information.

And as for that, she sent her mind out to the children and all responded. She understood the undercurrent of fear that rippled through them as one of their number had been cut off but as long as they stayed out of the city inner ring they would be fine. But the messages came back that even on the fringes as they were, the town was also in danger as knights pursued people far through the gates. Buildings also were on fire down there and as many of those were made with plenty of wood, they burned more easily.

Then run, get out and run. She told them.

And she felt herself believing it, that they should all get away from here and run away, she felt her legs wanting to run but there had been enough of that getting away from where she wanted to be already and hoped that she would meet them when she got past that wall standing between her and everything else. This ruckus was nice but it would not do on its own and was especially a little too immediately dangerous for her liking.

I wonder who else I share that thought with? She wondered.

There had been no sign of the king having come down from up on high and the Minister had disappeared into the shadows.

That man can wait. I'll deal with him when I'm all finished here.

She honestly couldn't wait to run into the king, no matter how unlikely it was that he would show himself.

I wonder if I should introduce myself when we meet or get everything out of the way?

Kieke had not spent a great deal of her time wondering just how everything was going to play out, that type of romanticism escaped her and in the beginning she had considered it a rather simple matter. She wasn't going to start ruing his existence for the way her life had turned out in an effort to make herself really feel that the kill would be worth it. If anything she wasn't considering herself in it at all. She was so much more than a happy little pawn anyway, not like all these people who stuck to their kingdom for reasons that confounded her to this very night.

She did not have to wait long to run into someone, she quiet even ran head first into them before she knew it.

He looked exhausted and ill, with dirt on his face, but Brodie was there in front of her. With his eyes darting around she could tell that he was not believing what he was seeing. He was distraught and she held his shoulders to stop him shaking. This made his eyes stop moving about to focus on her. His voice was cracked and it seemed he had swallowed some smoke.

"You're exactly who I want to see!"

"Brodie I'm happy you're alive but I've got to run."

"Me too but I've been looking all over to tell you. There's a way into the castle. I've found a way into the castle."

A shiver fell down her spine.

"Wait, the gate is open?"

"No, there's another way in I've just discovered and I didn't mean to find it either. To be honest I was hiding. Look, the king is still missing and needs to be found to put an end to all of this. Honestly from what I've heard the church has gone mad and seriously looking at all this it has to stop, tonight or right now I don't care but this isn't right and shouldn't be happening. I'll show you where to get inside the castle."

"You'll rely on the king?"

"I'm relying on you first."

They were moving further away from the gate than she had thought, having had to climb a little while up and around meant it was rather far away from the path carved out from the violence, so the city was quiet even if there was this buzz of something else behind their ears. It certainly wasn't coming from this street, more abandoned places where people had vanished.

Together they looked out at the orange glow of the burning city. After a while, he realised that she had gone without speaking for the longest he had known her.

"You're very quiet. What are you thinking about?"

Her voice was slow, tired.

"I remember first coming to this place. I remember seeing it without those outer walls. It was a beautiful sunny day. The people were quiet and hard working, living in this place without shadow, *'where light would always shine'* so it is supposed to be said. I remember thinking to myself, that I might have found a place all for myself. It didn't matter that this was where people sent their orphaned and abandoned, because here people knew, they just knew, that there would be those who would help them. Some here found that they could help them, such as myself, from a life cold and dull and short."

"I suppose this means the orphans are safe?"

She nodded.

"Oh I know they are safe, all but one. I could not save one today, the newest, who's parents were still who she looked to for her light. And I look and see all this place burn and think to myself, what happened here? She was treated so cold for her wish, and now she is just as such, cold and nothing more than someone's regretful wish turned sour."

"How did she die?"

"The church cut her down and then came for all the others. In a way I'm responsible for all of this. Even if it is good to see a bit of life around the place for once in a long time."

"Don't say that, I share some of the blame. I trust you to do what I can not and face the king and get him to restore order."

"You don't have to compare yourself to the others and be dead. Come with me and we'll see the king together."

He looked back to where the lights glowed, worry on his face.

"Compared to what you do I'm not sure he'd even see me. So I can't come with you, I need to go back and be where I should be, with my people."

"I suppose they are yours more than mine tonight. Putting the hope of you all in the hands of someone like me who comes from so far away, it might be that those out there would never allow what you're doing if they knew."

The way in all along turned out to be a house among all the others sitting up directly against the wall bordering the castle grounds. There was nothing particular about it that made it different from any of the others but perhaps a noble once lived there or a military man. If you knew where you needed to go then it can't have been too hard to remember the location.

The noise and the shouting flared louder and Brodie gestured to inside.

"It is here. Straight down the back."

Kieke looked at Brodie's bare hands.

"Did you come with anything to defend yourself with?"

He frowned.

"I didn't think something like this was going to happen. Anyway, I was hiding away in here which is how I found it."

That's a lie but I don't want to have to lie for much longer. He thought.

At this Kieke smiled sadly and reached into her belt. She pulled out a dagger and toyed with it between her fingers.

"How true. Here, this is for you. It won't do much against all that armour but it has been very helpful in keeping the less armoured people off me. I don't want one more dead kid on my mind."

She pressed into into his hands and he looked back at her most sheepish.

"I'm barely a kid any more." He said as he took the dagger anyway.

Kieke shook her head.

"But you're sweet and I don't want some riotous person getting the better of you. Much better to hide here, but if you insist on going back out there do be careful."

"I can't stay and wait here, I have to do something, I have to see what I can do. When I realised what I had found I just didn't care about the danger any more."

I'm not really lying about everything, I just want someone I can trust doing this for me and I want them to try and be safe. I don't want to see her body on the streets like so many others.

He looked up to the castle.

"What about yourself?"

She just smiled at him.

"You really are so sweet. I'll be fine around the castle and I will find the king and save us all."

She messed his hair and both of them went their separate ways.

He really must think that he can make a difference. Any other time I'm sure he would have felt something and would have guessed that it would have been better to not go back out there.

She made her way inside, where there was nothing but cold walls and empty crates and put her mind to the task of searching for the way through and there in front of her it was. At the back of the wall was a wide open door that opened out directly into the wall surrounding the castle grounds. From inside the wall she could see that it had been built in a deliberate way to allow for this tunnel.

On the other side was a wooden door that led to another small room. There was another door which swung open and this led to her taking the first steps onto the castle grounds that she had in years.

Kieke had always wanted to use the main entrance but on emerging found herself not minding as she faced the left side of the castle. In front of her were the wide open grounds that followed the walls to the left and the right. She could have followed them along but who knew what she would find. Why take the risks associated with the unknown when right up ahead of her there was a ramp built into both sides of the castle that she knew led right to the top which also had ways inside?

The iron gates that had locked away the ends of each ramp were falling off their hinges and she could make her way through them with no trouble. What a mess this place was now!

Kieke knew she should have paced herself in the cold weather but she ran as fast as her legs would take her and the moons lit her path. As she ran up the ramp that led to the top of the castle, her legs and lungs burned from the effort of the climb and the effort not to laugh. A leisurely stroll this most certainly was not.

Looking far down to the city below as more parts of it began to burn, she almost felt like skipping as she ran because that sight was glorious to see. What a waste this would be if she couldn't shove this in the king's face and force him to stare at the sky even if he could not see that vile darkness and tell him what he had done and that it would all soon be over.

Her face certainly was hurting from all this grinning. The view was left behind as she skelted around a final corner and the ramp plateaued out on the left against the castle wall to create a little square space where people could have done duller things than she was doing right now, such as stop and take in the scenery. There was no reason for her to stop here, because the path actually continued forward, rising slightly higher to then run straight along the length of the castle's face and there was a door up ahead as long as she was remembering correctly.

A row of small bushy trees that didn't mind the weather were lined up the whole way alongside it. Because the castle itself blocked the moonlight there was no light along this path, just a single square of it down the far end made by the trees against the castle and she came to a screeching halt as she made to race up to the path.

Steps shook the ground as out from the shadows in front of her trod a huge knight clad in black, with a curved, gigantic black sword longer than she was tall poised and ready. Without a word did the knight tread the few remaining steps needed towards her. Kieke called up watery bindings from the air to halt the knight that clasped his arms and legs.

And these did nothing at all. In an instant the knight was over her and the sword, moving with the motion in his stride was coming down. That instant was all she had to fit together a barrier of a most rudimentary magic that she had learned but it was all she could use and she all she could do.

The barrier saved her life. The force of it breaking through the swing of the sword with a loud crack and a small flash of white light threw her backwards beyond the foot of the landing and she yelped as she attempted to stand quickly on a crooked ankle.

None of this hindered the pursuit of the Black Knight, who stomped over with purpose to the woman with his sword raised again and brought it down and indeed all the woman could do was look up as the blade came down.

But something stayed his blade mid swing and the Black Knight found he could not move, frozen not from watery magic as a far more nefarious weight held him in check and without a sound the world around both he and the woman beneath him suddenly melted into a place entirely different.

Gone was the darkness of night with the moons shining down and the castle to be replaced with a bright place which was nothing like where they had been, a realm of a great sky with reds and oranges and yellows of a promising sunrise, yet there was no sunrise as a great silent maelstrom of deep reds and orange sat swirling around the horizon and reaching far up into the sky, pressed into a great dome. Against that there shone a ball of light in the sky, great and yellow sitting higher than any other he had known that lit down to a depths that had no end, if that really was what he was looking at past the edges of the ground beneath his feet.

The ground he found himself standing on was flat and blandly dirty. He could not tell if he was on a circular floating island or a land surrounded by a great golden sea as the horizon was reflected so clearly. While there were edges, whether they held a lake of clear liquid that reflected the sky or plunged into nothing could not be judged, but there was a shimmer as if light was indeed reflecting off something.

The far end of the circle stretched far away and curved high up, slowly increasing in slope and crumbling away until it was swallowed by the clouds that swirled great and ominously despite being so far away.

The Black Knight could not move but was able to at least see in front of himself and he saw the woman was laughing and whooping to herself in celebration. The witch was almost dancing around him, as much as she could on that ankle while giving thanks to her master as she went. No doubt she was savouring the feeling of coming away from her death but it was strange how some always acted in such a manner when they did, like a fool.

He tried to move again but the armour would not obey his commands.

So I am bound by some force here that can stop even me. While aggravating that I can not finish my task of ridding the world of this filth, to go to such lengths to stop me...I'm not surprised that I have been halted. Such a thing should probably be possible.

There were few things that could, some he supposed he wasn't aware of. This certainly would be one of those things, yet not entirely unexpected. Whoever her master was must have been rather powerful to do all of this, for he knew of those with similar magical talents to create their own sanctums and magical wells but nothing quite like this all at once. That bothered him more then the fact that he had been manhandled as he had. Perhaps she would tell him?

With his deep voice echoing from within the armour he spoke.

"Who is your master? It is right that you thank them, for without the power being granted to you, you are nothing but a spineless girl not deserving to fight the fights you find yourself amongst."

The woman stretched her arms as if she were merely waking up. Indeed her voice sounded relaxed and amused.

"What, fight you? I don't intend to fight you. My master tells me you can't even be killed so I'll just leave you out of the way somewhere, so you can't interfere with his plans and there's no place better than nowhere. You're not exactly going to liven up the scenery as you're a bit of an eyesore to be honest and as much as there's all these things we could talk about, I really can't waste time talking to you right now, bye."

The woman giggled and waved a hand as she dissolved from the plain the knight now found himself in.

A moment later he felt the weight lifted from him and was freed of the spell that bound him. His feet scuffed the ground and the armour told him all he need to know. This was not an illusion then. This utterly was somewhere else entirely, certainly made by magic.

Free to move about, he surveyed his surroundings.

Did your master see no need to burden themselves by holding me considering there appears to be no escaping this fanciful realm of theirs?

There was a presence in the distance beyond the furthest clouds, yet even when hidden by them he had only to focus for a moment to pinpoint the source. How foolish they were to both leave and turn away from him as they had done, as turn away from him they had for he could sense from it no watchful eye in his direction.

The Black Knight spoke as he stared at the presence.

"You can't even hear me, can you? As for you, fool girl, you may have thought to keep me out of all this, delivering me to the land of your master, a distance unfathomably far from all things. You are ruled by one who believes that they can play with the fate of the world and use you to place it in the palm of their hands. Do you honestly believe there are those who would stand to let this happen?"

His grip tightened on the hilt of his sword as he looked up to the sky that he could see. It was all coming together now.

"It does not matter how far you run and you can not hide for I am here, placed by your own arrogance. For these eyes see beyond the shroud to what is hidden beyond, may it be that I see even further than you could have possibly dared to realise. Yet I am not surprised by you in the slightest, for even when facing the executioner's block have many remained ignorant and blind to their last breath, keeping to their ways even as their heads have gone from their necks."

He hefted up his sword and from deep within called out so loudly a sound as if to reach that very place beyond the swirling clouds.

"To that I say hark and behold! For this black blade was made for such a purpose as to be the end of you, and with this blade shall I slay your master myself!"

Chapter Thirty Six
The Long Night

Bernard could feel that something was off about this night. He often felt worldly stirrings when the nights appeared particularly still and calm, such stillness and calmness was rarely the case in his experience, as much as he would have rathered not been the one to have had such experiences. There was a rumbling in the air from distant clouds that had been threatening rain, which really should have been nothing to worry about on such a night. Out there in the sky were two moons that did not care and on those moons there was a lot of time to spend looking at them absorbed in thought. Rather them than many other things, honestly.

Yet distractions were there for when they were needed in moments of pensive silence, not when there rang a sound that rattled down to his bones and refused to be ignored.

The sound was doing a better job at being noticed than the food on his plate and he found himself looking down at the plate in front of him remembering that there was food on it while not at all feeling hungry. He still had to eat, in case he was on the move again where food would not be easy to come across or pry from trading merchant's hands, even with the coin.

He could hear the accusing voices in his head, might people be so bold these days as to accuse a wizard of anything, even if there was much truth to be had in the matter. Those voices said words such as *'Aye your coin will just vanish on me after you have made your way'* or *'why don't you just use magic to create food out of nothing? You'd all solve the food issues for the poor if any of you cared'*.

He had heard those words before and was sure he'd hear them again in some way from ignorant people with loose mouths. He nearly shuddered at the thought of such interactions which deepened as this sound refused to leave his ears alone. Really now, what was this unsettling buzz?

Bernard got to his feet and slowly walked over to a window. It was dark, late out and he was tired. Looking outside down below he saw not just the street lights, but other burning lights as well. Not only that but people piling up wood and timber as they went spilling lanterns on them where they blazed into an inferno.

He watched as up and down the street people were doing this and could see the orange haze across in other streets along with the firelight of those taking sticks from the fires that burnt.

There was something deeply unsettling going on, he decided. He nearly staggered out the door before his stomach protested most loudly that his feet be made to walk their way back to his plate and his meal, which he did with reluctance.

It was the cured meat of some long dead creature by the smell of it, wrapped up with grass that he had found as there was no bread to be had. He had eaten worse and devoured the lot while his eyes darted about looking for other eyes that might be sinking down from the roof or rising through the floorboards below. No, there were none and with that he was going out again, even if the eyes were to follow him. Maybe now he would feel better, so even though his stomach was heaving he forced himself outside, stave in hand.

Up at the sky he could not see anything out of the ordinary, dark clouds and stars above, the moons greater and lesser too. Down below far in the distance the sounds and sights reminded him that all was not well with the night as he could hear noises of fighting and clashes of metal on metal and metal not clashing on people at all with the slick, horribly juicy sound.

He raked his hands through what was left of his hair at the destruction and looked to one man with a burning stick.

"What's going on here? Are we under attack? This appears to be no siege as you are bringing down your own homes and why you would escapes me."

The man shook his head.

"We heard that an army of knights had marched out of the church to enforce order. But they were butchering people and are continuing to do so with no mercy or reason. I don't understand why people are being cut down where they stand, some are already fleeing out to the farms but beware, for we heard the sounds of screaming death beyond the outer wall even still. You should find somewhere to run and hide old man, before these butchers catch you for unless we have all gone mad the church has turned on each of us and honestly such a thing might make us mad before this is all over."

The wizard would not run, nor would he hide, from such fortuitous circumstances.

If there were any taller buildings that I could get into, I would like to watch this callous and depraved notion of zeal and divine favour fall from the eyes of all here. And yet, I do not know if people such as these can be relied upon to fully complete the deed I would ask for.

He shook a raised fist upwards while holding onto his stave with the other.

"Madness has gripped the church, not you I say. Beforehand, there was a calmness about this place that I found suspicious but perhaps it was all in vain as a disguise. One cast aside so suddenly and clearly that I must suggest that someone in the church has become overburdened with the monotony of power and has granted their own wish to exercise it."

"How dare you say that?" Said the man, aghast.

Bernard sighed, exasperated.

"You still you cling to your belief, even as it burns you. Well then, be away with you from my sight, for I very much doubt this will all clear over, although I must say that it is hard to blame outsiders for this now, isn't it? Who's words do you trust now that your doom comes from within and who do you look to when you see the sky is falling? Do you help those around you or do you bury you head in words that you can not eat or use to warm yourself with? Too many of you believe in your ways absolutely but you fail to believe in yourselves and even now you seem uncertain in my eyes. Let me tell you about which I am uncertain, as I wonder if the king still lives at all. Now put that stick down and help defend yourselves in your own name or in the name of this place and cast aside your vile downturned eyes to ones seeing all of this."

Bernard began to leave, to march onto the church. As he did, the people behind they called out after him.

"And who might you be, to demand all this of us during this madness?"

He turned back briefly.

"One who has seen the end approaching and is doing what must be done to stop it. I can not do this alone for the words of one man mean nothing and should they not? It riles my stomach to think that those here would call this madness. No, I would call it waking up. There are only bright days ahead but this night must end with your lives intact."

And then he left before such a group might turn on him.

At the very least the work I set out to accomplish is in motion, sadly through no part of my own actions, as far as I can tell. Martyrs often lead the way for such disregard of the rules and structures that they found themselves caught within. I have seen it myself and all I can wonder now is what their name shall be. What a thing to witness. I should not have to take myself and upend the church building itself, assuredly I have no wish for my magic to be mistaken for that in the hands of a layabout ruiner of things, but something must be done.

And what of those who commanded such places as the church? Where were they and what might they say to his words that sought to stand above their own? He could not guess and would look to ask them in person if at all possible.

Is that why the head does this to itself? Like the snake that eats its own tail, perhaps the two are far enough apart in who they are for one to care about the other. Now shall this place choke or spit out its pride and live amongst the ruins it made for itself or shall another descend and attempt to save them all by breathing new life into the corpse of this snake? Ahh, but I fear that if it were to be reborn it would do so as the phoenix, and the snake would become a mighty dragon breathing fire over all. Then reverence would come from those most twisted corners and the only thing to do would be to bring the sky itself crashing down upon its head before it could take flight and sow chaos across all the known world.

That would not do. It had to be him to end the church, he had been so ordered by the wizard's tower and had then sworn to himself that he would make the act be worth the journey getting there. Others with the chance to do so had chosen instead to be solemn and quiet and watch the world make of itself what it willed of its own devices, even though those others had a responsibility to their knowledge and power held, to then uphold as themselves what was good and right in the world.

To not do that ended up with people like him crossing the lands, left chasing after the tasks left by ghosts. The dead would certainly forgive him for leaving, with this job well done by others. But he would not forgive himself if another would be sent, in the future, to do his work anew if he was to falter or fail or turn around now. The last stone of that place would be ground to dust under his foot. The last dried out bone, the last beating heart that did not beat with honesty but that dark sunken power, that grabbed you by your neck and demanded you wallow in your sadness as a means of showing your faith instead of looking ahead and using each new day to move on, that would be what he would remove from here.

The cure for such sadness was not a finger pointed in the direction of another. If someone wanted another to blame they only had to look to themselves or the words on which had been written who to blame for the fault of all things. Even if there was nowhere here left to live he would see the church gone. But if he found one as he had found amongst those angry few so far, who wanted to remain, he would not blame them. There was only so much he could do after all as he had said, as one man. That was not his fault or any other from the wizard's tower.

He could not command the mountains to spring forth from the ground or call the sky down on their heads alone. No, if that was not the unchained will of the people then he would see to it that they could do as they saw fit. But no home of blind minded depravity would he save.

He would not run and escape, he knew the church would have to be looked upon where there was fire as there would be a blaze and the people of the city were aglow of it and had to be turned rightly from their wrong path lest they fouled the source of their illumination. This was no test or sign, but their own fire, their own flame.

As Bernard had wandered and watched on his way, listening to others and seeing horrific sights he wondered. Was this really what the people wanted? The flames reaching higher, but none reaching the church that was higher still that stood above it all. They had lived their lives with their everyday hopes taken from them, held above them, demanding that down on their knees was where they could reach for it with outstretched arms. Now those arms reached for whatever weapons they could, because of course they did.

What most potent light was there that was not fire forged in the bellies of those with truly righteous rage and fury at being wronged for the last time? It was all their own as well, no mage could hold this ideal up and tell them to worship it. He wouldn't start, at least.

Really now, he had heard that the gates had been breached but none could have passed through the inferno gathering at that gate. Certainly not a blaze that had been born from the wish of a dead girl and all those who had followed her. Almost as if someone did not want him to approach.

I feel as though I have just opened a trap and am waiting to see if the creature caught in the snare still lives. Will it lunge at me with teeth bared or will I be faced with the stench of a corpse? Certainly not for this beast to cower in the back of the cage. I must approach with caution but am worried for all those who may have gone on ahead to rest their vengeances unawares, unless they did not get very far.

If he had to think about it, people had been taken away for some time, so it could have been set in motion long ago. He had heard the rumbling in the streets, the sounds they were making, such a loud noise. He had been too late, he felt, as the disquiet turned into something else. He saw that people were chasing each other in the streets, the ordinary people. Back and forth they went as the place went up in flames and choked the sky above.

Up there in the sky, wasn't that something else moving through all the darkness that he saw? Well in that case it was all the best for him to do what he could to help those who still had heads on their shoulders. The church was nothing more than a building after all and he had plenty of time to destroy it. The self determination of people was not something that could be put back into those who lost their lives.

As he made his way through these glowing streets he saw there were people carrying a water cart, desperately trying to put out as much of the fire as they could. All in vain but the effort was telling and effort was all he needed to see with his eyes and understand, even as knights of thickly armoured brown charged at them fiercely in a mob and from up the street came another group of these peculiar, graceless knights, moving in and blocking their escape.

Then the ground rose up into great spears made of dirt and paved stone, crushing them. The citizens cowered at this new forest of blades as was mostly right at the power he commanded, however this was not the right time in the slightest for his liking where he could make the most of that fear.

He walked over to them.

"Are any of you hurt or injured? I can not stand idly by and watch this city burn and I see you are doing the same. I shall help while you work. This is not what I thought was expected of me when coming here but I must do all that can be done with the choices of those in front of me."

One man looked exhausted but spoke up.

"We're the only team left, the others have been cut down but there's nowhere to flee. Shouldn't a wizard be leading an army rather than helping us out? The city is done for anyway if we lose the battle."

"I am not taking sides, for I can not take the sides of your minds and pit them against each other. If you care about the place you should be thankful in the end that it remains standing."

Wasn't this what I wanted? To topple this thoughtless, cold place of stone faced fools and fervour that tore at the freedom of the world? Will I just be left with a shell in the end after all with the people gone and forgotten? It was never my intention to create a wide open hole in the world where others might scramble for power.

The wizard took up the place of the exhausted man pulling the cart, the younger man next to him on the other handle, who seemed vaguely familiar, pulled a long face.

"If I fail, please don't turn me into a snake."

"I will not, as there are snakes enough about already. This night is rather dark and these hours long, yet there will be a morning waiting for us I hope that will not involve stories of mages throwing men into the ocean, thank you very much. Regardless of the truth to those rumours, do as others have already done and flee when you are able, I should think not far beyond these walls if what I have been told is to be believed."

If the next day came, Bernard knew that what he might see beyond the walls would not at all be nice or pleasant, but those outside were now beyond help. The moonlight might as well not shine down on anywhere else than where he walked.

The wizard was not the only one who refused to turn away, as despite having his eyes looking above, Rin was not seeing the moons, his mind elsewhere.

"No, I would not be safe. I long to be free of this place but now have no thoughts of running but making sure the mess does not spread. I'm afraid that leaving this place would not help anybody. As much as I hate the walls inside which we all burn I can not allow the people here to succumb to this madness."

"Very well lad. What is your name?"

"Rin."

"That's the name of the young prince, is it not? You should call yourself something at least a little more convincing."

"I probably should but there's no reason for me to care any longer."

"I do not take it to myself to help out the courts and kingdoms of the world. No matter that some have in the past held great fortune and esteem through such services, I am not of that persuasion and you will not persuade me with such a name regardless. This world is set to fade and it is all moving faster towards that end because of those in their castles turning their lands dark and foul while things you could not even begin to comprehend watch on."

The wizard scoured the sky but could see no sign of that blackness he was sure was watching on.

Some of us can't even guess at the most basic of answers yet it is the best we have. Until we find just what it is that lurks shrouded in the dark.

Rin pulled out the dagger that he had been given.

"Well then, whatever shall I do with this? Is all I am to do here merely watch? No, this was given to me to defend myself from harm. I could have gone down fighting aimlessly at this time but a part of me wonders where else it could be this dagger would go if it was needed in the face of other harms."

The wizard was frowning sadly.

"And yet look what has befallen you in your attempt prove yourself to me. Is this what you think the people here need?"

"This is not how I want to be treated, with those words such as yours. Are you saying that you might ridicule me in front of everyone when the time comes? Not that now is even slightly the time for it regardless. It is not up to me to care. Those around me will tell me how much I am needed."

And they had better. He thought.

Perhaps in the future you might just take it upon yourself to help me out. I'd quite like someone with such knowledge close to my ear.

A wizard by his side might help in getting any nervous people to come about him too, he thought. It was all theory in his head and he wasn't sure quite what he could offer the wizard but the possibility sounded better and better the more he considered the prospect.

Bernard was still frowning.

"You mistake my words. From where did you get that dagger? You don't feel magical, you don't smell magical but that dagger certainly came from one who was."

With Rin still gripping it in his hand, Bernard held up the blade of the dagger to peer at it.

"Yes, so now I also have a witch to contend with, that's just grand. The more I know I suppose."

Rin stumbled back and dropped the dagger, treating it as one would a diseased thing.

"What? No, that can't be. I've done something very bad if that is so. In my defence, it is not easy to tell if someone a person might come across might be any sort of anybody due to trickery. A vile temptress she nearly turned out to be."

"Only for some, lad. And what do you mean nearly? What did she want?"

Rin's jaw clammed up a little as he tried to remain calm.

"Ahhh I think I have given her what she wanted already! I needed to get someone to see the king, my father, who wasn't me and I thought I could trust her and she was trying to get into the castle to see the king and there was nothing wrong with that I thought."

"Slow down. Why do you believe so much in someone who is little more than a title at this point? Surely you know what truly pulls the strings of this kingdom."

"You still don't believe me? It's because he could put a stop to all this church madness, the people need to believe in him. I believed more in another but I did so most wrongly it now seems."

Bernard gripped his shoulder.

"There is no hope for this place that a king can fix. Now where did you leave this woman? You need to stay away from her, as you may fall further into her snare, whatever her plan was for you. I suggest you run and hide after all here is said and done for you will be taken in by the people and executed if this gets out truthfully and I will not help you."

"Well aren't you helpful?"

"Do not mind me, lad, but there would be those more than happy to do the same or worse to you whether you deserve the undue attention you would be getting or not. Even if you are not who you claim to say you are, those around you don't appear to care. There is no need to be any more helpful than I already have been. You may have played a part in unleashing a darkness on the world you could not possibly imagine, after all."

Rin wrestled himself free from the man's grasp.

"All the more reason for me to go back after her even while now feeling so sick. What if she has found a way inside and is not languishing at the doors? Oh with such a kingly fascination as hers whatever have I done?"

So now we're all in more danger. I was so happy removing my worry with these fires but it was all for naught in my ignorance because none of that is going to matter at all if I don't now confront two people when I thought I could use one to not have to confront the first so soon and yet now I must come to terms with two such confrontations now.

Rin didn't want to see his dream fade away and with a burning anger he now felt he understood others for having, picked up the dagger while trying not to gag at its touch and ran back up the streets while the city fell to chaos down below.

The wizard watched him go, not amused at the stupidity of people.

"Go then, to your death, as I am more preoccupied here and would seek to shield those with something about themselves worth saving."

***

The front gate had been abandoned and forgotten when Rin reached it. The events of the night had been left to those below and had the gates not been wide open and a few bodies on the ground there would have been nothing untoward about what he found there. He took a moment to consider that the open gate was some sort of trap, but then again were that the case he would have needed not worry, for those who might create such a trap might have known him and he doubted those stocky knights were smart enough to think of one themselves. They had seemed more likely to just mash him into a pulp and had done so with many people already.

He was doing his best to concentrate so that his thoughts were not like pulp. He could stutter and stammer over his words otherwise or put himself into danger.

What will I do if I find her? Should I play dumb? If she turns around and said I helped her well she'll be in for a shock when she finds out who I really am. She might even think that I've betrayed her and maybe I have...well it doesn't matter who I am, Kieke was doing the wrong thing anyway. I wasn't brave enough to stand in front of any of those men with swords but I shall not blame myself for that. After all I've got a witch to deal with. This night keeps getting worse.

Rin ran out into the castle grounds, illuminated by the moonlight above. He did not care if he was spotted, if anything let him be spotted, for he had words to say that were most important.

The front doors were ahead of him and while he knew they had to be locked he was insistent on trying them anyway. No one had come up to him or bothered him since he had made his dash across the grounds, which he took as a good sign that no one was watching. And as he pulled at the double doors, they clattered stubbornly in his hands and remained closed.

He felt rather far removed from the goings on below, even though the closer he got the more keenly he felt an ever increasing sense of dread. It seemed the ones inside had finally forgotten about their own people and were just content to let them be killed. He wondered how many other people had stood where he now did and demanded that the doors be open for them. How many messengers and people had come from far off lands well meaning, only to meet their end facing these two doors? There were few places these days he would consider well meaning and fewer people, as it had turned out.

You couldn't rule over a mass grave with no people to do your bidding or listen to you. *'This world is set to fade'* that wizard had said and Rin could certainly see now what he meant. For a moment the sounds silenced and he shuddered at what that might sound like more permanently. Who would want to live in a place so accursed after this? Such had happened to Hurstag, cleared of its wealth and remembered only for his mother, who had then been taken away.

He hammered on the doors with his fists in frustration.

Even when doing the right thing it all turned out wrong, because here I am, trying to help. What kind of kingdom have I been living in? Did I seriously think it was all suddenly going to get better one day, that the skies were going to clear?

Rin rested his bleeding fists against the wood as blood tricked down from his knuckles. Letting it all disappear would be far too easy. To give someone what they wanted just to spite the world was a terribly defeatist attitude he hadn't put consideration into. Down below him were all these people now coming to that conclusion, but maybe too late.

I really need to sort myself out somewhat.

He was glad his mother wasn't alive to see any of this. Nothing left for her, nothing left for him as all of who they were was becoming wasted in the darkness, now wasn't it? What was wrong with just wanting to live and getting what he wanted? Why was there all this darkness and fear? Something was off, foul about this world, he realised. It had even turned him into one of the things he despised in that he couldn't even trust himself.

Stalling at the doors hoping that someone would open them and let him off the hook could only last for so long. He resigned himself to another type of effort that he very much hoped would get him somewhere further. He couldn't get in through the front so the next best way in was to the right side of the castle, the sit in barracks.

This was the most direct way into the castle after the front door that didn't involve him scrambling up along the sides. Across the grounds was the back of the church where he could see the arch in the wall that allowed people to come and go from it.

Then he had a sudden thought.

Where *had* those knights come from? There was nothing to say that they had come out from the front door because of course not, that would have been ridiculous. Most likely they had come out from the barracks. They certainly hadn't come from outside Churl then marched in, as anyone would have noticed and despite being shut away he would have certainly heard something about it before now. Unless all the people going in were only now coming out.

On this possibility, Rin found himself caught in a decision. There was no sound coming from the barracks. There were no footsteps, no voices barking orders, simply his breathing and the sounds of his own feet were all that was loud in his ears.

It feels like I'm close to uncovering something about all of this but a part of me slows my feet. I really don't want to make the wrong choice here.

Next to the barracks was the right side ramp that appeared to welcome him above, but the doors to the barracks were open. As he walked closer the sound of torches crackling could be heard within against the walls and a part of him wanted to go inside simply to be closer to that warmth. So he stuck his head inside, into an empty room.

Wandering around the stone entrance hall he found that there were weapons and armour strangely laying about most haphazardly, the same kind given to the ones that had put his people to the sword. He went to pick up a chest piece and he strained to even lift it. No one should have been able to walk around while wearing this. The swords were the same which he found extremely frustrating.

Here I was hoping I'd get a real weapon for once.

He looked at the dagger, knowing he could not trust it. It appeared normal enough to his eyes, but he had been told enough about witches and other foul people to know that their influence couldn't always be seen and known. It was possible that Kieke had been doing something to him without him even realising it. Even if the old man was mistaken it would have been an utter fool's decision to not do everything you could to protect yourself from foul magic.

This had better not all have been about magic. When I find out the reason for all this madness I'm going to make sure none of it ever happens again.

Least of all what he wanted was to stay out of the world's way. Going to get executed by the people would he? Well perhaps he could blame the night's happenings on that woman but he needed to be sure first of exactly what he was dealing with.

What did I need her for again? Why did I bring this person here? They can't help me. I just wanted someone to know me, so that if I died while doing this I could be remembered. Didn't actually think anyone else would believe in me but who's here watching now? No one, not here. All because I wanted to be remembered I've gone and done it, having brought someone else in here because I got caught up in the moment and let out a secret in my confusion when I wasn't thinking straight. Let it just be that. Let her not be a witch and the old man be mistaken.

He wouldn't be able to stomach what ever else happened if it was because of him and she had a great head start on him now, to the one who had all the answers and he didn't know what Kieke was truly going to do when she found his father. He would stop her as only he would be the one to get what they wanted from that man, no one else.

Rin was snapped out of his thoughts for there came a strange sound from further within, a howling that wasn't from any animal, sounding as if it came from some strange creature, some odd yowling pet. Then he opened the next door and came to a stop.

Needless to say, when someone comes upon a scene thoroughly unexpected, such as a host of slain soldiers, folk and all sorts of people and individual bits of people, all forced and crushed to fit inside suits of armour, they do tend to stop.

The sound was coming from one such of those knights, but they were not walking as a person did, they were moving on all fours, perhaps learning to walk or not fully being able to, as their limbs had expanded, meat overflowing the armour to be much larger and a sword dragging in a fleshy chunk where a hand should have been. The head wasn't a head at all, a faceless lump of flesh that had expanded over the helmet, with the rest of the armour not faring any better. Through the cracks there dripped a terrible mess of blood, meat and mud.

Then, when some of that mess forced into armour gets up and notices that person, moving and contorting in ways human arms and legs could not while howling at him, someone would tend to do something else entirely than stand still. Run.

And he did, back out the way he came and up the castle. The creature had been bounding on all fours after him, the sword still held fast clattering against the ground as it did so, occasionally taking swipes at him and some had gashed him as this creature moved horrifyingly fast. Soon enough, Rin was bleeding from a cut on his right calf, his right shoulder and a graze along his back that had just barely missed his head.

It had trouble turning corners and had seemingly lost sight of him more than once as he had run up the ramp, giving him some time to get a lead but he found himself rapidly losing energy and his head was feeling light as he left a trail of blood behind him.

This is bad. I can't keep going for much longer.

The steady incline which hadn't at first been a problem was now admittedly taking a toll as he dragged himself further, that crunching and scraping always behind him getting closer for another mad swing and one would be the one that would kill him sooner or later.

He had thought that he could have climbed over the metal gates to avoid being followed but there were no gates blocking the way up the side any longer and the creature was just barrelling through the metal walls unobstructed.

Directly ahead there was a crossed iron wall, the path beyond it wrapped around that side of the castle to the back. Rin found he could not pull himself up to climb it with his leg and back in the condition they were and his hands were covered in blood that made them slippery.

Only a moment away from being crushed he dragged himself away from the wall as the creature collided into it with a howl and left the iron dinted.

To the left the path split and continued upwards and as Rin limped up the ramp on the left of the wall he wondered if he could climb the trees lined up on the same side.

Oh, I'm nearly at the top. He thought.

Rin reached the top of the ramp as his vision began to darken ever so slightly and his heart sunk at the long, flat platform in front of him that was covered in shadow. His legs gave out, forcing him to crawl and he turned to see behind him the creature readjust itself to aim straight at him. It begin to charge.

This is it then. Stupid, stupid-

He felt blood and sweat rise from his skin. It lifted off his body dripping upwards, twisting out into a spike that pierced the soft head of the nightmarish knight, right through a split in the armour to skewer it and the body collapsed in a heap.

Rin was only staring at his hand for a moment when he noticed there was another person on the platform. He put it down to support his legs to help himself stand, because he refused to be seen as helpless in this moment and staggered to his feet, to stand in front of Kieke, who was looking mildly surprised.

He could have asked about her bent ankle but knew that wasn't what he truly wanted to say, so he didn't say it, even though he knew less about the answer to that question and already knew the answer to the one he was about the ask.

He was shaking in the cold and could barely get the words out of his mouth.

"Are you a witch?" He asked.

She shrugged a shoulder as she nodded, face abashed.

"We don't go around calling ourselves that though. Not quite the same even if you would think it. I suppose such talk close enough for now. What are you..?"

Kieke could not finish her sentence. Both of them knew the answer.

"What I'm doing here?" He said.

He pulled out the dagger and pointed it at her.

"I'm here to put a stop to you. Are you responsible for all this?" He waved an arm down below.

She shook her head.

"No. That's no to both. I'm not going to let you stop me, but I didn't do all this."

"Then why bother with me just then? I could stop you right now."

"It's what I see in you. When you become like me you get a certain attachment to people. There's nothing wrong in wanting the world to be one where you get what you want."

"Get out of my head, I'll never be like you and stop thinking you understand what I want."

"I'm not in your head and don't be like them. Not like all of them down there. I just have something to do right now that means a lot to me. Come with me and you can understand it better."

She took a step forward but he took one step back and held up the dagger.

"Keep away from me-"

Rin took a second step backwards but was not careful where he placed his feet. Slipping on a trail of his own blood, his legs slid and he was left to cling onto the ledge. He held on with both hands then his right hand gave way and Kieke fell to reach out to him.

"Take my hand."

She could see the doubt in his eyes, just waiting for betrayal even as he barely hung on for his life.

"I don't know if I should."

She felt a sudden stab of fear that was not hers, the voice of her master urged a command in her head.

'Save.'

I'm doing this. Is he important? Tell me.

'Save-'

I'm doing this!

'You will die!'

"You can trust me!" She shouted.

Rin hesitated, his eyes bleak.

"I don't know. Is death better than being tricked by a witch?"

"I'm not trying to trick you I want to save you. I don't know who you really are, there I admit it but you have to live. Please take my hand and live."

'Save us, child.'

What?

Rin reached up to grab her hand as Kieke's world ended. The sky heaved as a blind terror sunk her mind as brackish water exploded out of each pore, blood burst from wherever it could find as strength and life left her body with a scream as she became a shrivelled and dried husk.

For Rin, whatever strength had remained was now gone too with his mind quite blank and he fell far, far below, where the fires below became obscured by a cold wall of darkness, then a cold darkness of another kind.

Chapter Thirty Seven
Walking in the Darkness

Nasker had been asleep until he felt a harsh light against his eyes. Was it sunrise already? That could have been a possibility but along with the light was the warmth of a scorching wind against his face and the rushing sound of it in his ears. These did rouse him more fully from where he lay. When he opened his eyes to find the light was an endless wall of fire that was harsh and orange, he frowned a little. This wasn't how he had left everything to be.

He sat up and looked at what he had been laying on, a patch of bare hot ground jutting out from a jagged cliff, the only flat piece of ground he could even see. At the edge of the cliff only a few paces away the ground dropped to where there was nothing below and nothing above either for that matter, only an expanse of open emptiness and the fire that had swallowed all else around it. The blaze could have been near, it could have been far, but with no way to judge the size or distance of it there was no way for him to know as the deafening rush of sound coming from it filled his ears.

He did not want to get closer to that edge and began to push himself back against the face of the cliff. As he did so a great rumbling shook the cliff and he thought the ground might collapse into that nothingness below. Dirt crumbled off the edges and also came rolling down from above, but there were no handholds to climb that sheer face.

Looking back down drew his gaze away from the endless inferno and to the solid ground he found himself on. Along the cliff to his right he saw the backs of four people, none of who were wearing any clothes and despite the blaze were openly facing the flames.

Their bodies were a smeared grey the colour of ash and held little dark fissures in their skin. Then those bodies began to crumble into the air, ash flaking off to nothingness, a burning log on a fire burning away to coals, steadily disintegrating until all but one had disappeared. That one slowly turned their head to face him and Nasker could barely make out her features, speak, or even hear his own words over the wind.

"Zelda is that you?"

Their charred legs crumbled and the body fell to the ground yet once there they crawled in the blink of an eye to lunge at his throat with a scream in theirs even as they fell apart and Nasker awoke with a jolt in complete darkness, with the shuddering sound of his breathing loud through the night.

Despite the cold he was sweating and had to scrub himself to quickly remove the sweat as he would certainly be grasped by a deathly chill otherwise. He felt sick and it took a few seconds for his eyes to adjust to the dark, even if there hadn't been any light at all.

After a few moments sitting up he looked around. No one else had been disturbed by his sudden waking. But wasn't that the back of a figure, ashen and burnt, that he saw walking away into the trees, into the shadow? He took another deep breath. He was imagining it possibly. Hopefully. Hope on its own wasn't good enough for him, so while everyone else was still asleep and appeared perfectly normal, he wasn't going to get any more sleep tonight or this morning, whenever it was.

He thought about what he had just seen and thought of Zelda and looked around for her. There she was, so strange that one, to be like the others.

Could it be that I'll have to be keep a further eye on her, or is another looking down upon us to guide her? That is what I saw, more than just a bad dream, surely. She can't see through me, but if one day could be that day then how much longer do I have? Even if she is so much like them in her ways, of course because through them she has been taught, I can't have her as this unknown participant here I can't work around.

Such thoughts swam around his head until the grey texture of clouds that passed for daylight travelled through the tree tops, a daylight that day after day was becoming an ever darker shade of grey, something they all had to admit.

Descending deeper and further into the forest did little to shrink the growing of the dark, their presence not enough to lift darkness from the trees and bushes around them. Most recently, Zelda had begun to feel strange, if only briefly, in the way one might feel another breathe down their neck in the most unpleasant way. Yet she would look back and see nothing while feeling her heart beat just a little louder in her chest every time that she did. The strangeness became a drumming so that she eventually put a hand to her head.

"Are we on this path until we fall to pieces? I would have thought that the forest would have protected us from many things but as it is I find that not so."

She had not asked this to be so sombre but realised after speaking just how sad of mind she sounded, even if she didn't feel it quite that way.

Gunter spoke to her.

"Never again shall the forest be so if we fail, or anywhere else. All the world will fall to the darkness of which we have seen. All around us it chokes the life of the world. It is that which ails you and may continue to do so, in which case you should steel yourself for further misfortune if you allow it to strike you about your head."

"Well I wish it wouldn't worry me so, as by itself the darkening of the sky calls for concern, yet it is hard for me to judge as I have not lived through this time of year in the forest."

"You will need to be aware of all around you to learn as much as you can. Other inhabitants of this forest are the ones who need not practice and learn, for in their entirety that is who they are and all they should be willing to know. The world beyond is dark and barren to them yet the times we find ourselves in may not effect them in the same way as us and such is the way when the world turns slow."

"Our magic is almost gone then." She said sadly.

"Can you feel that numbness at your fingertips, that last breeze of warmth that comes from nowhere? It is all that seems to be left to give the barest hint of magic when held against the ground or brushed against trees. Still, inside I feel it holding my heart in place and for that we shall go on knowing all is not lost, do not keep your worry about you. Ah, but I hear someone coming, you will see."

Zelda kept her arms crossed as forest creatures came into view.

"Well I don't like what I see. They look like a bunch of suspicious thieves to me."

That they did, all eight with distended bellies, stocky grey limbs with scaly bumps on them and stumpy fingers, these creatures had appeared clambering through the trees. They were hairier then all of the druids, and taller, despite being hunched over and over their thick shoulders each had slung a sack large enough to hold a whole person inside, which was rather concerning considering the faces of the creatures, which were flat with a stumpy nose and two thick teeth poking out at the sides of their mouths.

The leader was bigger than the others and was smeared with mud. His acorn coloured eyes and that of his fellows somehow gleamed despite the lack of light. His voice sounded at once the same as the croak of a frog yet far more refined and capable in speech than a frog. His breath wafted and stank so Zelda wondered if from that mouth would come vomit at any moment.

"And what do we have here?"

Findal raised his eyebrows.

"Always fascinating to see the ways of the highwaymen that pilfered up and down the great trading road, where once even there was a great stone bridge that connected both sides of the world, being copied by beings of nature. Just as we seek to be more like them they have sought to be more like us than any others I have seen but I had not guessed that I would see trolls here, distastefully civilised."

The leading troll snorted.

"Scoundrels we have been called in other lands, but have you been called such even once? Not by those among yourselves, but others involved in the finer things. Things that you seek to leave behind for a world more alive in the minds eye. Yet for now, time falls hard on those human lands, as it once did when t'was elven lands, before you ate them up on the chase out."

Findal scratched his jaw.

"The world is in a vast and unimaginable peril beyond that which befell the elves. The spirit, the very core that holds together the strength of this land has become lost and we must find them again. Surely you know of this and you venture further than most. Have you seen them or caught a whiff of their presence?"

All the trolls shook their heads and their leader spoke.

"Not at all, not at all, not the least reason being that we have no need. We're here in most part while we wait for all this above to change about you see. Less people along the north road these days means less people to steal from. You need to watch out, for although my people put on a good face we are well aware all is not as it seems. I refer to what lingers in this forest. It is strange, this darkness I feel. It is like a breeze sounding of a cry barely on the wind that I hear when I look deeper in and is ever present when I go there. Yes indeed there is something dark in this forest but I wonder that it could be part of the cycle that turns, more ancient than us all."

Gunter shook his own head.

"No matter what you see or hear, outside this forest the darkness that lurks within is not present but it is reaching out across the world and that may bring attention here most terrible, as many fear a repeat of the war that threatened to plunge the world into darkness many years ago. If we find the source of it we should look into it, for all in this forest should feel the dark that spreads itself, looking outwards for new lands to make just like this one beyond what has been seen here and of a like not yet seen beyond it. The world is slowing and the cycle will die along with it when it does finally cease. Others may be off on fools' errands but we know on what the world turns and as we see it slow know what must be returned to see the world be right once again."

The troll pointed at him with one stubby finger.

"Who is the fool here I say? This is part of a cycle that spun when the stars first came and all who lived were young. This could be naught but a beginning, I do not expect you to understand, for humans fight over many petty things, including the comprehension of right and wrong, to which it is almost natural. Even if it is not so you must think of the reason why humans do. We have not seen a dark like this before but we do not fear its coming. The sun will rise another day and perhaps when it does all you will see was that the dark was waiting for the light all along. Whether that light shall come from the sky or from gold, we do not know. Just as the forest is, the shining light from either is a friend to us, one that is ever helpful. Look to that which shines to find yourselves a waiting friend in kindness."

Gunter pointed right back at the troll.

"There is no kindness in nature, so whatever darkness has gripped this forest is blind to you in your madness and shall not be a cause for further discussion amongst us. Nor the uses of gold. Around you is the waiting ruins of the world and your pathway along regret."

The troll lugged his hulking shoulders.

"So it may be for us and you, that is if you survive at all. Caution must be exercised the further along you tread if you hold such worries. As such you should leave to be on your sad and lonely way, for all you shall find in this forest is loneliness amongst the trees if that is your opinion and should it be that you come back crawling, know that we who have previously been kind and open may not be so on our next meeting."

With that the trolls continued on their way past the druids. Then the head troll paused and turned back for a moment.

"For instance, we're after more things that shine, but we know that you have nothing of interest which is why you're still alive. Such a sad way to go, to leave it all behind, in more ways than one."

Then the trolls disappeared and Zelda was left wondering just what else the forest could hold. Gunter was nodding.

"See Zelda, even they know that there is no purpose to carrying their worry around. Despite their less than pleasant ways, you will always learn something if you take your lessons from those that are from nature."

It appeared that he was taking her silence to mean that she was accepting what he was saying, but in fact, Zelda was trying not to worsen the pressure on her head that was becoming a rather persistent little thrumming. She found it was coming and going, in its own little cycle, but that didn't mean it was a good thing or that she should have to wave it away. Ignore it and put up with it for a time certainly but no good could come from simply ignoring whatever it could be and going about her day.

After a while of walking through the trees the forest became ever darker as the canopy variously knitted itself together to provide them with patches that were dark and shaded. Underneath one such of these where the sky was hidden from them they all were stopped in their paths at the sound of breathing. In the dark spaces and holes which they could not see into, such as in the ground and in tree stumps were the noises of creatures, although hiding in wait or sleeping could not be known as reaching out left them with nothing to guess at.

Survel had pulled out his sword, to be used for investigating those dark spaces as they went, leaving Zelda to wonder if he might accidentally poke something with the end of it, which all seemed a bit much. They were not trying to locate someone hiding from them in the dark after all.

"Who hides out there in the dark?" Survel said.

None of them could pierce the darkness that came out from those holes, the hushed and shivering voices of those within answering out in a timid attempt to not be heard by whatever else might hear them.

"In the dark? No, we are hiding *from* such darkness around us. The night comes and goes but what approaches is something more. We feel it in the ground and have been told of it in the sky. Here we hide, for we do not wish to stand against it for we have no power over it to do so. Please, let it all pass us by and never have it come again."

Zelda was squinting in an attempt to see just what was making the noise, because it would have been rude for her to just ask what was and she didn't want it to appear as if she didn't know something such as this.

"I can not see you." She called to the shadows.

"Come out and speak to us, for you may do so freely as there is no cause for alarm to be amongst us."

The voice spoke back.

"There is nothing to be done now that the world is on the edge of ruin. For within our forest home is a dark and awful power and beyond our forest home far above there is a dark and awful power just the same. Can you really not see? Yet do not look at such a darkness for it will see you and then you will be no more."

Survel scowled.

"You look too deeply into us I think, to accuse us of not having our eyes open, for it is necessary to have them wide open. While the dark we see above surely does bleed the sky of any comfort one might find in it, looking up all the time does little more than distract from what is on the ground, which is where our minds and hearts should be."

They had better not accuse us again, or I shall be back for them later and they shall regret their words of weakness. He thought.

Gunter stroked his beard.

"I believe they may be confusing the two. Surely it is that the darkness hiding above serves only to mock us as the world ends. That end itself is its own darkness and it would be a folly to think otherwise."

The creature continued with a pleading voice, a shaking edge on the verge of tears.

"None of it shall give us harm if we hide away and make ourselves small and as nothing in whatever eyes it might have. Are you blind to the thought that to hide is to save oneself from the dark? It comes, it comes and yet so loudly do you make yourselves known here. Turn away and be still as we have and do not see it. Yet as you are you might already be blind enough."

Are they unable to convince themselves? Zelda wondered.

She could not help but note that Gunter raised his voice slightly on his reply, which made her frown and was glad for the dark to hide her expression.

"So we are to be blind and loud while the dark has eyes? What nonsense that is. For that matter, do not compare us to those others behind their walls and high up in their castles who let the world and all they have uselessly hoarded in it pass on by. Too long has the world turned without its rightful guidance and has become unbalanced. We shall return it to that time where all shall be as the ground, sea and sky commands by our voices. Do not fear, or if you must, know that you will not have to know fear for long and you will not have to hide when we are done."

Zelda nodded, the knot that had begun to lodge in her stomach loosening.

"Such is something we all hope for." She said happily.

This was met with nods from the rest and while they were all in glad agreement the creature however sounded unconvinced.

"The forest will protect us even if it will not protect yourselves. It has been a good friend to us even if not you to it. Please leave us be, for I would not like to think that the forest of all good things would turn its back or reveal us from having conversed with you."

Another one, their voice lighter, came out hushed from a hole.

"What can we do with these foolish humans? They aren't of the forest and are going to doom us all."

A third desperate voice up in a shrouded hollow called out.

"Can't we all be quiet and do as we were able? We'll be found here if we make too much noise. Please I implore you, do leave us be."

"Yes." Said the first voice.

"We have not seen a dark like this before and we fear its coming. The forest is becoming cold and quiet. Whether that is the way of the forest willing or the grasp of darkness, we do not know. The forest when at peace is a friend to us, one that is ever helpful. Hide away in that silent peace to find yourselves a waiting friend, in kindness."

Voices popped up all around them, saying the same thing, which made them all wish for silence as the voices were not echoing and followed them for some way, so they they knew they had been surrounded by the creatures in some number until the hushed whispers were swallowed into the dark and were not heard again.

Zelda found the silence to be a welcome relief as there was less noise crowding up her mind. Her head still thrummed but there were moments when she could not worry about it. She was not able to keep to herself however as Gunter was peering at her out from the corner of his eyes.

"Hmmm, something tells me that you did not know who those creatures were. Well it was best that they were hidden. Not terrifying of visage are they but some things are best presented to you when one wishes it to be for themselves, not for others to demand and if it never does then it never shall be. That is one of the unknowing ways of nature that must be respected, otherwise respect might not come to you. Vast memories do some of the inhabitants here have and it would be a shame for your meetings to be ruined with just some careless words from long ago in your life. It would be a shame too for any of us to tell you of them. When the time is right I am sure they will reveal themselves to you."

Lessons were all well and good for all who could hear the words, however Zelda wondered if they would have all been right to have some silence in case something out there did come down and find them in their current weakness. She decided on keeping her words to herself though. She certainly could not find within herself the need to speak up on the matter. If she did, she would just be speaking more words and did not want hers to be whatever brought down the darkness onto them.

A darkness did come, which throughout the day's travel wound around the ground and the sky, hanging in the air making it thick and hazy. Among the haze up high through the clouds from time to time came that dark and writhing warning that they believed heralded the end to all things, such a dark and mocking thing in defiance of the world.

That was not all that they came across which mocked them so, their next encounter used words rather than rely on a mere foreboding presence that when it came was dark, musty of smell and all together mysterious.

A group of five strange creatures appeared before them. There was nothing to be seen of them other than a dark shrouded garb of dark green moss draped about them that could barely be seen in the gloom, drooping down and covering their features, hiding their heads completely in blackness. However sticking out were thin brown limbs like old bones, thin yet strong, shaped in bark. Their legs bent backwards as those of birds and on their long arms that they wrapped in the moss were hands that held sharp, hooked claws to be movable talons.

Their voices from within the shrouds were the rustling of leaves scraping over a frozen lake, with the whisper of a wind just as cold following in their wake.

"Come now, who is here? I sense those who find only folly in the forest. Indeed do we look before ourselves to see that humans come, searching in no doubt for their light, as all things do, their sun. Your paths here are dark, humans. Do not be alarmed if you can not see further towards whatever it is you seek in this forest."

Gunter stepped forward, but it was Zelda who spoke first.

"Our need is the need of the forest. Do not tell us in so certain words what we shall not do."

The creature rolled its sly words yet still held them with an icy seriousness.

"Then whatever shall you do, for do you hear the wheeze of death across this forest? It comes for all with many a tool to use at its employ. By which you shall fall can not be made certain."

"So not by your own claws then, you mean to say, unless you would take upon yourself the duty of this death you so speak of?"

"Or perhaps it can, ah or then not at all, for that fate would be a mercy upon you most undeserving."

Gunter then found his voice.

"Then let us be you wretched creature. We will be gone soon enough but not in the hidden manner of your own twisted pleasing. The darkness in the sky is a warning, to all a reminding harbinger that tells of darker days to come. We must stop the fear it brings from coming true in the eyes and hearts of those who live and believe in the promise of a new world."

The creature clicked in its throat.

"It told us all about this blasted world, the darkness did, all we would ever need to know. Now we find you here and while our friend the forest might not come to you, we would anyway ask if you would be so kind as to join in the night time turning above, you who would think to march forward into the dark most unaffected."

"We are far more than the people who live only for their kings or the power they hold in their hands which is the darkness that holds this world to the ruin coming from your mouths. There are those out there who would rather not be seen and are capable at doing just that. This darkness you live in is merely an effect of the rule of kings and fools which has no place in this forest and should not have ever existed. Under such rule does power come from words of lies and deception none too different from hiding away in the dark. Nothing more is quite so wicked."

"There are ones who are more so. Think of those who would go on and travel to other lands as elves did. They who had remained in this land, who have since now fled, knew what it was they stayed for and now perhaps too late is what they have run from. You know of their foolish past wickedness that rid them from this land yet who knows what worse they have done?"

Zelda huffed.

"I'm not going to let the forest burn down if that is what you are insinuating, for we amongst ourselves have no knowledge of the use of such things as the elves had and know keenly quite how it can corrupt and hurt. If the darkness comes, I'm not going to let fire burn everything down just to make a light for finding easier that who we seek. You clearly have no love for where it is that home rests in your hearts."

"I wonder how much what you say is so. Who is to say that we are wrong for what we do when knowing the ways of you and yours and theirs are a mystery to us as the workings of a beating heart. Who do you live for and where do you return to when a night such as this falls? When all the world you see about you is a land that has been plunged into darkness, who can say that you are not already home, where ever it is you may be? We had lost our own ways and had not known that we were waiting for a darkness such as this to come and we welcomed it for giving us new purpose and reminding us to be strong. Whoever will join us in this most gracious night we do not know, when there are those who think that only the forest can be helpful and the darkness never so. Yet it can be a friend for you, helping you find your own purpose. Embrace the dark as you did the forest to find yourselves a waiting friend, in kindness."

Nasker moved himself between the lot of them.

"Remember this well." He said, turning to the creatures.

"Those who hold onto power often forget that when they hold out their hands to power, they weaken themselves by giving themselves something to lose, something they can be made to let go of which they never had to before."

He put his hands around his companion's shoulders and eased them to move on.

"As for us I think we have squeezed the last of the friendliness that this place has to offer within reasonable bounds. Let us leave them to their fate, whatever it is they have made for themselves they deserve it wholeheartedly."

There was no retort from the creatures for this so they walked past those strange wooden forms, who let them go without any other further words.

There followed the party a silence that was most absolute, the forest drained of all sound but for their walking steps. In the wake of the creatures it could have been said that the forest became darker still, were it not for all the forest around losing light, even as they slowly were walking upwards and there were dips and hills all about which they tried to stick to the least steep routes to keep up their energy and keep themselves in high spirits as best they could. What else they would find ahead was a matter of dread but at least one of them was still focussed on the creatures they had just met beforehand, for surely such dark creatures surely should not have taken their refusal lightly.

Those who wanted power were not likely to share in it. Then for other foul reasons must have it been offered to them, so Zelda figured. Then again it could have been just as likely that they all must have appeared too weak to be bothered with and that any further insistence would be a waste of that chill breeze the druids refused to let settle in their own chests. Or maybe they had appeared too foolish to be amongst those who had found a home in the dark, as others had thought of them fools for treading this far into the forest. Yet further in they tread, without meeting a soul or a spirit and Zelda felt hers lessening, feeling near powerless and uncertain again.

"Why would they be so afraid to the point where they would have to take what the dark has when they must have known that surely a cruel end awaits them for doing such a thing?" She asked.

Again it was that Gunter had something to say to her on the matter and she quite began having her head throb with a second pain that wasn't what she wanted at all.

"You have seen those who would meet the same fate since the start of your journey. They are no different from those in their castles using such advantageous situations for their own good where there is no good to be had. That does not mean that they are afraid. Do you not see the lack of animals and others of nature's children? There you shall see those who are scared and afraid, as the dark searches for them as we have been told, as prey and in such forms it will search for you too for the same foul purposes. So it is that creatures who were never prey use these dark times to keep themselves where they are in a weak imitation of strength that can clearly be seen."

Zelda felt her legs twitch, which was a rare occurrence not having happened for some time. The scars themselves, which were nothing more than little lines had done little to bother her here and there but did remind her of when it was she had been grasped by something with an intent to take her down a certain path and this was quite the same. The two experiences felt remarkably relatable and she frowned.

"I find myself being more wary in what perceived strength they may gain from these sad times. Imitating means nothing, as we have been told who we must be when we look to nature so then we must be. Which makes our weakness all the more hurtful for, not that I would try now, we can not convince others without possessing that we do not have. I do wonder how much all around us is merely smoke and mirrors but that still can be a means to an end for some when there are those weak willed beings enthralled by such appearances. I do not doubt that the kings and lands of falsity must fall and be replaced with the natural turning way of the world but I also do not doubt the possibility that some of those might actually have the power they appear to hold onto. We might find ourselves caught otherwise, to ignore it."

"None of us should ever take our strength from such appearances." Gunter angrily said.

"All of us here are exactly who we set out to be and everyone else out there living in all sorts of blind, wishful lives shall be crushed under the weight of whatever it is they choose to hide with because they are weak no matter what it is that causes them to give in."

Zelda shrugged.

"We could be weaker than those we have just passed. That thought does hurt my eyes wherever it is I look. Then perhaps I shall look above, to sights that hopefully bring some much needed relief."

"You mean to climb a tree?"

"No, I mean to fly."

"Do not attempt to do so, for even if you can, you see the dark above that would use you as its food."

"Yet it has done nothing but scare us from time to time and that is all it shall do. If that is really all it has over us then it can not harm me for the loss of our world drawing ever closer scares me enough already. However much fear one must suffer through in their lifetime I do not know."

"If you don't do as I say you will never truly understand."

Zelda feared in that moment, a rush as if she were being left behind came quite unbidden and that moment felt heavy chains about her that weighed her down and an urgency inside her begging them to be removed.

If I am to accept all this, then what will be left for me here or anyone else who refuses to listen? Ah I'm at the end of my tether. I need some space!

She looked at what she could of the sky, trying to see beyond the dullness to what it was she could feel. As she expected there was almost nothing for her to reach out to around herself as there was that deeply unsettling black murk. Yet she found herself searching through the hurt inside herself for a moment of clarity to see beyond the grey above and in doing so found far above a lightness in which those chains about her fell. With that she became a crow as black as the times ahead she felt obscured from knowing the ends of and soared up into the sky.

Down below she could see someone shaking their fists but she soon left thoughts of them behind and looked to the sky. The pain was all gone and with her bird eyes she could see clearer and further and she circled and flew so that she could see even further over land. Her mind felt clear but it was a frightening clearness the way near freezing water was dangerous yet fascinating.

No, she would not be afraid, not of this. She was flying on her own, with no beat of the land far down below rising up to comfort her. Oh let that not becomes the constant reality that all must face! Let them triumph over fear but not by knowing it in this way.

Such were the thoughts in her head as she looked about her. There far away she could see in the north something flat and glinting that caught her eye in animal eagerness and her own. On the horizon it shimmered and moved and there was no doubt in her mind, that blackness lit by the moons must be the ocean. The ocean! Briefly did come the urge for her to go there and set her eyes on such a thing, to see a shore and set her feet upon it and feel what sand must feel like under her feet. Only but a moment did it last, for the need for selfishness was not so large that she would not want the world to see another day.

Even if to the north they were running out of land this was many days, perhaps weeks walk or more. While to the west there was no end to the forest in sight, the thought that they may indeed have to cross the remainder of it and then search elsewhere filled her with a sadness and apprehension at how much time was left for what needed to be done.

From up on high she turned to look down below and what faced her was sudden utter blackness. It shook and it shimmered and for a moment it was a flat surface like that of water reflecting nothing before it sunk into the sky, something alive that then burst outwards to become again a streak of surging wetness that defied her eyes as she tried to make sense of what could cut open the sky in a trail and make it bleed black, then close it up behind it. Only to have it appear again, travelling in all directions while being in front of her. Or was it behind her? Wherever she looked it was twisting to meet her, closer yet further away, always in her vision. She could not even flee as there was something important to do before she could do that. Her wings had to work.

They were heavy, not from any magic she could feel or any dampness but heavy none the less, a tree stripped of its leaves and that black thing refused to leave her mind's eye alone and in a way it was seeing her. There was no moving under the weight of such a gaze and there was no up or down that she could tell, even as she fell far down below. Worst was that she felt herself changing from the form she had taken that might have softened her fall. So with painful crashes and cracks did Zelda feel herself break through the trees with a brutal suddenness, so that her consciousness had left long before her broken human body hit the ground.

Chapter Thirty Eight
The Army of Kasynne

The sounds of three men walking through the scrub rid the forest floor of the silence that had occupied it before those men had been present. They were speaking in low voices to one another and had been for some time. Why should it be that they were to speak in hopeful tones? After all there was little between any of them that was at all well.

Their trek through the forest had worn them thin as such travel would do, while their minds had been on other methods of travel such as boats. To go so far away had become such a more likely possibility that it had become a conversational topic of grim acceptance. Beyond to the ocean might be what they were looking for, as in a way the need to travel beyond called to them more pleasantly than the thought of walking here. The land was no longer familiar to them, no longer calling out and they could not call back.

There far beyond the land might they find it again, to regain what was lost, but they had to get there first, wherever that might be and in no way could they ask the forest for guidance. All they had to rely on was what anyone else might have to rely on were they to simply go for a walk.

Survel was unhappy, more so than the others yet little more than any had seen him.

"There is nothing in this place not choked out by fear and longing aside from us. On we go and have kept going, yet all around I see whatever the shadows wish me to see. Whatever peeks out from them we can be sure of not finding what we seek. The spirit could be calling out for us or others and we might not even know it, to find or see such a core on what the world turns."

Findal responded slowly.

"What have we found here but the darkness that clings to the sky? We must be on our way and run as far as we can, for the dark clings to the trees too. Nothing is good, but we must keep going as we said we would, for I fear our journey was long even in the beginning. Worst comes of it that we reach the shores and find nothing, we can take ourselves further along them to the north and try the luck of the kings of those lands instead of setting sail as soon as we set our eyes on the shores and that dark horizon."

"We have all been to the north and know it a terrible place of towns and noise and shackled beasts. There is no need for us to go there if the last wisps of what was ours came from across the sea, or at least be a possibility where one might look."

"Hmm perhaps I was feeling the call of old eases more than I had thought. For some people a word is but a word no matter how you say it and that is all you need to say. I do shudder at the loss of our words however." And Findal did.

Nasker was walking along behind them.

"That said, do either of you even know how to build or even steer a boat? I do say that we might be walking someway along the coast until we find someone inclined to do the boating for us. For that matter the weather as it is does not suit for such travel so for some time might we find ourselves lashed to black shores else we be crushed against treacherous seas that I am not too keen on travelling regardless I must say."

They were not at the shores yet, not knowing of whatever lands they might find on the other side, but the harshness of winter would follow them there and out of the forest would mean into the wind. Here it was not making itself much known, for the trees did much to thin the wind to little more than a whistle when it picked up. Was that wind picking up a foul air from the trees or was it carried from beyond? It was a smell that clogged their senses and did not leave them in gladness of mind as that creeping, crawling sensation they were having from down below was much the same as the darkness above.

More than usual had they seen it lately, roiling around in the sky, but they could not bring themselves to even hate it, that energy was not within them to spare on such a thing. Days and nights had been spent suffering moreso the cold than they had been accustomed to, as no longer were they able to laugh off the concerns thrown at them by rain and sleet, or the chill that came from a frosty morning or long worn day. Such times they had coped with before but the presence of evil they felt about them in the forest would surely weigh heavy on them, just as it would do so on the rest of the world were the world to wish to be such a burden.

So onwards they went, where there was certainly no way for them to be knowing how much or indeed how little assistance they would be in keeping the world from falling into the darkness they found about them.

A deep dark pit had once been told of, to the far north east reaches of Malleau, where the Demon King had resided to grow his army and to those present to see such a thing it could have been said that they could understand exactly when such choking stagnation as that found in the forest was spoken about.

Of course, Nasker had vastly more knowledge about what the dark creeping up on them all to smother them felt like, but he kept this all to himself. He could feel the thing that was keeping him moving, that faintest phantom of hiding warmth that could be what he sought. He could not be sure, yet it was the best he could do where he found himself to keep going without giving himself away.

Burning down the forest would have been an easy fix for him but that could not be done now. He had not finished with the usefulness of those who he was among and although he did not need the magic of the world to find himself with a purpose in Auralin, hiding out among those who did was in its own way useful to him.

However long that would all last was up to him, as long as the wiles of whatever was out there did not ruin them all further. He could not be sure of the stability of the minds of those who had nowhere else to go. Those people had already ruined themselves, putting their trust into something so weak and without feeling as the world they now lived in. The world did not care, it wasn't something that could think or feel.

For all about them that differed, there were some similarities of mind, such as getting out of this place that had once given them a reason to move on. They would move on, past the trees and through the fir and bared branches to a place where all of this could be left behind for a time, intent on a world other than that around them.

Findal turned to the others and looked back slightly.

"I can only hope that what is here is not all we can see, for to turn back would be most tragic, were we to reach the ocean and turn around, or not. For in lands among such people that live on the west we may have to hide, if they will take us. The seafarers of Keen they once were and may still be and we might find them in winter's state of recluse."

Survel scratched his jaw.

"Cut off from the world after being stripped bare by those who dwell in Kasynne. It is they who stole the sea trade away from the north is my guess. Whatever we might find beyond the forest could still be as unwilling and as careless as anywhere else we have come across. Lessons learned mean nothing to some people and it is far too late to hope that they may care for anyone's words, let alone ones coming out from the dark such as ours. Even if we don't mean to, some may see us and think we spread it if they have watched the cloud over the forest grow. Too late we have been to choose this path so that other might take our words seriously while all around is swallowed up."

"Were that so then there would not be any backwards steps. Who is to say that we have not already been effected or indeed swallowed as you say? Who can see inside such a dark foulness to see to a future ahead I do not know. Our own ways are caught in it, effected by what I fear not to be evil intent, just sad happen stance along which path we have been forced to tread. The right one, but one seemingly greater than all others taken hostage in these dark times."

"Indeed. It is not helped by those who have found themselves peace in the dark which those who are not us smirk at thinking our time has come."

Nasker was looking to the ground and spoke quietly, almost to himself it could have been said, were it not for the silence allowing him to be heard by the other two.

"It has come for some, of their own choosing and following in that choice are reasons best left avoided. Best then that we keep going as we are and ignore those with such wrong opinions. It doesn't matter what people think they see, for many and all sometimes see in others only that which they want to see, it is the wishes we hold within who keep us who we are. Those saying otherwise are simply saying otherwise and no stock should be taken of such words."

"If they intend to harm would you think nothing would be done?" Survel asked.

Nasker shrugged before replying.

"Well then, that's an entirely different problem. If that happens at Keen then we'll worry about that when we get there. There can't be too many others blaming us for all of this and certainly others have found blame in these times among those they feel it can easily be placed upon."

Ahead of them scrambled a noise and out came Gunter from the trees.

"You should all come and see what I have found." He said.

The four of them walked only a little way further ahead and onto something strange. It was a road that they had come upon the edge of. Not a paved one, but a great dirt road underneath the trees, surrounded by mist and lit in grey gloom. The far side was in shadow, as fifty men could have stood on it side by side. Both directions along it left and right could only be seen a little way before disappearing into the mist.

"Well this is a strange sight." Said Survel.

"I'm scratching my head too." Replied Gunter.

Findal was squinting to the road's right.

"If my head is right, one way seems to lead back to Kasynne at a guess, although that is only a guess. It would make sense for them to have done something like this but I'm left wondering how the cowards would have made it so far into this forest. Rare are the tales that they venture within."

Then there came a familiar, now husky voice of that young woman, who had not done what she had been told.

"And yet, the question remains what road is this we find ourselves on?"

Zelda was still going against the advice given to her. She was only able to move as fast as her back allowed, as it ached. She had been given an old branch that could take her weight as a crutch and was relying on it heavily for her left leg. So it was just as well that her left arm was not the one that was broken in both parts.

Her right eye was the only good one after the left side of her face had struck a tree branch on her fall and she had even lost some teeth. Her breathing through them was shallow and breathing too deeply prickled her ribs with pain. Battered and bruised she was quite the sorry sight even so many days after and on some days she had to be carried.

With one side of the branch she rubbed the back of her neck to relieve the throbbing pain that had risen again while trying not to look at anybody, but Gunter had his arms crossed.

"Still following us? I have said before many times that you can rest if you would wish to rest. There could be a darkness about you now, yet still you follow."

"Day after day you have said this. I am following and am still sorting out my mind." She said.

Her words were thin, strung out and tired and inside she felt that way. Speaking only made it worse but she did not wish to appear silent of mind.

Survel shook his head.

"Zelda, is it time for me to carry you again? Do you feel the evil closing in about you?"

"I do not need that nor do I feel that." She said with a tired sigh that rattled out of her.

I'm not feeling anything around me at all. All due to being incomplete, really. An awful thing, to feel this way, without knowing that I will ever feel as I have again. I suppose the others are quite the same. Ahh, but if they are not I'm only making myself appear more weak and useless, but then again haven't we all been weak and useless? For we have not been where we should be nor been doing what I had imagined should be done. Our time taken up helping ourselves when we should be the ones offering it but there's nothing to give. Not right now.

"Then that's enough." Gunter said suddenly, snapping her out of her thoughts.

"None of us are suggesting that there is dark within you, only that it may have effected you so that your mind is unclear and scrambled. You're rather particular in where you place your stubbornness. That being said, not just anyone should be able to follow us and keep up from time to time, or even have taken to the skies when you did when the rest of us certainly were not able. It does make me wonder about you. For now, look at what we have come upon and wonder yourself at this, a great road that I can not recall. Such a thing in this forest should be known to us."

"I don't remember seeing one from where I flew." She said.

"Seeing that the trees reach overhead somewhat I do wonder if I merely missed it. I had never seen the ocean before and I suppose that held my gaze from other things."

"Well we are not going to be able to see such sights when all the light drains out of the sky forever."

She heard their words and the pain she felt was great, greater even on remembering the dark and her eyes were looking for anywhere other than that dark if she could, which swallowed anywhere she could tread. All of it made her feel sick, an illness inside, a wrongness that was sometimes a dull throb and other times a sharp pain that put lights in her eyes and when they left, everything always seemed duller than before. The world really was fading as the days went by and she knew she would need to be stronger to overcome this.

"I feel that warning above is following, could even be chasing me across the sky and I can't help wonder if all this is but an illusion for such black stains if it is as you say that this road should not be here, shrouded amongst the trees and mist. But I still want to walk, it gives me something to do. Even if that which should only be a warning is in fact something more and has taken an interest in me, I should be fine now even if I find my wings clipped, altogether not as I am."

What else could it be, up above? Is this just one more thing I don't know or is it something that can not be known? The darkness was so strange that I now have more questions on what we really understand about it.

Zelda suddenly caught herself then thinking unbidden of the elf she had met. One day she would ask the spirit for the real power of the druids, whatever that truly would be. She was sure that it would be magic that could not be taken away from anyone, for any reason, real knowledge she could keep for herself so she wouldn't have to rely on the advice of others that could be skewed without her knowing.

Findal checked the strength of the crutch she leaned on, deciding that it must still be suitable if Zelda did wish to walk.

"Don't want you falling over when you're so out of sorts. That's not saying much as we're all out of sorts right now but not for long, we can hope. Now we aught to make a decision about this road we find ourselves on. I suppose we could ignore it."

Nasker was looking left, down the road.

"I say we see where this leads us. We can always walk off the road if we need to."

And then we'll just find another road, if the maps I once read are still accurate. That is if we don't hit the coast first. Even if I think we're a fair bit too far west for that to happen I can't be sure.

While it appeared that nothing had tried to reclaim the road itself, on the edges were the twisting, creeping roots of trees that never quite appeared to remain still, or so it was to all their eyes as they walked along, keeping them in the middle. That was not the only thing most grim, as the road did twist and turn here and there meaning they would all be walking into deeper shade every once in a while where anything could lurk.

None of them trusted that the trees would stay where they were and could imagine them creeping in, walking on those roots to make the road smaller or crush them in all at once to reclaim the road. Such was the right thing the forest should have done, but with unease did they keep their hands close to their swords, were anything to jump out and get them and the forest provided no clues. It was deathly silent, whether it was for the lack of living things or that invisible eyes watched while remaining still and motionless without a sound they could not take chances on.

Zelda tripped over a stone and stumbled, managing to catch herself from falling and the resulting sickness from rising too far up her throat.

"I am fine, really." She said.

"It would be a shame for me to go all this way only to not see the spirit with my one good eye. Do not worry that if you go too far or walk off the road I might lose your trail and never pick up where it is you have gone. I am sure I shall find the way."

Her words were not believed, and Survel scooped her up and she briefly found herself protesting before giving up. If they were all going do what they could to keep her along then the least she could do was make the task easier for them. And besides that, with the absence of the heartbeat of the forest, she found his own heartbeat to be alive enough without trapping her in darkness. She did sometimes find herself dozing off in those sturdy arms.

I wish I could do this myself. No need to rely on other people and carry myself and others.

Others? Why would she want someone else to rely on her so much? She wondered at this. Certainly not in such a way as she was now could she be reliable, being so sore, but maybe one day she could be the thick tree branches someone else needed.

I miss the heartbeat of the world. It must be returned.

She thought this to herself and put a hand on her head, because she felt odd thinking about it so suddenly, missing resting up a nice solidly built tree so much, if that was really what is was, to feel that way about a tree again. She could not go back to simply having trees as nothing more than wooden, unfeeling plants. That she knew for certain.

***

Further along the road they all went, spending days and nights in its middle. During one dull and dreary afternoon they heard a rumble coming from behind, that could not be felt coming from within the ground itself but on the ground, where along it could be heard the sounds of marching feet that clinked in boots.

The way back was obscured by darkness so they could only guess at what was approaching and Zelda was glad that today she was keeping up with the others and not swallowed up in those marching boots getting steadily closer.

Out from the mist the noise increased and there on the road was a great army of people together with their spears and musty yellow banners high coming ever forward.

There was no space on either side of the road, as they filled up the road from one side to the other and scraped the trees as they passed.

All but one wore armour of a grubby silver metal and open faced visors over black shirts and pantaloons of the same cloth. The swords and shields of those who carried them were simple and similar among them all, the swords stubby and double edged and the shields flat at the top with the sides angling down to the bottom to meet in a point. Dispersed among them were those who carried small brown bows.

At their head marched a king, who could be told was so by the gold crown on his head placed over his helmet, visor raised. His armour was, in contrast to his other wealthy fellows, coated in gold to match his crown and his own shirt and pantaloons were burgundy wine in colour. For armament he had a large round shield that was slightly domed and made of metal, where set into it was the image of a dragon, wings raised. The king clutched his sheathed sword, of a sort that appeared the same as those around him, at the middle, the belt unbuckled from his waist and swinging in his hand.

As the army came closer their faces could be seen. While they all differed in age, grim was every soldier under their helmet and none were more so grim than their king. While being a man not yet in his middle years, his face was tort in a creased frown that told of great concerns beyond his years which at the same time looked so at ease that it must have been an expression which rarely left him. The creasing aged him several years over with the slight fat achieved from overeating barely salvaging him from appearing even older.

A soldier next to the king was pointing out the druids in front of him and saying words that could not be heard, to which the king shook his head and brandished his sword above him where it could be seen. The gesture was noticed by his men who began waving banners as the command was passed down, far down behind, further than could be seen but the rustling of armour could be heard far into the distance even when the front of the army had come to a complete stop in front of the druids.

The voice of the king was dry and tired, but his blue eyes were not showing it beneath blonde brows as he looked down upon them.

"What do we have here? A bunch of forest folk. Honestly didn't think I'd come across any of you here as I didn't think you'd have the gall to show your faces. Not that it would be like you to do so these days regardless, the least that I have seen or heard, that is. Explain yourselves."

His eyes flicked over to Zelda.

"No, wait. What happened to her? Explain that. Not a captive, are we lass? You can speak before me."

"I took to the skies and saw terrible darkness, then I fell to the ground below. All my fault, really." Zelda said sadly.

"Only just noticing that now are we after using your foul magic trickery?" The king spat, with quite the sudden turn of mood.

"Did you not look up to the dark clouds in the sky and think something is amiss these days? I wouldn't think so."

Gunter glared at the man.

"Well did you rip up the ground of this forest for this road? A reason enough for the world to hate you and take its dues in the lives of your slaves."

The king glared right back.

"Are you insane man? This road has always been here and the forest you are in belongs to me, Lann, king of Kasynne. We can do what we want to this place no matter what you say, but I'm sure talking to you about it would be quite the waste of my time. I have had enough of the horror and dark days that have begun to plague my kingdom as dark clouds encroach ever nearer."

"I thought those were your banners. What horrors might those you speak of be to a king who thinks so little of the ones he puts on his own people and those who spite him? You and all those who march alongside you are everything wrong with the world."

Lann scoffed.

"Whimsical people gone to the trees might ask, even if they know the answer already and I suspect this is all your fault, turning the forest itself against us. Some who would get close to the forest have gone missing, never to be seen again. So now we march to the darkness in this place that none of you would take care of and no one is getting out of here alive without it being dealt with. If Atwixie becomes a forest of ghosts then so be it. We have rather tried to avoid walking amongst the forest in the past and we have been marching on this road for some five days with little rest while my men have been beset by shadows and the very ground itself. *That* is something wrong with the world. Any magic is."

Zelda looked at the king.

"Are your thoughts on magic really the same as I have heard about your people? We are different from any other people you might meet so should not be judged the same."

The king sighed.

"Why does it seem like I am being scolded with that sad, ruined face of yours? I tell my people what to think, not the other way around. It was a person's own folly for a time to approach those trees but for no longer, for it shall not be my own folly for others to then say that I did nothing, and no one shall tell me that what I have done is wrong anyway."

Especially not these people. Then again, they might as well not exist at all, their voices meek and without worth. Walking in my lands are they? Well they'll have to earn their real worth to me.

"She should have elaborated." Said Gunter.

"The differences in our magic of the world to those of other kinds is so great that all others should be judged useless before us. We are necessary. I have not even introduced myself yet, for you to know who you should be listening to. My name is-"

"I don't care who you are." Said the king.

"You say you are necessary? You say you are different? With such a statement as that, surely you can back that up with some evidence, so why not prove it?"

So he asked, in a most drippingly arrogant way.

"Go on. Why not show all of us here on the front row as it were what your magic can do? Ah, I know why not. I will tell you, there is no use for it."

Gunter bared his teeth in a snarl as chuckles could be heard from within the ranks.

"Armed men stalking through the forest would do little to help in what we can achieve alone."

The king ignored the aggression.

"You have not been on the borders of Atwixie for a long time I see. For we are not alone, to say nothing of those natural beasts we find from time to time that are spread through all places and other far off lands. No, I speak not of them as for far too long we have seen black clouds over the forest to our west, and in our prisons those accused of being able to bring magic to muster were all saying the same thing. Do you know what that was?"

He leaned forward, leering, yet could not stop some form of knowing amusement twisting the sides of his face upwards as he spoke, quietly.

"That a darkness was coming out of this forest, one the druids couldn't or wouldn't do anything about. So despite being ridiculed as I may for heeding the mad words of prisoners, we watch no longer. I don't often hate being right, being the king after all means I get to say what is. Including the punishment for those who ridicule me, or spite me, perhaps."

He lifted his careful gaze from them and surveyed the surroundings.

"Such things must I do to protect my people from all that would seek to ruin them and my kingdom in which they live."

Zelda nodded.

"A rallying cry if I had ever heard one but you're speaking only to the trees and it is to them you must insist your reason to be left alone. The core of nature shall once again alight on the wrong world of kings such as yourself and cast off the shackles that chain those unwilling to act together. Only the righteous of nature will remain to guide all people, the rich and the poor, both meanings lost, as there is nothing divine about a right to rule or live over each other or over nature. When we fix the world it will be shown with whom true loyalty to the land lays, not in kings or rulers but in those of us who believe in a promising future."

Survel spoke.

"We all follow because we still trust in the promise that future. That is the nature of our belief. A future you can not fathom with your twisted ways."

The king frowned.

"I'm *telling you* that a kingdom works best together and that happens when people do as I say to ensure their futures. But enough, fathom this then, that you either keep pace with my army or get out of my way. I'm the one with an army at my back and you would deny the lives of every single one of them for the sake of whatever you think the world lives on. Ridiculous, yet you want to be useful so I will let you be useful, regardless whatever it is you are blathering on about. Your sad words will not reach me. If I might entertain your stupidity, I would wonder what the trees would say if they saw what had become of such staunch guardians as the druids. What might they tell me I wonder? Would they speak with words, or with a terrible dark force?"

Findal rubbed his hands together.

"Would you understand the meaning behind either, oh lordly king? Those who can make sense of it all for you are far away from your ears when you are back in your castle. Clearer voices than those you surround yourself with can not reach you, not that such tragedy is any different from anywhere else."

"And that's enough time spent entertaining fools for now." Said the king.

He raised his sword a second time and the army began moving again. The druids were worried about being trampled and had to walk along the forest edges as there was no space for them on the road. Gradually as night fell, with little torches lighting up along the snaking line of soldiers they were able to keep pace as the soldiers' armour weighed them down from the march as the road gradually began to slope upwards.

The druids were able to regain the lead on the road and walk near the middle to be closer to the king and the occasional bitter hiss of a revolted soldier. For his own part Lann did not seem to care, he seemed more focussed on the sky above that was turning into a terrible blackness this night indeed.

They all should have been happy in what little warmth and light the torches gave yet such light seemed so small. Then alongside the burning torches came green orbs of luminescence and with the air filling with the sound of beating wings, pixies appeared around them.

Some men went to swat them away with no success but the king did not join in. His face, however, was twisted as far as the pudge would go in annoyance after being distracted from wherever his thoughts had taken him.

He called out to the pixies.

"Where is the one among you that sought to provoke me at the edge of the forest? The one who would be bold enough to tell me that all found in this forest is not mine to take?"

The pixie king appeared before them all, with his own little crown on his head, which almost would have appeared to be a joke were he not taking his role so seriously.

"If there was anything for you to take, you would carelessly take it and destroy all in your wake. It was more of a feeling than a sight to behold, that which I had, to keep an eye on you to be sure. You have the look about you to cause trouble."

"So you've been spying on me? Certainly nothing I can stop, but I'm sure you only see what you want to see about the world, however little and small that is. Quite like this bunch." He gestured to the druids in front of him and turned back to the pixie king.

"You can't see inside my head so let me tell you what it is I am thinking, that my men do not like you insects and wonder if they will come out with additional limbs or extra heads for merely being in your presence."

"It could well be that you keep your limbs at all due to us allowing you to travel through the forest. But we are not insects, we are creatures of this forest itself and can not afford to be picky with those who come when heeded in these dark times. Especially when we stand to lose more then you and directing you is all we can do. We would lose our very selves and do not wish this to be, so we might see ourselves as being helpful."

The king waved them away with a dismissing sweep.

"I don't care about pixies. I would find myself in such misfortune to walk alongside mystics and vagrants to set my sights further within such a foul place and that is enough in my mind for the moment without your racket. If the forests were to fall, where ever would you go then? I'm hoping you would all just disappear and not come back to let me claim all here that is mine, all that lives in my kingdom, in peace."

The pixie king nodded his little head.

"To such a place that the darkness of the sky does not reach. Whether or not you know the tales is not for me to care. But it is where we are going. Of course we will go, to where those who can not search, will never find."

A little way ahead, Zelda wondered about what she had heard.

"Does that include us?" She asked.

Nasker had been peering back behind them.

"I don't doubt it. To both the human king staking a claim to us and the pixie king telling us we will never find his true home. People as personal property isn't so unusual. It all depends on who owns who and how far the people around them are able to let that carry on for. I'd be careful, if I were you, not to get too close. As for where the pixies will go, some answers honestly aren't worth worrying about in the face of darker things."

It certainly would not have been worth getting close enough to Kasynne to test whether they would be treated as people or thrown in gaol. That had already happened before and to the eyes of the king, Zelda doubted he would see her as anyone different in that regard. If they had just stumbled into the more populated lands she could see herself being locked away which she did not want. The fact that they were not being apprehended now told her that this road was not going to one of those places where people were living.

Gunter spoke briefly to the pixie king before they were left alone. Neither of them wanted to share information with the other, by the sounds of it.

"That tiny king couldn't even warn us earlier." He said.

"Remember how important it is to keep your wits about you around the people of Kasynne and do not let your wits leave you."

The gradual climb had led to the top of a hill and the road without warning opened up in front of them to the bare slope below, steadily dipping downwards to create a hillside that had been cleared of trees.

With a free view of the horizon, the moons could be seen shining through the clouds but it was a dim light indeed. Even with that being so, anyone could look to their right, far to the north and see the forest suddenly stop, to be replaced with a black sea. To the left there was a branch in the road leaning off towards another part of the forest.

At the bottom of the slope the forest resumed in a wall of trees which the road continued to snake through until turning out of sight. Beyond that the forest flattened out and there could be seen another patch of forest cleared off in the distance and a soft orange glow filtering from within, the source of which could not be seen as the trees shielded it from view. What could be seen were little black towers sticking up out from above the trees, only in thanks to the orange light coming from underneath them.

While this was all something most people could see, Zelda found her vision blurring again and blamed her limited ability to breathe.

That hill took a fair bit out of me. She realised.

I can't rely on myself for much longer.

At the king's instruction, his men did their best to hide their torches and lower their banners. As there was not enough room for all of them down the slope, some split into formations neatly along the right side, filling half the space by positioning all the way back down to the forest. Even with a fair number still waiting behind on the road there was at least ten thousand men lined up.

The king was strolling up and down the formations, pointing at the next area free of trees to each of them. After he had done this a few times, he stopped in front of the druids and thought for a moment.

"I am not sure what we will find ahead, but more readily overhead there is a dastardly dark night if I ever saw one to remind us of why we are here. Merely glancing above sets my mind down a path of turmoil most unbecoming of me with no other explanation."

Zelda found herself blinking.

"But that is because balance of the world has been poor and it turns ever so slowly while relying on nature's power, which governs all things. We will return the wind, the water, the mountains and the trees to their rightful places in this world, to see it turn again as it should. None of you are seeing anything right now as it really is."

The king sighed and rubbed his temples.

"Again with these words from you? It is a sad fact that I must find myself associating with such mad people as yourselves for the sake of my own good people. My ways are their ways I shall have you know, so you would speak as if to call all my people blind. Not that we believe in that rubbish coming out of Alegan."

There was a ripple and murmuring sound throughout the rank and file, to which the king nodded in satisfaction.

"Let me make this even clearer. My right to rule is through my father's line, not some prophecy or some ordained phantasm making it true. I have no interest in magic or your foolish ways, yet if you say you have merit then surely it was not on display in these most recent years as the forest and all surrounding lands of my kingdom have become a place for evil to lurk and no other."

"Sounds awfully familiar." Said the pixie king.

"You have nothing to say." Lann said, most dismissively.

"Druids, you saw what rises from that glow that could be spotted from back up the slope? Watch towers at my guess, black and crude, yet perhaps too black and crude for bandits. I don't want anyone getting away from me but I worry that my great army will be spotted due to being given a sharp eyed warning and as we have been walking for many hours we need a rest."

Gunter spoke bluntly.

"Then I have decided that we will go take a look to see what can be found by taking that side road, which should position us around the side and not at an obvious front entrance to spot out what we can. However that is no assurance that we ourselves will not be spotted."

The king narrowed his eyes.

"Why not just fly over if you can so easily turn yourselves into birds then come back? Rather suspicious that you'd walk but suit yourselves in that regard as long as you return with some answers as to what we should expect but be warned that I don't intend to be kept waiting for longer than I will rest up my men. If we are forced to move without you returning and fall into a trap or have anything else go wrong then all the blame will be on all of you and any others like you."

Gunter frowned and motioned his head in Zelda's direction.

"We may have one to return for rest, depending on her condition."

"I don't care." Said the king.

"She might even find herself alone if she returns late and then whatever will she do? If any of you feel the need, turn back if you must or flee into the forest to stay out of my way but don't leave yourselves here in front of me now. If not getting me the answers I seek then what good are you?"

It was decided that the further retorting words of the king of Kasynne were best left unanswered. Not the least reason being that they had to remove themselves from his presence, or rather the presence of all his men with all those swords, spears and bows which seemed much more dangerous than the words of the king himself.

Without one more word from any of them, the party walked back up the slope, taking one last look at the view and Zelda one last wistful look at the ocean before leaving the king and his men behind. The pixies remained surrounding the king and his fellows while more soldiers poured in from the road they had walked in on.

As she descended down the road the forest quickly obscured them all from view while the druids headed towards that distant glow. This seemed rather strange to Zelda, as all things considering and surely with the sky above being so dark, they should have been heading towards something that would not have tolerated such a glow in the slightest.

Chapter Thirty Nine
What Lay in the Forest

The army had been left behind and the dirt path had been steadily taking them towards the mysterious glow. While the glow did provide some relief from the night it was slight, for overhead the black clouds hung in the sky and anything could have been hiding amongst them, just as anything could be hiding amongst the trees. There was a rumbling sound that could be heard faintly from the sky. Even though it might have been threatening something other than rain, all of them knew that looking ahead was the most important thing to do.

Not all of them were doing that however. Findal was looking to the edge of the forest, trying to gauge where the king and his men might be.

"I worry for all of us if we are to meet the king again." He said.

Gunter shook his head.

"We don't have to do as he says. It was merely enough to tell him what he wanted to hear so that we could leave. Those soldiers may destroy anything they might find that could prove helpful in our search."

"I wasn't expecting to follow his words. The plan is sound after all, to leave them to their own devices but it was a rude reminder of what must be left behind, all that foolish power. At least we can get a look into this cloud ahead before moving on. We should sort it out if we can but lingering too long will mean there will be no forest of any sort for us on our return."

Zelda sighed, which came out more as a coarse whistle from her mouth.

"I don't like the idea of leaving this problem unaccounted for either, as certainly it is effecting the forest, because that would mean having to leave this place in the hands of the king. Perhaps he will appreciate it more if he fights for it but just as much I dislike the thought of him strangling it further. The world will keep slowing due to the continued existence of this kingdom and its own dark influence but that can not be helped."

"The pixies fear for their own selves and their lives in the forest with the darkness overhead being so threatening but there really is so much more outside the forest than they know. They are clueless, all they care about is this forest, when there are other forests and a whole world in peril from those as the king, who he would speak with. There isn't just one king set to rule arrogantly and without care, there are many others in other lands. I don't understand why rulers would do as they do if they knew they were only making their lands worse places, where evil grows from them."

Findal remained troubled, but tugged his gaze from the trees to the path ahead.

Really now, we need to get out of this place. Can't anyone else see that there's trouble here? Having a kingdom that is already so lost in its own ways so close to the forest means that the forest will never be safe. I had thought that there'd be some difference in protection for it over all other such places. I guess I was the one with the foolish thoughts as the one who made this forest special has long left us all. We'll put it back to the way it is meant to be and I don't care what state this forest is in when we do. Some things we shouldn't have to fix ourselves. When all is good and well again let nature have its own way as all of nature should.

After not too long they all had to stop, as Zelda stumbled suddenly and fell to the ground, the stick clattering next to her. The world appeared rather grey with a haze across all she could see.

From the ground she did speak, feeling sad.

"All of a sudden I quite feel the day catching up with me, racing to meet the night we find ourselves in. Maybe I shall head back to be on the tail of that king, slowing you down as such would not be just to our cause."

She attempted to right herself but was shaking as she did so.

I'm not going to make it much further. This isn't a tiredness for lack of sleep but an exhaustion I can't shake off. Why? What else is wrong with me? Each breath taken makes me feel sick not just to my stomach but to all of my insides, they protest me doing anything at all. My limbs are broken but that should not be enough.

"You'll be carried by one of us if you have to be." Findal said.

Zelda looked to Survel but while he spoke he was peering off into the distance at those stone towers.

"I hope your legs begin to improve so you can walk. Keep looking to yourself. Look back too much and you begin to wish more for what you could have changed rather than what you still can."

She shook herself out of that odd returning feeling, as she aught to be looking ahead too she knew, but could not turn away from the lonely emptiness below her.

Underneath her there really was nothing more than silence.

Why did this happen to me? I should be able to fly but that creeping watery darkness took all that away. I know I should have stayed on the ground, should have listened, but I felt so close to knowing and understanding something different. I don't want anyone else to feel this way with the world so cold and that's why I'm doing this, for a world that's better and for that I have to be better.

She spoke resolutely to the ground.

"I do wish to continue. I want to feel the world's heartbeat again."

Zelda lifted herself up and followed the others as the dark clouds rumbled again overhead, threatening rain that she suspected would not fall. Rain from such dark clouds that surely held more than rain would do no good.

Let that darkness stay far away from us.

So she thought, and the sky rumbled further in response.

The rumbling sound stayed with them as the dirt path dropped steeply and simply ended in a manner it had before but not by breaching the top of a hill, for where they found themselves was next to a wide, round field and everything about it was wrong.

The dark greys and greens of the forest were gone as the druids found themselves bathed in the glow of that orange light they had seen and something else unexpected, a warm breeze while standing on the outskirts of a wide, bare circle of hard baked ground that was dusty and pale.

The ground was not completely flat as it followed the curve of the land itself, the edges dipped away from it and the furthest edges could not be seen from where they stood. Shallow channels crossed all over the ground like scars and closer now they could see those towers which had been poking above the trees as black monoliths of cut stone that reached into the sky and were placed variously around the circle. The middle of the towers had been cut out from them and fire burned within each, which was the source of the glow. There were enough of these scattered around to light all the ground so that there were no shadows nor anywhere to hide.

Yet the place appeared abandoned. No one revealed themselves out from behind any of the pillars, even though the party was so visible. The warm air, which would have been nice were the scene not so grim, was what spurred them to move on, for it was mysterious that there was any breeze at all. It did not match the darkness above, the forest itself or even the time of year for such weather.

When they stepped onto that hard ground they found it warm as well and the air became only more arid as they went. They clung to each other, Findal on the left next to Zelda, who found herself next to Nasker with Gunter and Survel next to him.

Nasker appeared distracted, his eyes searching from his position in the middle of the party.

"Well then, I'd almost believe we are being welcomed in." He said.

"Almost?" Enquired Zelda.

He nodded.

"Take a look around you, we're not welcome here."

"As if that is a thing that should ever have to be said in this forest." Gunter grumbled.

"This is our forest and it does not matter what anyone else says. If nobody is here then we shall help ourselves with knowing what is here now and move on with thoughts of rectifying it in a most speedy time later. If it turns out that someone is here I would quite like some answers, from whoever did this to the forest."

"Just our luck then that no one is here to answer you, to say quite what it is they have done." Said Findal.

"Otherwise we might be here for a very long time indeed getting those answers."

Walking further in they could see that at the base of the black pillars glowed a red light from each that was a sinister glow. On closer inspection it could be seen that the scarring ditches in the land appeared to cross over each other from tower to tower. Some of these lines split and led into pools of a tarrish, bubbling liquid leaking into those scars and the fumes so that the land itself appeared a diseased thing or one afflicted with a foul curse.

They found more of these pools but it could not be judged for what purpose such a vile substance was being used nor did they want to get closer, having to step over some of the ditches was close enough without having any of the black liquid boil up underneath them or further stain the ground on which they walked. The smell was horrible enough for them to not wish to stay near them for long.

The hill began to flatten in the middle and a slab of black metal was coming into view. Before they could get there, the party came across something strange, as even among all they had seen there was still room for them to be surprised. In front of them were five lumps, thick black cloth sacks half buried which were sticking out of the ground.

"And what are these?" Said Findal, curiously.

Either at their curious approach or at his words the sacks were roused from the ground, rubble cascading off the arches of their backs as they stood, five haggard frames. The sacks were coarse robes that covered the burned, smeared skin of their bodies and most of their faces. This might have been well, for their mouths were of few long teeth and would have been horrible to look upon more, as they were horrible enough for what could be seen, and heard with haggard breathing, too.

Their movements were stiff, moving whole limbs as one, then twisting their joints slowly one at a time as if such movements were the only way they could command their bodies to do as they wished. All of them dragged their bodies over to stand hunched before the party, pointing with their long, crevassed fingers that ended in points even with no nails to sharpen.

The first of them to speak was the one in the middle, although he bore no discernible difference from the others. Their cracked voices, slurred and raspy from few teeth spoke each word on their own from deep within their throats, yet quickly in turn with words clipping off from one another.

"We are the ones who welcome all those who tread upon the door that leads into greatness. Finally have you come to the place of your salvation. Still we would ask you to answer. What are you here for?"

So spoke the first, to be followed by the second, to their left.

"Welcome. Do not fear if you have no answer, for the lands beyond our door turns such nothingness into a whole and you will have your answer and more."

So spoke the second, to be followed by the third, to the middle's right.

"All you need to see is right here to take away your loneliness, for when consumed by emptiness you will find you were not alone when graced by the path ahead. Now speak."

"Speak, speak." Repeated the fourth and fifth, again and again, not as one, but as ravenous young birds in a nest, bobbing their heads.

So it was that Gunter spoke up on behalf of them all.

"I do not know who made this place yours." He said.

And this quenched the speaking of the last two, who each lapsed into a long drawn out guttural breath as if disgusted, heads low as if sulking. This did not effect the first speaker, however, who responded to him no differently then he had spoken before.

"It has always been ours, we of the shores have been welcomed into this special place of belonging. You too can embrace it, so close as you are, so nearly home."

"Home is where we decide it to be. That being said, some don't get to make that decision, not while I am here. You're fouled, wretched creatures who have taken upon yourselves awfulness that has left a dreadful mark on the forest. It has even brought the attention of a man who- actually, that is not important."

He stopped and shook his head before continuing on.

"What's important is that you leave this place. Do not concern yourselves with the particulars in your leaving and just begone from here. You're a further strain on the balance of the world, already it turns so slow that any day now it could fade into nothing and that can not be allowed to continue."

"We are the welcoming heralds of one who would not seek that end. Yet you would reject what is being offered to you to, that which would save you from yourselves and instead leave such a gift laying at your feet?" Rasped the figure.

Gunter gave no indicated he agreed.

"A gift would have been you not being here at all. At first I had thought it best to leave this place be as we went on our way but it is plain for me to see that this is some troubled place of malcontent evil that goes against the balance of our world. While people fight against each other we will move on to fix the ruin they set upon us all, yet we will not allow your evil ways to carry on any longer."

He drew his sword but was not able to do anything with it, as a voice came that was at once like the wind because it was everywhere, or a rushing stream that flowed and gushed. The sound of that voice carried, whipped up off the blistering air now around them, reverberating through the ground that they could all feel.

"Is causing ruin not what all who live in every corner of this world do?"

The cloaked figures cowered down and each faded away into a black mist, as far back on the slab did a giant shadow rise to its feet.

Gunter took a few steps forward, with Survel behind him.

"I should say that it can not be, as I do not know how is it possible that it can be, but I knew I would know you when I saw you no matter what form you took. I must ask how can it be, spirit, that you are here in this forest?"

The spirit was at least four times the height of a man and while it took a similar shape, there was no flesh to speak of, only charred wood that creaked and groaned, split open so that the insides could be seen. Grafted to each arm and leg were four pieces of black metal plating which on its arms took the shape of thick, clawed gauntlets while elsewhere the metal was nothing more than crude slates bolted to the wooden pieces of it which served as either a mockery of armour or to hold its form together. It could have been both.

The same was true for the beams bolted into its back to make a spine and there were metal beams sticking up surrounding its head on which it had no face or mouth through which to speak.

With every step it took on cloven shaped feet, the air further became a haze of heat, with dirt rising into the air around it while the voice coming from within its very body that could still be heard from all around sent ripples through the air.

"It took me so long to understand that this world is a stain. Untold years I had wasted, gladly, without knowing because that was my place in the world. But I know now, that I *am* the world and I will not be used again. That is what you are here for and I say never again!"

The air became a scorching wind that stung the eyes and chaffed bare skin and Zelda felt her conciousness slip as the shaking in the air began rattling her injuries. Those loud words were sitting inside her head and she could not get them out. Her own body did not feel like hers and her voice was a small sound, one barely heard over the wind.

"What is this? I can't see."

She said this sure that no one had heard her, and none of them had.

The spirit raised their left arm to reach to those black skies and with a great thunderclap did the blackness fill with lightning to strike down into their clawed grasp, a bolt which surged and twisted before vanishing into the shape of a savagely tipped spear of black iron, wreathed in a foul smoke as it cooled.

Holding the shaft aloft did they then bring it down to smite deep into the ground before them and all the ground around which they all stood shook and cried at having such a foul thing dug within it, with the ground around the tip melting as the spear was dragged through it and then swung up.

From within the ground a blazing blade emerged and the spear had become a great halberd, the head burning orange and red in its newly forged state, with excess dripping from it to cool on the ground below.

The tip of that wicked weapon was then pointed aside from the two druids in front of the spirit and a great burst of flame came from that tip that struck through Findal who with a scream fell in that moment, the sound, heat and smell so close and all of it instantly intolerable.

Zelda collapsed, falling to her knees as the lame leg gave way in the instant it took for the wind to change direction to blow against her back. She dumped what water she carried onto the ground in front of her trying to call something, anything to her aid but there was nothing, nothing at all. There was shouting, the words of which she could not hear and of the puddle before her it could barely be seen.

The puddle dried beneath her hands, having done little more than smear them with mud that became dirt and in the back of her mind came a dark shadow that she had felt a few times before, that horrible dread. Only this time there was no way she could see a way out. She could not even cry tears, as the burning air denied them to her.

I'm going to die here.

Then the air stopped and all was still for a moment until the spirit let loose a terrible, ear-splitting roar from within it. That sound cracked the ground and a great explosion of fire burst out from its body that engulfed Gunter and Survel and knocked her to the ground while it burnt her skin and was felt down into her lungs, as the air in the fire's wake was thick and scorching.

Before she could even react, the ground where the puddle had been became wet again and out burst many arms of mud with grabbing hands that grabbed hold of her body and began dragging her down. She couldn't even scream as one clasped over her mouth but she tried to reach for Nasker's outstretched arm that flung into her view as he dove to catch her, too late.

Zelda was dragged down below into the darkness where she couldn't breathe, surrounded by a mire that surely had no way to be there or reason to exist. But then there was no way of getting out to worry about that. A peaceful chill sank into her bones and Zelda found in them a silence that sent her off to rest.

***

She awoke in darkness. The ground against her back was hard and she felt her fingers move over smooth stone which was cold to the touch. Cold. The strangeness sent a shiver through her and she breathed in deeply a cold air that made Zelda open her eyes.

There's no reason why I shouldn't be dead, unless this is the land of the dead itself.

An empty, dark sky loomed above, where there were no stars and were no moons, no clouds. There was not a single sound, and she found herself not making any noise. Zelda could see the grey ground at her sides was indented with strange circular lines and when she looked up as she lifted her left arm could see through the dirt that covered her the burnt patches underneath which covered her body.

The burns stung and itched against her ruined clothes. Where those hands had smeared her with mud when they had pulled her under could be told from the rest of the mud she had been soaked through with by those darker dirt handprints.

Why is my body here? Is this part of some punishment, to forever remain in this dark place while I lay here, eventually going mad over boredom or pain?

She lay there and suffered in silence as she looked to wonder at the sky far above, a high blackness that stretched beyond her reach.

I was sinking, so am I still underground?

The air did not smell musty and as her eyes began to adjust she saw that the sky wasn't completely black after all, instead a deep blue and while that deep blue of the sky was empty, she could see thin shadows that stood around her. These appeared to be thin pillars, perhaps of a grey or white colour.

She could not see very far in any direction, so maybe, she thought, that she was on top of something while everything else was below her.

Zelda sighed and closed her eyes.

I'm in a circle.

Then she heard a voice, and the voice made her raise her head. Because it was her voice.

"What a pity."

Standing to her left was a person who looked like her. The only difference was their shameless nakedness and that their skin was grey, the veins black and the eyes while smouldering like twin pieces of coal appeared dead, with no light coming from them.

Such was the graven image that Zelda recoiled slightly, a vision she imagined to be an image of her own doom. On doing so, that other face twisted, head tilting in confusion.

"So she finally wakes and on seeing herself is disgusted, but why do *you* shirk away from yourself when you don't even know how *I* feel?"

It spoke quietly, exactly as she would with her voice.

Zelda could not see how it could be more obvious. Staring at this double of herself, Zelda found her breath and her voice.

"You...you are not me. Who are you?"

"I am you." The other replied.

The mouth twitched up into an amused smile on hearing itself speak those words, the face twisting in a way she was sure she had never done to her own face before. It was not unkind, just arrogant, which regardless she didn't think suited her at all.

She got to her feet as best she could, having to stoop, supporting her weight on one leg. Anyone might have thought her to be the crude copy, the one with broken parts.

"You can't be me. Is it you, spirit, the one who attacked us?"

"Oh I'm so much more than what you all thought me to be. I am the world itself. Not just a part of it, all of it."

The face became sullen.

"But then, if I am the world, why was I given this life? It was not needed. If not to suffer then why?"

Zelda looked down to her feet, to the strange swirling pattern of circles on the ground. It was meaningless to her but not without concern. Was there a reason she had been brought here?

"Well that was a good guess on my part. But I have questions. Are you really the world or just a part of it caught in this terrible time?"

"I don't know." It said.

The face suddenly brightened up in realisation.

"I know. I am the world."

Zelda spoke slowly.

"Then why stop the cycle turning that all life relies on, or was there some other who did this nefarious deed?"

I have a very bad feeling about this. She thought.

The spirit began to pace.

"The world is a cold, dark place. For the longest time I did not have to do anything, as surely you know the way of the world by now. The world doesn't need those who live on it to tell it how to live, but I do. If all they do on it is fight and die and scheme then why should I appear any different? I am compelled to appear as they are and give them what they want. But I don't want this world, and I won't let you have yours."

The place she found herself in certainly was cold and dark. On her feet Zelda could only see a little further than she had before. They both appeared to be on some sort of disk with anything beyond ten feet being out of sight unless there really was nothing beyond but deep blue nothingness. She returned her gaze to the spirit and doubted that it would allow her to go exploring and Zelda did her best to make sure she wasn't helplessly begging with her words.

"Please, we only want our understanding back, so we can all feel the heartbeat of the world and keep the cycle going, to make sure that the world won't end."

"Wrong!" It yelled.

The sound was swallowed by the void around them. The spirit slumped, their face one of sad despondency.

"How little you knew. The one who led you on your journey would have me dragged back to that place where I was born. Where the roots of my being would dig deep and the world would be torn asunder, made anew into a new world and through me they would control it."

Zelda's eyes widened.

"That can't be possible. You're lying to me or are at the very least mistaken. You were to return the world back into the old ways where all people could understand each other."

"I see into you heads." It hissed.

"You would look for those fools for guidance but all they want is to make you all blind again for some sickening sanctity of life that I can not fathom and is in no way part of my being or the world. You talk of the old ways without even knowing what they were, how boring they were, yet that's all you wanted. Preaching and talking and revering day after day while the world around you moved forward with the wars and the darkness and the fighting and they forgot who they owed it all to, who made their crops grow and the rain fall. All me! I was doing everything I was told to do."

The spirit gave up pacing and just stood, glaring at her.

"Then over the years I was left alone. Why was I left alone? Why was I abandoned to this life? Why? The elves had no use for me, discarded me and not one of them stayed by my side. I was still here feeling the dark and hatred build up in the hearts of those who lived on the land and I felt it grow over untold years and I thought that surely sharing what I knew would fix this within me but I remained disturbed to my core. So I slept, wishing I would never wake, always aware of the waking nightmare that would always be waiting for me as even sleep gave me no release from those words and thoughts. How I begged for rest, a silence that never came as the same questions were asked of me again and again, even when I could not move against the confines of that damn tree which was my prison."

It closed those smouldering eyes for a moment, reminiscing, before looking up at the wide above.

"I told myself this life would not continue were I to be given the chance. I knew if I were to not destroy the world then nothing would change, the damage would still be there, knowledge waiting to be discovered and used and for me to be ripped up and torn apart time and again. Until one day a darkness found me and I was shown that there was a way to end this diseased and rotten world, one brought by my hands. In the end when all else is gone I will destroy myself to ensure that nothing ever returns. It's all so cruel."

Zelda had to still her shaking, she had to or she would fall over again.

"What you brought us all helped me understand life better than I could have had any other way and I know that's the way to changing the world to be as it should be."

"You want to feel like me? As I did? You're a truly disgusting creature. I didn't need to feel. I didn't need to understand. All that has done is give me a burning desire to know why such a cruelty needed be given at all. All anyone does after defiling me is that they turn on each other in turn to make sure all are covered in scars. Even as they dig into me, elsewhere there are those that fight among themselves."

Zelda shook her head.

"We're not all the same and not all of us wish to solve their problems by fighting or through greed. It is true that the world is full of fighting and disagreement but that's why I went searching for you, to get the words needed so that people would listen and to stop the end of the world brought about by selfishness and evil. If the cruelty is what's hurting you then why should we not have it brought down?"

The spirit staggered.

"Enough! You can do nothing. I heard the pleading of the world itself and it seeks death! With the way it has been treated, no more shall it provide for those who live on it, to which I will do my utmost to grant that wish. I am not going to be used to change the world any longer."

The two stood apart, facing each other. Zelda wearily faced her double.

"All this for a world you believe has to be destroyed because it is far beyond hope?"

"What is hope?" It snarled.

"There is no reason to live in a world that destroys the future set out by those who came before. My body is being spent and yours should do, for I need the pieces of it. Through you we will both get what we want." Said the spirit.

Such words should have shaken her but Zelda spoke quietly.

"You've got a good enough copy. Are you are compelled to appear as me? I want myself to be whole and able again, but I don't want that which you say. If you should try then I think death would be preferable for one of us."

The spirit shuddered.

"I don't understand. You were supposed to be exactly what I needed. Why are you like this to me? You should have wanted this. You should have been perfect."

"That's not a word I've heard about myself before. How did you figure that out? You are wrong about me and what I want. Also do not think that by simply copying my body that makes us alike, for we are nothing alike."

"This is all wrong!" Yelled the spirit.

"I know it is wrong." Zelda said.

"But I believe I can fix this on my own if the choice is between me and you."

The spirit, however, did not appear to be listening.

"Why won't anyone answer me? Why?" It raged.

"No one listens. All anyone does is fight one another over land while they poison it, poison me who hears and feels all their words and thoughts and I can't make them stop. Only when all is nothing will I then find my peace in death!"

"I guess we will never come to an understanding." Zelda said sadly.

As she said this, she felt something cold drip onto her head. Her hand came away black and more of it dripped down from above. She was disgusted at the colour of it.

Then more cold black liquid gushed up from behind to her ankles.

Where did that come from?

Zelda turned to look behind her but as she did the spirit jumped at her and both fell onto the ground, into the liquid that was rising everywhere out from the stone floor. There was something horribly weighty about it even though it flowed like water and was less than a foot deep. With her battered body, Zelda could not fight against herself, especially one with an incredibly tight grip but neither struggled for long as the stone ground melted away beneath them.

Both fell into a pit of blackness and she could feel the copy disintegrate in her hands and the blackness became hot. So hot that she curled into a ball. Zelda couldn't see or breathe, but something was different from before.

She felt like a seed with a profound aliveness within and she remembered the time when she had been earnestly worried about becoming a tree, even if she had found it only the most slight bit amusing. It was still amusing. Underneath her eyelids she could see a split in the dark which became lighter and lighter and she reached out for the light with her hands in the same way a tree grew towards the sky.

***

With a deep breath of hot air she breached the surface covered in mud to be met with blasting waves of blistering heat, the sound of distant yelling and the crackling of fire along with a scorching, harsh light. Zelda felt mud dry in her ears and tasted it in her mouth and she could smell it but overwhelmingly a more awful smell comprised of the tang of metal and burning meat made her gag.

She tried to clear her eyes to see but all she did by rubbing them was make them sting with dirt and the heat which bared down on her with a blazing intensity from all sides.

I still can't see properly. She thought.

With bleary, heat stricken eyes did she try to look out of the small dirt patch she found herself in, but all she could see surrounding her were mounds of black and red and fire. Zelda was thankful she wasn't on fire, even as the heat meant the new mud had turned to dirt and this had left her legs partially buried.

Zelda tentatively began trying to pull the rest of herself free, bracing for the pain she knew would follow for trying to shift those broken limbs but there was no pain as she did so. On that surprising realisation, Zelda felt for missing teeth and found that they were back where they should have been.

Strangely, freeing herself made her feel heavy and she suddenly began to feel more aware of other things such as the little metal parts of her utterly ruined clothing that burned hot.

I need to fix my eyes.

It was as she thought this that her vision sharpened and those eyes widened in horror, for she was surrounded by sad mounds of soldiers, not all of them who were whole but in pieces, but the very same who had marched along the road.

Crackling sounds came from those bodies that lay there burning with others further beyond heaped even higher, so many more that she could not see the trees or those pillars that should have been around her.

She could not bear to look upon those piles around her but was forced to look above as in front of her there came a crunching noise of bodies being crushed and over the top of one pile she had to look. Bodies were thrown aside with ease while others tumbled downwards and there the spirit was, or what was left of it, for there was now even less of a body that was bearing down with fiery hate before her.

Scarcely all that remained of the wooden pieces of it were charred logs split right through to their insides and those insides were burning with a vicious red glow where streams of shining yellow light could be seen. Even the black, dull metal that held its remaining pieces together was dinted, warped and cracked all over and where that metal still touched the remains of wood it was not black but burning red hot.

Dragging that awful weapon along behind it, which was bent and notched, the spirit appeared pained as it crawled and splintered, creaking towards her as pieces of itself too far gone to charcoal crumbled from it, the smallest of those flaking away into embers flying off into the sky. The same sky that its voice howled into.

"Look, this is all the world you have left and all that is left of me. This is the consequence of your refusal to accept the death of the world. You see it. You'll die alone wondering why you had to live at all. You almost deserve that suffering endlessly, yet I must try for the sake of the world to bring it death, starting with yours."

Zelda found she still couldn't get to her feet, however she could speak with her voice clear even if she could not remove the upset from it.

"But you're not part of the world any longer, and who knows if you ever should have been. Just look at you. Look at you. You're nothing more than a tired, burnt out phantom. Even if what you've done to the world means it's too far gone I'll decide what to do with it myself. You can rest now because I feel what you had is now mine."

"I don't know why you won't let this world die."

"You've seen into the hearts and lives of so many before I came along and you say that as if you don't know? Why else would I remain here before you? Because I'm here to save the world."

The spirit shook and the air itself hissed and sizzled on their words.

"No, not while I take part in this wretched life. I'm going to stop you. You'll never save it. *You'll never save this cruel world!*"

It raised itself to swing the halberd and there was nowhere to hide. Zelda was left thinking that for all she had said and all she had done, this quite might be the end. She didn't have her sword with her and she figured there was little it could have done anyway.

She did not have long to think on it, as from behind her came noise, of yelling and clambering from a blonde man with a large, round shield held in both hands and a bent crown hanging from his belt.

He charged in front with all his might to intercept that terrible blow, and the shield glowed with a golden light as it deflected the weapon with a boom that shook the earth, shook the air and staggered the foe back.

The king of the north collapsed down to his knees next to Zelda, leaning against the shield while some of his men still holding spears ran up beside him to help hold it for what little good any of them might do.

With an infuriated roar, the spirit picked itself back up and brought surging, spiralling lines of crimson fire from within the yellow light, fire that leapt up into its arms and the metal groaned as it burned red right through on the calling forth of this awful heat.

Then the fire which it held up burst past its warped claws, burning brighter and the sound from the spirit became angry, those arms thrashing around as the fire spread to no avail as the fire would not leave it and the metal plates began to bubble. All of a sudden the spirit found itself burning too hot, the flames turning white and the metal set alight to follow suit.

With nothing left to hold itself together and the world having rejected it, the last remnants of a body crumbled into coal as molten white gold metal poured to the ground and with a final scream the creature that had once been the core of nature exploded in a burst of orange light and was no more.

All that was left was the stench of death and the crackling of fire.

Zelda lay on her side with her face in the dirt. She guessed a little more didn't really matter, because she was covered in it, but still rolled onto her back.

Far above, those black clouds had already begun to clear. There shouldn't have been much to see, as it was night after all and they were surrounded by all this glare. Yet up in the sky an aurora danced with sweeping waves of orange and underneath it, little red embers danced below that she could almost reach out and touch.

Zelda giggled a little. Now when was the last time she had heard herself laugh?

Even if she felt stuck to the ground, that made her smile and her vision began to blur up as the dirt on her face was being mixed with...tears?

Ah, finally.

A part of her wanted to get out of this terrible place but her head felt rather sleepy and her body rather heavy. Zelda didn't even bother rubbing her eyes clear as she drifted off, even though they stung. There would be more tears for that, which to her was just fine.

Chapter Forty
After the Confrontation

Zelda awoke, not solidly on the ground where she had left herself, rather to the swaying of being carried on a stretcher, covered by a blanket. Her ears filled with the sounds of burning wood, murmuring voices, heavy breathing along with every marching footstep taken and the sounds of other creatures besides. So too could she feel every fibre of the cloth that supported her and the bristle of the blanket that covered her. It was her skin that she felt most of all, because it hurt.

I still feel so heavy. And why do I feel burned, as if I've been set on fire? No, wait, I am on fire!

She tossed the blanket off her head and found she wasn't on fire at all, nor was she burned again, at least so far as she could tell beneath the thick layer of dirt covering her skin. She found herself breathing shallow and she sank back into the stretcher found to be made out of one of those yellow banners.

There had been a victory, yet around her was a sadness as she looked beside her to find the forest crackling in a fire while smoke filled the sky. Zelda looked over the forest wearily while her nose stung. They were on some dirt road far smaller, thinner than the one she had come from. A much more normal sized road for several people to walk along.

And so despite our efforts the green will wither away in the heat until it becomes nothing more but grey and black. Many creatures sleeping in the forest throughout the winter will die.

To distract herself from her sad thoughts she looked around at the armoured men who carried her. It seemed ridiculous that they still wore their helmets. Their eyes, she could see, were looking right ahead, until one dared a reluctant glance down and strangely to her, those eyes were showing fear. She could feel his heart beat faster, grim acceptance all over his face even while those walking on did their best to look anywhere else than below.

"Go tell the king she's awake." The exhausted voice of that grim man said to another of his fellows.

"Not much good that'll do right now." Said the shaking voice of the one being spoken to.

"I think he would prefer to know regardless, now go do it."

"I don't want to-"

"Do it! At least you won't be the one who has to stay behind and look after this monster, even if you run into another one."

Monster? Zelda thought.

She could feel out of the heartbeats around her, one of them getting further away, but one amongst all those many was no relief at all, for without meaning she felt a sensation of something crawling all over her skin, in a way knowing that meant people marched in front and behind.

"We're keeping our eyes on you." Came the voice of another one of those bearing the stretcher.

Zelda did not respond to say that he had nothing to worry about, as she was unsure that he would hear. That voice sounded far away indeed, as if they were several more paces away and behind a door, not right beside her. Every sound of any living thing was fighting for space in her head, every crunching footstep, every breath and nearby lick of wind.

The distant voice of Lann, king of Kasynne, was added to the wall of tumultuous sound and the metal sound of his boots came closer.

"I see she's still alive. Good job well done for not killing her in my absence, everyone."

There he was, still with that shield held tightly in his grasp.

Zelda sighed.

"Even if it is quite so apparent that I am out of sorts, that doesn't mean I can't hear you."

"Then you can hear that you are in good company, of those who will do as they are told, not that anyone needs to be told to get out of the forest now that I have allowed it." Said the king.

Zelda thought that for the best for the king and his men.

"I would like to use my own feet, yet some deep and powerful worldliness keeps me low that I feel even in my mind. But enough of me, with every breath I know where I am, where are the others? Do you at least have their bodies, of those others I came with?"

The king scoffed.

"Ha! Amongst the some twenty five thousand others I left behind? No, I do not."

His face darkened as hers fell.

"What now?"

"I'm just disappointed, that's all."

"Disappointed?" Said the king, his tone sounding most incredulous.

"You should be thankful you're still alive. We can't truly know who you are and whether you are attempting to deceive us even now. That's why I'm keeping such a large guard on you, for oh I didn't trust you and we made our own way along a road that still led us right to you and we were close enough along the road to see a sight. Of the first two, I don't care much to say but yes they both fell with the first, against such a beast there is nothing any man could do alone with no special protection who was just a man, burnt down where they stood. The last one though is why we keep you under such eyes.

"What do you mean to say?"

"I'm saying that your last friend was one of that most vile, devious kind who burnt away the shining light of Malleau, what even could have been that in all of Auralin, the pyromancer."

Her hands went to clutch at her head.

"Ahhh! What is this? What? A betrayal such as that? And one that could have come at any other time than now when I would most prefer not to be doubted."

"Indeed. That being said there was no friendliness between him and the beast who seemed to use that same awful magic among others, which I found most peculiar before I heard what came to pass between you and it regarding the world. Honestly, that you yourself now contain such a worldly magic is something I suppose I will have to come to terms with, considering what I saw with my own eyes."

He looked down at the shield.

And I might have never known of that usefulness in my own possession. I wonder what else I have amongst my treasure, just waiting to be found?

Zelda blinked.

"You are not the only one coming to terms with things, now on multiple fronts. Nasker had travelled with us for some fair while and never seemed of that horrible sort."

"And yet he was. I'll have you know that when we intervened to lay that beast low, instead of running off and fleeing he stayed about hiding, stalking around the growing heaps of the fallen, even adding to the number whenever anyone got too close for his reckoning as he did appear to be searching for something. Yet whatever his quest, it still was not complete when he was captured."

At this, a soldier began shaking and the king rounded on them.

"Why are you shaking? Tell me you've still got him held properly, man?"

The soldier shook further and stammered.

"Actually no, not well for the guard is slight. But please, it left us terrified to do so, for no man should be moving let alone living with such burns inflicted upon them. Yet it is an injustice to call that monster a man and say he should be dead, for when all about us our countrymen were cleaved in twain and burned, those that burned alive screamed and screamed and then no more, even as burns savaged their bodies still. Yet that vile monster feels nothing of that same pain that should be scourging him, I am sure of it."

The king stared at him, flabbergasted.

"Well don't just stand there, go stand an extra guard on him and hurry up about it before he makes an escape."

When the king said this, Zelda saw an image, fleeting behind her eyes of a small black stone slab of a monolith that stood out alone in the trees. On that stone hung an emaciated man elf, chained and bound to it by their wrists and ankles and while he still yet moved, from that elf came the smell of death and she recoiled back to her many senses.

What did I just see?

Zelda then felt the hair on the back of her neck stand up and prickle as leaves on a fire crinkling over. As she felt this ominous feeling, off to the left through the forest there came a fireball glow of heat that filtered through the trees and up into the sky burst a burning orange line of fire, far, far above where even the clouds would have been. While the procession of men halted and all had looked upon it for none could miss that pillar, in a second it was gone as if it had never been and the king appeared tired and resigned to what he had seen.

"Someone who isn't me can go find out what that was." He said.

"But I think I know. That weasel you had amongst you has already fled. Can't blame people from wanting to keep their distance from monsters. Not sure why that happened, though at least I don't hear any screams."

"He got what he wanted." Zelda said.

"Now he can leave us alone, unless he intends to set more of the forest on fire. I suppose we'll have to stop him then and I'd rather not do that laying down."

Zelda made a place for her feet and found that she could stand. As she did, the dirt grew into her mind and it was with a great effort that she was able to move her legs off the ground, with a part of her insisting each leg dig deeply so that she would become as a tree. She supposed that this was what it must feel like to be a giant, following along the resumed line of men, now thankful to not be carrying her but still scrambling to get out of her way despite her currently preferred harmlessness.

Well they can do that but I don't want to just stay here. I want to move because this is going to be my responsibility if I am to stop the forest burning down any further than it already is. Now, if I am needed to do so, what might I need for that?

Among the haze of sounds and sensations, a clear noise like a chime rang out and ran through her, a sensation demanding that she follow it.

"What is it?" The king asked, noting her interest in something with a tone of annoyance.

"There's a river somewhere and I want to get closer to it." She replied.

The king sighed.

"Just don't think of running away. I already find it difficult enough to trust you without the possibility of you running off, never to return."

"Then why not just leave me here and carry on home? If all I need to do to gain your trust is prove that I can indeed be trusted by returning, I should find that rather easy. Feel free to ensure such a thing yourself but I'd rather not be pried upon if I'm going to be taking a bath."

Zelda took the blanket and men let her pass as she walked off the road and through the trees.

The glare of fire glowed through the trees and it made her feel restless so she tried to relax by following the liquid feeling that flowed through her to the source. Quicker than had been expected she found a running river that led out north. The end of its journey must not have been much further away before opening up into the ocean.

Zelda inspected herself, covered in dirt with the burnt ruins of her clothes hanging off her, then looked about to make sure once again she was alone before removing those sorry, frayed remains. Some outer layer of dirt had been coming off but much of it had refused to budge as if it were her own skin.

I was meaning to think of water, but now that I am here all I can think about is the mess I have made of myself. I really do feel like a mess.

She had also been thinking of the little snicks and cuts and scars here and there which she had accepted she would keep as part of the rough and tumble of life, only they were no longer there, her body all as good as new.

That's all fine as I suppose I did get put back together, but does this mean that I can't get injured or that my body doesn't even matter? Am I really me under all this dirt or did I die and am nothing more than the world starting again after all?

Zelda paused by the water's edge and wondered what would happen when she got in. She needn't have worried as it turned out that she could easily walk into the river and even though she should have been carried away by the current, especially where it got deep enough that she had to start swimming, Zelda did not feel like a piece of wood cast into a rushing river, not at all. If anything, she could halt her own body in the water against the current, her mind resting in it as the water flowed not around her but through her, which was all quite strange to feel.

Never the less, she was thankful to find herself absolutely still quite solid, as a part of her objected mightily to being thrust into such freezing water.

But that did not matter to her, because Zelda was having a bath and nothing was going to stop her.

There in the river she had a moment of indecisiveness as she didn't even know where to start scrubbing. She didn't even know where to start doing whatever she could to fix the forest either.

A moment was spent contemplating this when out from the sky fell tiny red embers that she had seen floating in the sky before, now gently descending down much further, around the trees.

They were rather large for embers and glowed much like fireflies, she thought and was surprised as one of them began to speak in a lightly pitched voice, sounding like a pot hissing over a fire.

"If one knew no better they might say that a pyromancer caused all this. But we know better, don't we? That it is not them but the fault of the spirit's wild blows and my people."

"Who are you?" Zelda asked.

When they got closer she could take a better look at them as many were the ones that hovered about her, wings that were little more than licks of flame quivering, in a most disheartened way. Their inners glowed around their amber bodies with a fiery red glow that when she focussed, found was not the same as fire at all. It was their very insides that bubbled and burned and surged about confined, each appearing as little round bottles of newly blown glass. Yet such an existence was not hindering them, these little beings.

The one who spoke whirled in sadness, arcs of fire rippling through the air in its wake.

"We have spoken before. I am the new king of the pixies and these equally sorry ones about me are my fellows. We are alight and I have felt my kin cry, for I am the new king and have been given the magical duty to feel such things among all the others. Tethered as we were to the spirit, brought about by a wish did we see our own creation many fathoms ago at the base of a great tree. I have been using my magic to calm them and make them understand. Those who do not hopefully will in time."

Zelda turned to see the flaming pixies settling into the water around her to douse themselves, perhaps trying to see if they could scrub away at what they had become. All this did was rapidly warm the river, making it bubble and steam around her.

"So you were a creation of the spirit all along." She said.

"Us and many besides at the behest of the elves or perhaps others. It was all too long ago and the tales are old and wrong. While as was seen that a darkness pervaded our maker, our king did shield us from that to avoid joining it in such a foul way. Thus by using his strength of will did he keep not only us but the power of that tree from a dark ruin. He was struck down most terribly and in that same instant we all fell and feeling the fire amongst us as one we were turned into creatures of the same such awful ignition. Which reminds me, while I speak of awfulness, I must find where that human king went."

"He isn't here but you can look around for him if you will." Zelda said.

The pixie continued to hover.

"First I must ask you, the one who has taken up the mantle of the forest and the world. Do we live? I ask you, do we yet live or is this nothing more than us waiting for our end to burn to cinders?"

Zelda eyed off the pixie king.

"I certainly did not mean to call upon you with the intention to answer such a question for you. On other matters, I daresay asking you to stop what you have helped start is a moot point, it would seem."

Whenever a pixie flew out of the water and shook themselves off they promptly burst back into flames again. The pixie king slumped sadly in the air.

"See? Look at us with your eyes properly and behold in them the forms of creatures that no longer have homes amongst trees."

"Hey! I'm not stupid. If you are so conflicted then tell me, what do you take for all this talk of pyromancy?"

"I can not say any more other than I oppose it still, even though such talk may make a liar of my continued existence, for all we touch singes at best and turns to ash at worst. Yet there are stories of those out there with the touch who are not guided in ways so cruel and never was it or perhaps even is it considered so."

"Then if you do not count yourselves among those who would use such magic unjustly, oh friends of the trees if you still would wish to be, could you find Nasker for me? He can't have gotten far. Can I count upon your honest help?"

The pixie king turned up his nose.

"Only for him to be placed into the hands of that king, one who would not do as I say, despite what I say meaning so much for my people."

"Really? I will have to see about that as your words leave me curious."

Then in her mind a flash of light caught her attention and flung it far out and away to the depths of the ocean, where she felt life leave something monstrously large within it.

As that life was extinguished, the land far away seemed to fall as great fissures so deep came rending that she could feel them in herself with great fires bursting forth and the ground shook and a sound split into the sky as it too ripped and tore.

Zelda could only watch as she felt it herself, while holding herself together as even here could she feel the ground shake and hear the distant rumble and cracking of it.

This is not my body. This is not effecting me and I won't allow it to.

But all was not over as back where that calamity fell, where the moons were unobscured shining silver light down on a sea that had risen itself far above in anger, within the sea she saw the source. From the deepest depths where the water was not blue but black were two red eyes that glowed through the deep.

Rising in that blackness it surged up with the tide to touch the sky and each side of the horizon. With a great roar the sea lunged forward at its command to swallow the land as the creature fell back to the depths which would be its tomb and the tomb for so many others who had thought their land bound lives safe. She did not recognise the land that was to be swallowed, for she felt it to be far in the north.

Well that's certainly not my fault. That's absolutely not my fault. No one had better say that this is my fault.

Her reaching mind did then feel to be receding to where it should belong, yet it first came across the hum of life brought together in a low lying seaside kingdom seated in a bowl between the split of two ridges and a forest which burned that faced the ocean.

There, although diminished, were floods converging onto that kingdom she had never walked along, but due to feeling out the land's low lying nature she wondered how it would cope. If she told the king his city was in danger, she did wonder what danger that might bring her. However, he would find out sooner or later.

Her vision was brought back to her eyes and she found the pixies were gone. Zelda got out of the water and wrapped herself up in the blanket, carrying the bundle of her clothes in her arms.

"See?" She said to the king.

"I return and with a new image in my mind that the lands beyond here in the north are home to many terrible things and now more. For ruin has come to the north and the tremors of that ruin have come all the way to greet us. You might find it as such when you return home, as something terrible has happened."

To which the king simply scrunched his face in annoyance.

"I was wondering at all that shaking and I'd prefer you to be wrong about that."

As they made their way along the road that snaked over a ridge they could look down and watched water that went through the forest along the slope and they could see it through the trees and where the forest broke away, the moons casting a strange luminescence on the ground that otherwise would not have been.

The king was not pleased.

"Now what is all this? What have you done? You can not say this is not something you have done. Did you try and put the fire out by causing a raging flood?"

Zelda shook her head.

"No, this was not me, at least. The ground from the forest rises rather fast and we are a little way above, so I doubt the water will overcome us or provide much relief."

"No use telling me, for it much appears you're trying to destroy the world of others already. Just like that damn beast after all, even if you don't know it. Really though, you're such a small thing to worry about."

The king walked off to his soldiers without bothering to check if she was following. Zelda continued walking somewhat slower.

"Fine then, don't believe me." She called after him.

"But surely even you know, what a confused creature it was in the end."

Zelda wasn't confused herself, in fact it seemed to her rather clear what she had to do with what she now possessed. Even so, she thought of the one who had previously held such things sadly.

I wonder why it lied in those final moments? Even if I have spent time being lied to and having my purpose being lied about, that wasn't a compelling thing to say to turn me over as my head was not willingly buried. The world is so much more than what one sees and hears, after all.

Then she stopped herself, embarrassed.

Oh, I guess it is more than what one feels, too. That's important.

Chapter Forty One
Belonging

On a hill in the forest's north where the fire had not reached, all who could look back at the smoke filled sky and the barren surrounds that remained wondered if ever again there would be green forest. None of them could be sure and to think of it left them sad anyway and sad things were best left to be avoided as what this sadness was might have been nothing compared to that which was yet to come.

The air was rather sombre for all those present. It had been suspected and had come to pass that all the druids had lost their connection to nature and others who lived in the forest were of a similar disheartened state. Among them were the pixies who could no longer cause cheek by whispering into the ears of others, now keeping themselves at a distance.

As it was, Zelda's thoughts were far away onto other things. Having been given the title of head druid was not something she wanted, but she was left with that for a moment as she mulled it all over.

She wore an old cloak that had belonged to the seer before he had burned to death. It was made of autumn leaves of dark green with patches of acorn brown and orange, all fitted together with stitch of green pine needles. Zelda did not think she suited such fine leader's clothes even if they fit her. Even so, a new leader needed to have been chosen from among them anyway, as the old man and woman had slit each other's throats.

Peter looked over the burning forest bitterly.

"In the end we could only do so much. We made our way as far as we could and it is well then that you are here, for as absolutely as we all were joined, this dull fate was not one to suffer alone."

Talking to a group of people was difficult when so thoroughly distracted by the sounds in her head. Zelda was thankful that she did not have to fight her own voice amongst the din.

"Ease yourselves everyone. While I do hold what we have all known, such a thing should never be for one person to simply give out and is not mine to keep alone. Yes it is true I have taken up the spirit's mantle and while most apologetically so, as I'm sorry for what I had to do, sorrow did not shield me from what needed to be done. I found myself with that duty placed into my hands on the back of my wish to see better days and so it will be."

"Well where are those days now?" A lumbering troll asked.

"We need a new tree." Said one of those strange goat people.

"We need a new tree." Said a small furry creature with large rabbit ears.

"We need a new tree." Said another troll.

"I'm so sorry you have no tree." Wailed the new pixie king, shedding tears of amber fire.

Zelda sighed.

"There is no need to be spilling over in your tears for many times already have we heard that you and those around you don't think less of your kind for it. As for your question, troll, you ask where those days are and I say they are right before you. Here, watch me. I am unsure if the land will heal as much of it remains silent to me even now, so part of the forest might be doomed and there will be nothing we can do. If here becomes the new edge of the forest then is it quite some way back from where it once began so some who might find themselves still irritated by our presence can see those bare hills now in place of trees they would otherwise chop down. I don't mind."

Zelda knelt down and put her palms on the ground. She could feel that beneath her the world slowly turned, waiting.

We're out of the wind and out of the way enough of Kasynne. As much as the hidden nature of the old Great Tree was special, I think that here up on this hill might serve us all better. I suppose I could have kept the balance going myself but did I want to? If this is what the elf meant by knowing the world as the way to true understanding and power, then a real understanding meant putting the world in danger. In that case I don't want it, any of it to be given to me, that I can't learn myself.

She breathed in and breathed out and let the part of her that wanted to bury into the ground do just that.

I'm looking forward to getting this thing off my shoulders.

It did not want to let her go and Zelda knew what that felt like. At the same time, she knew that some things had to be let go of, which was often the first step to even better happenings, so she let that tugging grab her and take as much of her as it wanted.

She did not become a tree, but instead pulled her right hand away and inside her palm there came a dot of light, of shining green, yellow and brown that became a small light brown seed where there had been nothing before. With her other hand, Zelda pulled back the dirt and placed the little seed inside the hole. A moment later did a small sprout shoot out and it twisted up into a small green sapling.

All the clutter left her mind then, all the weight and the sound and she found herself free again to hear only her own thoughts and not feel the movement of the world unwillingly upon her. When she willed herself to do so looking down at the little tree, she took great delight in feeling just how sturdy the ground felt under her feet and the rushing of the world around her that told her it was balanced and stable.

The wonderful smell of it was second only to the feeling of those around her who shared in that connection and at this lifting of the mood around her she ventured some hopeful words.

"I think...that we will have nothing to worry about in regard to the world turning dark and dull, for the moment that is."

Peter hummed.

"I suppose I'll have to thank you for that. I had just picked up my old smithing tools again. Well, I don't know who they belonged to but they're mine now. Or perhaps not, if I don't need to worry about civilised life again so soon."

He settled onto the ground with his head in his lap.

A troll looked at him out of the corner of their eye.

"Making a thing or two might be helpful if you can sell it for a coin, something required in many cities to get anywhere, or even someone's ear, human or otherwise."

Peter shuddered.

"Peter there's nothing wrong with having a hobby!" Zelda said.

"However, I should not think that we would need to worry. After all, I'm taking this change to mean that our words are back, so maybe people will have to stop and listen."

The troll lugged its shoulders.

"And what an uphill battle that will be. Wizards and the like will doubtfully take kindly to the words of such wanderers."

While present, as he had demanded to be along with twenty of his men, Lann the king of Kasynne had so far remained silent. Even if he was holding a sack rather suspiciously, Zelda found that she didn't mind him being there. At the talk of these words, however, he now looked as if he had been standing around long enough and made to leave.

"Druids and their magic, is that it? Well I have no idea what just happened but for now we will leave what is left of the forest alone. Take my words truthfully however, that burnt land can and will be cleared, even if I like not how that burnt ground begins to crumble underfoot as if drained of all worth, as bad things are undoubtedly attracted to such foulness."

The tiny hands of the pixie king went to his hips.

"Who knows what shadows might stir in those smoke found hills and soon to be open plains? For regardless of our discontent it might stir enough with what have you there, human king. Do not aim to leave so hastily as you would. You took those cooled stones, formed in the creation of that dread blade used to slay our king and change our very selves. Why would you take such terrible objects with you?"

Zelda turned to the king.

"Huh, you weren't going to tell me about those? Despite all you have seen you would take something made of such foul intent?"

The king guarded the bag, huddling it.

"If all these do for you is remind you of your awful fate then why not let them go away from you?"

He took one out of the bag, a flat bottomed stone of a steely grey sheen which he could just barely grip in his fingers.

"Looks rather unremarkable, doesn't it? Yet great power surely runs through them all. I thought magic to be nothing but trouble, yet I realise that it saved me many times this past night and if only the same could have been afforded to those about me then with these it may be so, along with many other wonders. Before you talk I shall not care for your words saying that I know not in what I meddle, for I can call for those in the north who shall settle upon me the needed knowledge."

The pixie king buzzed and flared.

"What you hold there is not an object of wealth and your people will find it a poor comfort for all they have lost."

"My people need it with Kasynne city flooded, there being no sign of its abatement back beyond the shore and a pyromancer running free in my lands."

Zelda shrugged.

"For how much longer could be up to you, for the pixies here could probably find him, which would aid your peace of mind greatly. If they were to tell only me so that we could keep him here, we could then trade things of want. That is of course unless you would attempt to take him. So would you, you who hold yourself as king?"

His expression was stern and his eyes glared.

456

"Of course I would seek to take him from you. I have someone in my possession who can hold him."

Zelda sighed.

"Then leave my request be, I do not have a liking for fighting. Let Nasker go, or die, if he has not already, but keep an ear out besides for any goings on that might be attributed to him. Let us not end this poorly as we have come from a tragedy and we do not need another so soon. And this is too soon."

The pixie king looked to her.

"Then help us persuade this king otherwise with his treasure. Surely there something you can do."

"No, I shall not help you." She scolded.

"Your predecessor knew all along what we were walking into and we were not properly warned, nor even as early as any of us should have been. So in a way what has befallen you is a punishment for that, allowing us to walk into what I'm sure was judged to be our certain deaths. So I must suggest you help yourselves further instead, as you are no longer tethered to the world you may now do as you wish. In a way this will be a test to see how you use your new lives and newly fire borne natures."

"Then what can be done?" The pixie king asked exasperatedly.

Zelda looked at the human king.

"I will keep a close eye on him and his kingdom, don't you mind. For all people who would wish for peace and quiet should aim to keep it that way."

Lann clasped his hands and grated them together.

"Well then, we're leaving. Wouldn't want to be caught wasting time myself."

The pixie king was hovering overhead, sulking.

"Oh this is no matter for us, as we do not have the power to stop you. Take what you will and be done with it."

The king and his entourage left them alone, gone to help put his city back together that was the seat of his power.

"The back of his neck would look just fine along my blade." Snarled Peter.

Then he sighed and shook his head.

"But I won't, as that would not be right."

"I suppose I'm just going to let him go, too." Zelda said.

I suspect that no good can come from him taking those stones, but if we're all a bit more open minded then hopefully he can come to his own understanding with his new found belief.

She spotted a lump amongst the rags of her old clothes and pulled out her own little stone, quite different in size and given for quite a different reason than the ones she had just let go.

Watching her play with such an item, a woman wearing the black finery of a bird chuckled.

"Well *I* for one can't imagine this going smoothly."

"Are you always going to be this way, Shira?" Zelda said.

The woman chuckled again.

"Of course not."

The bear pelted man shook his head.

"Only if you choose it to be with that one, Hurnor tells you so and so the same is for me. Neither of us want to believe in a kingdom led world."

"So would either of you two like to be the next head druid to see that through?" Zelda asked them.

Shira shook her head.

"Oh no, that's perhaps a little too hopeful now. That task is still down to you."

"What? Fine then, can't I insist that you stay for a while longer instead of leaving?"

"No can do, we are late going places and in that we really should both be going."

Zelda's shoulders drooped but she wasn't feeling the disappointment she thought she aught to be.

"I want to learn more and make sure we're doing all this the right way, what for and all that. Not quite sure I can do that on my own. But who knows? Despite my actions I really think we should all decide for ourselves whether importance should be thrust into our hands."

The feathered woman tilted her head.

"I'm sure many would disagree with you. A power to make a new world, just gone like that."

"Indeed some would grab at the chance. For a time I was with those who would do whatever they could to get what they wanted and I had that which they always wanted in these hands. But I'm not them. I don't want to sacrifice the world we all live in for any dream I might have."

Peter snorted.

"I'm not agreeing with the disturbing way in which this was all supposed to come about by saying this, only, why give it away? Surely you had the power to make your wish real yet you just make it sound as if you never had a dream to begin with if you dared not wish to change the world."

Zelda shook her head.

"Not quite. There was merely a certain solitary sadness I did not want to become a part of. It would be a shame if the world was changed just for my liking. I like parts of it just fine and I'm sure there's people living out there who like it the way it is too who now don't have to worry about the world ending."

And yet I couldn't resist a peek to where I once lived and found darkness over it still. So I tried in my own way to selfishly make it right. Be that as it may, I can't keep looking that way to wonder, if I do I might go mad. Maybe I'll send someone to go look if they would be so inclined. Sometimes it is wise to put aside all that happened or even live with it all behind you rather than trying to make old days new again. A part of me wants to go back to my old days, but that's the part that doesn't take into consideration everything that's come after them to make me who I am.

Peter was mulling over his words, chewing them.

"In a way we weren't going to let people rebuild because we didn't want to be a part of that worldly lie but I don't see that I have the choice to follow that dream right through. I know we should be thankful we have what we have back again, I just don't see why that means others should keep what they have in such terrible ways."

"That's not to say I agree with everything as there's still plenty of wrong that only we can right." Zelda said.

"Of course I quite want to keep doing what we've been doing and while I expect that because of me there will still be those found to have such talents quite reluctantly placed upon them, I don't see any reason why I or anyone else shouldn't be there to help them leave their old days behind."

With that, Zelda put the little stone away inside the cloak. It was, after all, just a stone.

***

It was the middle of the night and the elf was by herself, walking in strange new lands and had done so for a little while now. She had even crossed a sea to come here and was finding herself at home, even if home was no single place in particular as she kept moving about day after day, or even as it sometimes was, night after night.

The night was cold but a simple human tunic was large enough to see her by as tonight the sky was not completely clear, with a few grey clouds here and there. But the moons were alight and the night was bright so the elf could see clearly the rolling hills around her. That green turned pale grey had patches of darkness where the clouds cast shadows down, yet there was silver amongst the grey, shining from the edges of the clouds and the bark of trees where off the moonlight struck.

Further out was the sea, yet not too far as she was still quite close to the coast and when she looked north, could see the glittering spread that had led her here and smiled at the new memory, looking forward to it becoming old and heartfelt.

Then up in the sky there came a sight that captivated her attention, for it was at once most strange yet beautiful too, an aurora of orange light which weaved its shimmering way through the sky. The feeling that accompanied her awe lasted only an instant before the center of what the elf thought of as her core exploded and they were consumed in a bright flash of fire.

Then the fire was gone and the night was silent and dark in places once again. As for the elf, gone was her golden hair for it had turned a shining moon silver and gone was her brown skin for it had turned black to a pitch to match the darkest hours of night.

All over her skin felt cold although her breath was warm. Ah, but it was worse than touching ice on the outside! Or was that pain? That was pain and she could not escape it. The tunic had been new but now it was ruined too.

Even though she held her hand up to her mouth to still her sobbing, those orange eyes blazed above with a scornful gaze of intense fiery defiance as she eased out the pain. Everything was sore but she couldn't help but smile a rueful little smile at the thought, if not sadly.

"Finally now, after all these years we are free of it, free from a cruelty that came from a pursuit of knowledge and power. If this is what being saved from ourselves entails then is it a price well paid but I shan't turn around to run from whatever this new me is. Ages upon ages of history were set out on a run, brought on by hopelessness, built ever on top of a mistake to be surrounded by darkness, refusing to believe that all the world's answers were not ours. How foolish that is, even now, as for what reason the sky turns black and pumps dark blood I still can not say, but my eyes don't need to see beyond that horizon. Why should they when I would not care for what they see even if it appears comforting and safe? The safe appearance of a home isn't one a person should necessarily turn back to. But an opportunity to make a new one? Now isn't that something far much more precious."

She could feel the grass and smell the air like any other, feel the wind against her skin and the ground she sat on without waiting for any of them to betray her or any others of her kind wherever it was they might be. The elf lay back on the grass of a hill most happily, making herself comfortable, pleased not with herself but another while admiring the view, waiting for the morning to greet her.

*****

The golden glow of early morning was shining over the frosty grounds of Churl. The city itself was a haze of smoke, as inside the city it still burned. It appeared besieged and perhaps it had been, from inside and out as the castle itself had begun to tilt to the side and sink into the ground. Outside the walls there were fires too, however these were from large groups of bonfires, stacked up high, where people were putting their ruined wood and letting it all burn. The crackling of fire mixed with the crunching of footsteps through chilled grass and people warmed themselves beside these fires.

They also heaped the bodies of the dead onto some of those furthest away so that no one would be downwind and nobody warmed themselves on those. Yet who was to say had taken part in the madness of the night before? On their way out after abandoning the city, the church had taken those who ran to the farms to the sword and others who had tried to escape, before meeting that end themselves. Their bodies were also on the fires and there were many of these scattered about as people brought more fuel to keep them burning.

What a cursed place this now was to the people of Churl. It felt unholy and even that was better than being hallowed by a light that was not there. They despaired that the hands which had shielded them from the horrors of the world had turned against them. Those who could, stood as one as they warmed themselves in the heat of the fire while being glad to do so, now glad to light a fire without being accused of dark intent.

And there seemed to have been some other goings on, as the great shaking overnight had brought around the walls a sight few could believe when seen in the light of day, the sprouting of giant trees. These were bigger and thicker than any tree anyone had ever seen, having those great trunks twist around the entire city, interlocking with each other, as if tamed by careful hands. Their deep roots came up in great tangled bursts to undermine those lifeless walled fortifications. They were looked on with worry and so if not lending their arms, near the bonfires was where most people preferred to stay.

Bernard the wizard stood amongst them. As much as he would have preferred to just be as any other person caught up in the morning, he had to admit that his stave and work during the night were likely reasons he had been given more than one weary morning eye. As such he had taken to instructing those around him. It really was his responsibility after all to see all this through and he knew he would not be leaving until he did. The people of this land would be safe with their eyes open by the time he was properly done with them.

"Continue to bring out all who are dead that you can find but do not stray too close to the castle again as though while the demons have stopped pouring forth, there could be some lurking within and you should not wish to draw them out. I shall say it again firmly, you should not wish to draw them out! Some of you went up and railed against the castle itself and know what you found, indeed some have not yet returned and why should they when dark shapes still roam within, that I now contain?"

People had been going about the morning, doing as he said. Some were collecting books of the church, wondering what to do with them, handing them around to those at the fires. The materials used in their making, leather and string, were scarce, so the valuable covers were ripped from the pages and being put aside into piles. Others were digging pits at intervals around the entire city that was where all the paper was going, for Bernard had instructed that the paper not even be used to write over, lest such words even be glimpsed again. He flicked through loose, unbound pages wondering how such words could have set the course for such an end.

"As for those books if you find them, bring them hither and about you. The past can not be overwritten but it can be learned from. Strip those words of their hide and cast them down forth, do not burn them or let any escape. Chase after them if they do as they are required for the spell I will cast around these trees that you will plant as the pits are filled in to further protect this place. The words within are lies and I shall use those lies to my advantage, use them to make the trees strong you shall plant, for demons can not pass through a ward of lies which is the best that can be done for anyone who would now approach this city."

One person approached him, carrying wood to heap on a fire.

"Was it really you who did all this for us?"

"Of course that was all me." Lied the wizard.

"I am a wizard who can do such miraculous things. As long as you stay outside the circle I am making you build you should have no trouble from the demons."

Best this place be abandoned entirely. In some rather simplistic way it seems that this city is being returned to the trees and groves of which it once was, a shudderingly long time ago and to most that will hopefully be unappealing to approach.

The thought of those long lost ages nearly did make him shudder, but he suppressed it, even though the air was chilling him.

A voice rang out through the air and a middle aged man came running and panting, short of breath.

"Please help, somebody help me. My child is seeing dark shadows in the sky."

"They are afflicted with a curse." Said Bernard.

The man's eyes went wide.

"What? Oh no not my child."

"The curse of magical potential." He clarified.

"Damn you!" The man snapped.

Bernard cast his hand into the distance.

"And all the promise that it holds. I should look them over, to advise you further on what must be done."

The man crossed his arms.

"For scaring me so I should think that you do just that. I don't want to lose anyone else. What could have happened to the Minister and our king and his family? Are they lost too? Inside the castle was where they would have been, which should have been the safest of places to be. To think that they are gone frightens me and many others who have no guiding hand left."

"Their fates have come to pass." Bernard said simply.

"There is no reason for you to go on thinking about them. Do not worry for their ends, for as you can see, there is nothing else for any of you here and there are other places you can all move to that are none too poor for anybody. Do not keep about you greatly the wonder of other people, learn to live for yourself and be concerned for your own self and that of your family."

The man appeared downtrodden on hearing such things.

"That's easy for you to say. This day has found the rest of us in a world unknowing without any direction. Must we have our purposes hidden from us, whatever they may be?"

Bernard simply shook his head.

"My good sir that is the very reason one must live. It doesn't matter who looks down and watches or who judges or at all what fate tells us who we should be. There's nothing easy about any of it, especially when people try and tie you to something as fickle as the threads of fate. Sometimes life just happens in certain ways and we all only have so much of it to do with what we can."

"Best we not waste our new morning then." The man said, turning to slowly walk back the way he had come.

As Bernard watched him go, a gust of wind set loose pages in his hands free. He smiled, looking up at those pages now aimlessly tossed into the sky.

"I suppose not."

www.ingramcontent.com/pod-product-compliance
Lightning Source LLC
Chambersburg PA
CBHW060812120726
47909CB00006B/1896